Praise for *New York Times* bestselling author
Stephen Frey and his
"ABSOLUTELY FIRST-RATE" (James Patterson)
thrillers set against the dangerous and deceptive
financial world

"*Forced Out* . . . may be his best book to date."
—Bookreporter.com

"Frey enlivens finance the way Patricia Cornwell does
forensic science and Dan Brown does medieval studies."
—*Forbes*

"The Grisham of financial thrillers." —*Booklist*

"Ruthless financial terror." —*Chicago Tribune*

"Frey has the undeniable ability to explain complex
financial transactions while at the same time providing
plenty of action and nuggets of insider money lore."
—*Publishers Weekly*

THE SUCCESSOR
"Frey knows how to deliver intrigue with just enough
thrills to keep the pages turning." —*Booklist*

FORCED OUT is also available as an eBook

STEPHEN FREY

FORCED OUT

A NOVEL

POCKET **STAR** BOOKS
New York   London   Toronto   Sydney

Pocket Star Books
A Division of Simon & Schuster, Inc.
1230 Avenue of the Americas
New York, NY 10020

This book is a work of fiction. Names, characters, places, and incidents either are products of the author's imagination or are used fictitiously. Any resemblance to actual events or locales or persons living or dead is entirely coincidental.

First Pocket Star Books paperback edition August 2009

POCKET STAR and colophon are registered trademarks of Simon & Schuster, Inc.

For information about special discounts for bulk purchases, please contact Simon & Schuster Special Sales at 1-800-456-6798 or business@simonandschuster.com.

Cover design and photo illustration by Jae Song

Manufactured in the United States of America

10 9 8 7 6 5 4 3

ISBN 978-1-4165-4964-2
ISBN 978-1-4165-7972-4 (ebook)

For my Diana. I love you, darling.
If you'd never convinced me to go to that game,
this book would still be just an idea.

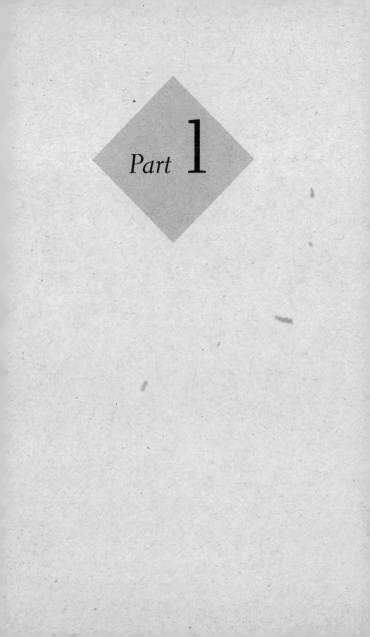

Part 1

1

FOUR YEARS. FOUR *damn* years since he'd been to a baseball game, watched one on TV, even snuck a sidelong glance at the standings in a summer sports section. But it seemed more like a lifetime.

Jack Barrett turned off the stadium's main concourse just past a tempting hot dog stand and limped up the narrow tunnel toward Section 121 on his gimpy knees, muttering to himself about this being a bad idea. His daughter and her boyfriend had finally convinced him to come with them tonight after badgering him about it all spring. But now that he was here, he wished he'd kept that blood oath with himself and stayed away forever. Nothing good could come of this.

As he emerged from the tunnel into the half-light of the Florida evening and that familiar panorama rose up before him for the first time in so long, Jack stopped to take it in. Felt that same intense anticipation and excitement building in the center of his chest, like he always had. He'd been to thousands of games over the years in ballparks ten times the size of this one, but this single moment always had the same profound effect on him. Always made him realize that his darkest problems weren't as bad as they seemed. Even now.

His emotion had nothing to do with the stadium. Whether it held sixty thousand or six hundred. Whether this was game seven of the World Series or a meaningless minor-league scrap. Whether there was a giant screen past the fence in center showing multiangle, slow-motion replays—or a cow pasture, like there was tonight. His reaction had to do with the field itself.

With the perfect symmetry of the diamond inside the nuances of the outfield and foul territory. With the contrast of sculpted brown dirt against a canvas of lush, carefully manicured green grass. With how lonely the snow-white island of second base seemed. With the sharp right angle formed at home plate and how the lines creating the angle seemed to stretch past the fence and the cow pasture into eternity. How frighteningly close the pitcher's mound was to home plate, but how big the entire field seemed. How only nine men covered the vast expanse before him, but how a batter who failed to reach base six times out of ten was a lock for the Hall of Fame. How each baseball field was a work of art, unique and compelling in its own right. Which made the game so much more intriguing, so unlike all other geometrically constrained sports. And now that Jack had suddenly reconnected with the game, he was forced to admit how empty the past four years had been without it. Forced to admit *how much* he'd missed this game.

Like you missed the love of your life.

Like he still missed the love of his life.

Even after all these years.

Jack glanced at the burning orange sun sinking toward the glittering aqua waters of the gulf beyond the grazing black-and-white cows. Nostalgia surging back at him from all directions as he inhaled the scents of freshly mown grass, cigar smoke, and those sizzling hot dogs all intertwining on the gentle sea breeze. It seemed like such a simple game—a man attempting to hit a pitched ball— yet ultimately it was so complicated. He'd been devoted to this game, given all he had to it. In return it had destroyed him.

He shook his head grimly. But here he was, back for more. In the end unable to resist the allure. Sometimes being human was nothing but pure hell.

"Come on, Pop, let's find our seats."

Jack shrugged Bobby Griffin's hand from his shoulder like a horse shaking away a pesky fly. "I'm not your *pop*," he said with a growl as the young man lumbered past.

"Be nice to this one, Daddy," Cheryl urged as she came up beside him. "I really like him."

Jack eyed an usher. The thin, elderly man was leaning over, his age-spotted forearms resting on a yellow-painted railing. A railing separating seven rows of box seats from the rest of the stands—the haves from the have-nots. The usher was wearing a short-sleeve button-down white shirt, black polyester pants, and a red cap with a shiny black visor. He looked more like a bus driver than an usher.

"Look, it's just that—"

"What's Bobby done so wrong?"

He was born a male and he's dating you. Isn't it obvious? "First of all, he keeps you out 'til two in the morning," Jack began, proud of himself for showing such restraint. "Which is way past your bedtime."

Cheryl smiled like it hurt. "I'm thirty-three, Daddy. Don't you hear how silly that sounds?"

"*Second of all,* he's only twenty-five. He isn't serious about your relationship." Jack hesitated. Talking about this with a woman wasn't easy for a man born into a staunchly conservative household on V-J Day—even when the woman was his daughter. Maybe because the woman was his daughter. "He's using you for sex." At least he'd made progress. Ten years ago he wouldn't have been able to say that. Not nearly.

Cheryl's expression tempered into one of sincere amusement, and she ran her fingers playfully through her father's full head of salt-and-pepper hair, then lightly down his grizzled cheek. "Maybe it's the other way around, Daddy. Maybe *I'm* using *him* for sex."

Jack groaned, grabbed his chest, and staggered forward a few steps. "You sure know how to hurt an old man, don't you?"

"You're not old, Daddy. You're middle-aged."

"People don't live to a hundred and twenty-six, Princess."

"Can I help you?" the usher asked in a voice that sounded like it needed oil. He rose slowly off the railing like his joints could use grease, too.

"We're fine," Jack replied, clasping Cheryl's elbow and guiding her toward Bobby, who was waving at them from up in the stands. "But thanks."

"You should think about doing that," Cheryl suggested, gesturing over her shoulder.

"Doing what?"

"Being an usher."

"Yeah, right."

"No, really. You'd be out here at the ballpark all the time. For free, too. It'd be perfect. You'd love it."

Jack rolled his eyes as they neared their seats—eight rows up from the railing on a direct line behind the third-base dugout. Cheryl meant well—she *always* meant well; she just didn't understand. Being an usher would be even worse than what he was doing now, which was bagging groceries at a local Publix store for ten dollars an hour. Not very long ago he'd been a top man in the New York Yankees' scouting organization. An important cog in the greatest sports franchise in the world—at least, in his opinion it was the greatest. He couldn't bear the thought of his baseball career ending as an usher for the Single-A Sarasota Tarpons.

"Maybe I will, Princess," he said softly, "maybe I will."

Bobby Griffin sat at the end of the row—he'd bought tickets for the three seats closest to the aisle. He stood up and moved out of the way as Jack and Cheryl approached.

"What are you doing?" Jack wanted to know.

"Letting you in." Bobby motioned for them to go ahead. "Look, I've got to sit at the end of the row, Pop," he pleaded when Jack didn't move. "I'm six four. My legs don't fit in the—"

"Well, I'm sixty-three, and I've got arthritis in both knees."

Cheryl grabbed Bobby's hand and pulled him toward the second seat. "Come on, honey."

"But baby, I paid for the tickets. I ought to at least get to—"

"Come *on*."

"Jesus," Bobby grumbled.

Jack sat down slowly, then stretched his legs into the aisle. No way Bobby was going to start an argument now. That might jeopardize his plans for later.

He shook his head, trying to clear away the bad thoughts. It bothered him to think about boys taking advantage of his little girl; it always had. Ever since she'd started dating. Ever since the first boy had shown up at the house with that hungry look in his eyes. Cheryl was one of the nicest, most sincere people on earth, and she always felt so much pressure to give the ones she liked what they wanted. She was pretty—slim with long blond hair—but she didn't pay much attention to her looks. Never had, really. Most of the time she kept her hair up in an unruly bun, didn't wear much makeup, and dressed plainly. But he didn't know how to tell her she ought to jazz it up. Truth was, he didn't want her to jazz it up. Then there'd just be more boys.

"How many people do you think this place holds, Daddy?" Cheryl asked when they were settled in.

Nostalgia nudged at Jack again. It was the same question she always asked the first time they went to a ballpark together. She'd done it since she was a little girl, since he'd first started taking her to games. The times her brother couldn't go. She had always liked getting a feel for her surroundings. "The capacity is—"

"Eight thousand," Bobby cut in confidently.

"Actually, it's sixty-two hundred." Jack moved his legs out of the aisle as a tall couple began climbing the steps. Hopefully they weren't going to plunk themselves down in the open seats in front of him. At this point he had a perfect, unobstructed view of the field, and he didn't want to have to move from side to side to see the action between their heads. "The number was posted on a fire warning downstairs," he explained, relieved when the couple moved past. "From the looks of things I'd say it's about half full."

The crowd mustered a weak cheer when the Tarpons broke from the dugout a few moments later.

As the players jogged toward their positions, Jack sat up and leaned forward, noticing one of them instantly. Before the kid even reached the third-base line on his way out to center field. He had that aura about him all the great ones had. An unmistakable charisma that caught Jack's trained eye right away. A confident, athletic stride that ate up ground effortlessly. A smoothness in everything he did—from handling the right fielder's bad warm-up toss on a short hop to adjusting his red cap with the smiling tarpon on the front after each throw back. An innate awareness of where he was in relation to everything else on the field. The impression he had a couple of gears in reserve he could call on if he needed to, and then you'd *really* see something special. And he had a gun for an arm, an absolute rifle. Of course, Jack had an advantage as far as recognizing the kid's ability. He'd spent thirty-four years scouting talent for the Yankees. Then the organization had turned its back on him.

"Yo, beer man!" Bobby shouted to a scraggly-looking guy carrying a tray of cold ones. *"Over here!"*

Jack covered his ears with his hands. "Jesus, you sure got a healthy set of pipes on you, don't you, son?" Bobby Griffin was big, blond, and good-looking. A sales rep for a Los Angeles–based sporting goods company, he covered the South Florida market. According to Cheryl, Bobby was doing pretty well for himself—which only made Jack feel worse. Successful, handsome twenty-five-year-old men didn't settle down with thirty-three-year-old women. They used them. "I think the *right fielder* heard you, for Christ's sake."

"Cheryl warned me about you," Bobby shot back cheerfully, handing the beer man a twenty and signaling that he wanted three. "Said you were kinda grumpy. But that's all right, I can deal."

Jack intercepted the first cup, brought it to his lips, and took a long guzzle. It was a hot May evening in Sarasota—still eighty-four degrees at seven-thirty—and the cold beer tasted damn good.

He glanced back out to center as darkness closed in around the small stadium. Strange, he thought. You didn't see many baseball players with facial hair, especially in the minors and especially the really good ones. But the kid had a full beard and a mustache along with a mop of dark hair tumbling down from beneath his red cap.

When the public-address announcer asked the crowd to rise for the national anthem, Jack did so right away. And he sang along loudly with the music as he always did, trying to make people around him feel comfortable about singing, too, though they rarely did. He'd served in the army before joining the Yankees, and he had a deep sense of loyalty to the country. His only regret with his military service was that he'd never experienced combat. Never had a chance to get to Vietnam to find out how he'd react to real bombs and bullets. He thought he knew, but you could never be sure until the chaos actually erupted around you.

"I hate the Tarpon uniforms," Bobby complained, squeezing back into his seat when the anthem was over. "There's too much red. Their pants, even. It's ridiculous. And that stupid mascot. A *smiling* fish. The whole thing's too loud."

"I thought 'loud' was your middle name," Jack shot back. "I figured you'd love their uniforms."

It was the first time they'd spent more than a few minutes together, and Jack caught Bobby shaking his head, like the young man wasn't sure he could put up with this for nine innings after all. Well, good. Bobby seemed nice enough, but it was obvious he was going to break Cheryl's heart at some point. The sooner the better.

It was going to be awful to see her hurt—again, Jack thought ruefully. To see the devastated expression, the tears streaming down her cheeks. Hear the soft sobs from her bedroom at night before she fell asleep, and again in the morning as soon as she woke up. It always made Jack feel terrible as he held her in his big arms and tried to comfort her. But the longer this thing with Bobby went on, the worse the pain would be. One of these times it was going to be too much, it was going to push her over the edge. It almost had with the last guy, and he'd been a loser compared to Bobby Griffin.

When Bobby leaned forward to check something on the scoreboard beyond the fence in left, Jack caught a familiar warning look from Cheryl. Thin lips pressed tightly together, one eyebrow raised, head turned slightly to the side, eyes intense like the blue part of a flame. Okay, okay, he thought. Maybe this one was different. Doubtful, but maybe. And to his credit, Bobby had paid for tonight. The first one of her boyfriends who'd ever sprung for anything.

Jack tapped Bobby's arm. "Thanks for the beer, son. Tastes good."

"Oh, sure."

"Ticket, too. I really appreciate it." It killed him to say so, but Cheryl was much more important than his stupid pride. "I don't make the money I used to." That one *really* hurt. "Every little bit I save helps."

"I understand."

Jack raised his cup and nodded. "I'll get the next round."

"Tell you what," Bobby suggested. "Let's bet on pitches for beers."

"What do you mean?"

Bobby pointed toward the scoreboard. "They post the pitch speed up there a few seconds after each one. Either of us gets the number exactly right before they post it, the other guy buys the next round. How about that, Pop?"

Apparently Cheryl hadn't told Bobby what her daddy had done before being exiled to Florida. Jack had asked her not to mention it to the neighbors, but he figured she was telling the guys she dated. "Okay, sounds good." He'd nail a few pitch speeds, then buy the next couple of beers anyway. To show Bobby his crankiness had its limits.

"*Play ball!*"

A chill ran up Jack's spine as he watched the home-plate umpire point at the pitcher from over the catcher's back, and heard the man in blue yell those familiar words. And he actually smiled inside a baseball stadium for the first time in what seemed like an eternity. More out of relief than anything else. Relief that tonight wasn't turning out to be so gut-wrenching after all. Relief that the bitterness wasn't crushing the experience. He took another deep breath of those wonderful scents and glanced around, his grin growing wider. This tiny minor-league ballpark was so intimate you could feel the action. Not just see it, like you did in the Bronx, because most of the seats there were so far away from the players. You felt like part of what was happening here, not like just a witness.

"Ninety-two miles an hour," Bobby sang out as the first pitch popped the catcher's mitt.

"Eighty-seven," Jack countered.

"You don't know what you're talking about, Jack. This guy's a fireballer, the ace of the staff." Bobby gestured toward Cheryl. "We've seen him a couple of times before. His first pitch is always over ninety. It's kind of his trademark." He smiled smugly. "Guess I shoulda said something."

"He's off tonight," Jack observed. "I could tell while he was warming up. He wasn't in his comfort zone." You never lost the lingo, not even when you were away from something as long as he'd been. Four years since he'd been drummed out, but suddenly it was as if he'd never been away. "He isn't just winding up and throwing the ball, he's aiming it. You lose ten to twenty percent of your velocity when you do that."

Bobby gave Jack a suspicious look. "How would you know?"

Jack shrugged as he noticed Cheryl slip her fingers into Bobby's—and Bobby pull his away a moment later. Damn it. Why did she fall for them so hard? "I guess I wouldn't."

The scoreboard flashed the pitch speed: eighty-seven.

Bobby hung his head. "Shoot."

"Lucky guess, son," Jack said, glancing out to center.

The kid who'd caught his eye was pounding his mitt and flexing his knees, getting ready as the pitcher went into his windup. "Let's go again. Double or nothing."

"Yeah, okay." Bobby leaned forward and concentrated. "Eighty-one," he sang out as the batter flailed at the next pitch. "That was a curve."

Bobby was right. It had been a curve. So slow it looked like it wouldn't have broken wet toilet paper. Seventy-two or seventy-three at most. Jack bit his lip. He was competitive as hell, always had been, but Cheryl wanted him to like the guy so bad. "I'll say eighty-two."

The scoreboard flashed the speed: seventy-two.

"All right!" Bobby shouted, pounding the arm of the seat with his big fist. "I was closer on that one. Guess you really were lucky the first time. Again?"

"Sure."

The third pitch was another curve, but this time it hung and the batter jumped on it, hammering the ball toward the gap in left center like a frozen rope. The kid raced to his right, dark hair streaming out behind him as he sprinted. Diving at the last second, going flat out in midair four feet above the grass just as it seemed the ball would shoot past him to the colorful, ad-covered wall.

But it didn't. It snagged at the edge of his glove, half in and half out of the leather webbing like a snow cone as he tumbled to the ground. The kid was on his knees instantly, holding up his trophy so the second-base umpire who'd loped out from the infield could see he'd made the catch.

"Jesus," Jack whispered as the umpire gave the out signal and the crowd gave the kid a smattering of applause. "That was unbelievable." He could have sworn the kid was off and running before the bat and ball even connected.

Of course, the great center fielders had that ability. Mays, Mantle, Blair, Maddox. They seemed to know where the ball was going even before the batter did, before everyone else in the park did. "These people don't get real excited, huh?" It had been a spectacular catch, but the applause had already died down. "What's the deal? They too old to clap or something?"

"It's not the crowd," Bobby answered, swirling his beer. "It's the player. The guy's name is Mikey Clemants, and he's a real prick."

Jack checked the Tarpon infielders to see if the names were stitched on the backs of the uniforms. They weren't, and he hadn't bought a program. They were four bucks, and he didn't have that kind of money to waste.

"Clemants doesn't give autographs, doesn't tip his hat to the crowd, doesn't do anything for the community," Bobby continued. "Skipped a team visit to a children's cancer hospital on an off-day earlier this year. Nobody likes him, not even his teammates."

"I know some major-league owners who'd like him," Jack muttered. "At least, they'd like him on their teams."

Bobby shook his head. "I don't think so, Pop. For every crazy catch like that one, Clemants makes five bonehead plays. Misses the cutoff man, tries a basket catch and drops the ball, doesn't run out a grounder. Plus, he's a head case. Doesn't listen to the coaches at all."

"Well, he looks like he could hit sixty home runs a year easy. That would make up for a ton of errors."

"He's hit three so far this season, Pop, and the Tarpons have played more than twenty games. That's only—"

"Yeah, yeah," Jack interrupted. He'd already done the math. "Nowhere near sixty a season."

"And he's only batting like two-fifty." Bobby shook his head. "Two-fifty in Single-A is like one-fifty in the majors. No way he ever makes it up there."

Jack gazed at his seat ticket for a few moments, then smiled wryly and slid it into his shirt pocket as he watched the kid toss the ball back to the infield effortlessly with that rifle arm. Bobby Griffin didn't know a damn thing. Mikey Clemants was the real deal. "I guess you're right, Bobby." Jack glanced past Clemants at the grazing cows, suddenly glad Cheryl and Bobby had dragged him out here tonight. For the first time in a long time there was a real reason to get out of bed in the morning.

2

JOHNNY BONDANO PULLED his gloss white
Cadillac Seville to a quick stop behind a rusty Jetta
and cut the engine. Then rose out of the Seville and
moved briskly toward one of the endless lines of row
houses standing beside the narrow Queens street like
clones. Johnny was thirty-seven and still in excellent
shape. He worked out every day and wore fitted shirts so
everyone could appreciate his impressive physique when
he took off his designer sports jackets. He had small, dark
eyes set close together, a pug nose, large lips, and he kept
his black, curly hair cut short—especially over his ears.
He was short and had a large head for his body, which
he was sensitive about. A few months ago the owner of
a liquor store down the block had joked about it behind
Johnny's back. Called him the Head instead of his real
nickname, which was the Deuce. It got back to Johnny,

and the man disappeared a week later. He hadn't been heard from since.

Johnny's nickname was Deuce because he always carried the same creased two of hearts in his shirt pocket wherever he went. Had for years but never explained why to anyone. When he went to a restaurant, he'd take the card out and place it on the table faceup next to his knife. He'd glance at the card every once in a while as he ate, sometimes touch it gently. Anyone asked him about it, he'd shake his head deliberately and take another bite of food. But no one gave him a hard time about it. No one gave him a hard time about much of anything—at least not to his face. He was one of the most feared men in New York City's underworld. A hired killer for the Lucchesi family, the most powerful mob in the five boroughs.

Johnny bounded up the row house steps, taking three at a time, then rapped on the door, checking the dimly lit street while he waited. He didn't see anything suspicious, but you never knew these days. The feds and the NYPD detectives had gotten slicker lately, gotten better at blending in. They were constantly on his ass, but so far they hadn't been able to prove a thing. They'd hauled him into court a couple of times but never had enough to make the charges stick. No body, no murder weapon, and *never* a partner who could testify against him in exchange for immunity. He *always* worked alone. Always had, always would.

Of course, the Lucchesi family retained good lawyers, too. Harvard boys. Best that money could buy.

After a few moments the door opened and Johnny moved into the modest home. The young soldier standing inside was named Nicky. Nicky's only job was to protect this entrance—to the death. It was a high honor in the Lucchesi family, and it meant the bosses had big things in store for him.

"Hi, Nicky."

"Hey ya, Deuce."

"Yeah, yeah, hey. Look, the number's twenty-seven tonight, right?"

Johnny was there to see Angelo Marconi, the number two man in the entire Lucchesi organization. Marconi was paranoid about everything and everyone, and you had to know the two passwords of the day or you didn't get in to see Marconi no matter who you were—no exceptions.

"Okay?"

"Yeah, okay," Nicky answered, head tilted slightly forward out of respect. "You know where you're going, right?"

"Yup."

Johnny brushed past Nicky and headed up the creaky stairs toward the back bedroom where Marconi conducted business: settling territorial disputes within the family, getting his cut on every transaction, approving bribes for city officials. And directing executions. Which was the thing he was mostly responsible for. Making sure the Lucchesi family maintained its terrifying reputation for violence and vengeance. The Double V's, as they were called by the family council. The council was the Lucchesi governing body. It met once a week somewhere in Queens, though never the same place twice in a row.

Despite all his power, Marconi lived modestly. He didn't own big houses around the world, didn't have a yacht moored in an exclusive Hamptons marina, didn't take luxurious vacations to exotic destinations. In fact, he almost never left this house. A few times a summer to see a Yankee game and to attend council meetings, and that was it. He was worth tens of millions, but he lived like any other blue-collar senior citizen. Like he couldn't wait for his next Social Security check.

When he wasn't conducting business, he watched television. He didn't read, didn't do crossword puzzles, didn't bother with the Internet. He just watched TV. Liked reruns of old sitcoms the best—*I Love Lucy, The Dick Van Dyke Show, Leave It to Beaver*—but he'd watch almost anything. Except soap operas. Not because he thought they were stupid. Because he didn't want to become addicted to one of them, didn't want to start planning his day around *Guiding Light* or *General Hospital.* Didn't want to have to explain that one to the brotherhood at a council meeting.

In front of the closed bedroom door was another sentry, a huge guy nicknamed Goliath. The guy's hands were clasped behind his back, and the bulge of a pistol was obvious beneath the lapel of his dark blazer. Johnny had no idea what the guy's real name was. No one in the family seemed to. But that was always how it was with the guy standing right outside Marconi's door. No one ever knew his real name.

"Noah's Ark," Johnny said loudly.

This was always the way. One password at the front door, one when you got to Marconi's door. The old man was bonkers about security.

Goliath gestured for Johnny to put his hands in the air—which Johnny did without hesitation or complaint—then patted him down. The procedure was entirely unnecessary because Johnny would never have been stupid enough to bring a gun into Marconi's home. Do that and you might not wake up the next morning, even if you hadn't meant Marconi any harm. Marconi had neither the patience nor the compassion for mistakes.

When Goliath was satisfied, he knocked on the door.

"What?" from inside.

"Bondano."

"Yeah, okay," came the raspy Italian accent. "Let him in." Marconi had lived in Sicily as a youngster. At fifteen he'd lost his homeland when he was forced to flee the country after gunning down three boys of a rival gang in broad daylight outside a crowded café. But he never lost his accent.

Goliath opened the door, and Johnny moved swiftly past. It was no Oval Office in here, but a lot of people in New York considered Marconi every bit as powerful as the president. Just an average-looking bedroom with cheap furniture from the seventies and a maroon shag carpet, it always reminded Johnny of a hospital. It had that disinfectant medicinal smell, and there were so many vials and bottles stacked on and around a bureau in one corner of the room you could barely tell it *was* a bureau. Since the death of his wife, the seventy-two-year-old boss had supposedly become a hypochondriac. Weak in the mind, people on the street were whispering more and more often. Maybe even delusional. But Johnny knew better, knew the whole thing was an act. Marconi's stranglehold on power hadn't waned at all over the past few years. In fact, it had strengthened. Even though he was officially the number two man in the organization, he was just as powerful as the don. More so in some people's eyes.

Johnny moved to where Marconi sat in his big easy chair, then leaned over and kissed the back of his hand.

"Hey ya, Deuce."

"Hey, Angelo." A rerun of *Family Feud* was playing on the old RCA.

"Take care of that," Marconi ordered in a raspy voice, pointing at the TV. He grimaced and touched his neck tenderly. "I think I'm coming down with something."

Johnny moved to the TV and turned up the volume just as the studio audience broke into a loud laugh. Now the authorities couldn't hear the conversation if somehow they'd managed to run a wire into the place during the past few days. Which was all the time there would have been, because Marconi had the entire place swept for bugs every few days. The row houses on either side of this one as well. He owned them, too. His sons lived there. Marconi was nothing if not careful.

"Sit, sit." Marconi gestured toward the other chair in the room. "Pull it over here next to me. Close, you know? So we can talk, Deuce."

Johnny noticed that Marconi had gained weight since the last time they met. At least twenty pounds. He wasn't tall—just five seven, a half inch taller than Johnny. But he had to be pushing two-fifty. And he still did that terrible comb-over thing with the few strands of straight, thin, oily black hair he had left. As if people couldn't tell he was almost bald. At least it was better than wearing one of those crummy toupees you could spot a mile away, like a lot of the older Lucchesi people did.

Marconi pointed at the TV. "That guy who's the host there. He's dead. You know that?"

"Nah, I didn't."

"Yeah, he committed suicide." Marconi shook his head. "He seems so happy on the show, always joking with the people."

"I guess you never know."

"Nah, you don't. Maybe he couldn't handle being such a little fucker. It gets to some men after a while." The old man reached over and patted Johnny's hand. Let a smile crease his olive-skinned, bulldog face. "But it's never gotten to you, Deuce."

Johnny took a deliberate breath, trying not to show how much the remark had irritated him. "No, it hasn't."

They were silent for a few moments.

"Why'd you want me to come over tonight, Angelo?" Johnny finally asked in a low voice. He'd learned how effective it was to speak softly now that he carried a big reputation.

Marconi patted Johnny's hand again. "I always liked you, Deuce. I always wished you could have been a real member of the family, wished you could have been a made man someday. You deserve it more than most of the jerks we make." He hesitated. "But . . . well, you know."

Johnny nodded. "I know, I know, I'm a quarter Russian. It can't happen." His expression turned grim. "My granddaddy couldn't keep his snake in his pants, so I pay."

"But I've always taken care of you," Marconi spoke up quickly. "Always thought of you as one of my guys. You know that."

There was something odd about this conversation. Like it was forced, Johnny realized. Like Goliath might bust in here any second and start shooting. Amazing how he could make the leap from a forced conversation to a hit so fast, but that's how it was with these people.

You picked up on subtle signals, or you died. He'd never heard of a hit going down in Marconi's house, and didn't know what he could have done to deserve it. But you never knew with the Lucchesi family. There was very little predicting. Which was the insidious part about getting into bed with them, and why you *always* had to be on guard. Well, if that was tonight's plan, he wasn't going down without a fight.

"You agree with that, Deuce, don't you?" Marconi pushed. "That I've always taken care of you? Always made sure you got paid good for what you do?"

"Yeah, sure. Of course."

Johnny made more than a million bucks a year working for Marconi. Thanks to the old man he owned a house in a quiet town out on Long Island's north fork and a condo down in Tampa overlooking the bay. In addition to the apartment he kept here in Queens. He'd never had to kill more than three people a year, and they'd all had it coming. All been scum of the earth.

Johnny always made certain of that before he pulled the trigger. Always made absolutely certain the men Marconi contracted with him to kill were lowlifes. It was important to Johnny that he never execute anyone who didn't clearly deserve it, because that allowed him to accept what he did for a living with a clear conscience. Allowed him to sleep soundly every night. It was his code of honor. And it could never be compromised. Not if he wanted his self-respect.

Everyone thought he'd offed the owner of the liquor store down the block, but he hadn't. You didn't kill a man for calling you a name. Of course, he'd never denied responsibility for what had happened to the guy, either.

Never admitted or denied it when he was asked. Just ignored the question the same way he did when somebody asked him about the two of hearts. After all, he had a reputation to maintain. The cops had hauled him into a precinct out near LaGuardia Airport to interrogate him about the deal because people on the street could never keep their mouths shut. But he'd just laughed at the NYPD boys when they got tough. They'd released him an hour later.

"You know I appreciate your generosity, Angelo." Johnny hated being so gracious, so respectful. It didn't come naturally. But he'd learned that it was the right thing to do if he wanted to keep making a million bucks a year. He'd never let his pride get in the way of that. "No question."

"Good, good." Marconi gazed at the TV for a few moments. "I'm going to ask you to do something, Deuce."

Now Johnny felt better, breathed a semisigh of relief. This was how it usually went, how Marconi usually carried on the conversation. And the old man's tone suddenly seemed more normal, too. The tension in Johnny's body eased, but he still kept an eye on the door. Of course, he always kept one eye on the door wherever he was. "What is it?"

Marconi gestured toward the window. "You remember that thing that happened in front my house a couple a years ago?"

Johnny's eyes raced to Marconi's.

"When my grandson was run over," Marconi continued, "when my daughter's only son was . . . when he was murdered."

"I remember," Johnny murmured, aware that Marconi's voice had cracked. It was the first time he'd ever heard the old man come close to choking up.

The boy had been the victim of a hit-and-run right in front of the row house while he was riding his bike in the street just after dark. Right about this time of the evening. Marconi had rushed outside when he heard yelling and cradled the battered little boy in his arms until he died. The ambulance had screamed to a stop at the scene a few seconds later, but there was nothing the EMTs could do. Nothing Marconi could do, either. All he'd been left with was revenge.

"What was the guy's name?" Johnny asked. "The guy who did that thing?"

"Kyle McLean."

"Yeah, right, Kyle McLean. Well, I thought that had been taken care of." Johnny was certain he'd heard McLean was dead. Certain he'd heard that McLean had died in a car accident the next night. Figured the real story was that some of Marconi's men had taken McLean out and made it look like an accident. "I thought it had kinda taken care of itself."

Marconi shook his head. "Turns out it hasn't. At least there's a chance it hasn't. A *good* chance." He pointed at Johnny. "I want you to find out for sure. And if it hasn't, take care of it for me once and for all. Make sure McLean gets what's coming. I'll pay you a million bucks for this one thing, Deuce. You'll do it as a personal favor to me."

So this wasn't something that had been sanctioned by the council—which all killings related to family business had to be. This job was outside that. A job Johnny had to do out of respect for the man who'd made him a million-aire. Even more important, a man who'd picked him up when he was on his ass and helped him climb out of the depths of despair. A job that would be ten times harder to refuse than any family contract.

"I know you want your marks to deserve what they got coming," Marconi said evenly. "I know about the research you do," he continued, "and the judgments you make in each case. I know about your code of honor."

Johnny pursed his lips. He'd never had any idea Marconi was aware of all that. Now he understood why the man was so powerful, what set him apart from the other wiseguys. He saw all the things they did—and all the things they didn't.

"Johnny."

Johnny's eyes rose slowly to Marconi's. He couldn't remember the last time the old man had called him anything but Deuce. "Yes, sir?" And he couldn't remember the last time he'd called Marconi sir.

"I just want you doing what I say. I just want you to kill Kyle McLean. You got that?"

Johnny had been told from the beginning that sooner or later this moment would come. A moment when he'd have to compromise his code of honor. When he would have no choice. But he'd always believed he could keep the relationship on his terms. Always felt like he'd be able to make the ultimate decision. Now he realized how naive he'd been. The people who'd warned him were exactly right. Everything would always be on Angelo Marconi's terms.

"Yeah," he finally said, his voice barely audible, "I got it."

Marconi hesitated a few moments, then nodded. "Good man."

"You got somewhere for me to start?" Suddenly Johnny felt like he couldn't get out of here fast enough. "Some way for me to pick up the trail?"

"Yeah. There's an ex-cop named Stephen Casey, who I hear may have some information on McLean. It won't be easy to get it out of him, but you're good at that. Getting dirt out of people." Marconi snickered. "You know, you're good at putting people *in* the dirt, too. Funny how that goes, huh?"

"Uh-huh." It wasn't funny at all.

Marconi reached into his pocket and handed Johnny a crinkled piece of lined yellow paper. "That's Casey's address down in Brooklyn. I want to hear back from you by tomorrow noon. No later than that, and the earlier the better."

Stephen Casey might be on vacation, might be staying at a girlfriend's house, might be working the graveyard shift at whatever job he was doing now that he'd quit the NYPD. But none of those things mattered to Marconi, not in the slightest. The old man had achieved a position in life few men did but all aspired to. He didn't accept excuses from anyone—even if they were legit. Because he didn't have to.

"Deuce?"

"Yeah, okay." At least Marconi was calling him Deuce again.

3

As Mikey Clemants ambled toward the plate—a forty-ounce ash bat slung over his right shoulder—a few faint cheers rose from the crowd. But they were quickly smothered by a chorus of enthusiastic boos and a loud chant of "You suck, Mikey" rising from several rows directly behind Jack. Growing in intensity as more people joined in with each chorus. The beer taps didn't close after the sixth inning here, the way they did in a lot of major-league stadiums, and the fans had turned rowdy since the seventh-inning stretch. For the owner of the Sarasota Tarpons every day was a financial struggle, Jack assumed. It was for most of the Single-A independents, he knew. The guy needed to make money any way he could, despite only paying his players $1,500 a month on average. So he kept the beer taps wide open until the last fan was gone.

"Clemants is gonna ground into a double play," Bobby predicted, nodding at the kid, then at the runner who was creeping off first to a short lead. "Betcha."

Maybe Bobby had been right about the kid after all, Jack realized. Maybe Mikey Clemants wasn't a diamond in the rough, wasn't the next Single-A prospect about to burst onto the major-league stage like a fiery meteor out of the night sky. Which was difficult for Jack to admit. He'd been so sure watching the kid head out to center for the top of the first that he was the real deal. Even more convinced after the circus catch a few moments later. But since that first inning Clemants had done exactly as Bobby had predicted: played like crap. He'd grounded out to short, been called out on strikes, and hit into a force play in his three at-bats. And he'd turned a single into a triple for the visiting team by botching a routine line drive over the second-base bag in the fifth. Thanks to which the Tarpons were now down a run with one out in the bottom of the ninth. It looked like they were going to hang a big "L" on the broad shoulders of Jack's can't-miss kid.

"Betcha," Bobby repeated. "Come on."

Jack would have taken the other side of that one in a heartbeat after the catch in the first. Not now. "Nope."

The kid popped the first pitch up. A moon shot that rocketed into the darkness above the stadium lights for a few moments, then came screaming back to earth and caromed off the yellow railing in front of a gang of young boys who'd raced out of the stands to shag it. The ball nailed the railing right beside the cowering old usher, glanced off one of the boys' arms, bounced on the fourth step, and smacked into Jack's outstretched palm. The crowd roared its approval at his barehanded catch. It was the loudest cheer of the night.

"Nice catch, Pop." Bobby patted Jack's shoulder. "Take a bow, old man."

Jack hated attention. "Nah." A second later the boys were in his face, begging and shouting for the ball. "Get out of here," he said with a hiss. "All of you."

"Please, mister," one of the boys yelled, lunging for the ball. *"Please!"*

Jack yanked the ball away from the boy's mustard-covered fingers. "No! Go on, get! I said, *get!*"

The cheers turned quickly to boos as the boys sulked away empty-handed.

Bobby patted Jack's shoulder again. "Nice going. Good luck getting out of here alive now. And don't expect me to save you, Pop."

"Oh, I won't," Jack muttered as the pitcher wound up for his next delivery. "Believe me."

The second the kid swung, Jack knew it was gone. From the distinctive smack of bat slamming ball. From the way the opposing pitcher hung his head and started for the dugout without even looking at where the ball was going. From the way Clemants flipped the bat play-fully in the air as he started his home-run trot. It was a herculean blast that seemed like it was still climbing as it sailed over the center fielder's head, then landed some-where out in the pasture, startling one of the cows graz-ing at the edge of the stadium lights. A five-hundred-foot blast. At least. And it didn't even look like the kid had swung that hard.

"Incredible," Jack whispered, feeling vindicated as the kid circled the bases. Clemants had made two of the greatest plays Jack had ever seen on a baseball field in one night, and he'd done it in a Single-A stadium. Admittedly book-ending an otherwise bush-league performance, but still. "He's got so much talent."

It was strange, though. The kid had just smashed a walk-off home run—the most dramatic play in baseball— but there was no one at the plate to congratulate him. No teammates, no coaches, not even the guy he'd batted in. Just the umpire standing by with his mask off and his hands on his hips, waiting to make sure the kid touched the plate. The fans were finally whooping it up, but Clemants's teammates didn't seem to care at all. Typically, the whole team would have been there. In fact, most of them had already exited the dugout and were heading to the locker room.

After the kid crossed home plate, Jack stood up stiffly, pulled his ticket from his shirt pocket, smiled at it again, stowed it in his wallet, then started limping up the stairs. He'd never seen anything like it on a baseball field before. Hell, Ty Cobb's teammates still congratulated him when he made a great play—even though they hated him.

"Hey, Pop!" Bobby yelled. "Where you going? Game's over. Let's get out of here!"

Jack kept going, ignoring Griffin. God, his knees ached. Elbows, too, all of a sudden. Old age was nothing but a legalized form of torture.

The little boy was sitting in the aisle outside the top row of seats in a wheelchair. Which, from the looks of his misshapen, gnarled legs, he'd never get out of. He was ten or eleven years old, twelve at most, but he looked like an old man sitting there between the chrome armrests. God, it was terrible.

"Here, son," Jack said softly, leaning down and handing over the ball he'd snagged a few minutes ago. He'd noticed the boy as he was climbing the stairs to his seat with Cheryl before the game. Felt terrible about the little guy's situation for nine innings—until he'd caught that foul ball. He'd known from the second it smacked his outstretched palm what he was going to do with it. He'd thought about coming up here as soon as he made the catch—which probably would have made him more popular with the fans—but he didn't want to embarrass the boy by making a big deal out of it in front of everybody. So he'd waited until the game was over. "Enjoy."

"Gee, thanks, mister."

"You're welcome." As Jack smiled at the boy's mother and straightened up, he rubbed his left arm, then his chest. Then he sank to his knees and toppled over, his head coming to rest against a cement step.

4

JOHNNY HESITATED ON the stoop outside Marconi's front door, checking up and down the street, trying to remember which cars had been here and which ones hadn't when he went inside. It was tough to tell much in the dim light coming from the old streetlamps, but he had a feeling something was wrong. He'd always had a sixth sense for imminent danger. A premonition of peril, he called it. And it had saved his life more than once.

He moved deliberately down the steps, then down the sidewalk toward the Seville, constantly looking around, his neck like a swivel on a stick as he walked. As he pressed the unlock button and the Seville chirped, he hesitated, wondering if someone had rigged the car to explode when the door opened. The meeting with Marconi still seemed strange to him; something wasn't quite right about it. But thinking Marconi had rigged the car to explode was stupid. The old man would never order so over-the-top an execution directly in front of his house. Would he? Maybe that would be the beauty of it. Completely unexpected, completely irrational. When they really thought about it, the cops would have to figure Marconi had nothing to do with it.

Johnny reached for the door, then pulled back quickly, like a flash of electricity had arced from the car handle to his fingers. This could be a rival family hit. He'd killed a captain in the Capelletti mob last year down in Staten Island. The Capelletti family was the second most powerful mob in the city, and they would undoubtedly take revenge if they found out who'd put a bullet through their man's head from across the street as he was headed into his favorite restaurant. But Marconi had sworn he was the only member of the Lucchesi family who knew Johnny was the killer, and Johnny was sure Marconi would never violate that confidence. If only because the old man considered Johnny the best hit man around and didn't want to lose the talent.

He grimaced as he reached for the door handle again. This was the life he'd chosen—and one hell of a life it was. Full of great things, including financial security, which he'd never known growing up. Then there were times like this.

But nothing happened when he jerked the door open. He bent down quickly and grabbed the Beretta 9mm he kept hidden beneath the front seat. He'd filed down the trigger mechanism so it fired almost like an automatic. It was his favorite gun of the fifteen he owned.

As he rose and slipped the pistol into his belt, he noticed a dark sedan at the edge of the glow from a street-lamp five cars up. His eyes narrowed. That car hadn't been there when he'd gone into Marconi's place. He pulled the pistol from his belt and took a step up the street. Instantly the sedan squealed out of the spot and roared off. He was tempted to jump into the Seville and chase whoever it was, but they had too big a lead. He'd never catch them.

Besides, the eerie premonition of peril had passed. Suddenly he wasn't worried about slipping the key in the ignition and turning it.

5

JACK OPENED HIS eyes slowly. He was lying flat on his back on the cement step—which seemed only slightly less comfortable than the cheap mattress on his narrow, single bed at home. Two EMTs in white shirts and dark green polyester pants were squatting beside him, pulling instruments out of bags. He squinted up against the bright stadium lights blazing down at him from over one guy's shoulders, then against the glare of the small flashlight the other guy started shining directly into his pupils. A stretcher lay on the next step down, and there was a small but growing crowd milling around, even though the game was over. They were sneaking glances, filled with morbid curiosity. Trying to seem like they weren't fascinated by what was going on. But Jack knew they were. People were always fascinated with pain and death—as long as it wasn't theirs.

"What the hell's going on?" Jack mumbled to the EMT who'd been blinding him with the flashlight. His name was Biff. The letters were sewn onto his shirt with thick blue thread. The other guy's name was Harry. "What are you guys doing?"

"You had a heart attack, Daddy," Cheryl said anxiously, her voice trembling with emotion. "At least, that's what they think right now." She was kneeling between Biff and Harry, tears balanced precariously on her lower lids. "They're taking you to the hospital."

"The hell they are," Jack muttered, pulling himself up onto one elbow with a groan.

"Easy, sir," Harry said soothingly, doing his best to check Jack's blood pressure. "We're just trying to make you feel better. We're just trying to help you."

The fingertips of Jack's left hand suddenly felt like they were going to burst. "I don't need any help," he growled back. Harry was overweight and had sad, sympathetic eyes. "Just leave me alone so I can—"

"*Hey*, why don't you just lay down and shut up," Biff interrupted, stowing the small flashlight back into his belt with an angry thrust. "Christ, some of these old guys really piss me off," he complained. "Why don't you just let us do our jobs."

"Why don't *you* go play in traffic, you punk!" Jack snapped. Biff was thin, with beady eyes. Red and road-mapped, too. Like he was hung over. Jack could tell Harry cared about what he was doing, even if he was a pain in the ass. But for Biff this was simply a paycheck. "That would make *me* feel a lot better." Jack spotted the pointed end of a knife tattoo on Biff's upper arm, sneaking out from beneath his shirtsleeve. He'd never liked tattoos. "A hell of a lot better." He reached for the black Velcro strip noosed tightly around his upper arm and tore it off.

"*Daddy*," Cheryl cried. "My God, what are you doing?"

"Princess, I'm—"

"Come on, Pop," Bobby cut in, "listen to them. Don't give them such a hard time."

Bobby was towering over Jack, silhouetted by the stadium lights. An irritated, this-could-really-screw-up-my-plans-for-the-night expression on his face. "Don't tell me what to do, young man."

"It's stupid not to take their advice, Pop."

"Don't ever call me stupid again," Jack warned, making it to his knees with a moan.

"I didn't call you stupid. I said it was stupid not to—"

"Not if you want to keep dating my daughter," Jack growled, brushing grit and a piece of old bubble gum off his palms. Harry tried to keep him down, but Jack pushed the EMT's hands away and rose unsteadily to his feet. "Are we clear on that?"

Bobby glanced at Biff and rolled his eyes, then turned and headed down the stairs.

"Don't do this, Daddy," Cheryl begged. "Please."

"Princess, these guys are gonna rush me to a hospital like it's a real emergency, then hand me over to some people in pale green outfits who'll run a hundred different tests on me. But they won't tell me anything while they're running them. Finally, around one o'clock this morning, I'll get a piece of paper with some meaningful information on it. It'll be the bill, and it'll be about two thousand bucks. After they stick me with it, they'll shrug their shoulders, tell me they can't find anything really wrong with me, and recommend that I stop drinking scotch and eat more greens." Jack shook his head. "Nope, I'm not going anywhere with them."

"I know you don't have health insurance," she whispered. "I know that's the problem. I'll pay for everything, don't worry."

"No, you won't," he replied, his tone easing. She was so sweet—which was the whole problem. "I can't let you do that." He'd stolen a look in her checkbook last week when she was at work. The balance was a measly $440. Of course, that was twice what was in his account. "I'll be fine, I promise."

6

GOOD EVENING, MR. Casey." Johnny's polite greeting echoed eerily in the small back room of the warehouse. Bare cement walls, dim lighting, bone-chilling cold, a rusty metal conveyor in one corner, a stack of rotting boxes in another, and the stench of fish and mildew with every breath. A nasty place for a nasty job. It was perfect. "Sorry to put you out this way."

"You're not sorry for anything."

Stephen Casey lay on his back, blindfolded and secured to a narrow piece of three-quarter-inch plywood suspended from the ceiling by four strong ropes. The plywood hung at an angle so his head was eighteen inches below his feet. He was much bigger than Johnny, but that didn't matter at this point.

Marconi had made a crew of Lucchesi soldiers available to Johnny, even though killing Kyle McLean wasn't sanctioned by the family council. Johnny had contacted the crew's leader and ordered him and his men to go to the address on the crumpled yellow paper and pick up Casey. Using Lucchesi code—because he was on a cell phone—Johnny had instructed the leader to take Casey to this family-controlled warehouse, tie him up in a very specific way, and leave. The crew had followed Johnny's orders to a tee. Casey was secured so tightly to the plank he could barely even move his toes. One thing about the men under Marconi's command: they always carried out his orders exactly.

"What do you do now?" Johnny asked.

"Huh?"

Johnny was leaning against the wall ten feet from where Casey was hanging. Damn, it was cold in here. He moved closer so Casey could hear him better, watching Casey's breath rise. "What do you do now?" he repeated, louder. The echoes were suddenly more noticeable, more ominous. "You were a city cop, but you retired from the force." Marconi hadn't told him what Casey did for a living now, just that Casey wasn't a cop anymore. The guy didn't look older than fifty, so he had to be doing something. Couldn't just be sitting on his ass collecting a pension. "Where do you work now?"

"Who the hell are you?"

"Calm down, Mr. Casey."

"Calm down? You pricks break into my house, tie me up, blindfold me, throw me in the back of a truck, drag me to wherever this godforsaken place is, and you want me to calm down? *Screw you.*" Casey struggled furiously for a few moments, pulling frantically at the ropes

binding his wrists and ankles beneath the plywood and straining at the rusty chain around his neck. Finally he gave up. "What do you want from me?" he asked, gasping. His struggle had only tightened the bindings.

"Tell me what you do."

"Why you wanna know?"

"I just do."

"I'm a damn security guard at a parts warehouse out at the airport."

"Which one?"

"LaGuardia."

"What airline?"

"Delta. What do you care?"

Johnny took another step forward, so he was only a few inches from Casey. "Why'd you quit the force?"

"I felt guilty, you know? I wanted to give somebody else a chance to risk their lives every day for fifty grand a year. Why the hell do you think I quit?" he said with a snarl. "I figured out crime *does* pay. I figured out it wasn't worth getting shot at by you guys when you're making twenty times what I am and ninety percent of the time you beat the rap anyway." He hesitated. "And I wanted to be around for my grandkids," he admitted. "I started thinking about not making it home one night. I started to get that bad feeling."

Johnny heard the faint sound of water dripping somewhere. So cops got that premonition of peril, too. "How many grandkids you got?"

"Two."

"How old?"

"Three and one."

"Boys, girls?"

"What is this?" Casey demanded. "What do you guys want?"

"It's just me here, Mr. Casey. Nobody else. The other men are gone. It's just me and you."

"That supposed to make me feel better?"

"No."

"You gonna kill me?" Casey asked, his tone turning less surly.

"Not if you give me what I want."

"What's that?"

"Information."

"Screw you!" Casey shouted again, his bravado back in high gear. *"I'm not telling you anything."*

So Casey was going to play tough guy. Which only made sense. He was an ex–New York City cop. He wasn't used to being pushed around. He was used to doing the pushing. It wouldn't matter, though, not one damn bit. Johnny had never failed to break anybody. Not using this technique.

"What information could I possibly have that you'd want?"

Johnny zipped the fleece he was wearing up to his chin, picked up a box of Saran Wrap off a stool, and moved close to Casey. Casey's head was level with his knees. "I need to know about a man named Kyle McLean." He let the echoes fade, gave his words time to sink in. "Is he alive?"

"I don't know anybody by that name." Casey suddenly shivered uncontrollably, and goose bumps rose up over his entire body. Marconi's soldiers had stripped Casey to his boxers, and according to the thermometer on the wall, it was thirty-nine degrees in here. His clothes lay in a wet pile in the middle of a puddle next to the stack of boxes. "I swear it."

"I've seen the police report," Johnny shot back, his voice rising, taking on a hint of anger. "Don't lie to me. I hate it when people lie to me."

"Look, I don't remember the guy. I was a cop for twenty-five years. I made a lot of arrests, filled out a lot of reports. I don't remember all the names, you know?"

"Sure, sure, except Kyle McLean was related to you." Casey's head snapped toward Johnny despite the chain around his neck and the blindfold. "He was your nephew." The obvious reaction of recognition a sure sign a nerve had been struck. "The report you filed says McLean accidentally drove his car off an East River pier one night a couple of years ago when he was drunk. And that he drowned. That jog your memory?"

Casey nodded as best he could. "Oh, yeah, yeah. *Now* I remember." His teeth were chattering so hard it was difficult for him to speak. "Can I have a blanket or something? I'm freezing."

"When we're done," Johnny answered, leaning down close. "When you've told me what I wanna know."

"You already know everything I know. Kyle accidentally drove his car off a pier near where they used to keep that old battleship. He drowned."

"Why would he do that?"

"They killed his girlfriend. He got stinking drunk and lost it. Couldn't take being without her. Missed a turn, went over the edge."

Johnny felt a familiar lump form quickly in his throat. He still hadn't gotten over her. Never would. "*Who* killed his girlfriend?"

"The Lucchesi family. The Mafia."

Johnny stood straight up and took a quick, involuntary step back. Then hunched over for a split second, like he'd been slammed in the stomach with a sharp punch. Angelo Marconi had left that little detail out. Unless this was an intricate dodge Casey was trying to pull. But the missile had landed too close to home, sounded too believable. How could Casey *possibly* have known he was being tortured tonight on direct orders from a Lucchesi boss? "Why would they kill his girlfriend?" Johnny asked, trying not to act like Casey's response had hit him so hard.

"Kyle owed them money, I think. Yeah, that was it. Like almost a hundred grand. He borrowed it from them to pay for his mom's operation. For my sister, Helen. She and her husband didn't have insurance, didn't have anywhere near that kind of cash. And the rest of us didn't have the money, either. She would have died without surgery, so Kyle went to the mob for the money. They were his only option."

"Yeah, but why'd they kill his *girlfriend*?"

No answer.

"*Mr. Casey!*"

"Okay, okay, here's how it went down. So they come looking for the VIG early, see, way before they're supposed to. They want some big extra payment they'd never mentioned at the beginning, too. A processing fee, they call it. Kyle keeps telling them he can't pay 'em yet, that it's way earlier than the original deal. But they won't stop coming around, won't stop badgering him, won't give him a break. It doesn't make any sense, and Kyle gets pissed off at 'em one night in Brooklyn, *really* pissed off. Tells the main guy to go screw himself. Tells him he's gonna turn the tables and come after him. So they off Kyle's girl-friend to let him know they mean business.

"Now he's going out of his mind because he feels so guilty and the main guy tells Kyle they're gonna start kill-ing his family next. Torture us before they kill us, too. Gouge out eyes with pens, pour acid on the wounds. Cut off body parts real slow. Real bad shit, you know? Helen first, then the rest of us. Yeah, well, Kyle can't take it, would never be able to live with himself. And he knows they're serious now, too. Like I said, he can't handle being without his girl, either. They were tight, real tight. So he goes the only way out he can think of. He ends.it."

Johnny raised his hand slowly to his chest, feeling the two of hearts in his shirt pocket beneath the warm fleece. "Suicide?"

"Yeah, right, suicide. Now, will you *please* let me go?"

"But you told me a minute ago that McLean acciden-tally drove his car off that pier. That's what your police report says, too."

"I forgot. I'm sorry. Kyle didn't want me to put sui-cide in the report. He didn't want his mother to hear about that. He didn't want his mother to think he mur-dered himself. He knew Helen wouldn't have been able to handle it. So I doctored the report after Kyle killed himself."

"*Doctored* it? Wasn't that risky? Couldn't doing some-thing like that have gotten you kicked off the force?"

"I'm his uncle, for Christ's sake. Kyle and I are close. I'm really like his older brother. I'd do anything for him."

There it was. The mistake Johnny had been hoping for. Casey's sliver of a brain hemorrhage. "If McLean's dead, how can you *still* be close to him? How can you *still* be like an older brother to him?"

Casey went silent. The only sound in the room was water dripping. He wasn't even shivering anymore.

"Answer the question, Mr. Casey."

"I don't understand. What do you mean?"

Johnny had always fantasized about being a trial lawyer as a kid. He loved watching Perry Mason black-and-white reruns after school on the old Zenith in his grandmother's cramped living room. But there hadn't been enough money for college, let alone law school. He still loved manipulating people into corners, though. "You just told me you're still like his older brother. How could you still be like his older brother if he's dead? How can you *still* be his uncle?"

"I . . . I don't know. I was just talking. It was a figure of speech, just something you say. Kyle's been dead for a couple of years. I was his uncle. That's what I meant to say. I was his uncle. Okay?"

"We dug up his grave." A bald-faced lie, but it sounded chillingly convincing in here. He knew McLean was supposed to have been buried, not cremated. And he knew what cemetery he was supposed to be buried in. "At St. George's in Queens. Way in the back." Johnny hesitated. "Guess what? No bones. Just an empty coffin."

Casey's teeth were suddenly chattering out of control again. "I'm so damn cold."

"You gonna tell me the truth?" Johnny asked with a snarl.

"He's dead. Dead, I *swear it.*"

Johnny opened the Saran Wrap box, pulled out a few feet of the razor-thin, transparent wrap, pressed the end of it to Casey's forehead and began shrouding his face. Over his face and under the plywood, over his face and under the plywood. Again and again as Casey struggled futilely against the chain and ropes. Johnny was careful not to cover Casey's nostrils as he wrapped. "One more chance, Mr. Casey," Johnny warned when he was done, ripping the wrap off against the box's jagged metal teeth, then tossing the box back toward the stool. "You gonna tell me the truth?"

No answer.

Johnny leaned down, picked up a bucket of ice water, and poured it slowly over Casey's face, making certain some of it went down his nose. Instantly Casey started screaming, his cries muffled by the Saran Wrap. It was probably already over, but just for good measure Johnny picked up a second bucket and poured it over Casey's face. Now the guy was really having a heart attack.

The technique was called waterboarding. Used by the feds to extract information from terrorist suspects in secret prisons around the world, it replicated the sensation of drowning perfectly. A friend of Johnny's had told him about it. Also told him that when the agents had tried practicing against it—in case it was ever used on them— the average agent gave up in fourteen seconds. Johnny had used the technique six times before, and each victim had broken right away. He ripped the Saran Wrap from Casey's mouth.

"I faked it okay I faked it!" Casey yelled. "I faked everything for Kyle, everything. I forged the accident report. Confirmed his death. I did it all. He was scared out of his mind they were gonna kill us all after they whacked his girlfriend. And they probably would have."

"Where is he now?" Johnny demanded.

"I don't know. *I swear to God I don't know.* I think he left the city after the whole thing. I don't know where he went. Nobody did. For all I know he's really dead now." Casey's chest was heaving. "I don't know what happened to him. As far as I know he hasn't talked to any of us since that night. Not even Helen."

It made sense that Casey wouldn't know where McLean was. That was the whole reason McLean had done what he'd done. To cut all ties so nothing could lead Marconi to him. The obvious risk here was that if McLean and Casey were somehow still communicating, Casey could warn McLean that people were looking for him. And he could make his getaway.

"Don't kill me," Casey begged. "Please don't kill me. I told you everything I know. I haven't seen your face."

"We're not gonna kill you, Mr. Casey," Johnny said in a tough tone, using "we" now because that was always scarier to a victim than "I." "But we'll be watching." He'd get Casey's phone records and check the numbers constantly to make certain he and McLean didn't talk. "And we're gonna *keep* watching. We find out you talk to Kyle McLean once, just once, and you're a dead man. I mean it, *a dead man.* You understand me?"

"I understand, I understand. I swear it."

Johnny started unfurling the Saran Wrap from around Casey's face, then stopped. Making Casey think his suffering was over, then snatching away the awesome feeling of relief. "There's a few more things I need to know. You give me answers I like, and I take this stuff off. You don't, and, well, you know what happens."

7

JACK STEPPED DOWN gingerly from the front seat of Bobby's SUV, thinking about how Biff, the EMT, had pressed him several times at the stadium to sign a form saying he'd called for their assistance. But he hadn't signed it. The whole reason Biff wanted that signature was so he and Harry could charge for their time. One thing Jack had learned over the years was that everybody was constantly trying to slip their fingers in your wallet. That life ultimately came down to one big, sometimes completely corrupt, chaotic grab for the dollar. Which was pretty damn discouraging when you really thought about it.

"Easy, Daddy," Cheryl urged as they moved up the narrow, cracked path. "Walk slow."

"I'm fine, Princess."

"Let's just get you in the house."

"Yeah, let's do that," he muttered, glancing up at the small ranch house he and Cheryl had lived in the past few years. Might as well call it the "coffin." This was probably where he was going to die. He'd been thinking about dying a lot lately, down to which room he'd collapse in. His bedroom or the living room, most likely, but maybe the kitchen. Maybe he'd keel over while he was fixing a sliced turkey sandwich for lunch one day. He loved sliced turkey sandwiches—though not nearly as much as he loved grilled hot dogs at a baseball game. "Let's get me in the house." He just prayed it wouldn't happen in the bathroom. That would be the worst. Sprawled out stark naked after collapsing in the shower.

He hated this house, hated the entire neighborhood. The people were nice enough, but it was so damn boring and bland here. A few storm-ravaged palm trees, some scraggly bushes here and there, and a sea of almost identical ranch houses built on brown, burned-out lawns along a perfect grid of ramrod-straight, potholed streets that stretched east–west and north–south as far as you could see. There was no character to it. It wasn't at all like the beautiful neighborhood he'd lived in on Long Island where the houses were big and different. Like the house he'd lived in back when he was with the Yankees. Back when he had some self-respect. But Cheryl's mother had grabbed everything in the divorce—including his self-respect. And this place had been all he and Cheryl could afford. Barely, at that.

"Don't worry about me, Princess."

"I always worry about you, Daddy."

"You want me to stay here tonight?" Bobby called, hustling up behind them. His SUV was still idling in the narrow driveway. "In case anything happens, I mean."

"Nothing's gonna happen," Jack said with a growl, catching Cheryl's eye in the light of the porch lamp. Making it clear he didn't want Bobby sticking around. "I just want to rest. I just want some peace and quiet." He pulled out his keys and unlocked the front door. "Cheryl can take care of me by herself just fine."

"Can I get anything for you from the store?" Bobby asked her. "Anything at all?"

"No, sweetheart, but thanks. I'll call you in the morning," she promised.

Jack limped inside, hesitating in the foyer so he could hear.

"Baby, can you come back to my place for a little while?" Bobby asked in a low voice. "I won't keep you long."

As far as Jack knew, Cheryl had never gone to Bobby's apartment. She'd sworn to Jack just last week she'd never been there when he asked.

"I have to take care of my father," Cheryl murmured.

"Just for a little while," Bobby begged. "Please."

"It's just that I have to—"

"I did pay for everything tonight. The tickets, the parking, the beer. And I tried making friends with him like you wanted."

She kissed him. "Yes, you did," she whispered, pulling back, "and it was really nice of you."

"I'll have you back in an hour. I just don't want to say good night yet. I miss you a lot when we're not together."

"Well . . . I guess I could come over for a few—"

"*Where's the aspirin?*" Jack yelled.

"Oh, Lord," she muttered. "I gotta go, Bobby. I'll call you first thing in the morning." She hurried inside, pulled the door shut, then trotted to their small kitchen and a drawer beside the refrigerator. She grabbed two capsules from the bottle of aspirin, filled a glass with water, then headed back down the hall. "Here," she said, holding out the capsules in one hand and the glass of water in the other.

Jack was just coming out of his bedroom. He grinned and took a sip of scotch from the leather-cased flask he'd retrieved from his nightstand. "The aspirin are for you."

"What?"

"Yeah," he said, hobbling past her. "I figured you might need them."

He caught sight of himself in the hall mirror and froze. God, he'd aged so much in the past few years. Strange how he'd never noticed it before. Maybe simply facing the day in the morning was such a grind he didn't see it in his bathroom mirror. Maybe the light was different in there. Or maybe he was simply looking harder right now.

He leaned toward the mirror so his face was close to the glass. His hair seemed grayer than it used to be, much more salt than pepper. The lines at the corners of his eyes and mouth were more pronounced, too. And his face seemed thinner, not as strong as it once was. At least the light blue husky eyes still burned bright—more so after tonight.

"You should go straight to bed," Cheryl recommended when she'd swallowed the second aspirin.

"Yeah, I hear you." He hesitated. "But I need your help with something first." He straightened up, pulled his shoulders back, pushed his chest out, and sucked in his gut. There; that was better.

"You're still very handsome," she murmured reassuringly, squeezing his broad shoulders from behind. "What do you need help with?"

Cheryl had a computer with Internet connection in her bedroom. Though she'd often tried to get him to use it, he hadn't. Truth was, he didn't know how to use it, and he didn't want to look stupid. Asking for help with anything was a challenge for him. Always had been. Just as it had been for his father. Of course, this had to do with technology. This was different. This wasn't like asking somebody for directions or something. He took a long swallow of scotch. And it might save his life. Literally. Might ultimately show some people they'd done the wrong thing firing him. He could damn well get past his pride for a chance at that.

"I want to go on the Web for a while," he answered.

"Really," she asked, surprised.

"Show me how, will you?"

She motioned to the flask. "If you stop drinking."

One of the images in the mirror Jack had tried to ignore was the spiderweb of tiny blue veins spreading out from both sides of his thin nose into his cheeks. That and the fact that his nose and cheeks seemed to be getting redder and ruddier by the day. He'd told himself the Florida sun was to blame, but maybe it wasn't. If she only knew how much he was drinking. But how else was he supposed to make it through a workday? He'd decided early on in his grocery bagging career that it was never meant to be done sober.

"Okay," he agreed, setting the flask down on the hall table beneath the mirror. "Done."

As he followed Cheryl into her room, he noticed a

heap of freshly washed panties and bras on top of her dresser and quickly glanced away. It was one thing when they were your wife's, quite another when they were your daughter's. Maybe he was too uptight. But he'd been raised in an uptight home, and he was too old to change.

It took awhile to get the hang of it, but when he finally realized that using the Internet was as simple as typing in a few words, then pointing and clicking, he felt damn stupid. "Great, thanks." He patted her knee gently and nodded at the door. But she didn't get the hint. "Can you give me a few minutes?"

Cheryl moaned. "It's almost midnight, Daddy. I want to go to bed."

Jack clasped his hands together like he was praying. "Please, Princess."

"Tomorrow's a workday," Cheryl reminded him. She was an administrative assistant in a real estate office. "I need my sleep."

"This won't take long."

She let out an aggravated breath and stood up. "When I get home tomorrow, we're moving this thing out in the living room because I can see where this is going." She tapped the computer. "You'll be addicted to it by the time I come back."

When she was gone, Jack typed "Sarasota Tarpons" into the search engine and hit go. It didn't take long to get to the home page. At the bottom of it was a team picture, but there was no Mikey Clemants. He was listed as "Not Pictured" beneath the photograph, along with an assistant coach and a trainer. Jack clicked to the kid's personal page, but there was no picture of him there, either. Just a blank screen where the picture was supposed to be. The kid's bio mentioned that he was from somewhere in southern Minnesota. From some tiny town Jack had never heard of—and he thought he'd heard of them all. Thought he'd *been* to them all at some point in his scouting career.

He scanned the stats quickly, noting the kid's last name was actually Clemant—no "s" at the end, as Bobby had pronounced it. Not including tonight's game, the kid had three home runs, fifteen runs batted in, and a so-so .254 batting average. He'd committed a bunch of errors, too. Bobby was right. This was nothing to write home about. The kid had all the physical tools to make it in the majors—the catch and the home run had convinced Jack of that—but there was something missing. Something very important. Hopefully it was something teachable. And Jack knew just the man for the job. That good-looking older guy he'd been admiring in the hall mirror a little while ago.

"Daddy?"

Jack whirled around. He'd been standing on the top step of the Yankee dugout in the Bronx, watching the kid's tryout. Watching the kid slam ball after ball over the blue wall. Enjoying congratulations from coaches, players, and front-office people. From all the people who'd been so skeptical when the kid was striding toward home plate at the beginning of the tryout. Cheryl's voice had jerked him away from that New York fantasy, jerked him back to his Sarasota reality.

"I'm done," he said, standing up. "I'll scram and let you get to bed." He kissed her forehead as they came together. "Sorry I kicked you out."

"It's okay."

He could tell something was wrong. "What is it?" She was moving from foot to foot like she always did when she was nervous. "Come on, Princess. Out with it."

She folded her arms across her chest. "Did you fake it tonight after the game?"

Jack chuckled uneasily. "Fake *what*?"

"Your heart attack. Was that all an act?"

He bit his lip, trying to mask the grin tugging at both corners of his mouth. "Well, I don't know if it was a heart attack, but I sure felt like I was going through something painful, let me tell you."

"Don't split hairs, Daddy," Cheryl warned sharply, using a tone she rarely did with him. "You know what I mean. Did you fake it?"

Finally Jack let the grin out of the bag. "Maybe I did, maybe I didn't."

She gritted her teeth. "Look, this isn't a joke. This isn't like when you rigged Billy Martin's toilet to explode and framed Reggie. This isn't like when you let all those snakes loose in the players' dormitory in spring training and scared them half to death. This isn't like that. This isn't funny."

"It's a *little* funny."

"It's not funny at all, *damn* it. It's my life."

She never swore, and it caught his attention like an Ali hook. "Princess, I—"

"You didn't want me going home with Bobby. That's why you faked the heart attack, wasn't it? *Wasn't it?*"

She was serious this time, and Jack wasn't ready for it. He'd never seen her like this. "I love you so much," he murmured. "I just don't want to see you get hurt, and I—"

"You don't want me to leave," she snapped, anger tears

welling in her eyes. "You don't want to see the person who waits on you hand and foot get away. You want to hang on to me any way you can. That's what it is, isn't it? That's what tonight was all about. That's why you scared Bobby off. That's why you scare all my boyfriends off. You're worried that if you don't, you might lose your slave." Her voice was trembling. "Don't be so damn selfish, Daddy. Don't try to run my life anymore. Think about someone other than yourself for once, will you?"

Jack shook his head. "No, no, Princess, it's that I—"

"You've got to let me go. I can't stay here forever."

"I, I—"

"You don't love me."

Jack's mouth ran dry. He couldn't love anyone more than he did Cheryl. How could she take his little prank so seriously? He figured she'd known from the start the whole thing was a hoax. At least suspected it was. "Princess, I . . . I love you so much. I can't believe you could think I'd want to keep you here like some kind of prisoner. Like some kind of . . ." His voice trailed off.

Suddenly she rushed into his arms, leaping across the sudden chasm. "I'm sorry, Daddy," she said, sobbing. "I'm sorry I said that. It was so mean, and I know how much you love me. You've always been there for me. Always." She looked up at him, tears streaming down her cheeks. "But I need to have my own life. I want kids, and I'm not getting any younger. I want to see you hold them. I want to see you teach them to throw a baseball like you taught me when I was little. I want you to go to Little League games with me and my husband. I want all of that, you know?" She pressed her face into his neck. "You aren't getting any younger, either." She sobbed loudly several times. "I'm worried that . . . I'm worried . . . Christ, I can't even say it."

Jack felt the awesome power of uncontrollable emotion bearing down on him. The twitch in his lower lip, the heat in his eyes, the mess in his mind. He hated being weak, hated people who were weak. He shut his eyes, fighting it hard. "I know," he muttered, hoping his voice sounded strong. "I know what you mean. And I know you want all those things. Every woman does. They're the most important things in the world."

She hugged him tightly. "I won't move away, Daddy, I promise. I'll stay right here in Sarasota. You'll come over every night for dinner. We'll have a room for you so you can stay over whenever you want. Bobby and I talked about that, and he's fine with it. I won't let you be old and lonely."

He'd never thought of that—at least not consciously. The possibility that maybe he wasn't scaring off her boyfriends to protect her, but to protect himself. He shook his head. That was insane; he'd never do that. Of course, the mind worked in mysterious ways. He knew that all too well. "I know you won't," he said, relieved when the emotion passed, when he regained control. "I know you want your own life. Damn, you can't be taking care of me forever. I know that."

"Bobby likes me." She pulled a tissue from her jeans and wiped her eyes. "I think maybe he might even love me. He could be the one."

That image of Bobby slipping his fingers away from Cheryl's at the game still haunted him. "Sure. I caught him looking at you tonight that way a couple of times. Like he couldn't be without you. It was nice."

"Daddy, I know I'm not the prettiest girl around. I know I'm—"

"You're *gorgeous*," he interrupted, looking into her eyes fiercely. "Bobby Griffin's damn lucky to be dating you."

Cheryl smiled. "Thanks, Daddy." Another small sob shook her, like an earthquake aftershock. She pressed her face into his neck again. "Will you *really* try to like him?" she whispered. "Please."

Jack tilted his head back and let out a slow breath. Sometimes life was so hard. "Sure, Princess."

8

JOHNNY DIDN'T WAIT around. Thirty minutes after dropping Stephen Casey off on a street corner twenty blocks away from the seafood warehouse—tied to a streetlamp, blindfolded, and still wearing just his boxers—Johnny was back at Marconi's row house. One thing about the old man, he didn't sleep much. Claimed he needed less and less the older he got so it wasn't tough getting a late-night meeting with him.

Seemed like Marconi was using a lot of those extra waking hours to put on pounds. It was one in the morning, and he was horsing down a ham and cheese hero. Leaning over a little folding tray table with a pastel flower painted on it that was sitting in front of his easy chair as he watched *Green Acres*, lettuce and tomato spilling out both sides of his mouth.

"I always liked the Gabor sisters," Marconi muttered

through his half-chewed food. "Always thought they were sexy."

Interesting, Johnny thought. He figured Marconi didn't have sexual thoughts anymore. Figured he'd left that behind. But maybe men never did. "Uh-huh."

Marconi put the sandwich down. "So what'd you find out, Deuce?"

"It's like you said," Johnny began. "Kyle McLean didn't drown in the East River after all. The car going in the drink was all staged with the NYPD's help. Casey faked everything for McLean."

Marconi cleaned off his onyx pinkie ring with a paper napkin. The ring was covered with mayonnaise. "Where's McLean now?"

"Casey doesn't know."

"He's lying," Marconi snapped. "He knows."

"I don't think so. I used one of the best torture techniques around on him. He told me McLean was alive right away, but he didn't say anything else about him. Even when I pressed." Even with a third, fourth, and fifth bucket of water. "If Casey knew anything else, he would have spilled his guts. Believe me, Angelo."

Marconi waved his hand angrily, then pointed. "I'll tell you who knows," he said loudly.

Johnny winced, afraid of what was coming. He'd already thought of this, just hoped Marconi hadn't. But the old man never missed a trick—or an opportunity. "Who?" he asked innocently.

"McLean's mother. She knows. If they're good Catholics, the kid's talking to his mother. You and I both know that, Deuce." Marconi grinned. "You may need to get the dirt out of her. Then put *her* in the dirt."

"She wouldn't tell me even if she knew," Johnny answered, disgusted at the thought of waterboarding a middle-aged woman who'd probably never even hurt a flea. Torturing an innocent woman wouldn't just break his code of honor, it also would disintegrate it. Make him no better than any of the other goons walking around New York who offed people for next to nothing regardless of who they were or whether they were guilty. "She's his mother. She'd die before she told me."

Marconi pointed a stubby finger at Johnny. "You know I don't condone violence against women, but this is my grandson. I can't rest in peace until I make this thing right. You need to do whatever it takes to find out where McLean is now that we know the accident was a fake. Even that waterboarding trick you do. You'll go after this woman if you can't find any other way to hunt him down. And you won't screw around. You don't turn up anything on McLean quick, you're going after his mother. Got it?"

They stared at each other hard for a few moments, neither one blinking. Finally Marconi picked up the hero and took another messy bite.

As Johnny watched Marconi chew, he tried desperately to shake off the image of a blindfolded middle-aged woman strapped to a piece of plywood. The image of the ice-cold water going down her nose. And the image of her begging for her life. "Casey did tell me something else interesting. Other than the fact that McLean didn't drown in the East River that night."

"Mmm. Yeah?"

"Yeah. He told me your guys killed Kyle McLean's girl-friend."

"Bullshit," Marconi retorted, smacking his lips. "We never touched her. She died in a car accident."

The old man had denied any involvement fast. Too fast. Like he'd known the accusation was coming. Or like he'd denied it before. "Yeah, that's what Casey said you'd say. But he said the brakes had been screwed with. Said the NYPD crime lab inspected the car, and it was pretty obvious what happened."

Marconi smiled, pieces of half-chewed food stuck between his crooked lower row of yellow teeth. Smiled like he was counting to ten slowly. "Maybe McLean screwed with the brakes. Maybe she did him dirty, and he couldn't take it. Ever think of that?"

Johnny touched the card in his shirt pocket. Christ, if he'd ever found out Karen was cheating on him, he would have lost his mind. "No, I didn't."

"Well, Deuce, that's why I'm where I am." The old man picked at a piece of lettuce between his two front teeth. "And you're where you are."

9

AS JACK HOISTED the last two plastic bags out of the shopping cart and into the Mercedes' trunk, a tub of margarine slipped out and tumbled to the cigarette-strewn pavement of the Publix grocery store parking lot.

"Pick that up."

Jack eyed the woman who'd just yapped at him like a Chihuahua on steroids. She was standing a few feet away. She was middle-aged, dripping with jewelry, and wearing huge Chanel sunglasses. He'd seen her in the store before—she made a huge production of herself whenever she came in—but he'd never had to lug her bags to her car. Somehow he'd escaped that pleasure—until now.

All the bag boys in the store hated her, cringed when they saw her come in. Just hoped to God she wouldn't end up at their aisle when she was finished shopping.

Supposedly she was a rich-as-sin widow, but all she ever tipped was a quid. Twenty-five measly cents to be her man-slave for ten minutes in the steaming hot Florida sun. It was almost like she enjoyed being cheap, the guys said. Said she smiled funny when she dropped the coin into your sweaty palm. Like she knew what a joke it was, and she was having fun toying with you. Well, the way this was going, he wouldn't even get a nickel.

He knelt down and picked up the container, feeling the flask of scotch in the pocket of his green apron.

"Let me see it," she demanded, snatching the container from his hand. "It's damaged. I want a new one."

Jack shook his head. "There's nothing wrong with it," he said politely.

"I *want* a new one."

Another bag boy was stowing groceries into the back of an SUV across the lane. A clean-cut, African-American teenager who'd taught Jack the ropes on his first day at the store. Jack caught the kid watching out of the corner of his eye, hiding a grin. "Then get it your damn self," he muttered. "And don't be such a *bitch*." The second he said it, he wished he could have taken it back. Not because of the trouble it could get him in, but because he'd let his temper get away from him. Because he'd stooped to her level and lost his grip on being a gentleman.

The woman dropped the margarine and pressed her hands to her mouth. This time the top popped off and rolled beneath a Toyota parked beside the Mercedes. *"What did you say?"*

The word had come out of his mouth with no warning, a knee-jerk reaction to her unbearable rudeness and arrogance. Helped along by the scotch, of course. For the past few hours he'd been sneaking a snort every time he finished stowing someone's bags, careful not to pull the flask out in front of the parking lot security cameras mounted atop the light poles. He felt bad because he'd promised Cheryl he wouldn't drink anymore, but forty minutes into his shift he'd known he couldn't survive the day without it. Besides, technically she hadn't asked him to stop drinking for good. Just for last night.

He leaned down and retrieved the container a second time. "You want another one?" he growled, holding it up so close to her face she instinctively backed up until her wide hips hit the Toyota. "You *really* want another one?" He turned and hurled the margarine as far as he could. Admiring its arc until it finally tumbled into the field next to the parking lot, startling a great gray heron that was stalking something in a puddle out there. For sixty-three he still had a pretty good arm. "Then, like I said, get it yourself."

She started shrieking at the top of her lungs as he stalked off.

He pulled the apron over his head when he reached his car—an old Chevy Citation he'd picked up at a government auction last year in Tampa for seven hundred bucks—and pulled the flask out, taking a long swig. His shift didn't end for an hour, but he wasn't going to get caught up in the firestorm he assumed the woman was going to create inside the store. Then he might miss the game. Nope, he'd just show up in the morning like nothing happened and see what was what.

From over the roof of the Citation he watched the woman quick-step back toward the store in her heels and tight skirt, still shrieking in a high-pitched wail. He took another healthy gulp of scotch. What a train wreck. No wonder she was a widow. Her husband had probably committed suicide. And he was probably a lot happier where he was now. *Wherever* that was.

Thirty seconds later Jack was wheeling the Citation out of the Publix parking lot, feeling that excitement building in his chest—and he wasn't even anywhere near the ballpark. God, he'd caught baseball fever again so fast. Last night had brought it all back. Brought back his incredible love for the game, the comforting feeling that he couldn't think of anyplace in the world he'd rather be. It was like being in the womb when he was at a baseball stadium—safe and warm. Last night hadn't washed away all the bad memories, but it had proven to him the truth to an old adage he'd never really believed in: if you really loved something or someone, time healed all wounds. The scars stayed with you, but you could forgive and move on, maybe even learn from the pain. Even at his age.

He eased off the accelerator, reminding himself to slow down. There was plenty of time before the first pitch, and he couldn't afford another ticket. When he'd been pulled over last month doing seventy in a forty-five on his way home one night, the cop had nearly made him take a Breathalyzer test—which he would have failed. Miserably, too. Fortunately the guy had shown mercy and told him just to get his sorry ass home and sleep it off. He'd always cursed cops before then. Figured they were never around when you needed them but were always around when you didn't. Now he figured maybe they were people, too. At least some of them. Despite the fact that the guy still had given him a speeding ticket.

Jack raced up fast behind a white station wagon. Too fast. Came way too close to the guy's bumper now that he was starting to feel the scotch. He took another guzzle anyway. Damn that Bobby Griffin. He'd gotten to Cheryl, gotten inside her head. That unfortunate reality had been tattooed all over her face last night at the game, then again at home. Bobby had convinced her there was a chance for them to have something meaningful. The end was going to be awful, but Jack promised himself not to give her the I-told-you-so speech when it happened. He shook his head and took another swig. At least he didn't have to worry about Cheryl moving out anytime soon. She was so right. That would be a bad day. A *very* bad day. Well, he was going to do his best to make sure it never happened.

He banged the steering wheel so hard he yelped at the pain shooting up his arm. That wasn't fair. If he really loved her, he had to let her go. That was the bottom line, what any parent eventually had to do.

But how the hell was he supposed to survive after that?

10

JOHNNY KNELT DOWN in front of the gravestone, laid a bouquet of two dozen red roses on the wet ground, then ran his fingers gently over the chiseled letters. Karen Nicole Robinson. She'd died seventeen years ago, shortly before they were supposed to be married. He'd never gotten over her, never been able to move on in that part of his life. His grandmother used to tell him time healed all wounds. It was the only thing he could remember her ever being wrong about. This wound would never heal. Johnny took a deep breath as he gazed at her beautiful name, pictured her beautiful face as she lay in the open coffin that day. He still loved her so much.

Marconi wanted Kyle McLean dead. Fast. The old man had made that very clear last night at the end of their second session, and the incentive to get on it right away was the million bucks. Which, after all, was a damn good incentive. It would be an all-cash deal, too—so no taxes. A million dollars with no need to cut Uncle Sam in on a cent. Marconi was going to move the money multiple times in odd amounts through several of the family's Swiss, Belgian, and Antigua accounts so U.S. authorities couldn't trace it.

The old man seemed obsessed with McLean. Like he couldn't think of anything else but the kid sprawled on the ground with a bullet through his head. Last night he'd reminded Johnny again to make no judgments, just to follow orders. Johnny shook his head. He was going to keep doing the things that mattered despite the warning. Coming out here was at the very top of that list.

Karen had lived in an apartment building across the street from his grandmother's place in Bayshore. They'd met one summer afternoon during a thunderstorm when they were both running home with schoolbooks over their heads, when they were both thirteen. They'd never dated anyone else, been almost inseparable from that moment on. They'd done everything first together: first beer, first kiss, first sex. He'd loved her so much and not because she was beautiful, which she was: a stunning brunette with long legs and haunting hazel eyes. He'd loved her so much because her heart was pure. She never hated anyone no matter what they did to her. She always turned the other cheek, always forgave, always figured they must have been abused as a child or were just having a bad day. He loved her for that because it was something he wasn't capable of. It wasn't in him to be forgiving or pure to people he didn't care about— sometimes not even to people he did—and he admired her deeply for it. Then she was taken from him with no warning. And that was how it all started.

Her operation was supposed to be no big deal, a routine appendectomy. But somehow something had gone terribly wrong on the table. When the surgeon came trudging out to the waiting room, red eyes riveted to the scuffed tile floor, Johnny knew his world had been shattered before the man even opened his mouth. There would be no wedding, no house in the country with two boys and a golden retriever, no happily ever after. Because he could never love another woman the way he loved Karen.

For several years after her death he'd tried going out with other women, but the dates had all ended up disasters. All hollow reminders of what he'd had with her. So he didn't bother anymore. Now he just called Marconi when he wanted female company, and Nicky arranged it for him. Whenever he did, he always took down the hundred pictures he had of Karen in the Long Island house. And the first thing he did when the girl was gone was put the pictures back up exactly where they'd been before.

The anesthesiologist attending on Karen's "routine" operation had given her the wrong dosage, though hospital officials tried to hide the truth. They'd tried to pass it off as her having a weak heart, just one of those unfortunate deaths. But Johnny heard the real story from a nurse who'd been in the operating room. A woman who was friends with his brother. It was his first lesson in the value of firsthand information.

He'd waited six months to take revenge. Stalked the anesthesiologist constantly so he knew the doctor's routine cold. Finally put a bullet through the guy's head as he was walking his wife's poodle on East End Avenue in Manhattan one frigid December evening. After the hit, he'd calmly tossed the .22 pistol into the East River, then slept the sleep of the righteous. Eight straight hours more soundly than ever before in his life. The doctor didn't give a damn about what had happened to Karen. Hell, he'd even had the audacity to demand payment for the operation despite what he'd done. Well, he'd gotten his money. He'd gotten justice, too.

The murder had been front-page news in the New York papers because the doctor had been married to a prominent socialite. A woman whose family had all the right connections. People who swore they'd track down the animal responsible for killing the gentle physician as they stood on the steps of City Hall in lower Manhattan two mornings after the hit, flanked by the mayor and the police commissioner. But no one ever came to question Johnny, and the crime went unsolved.

Johnny had never felt the slightest remorse, and he quickly realized where his talent lay. There would be no more stocking shelves at the Sears in Bayonne.

He rose up off the ground when the rain started to come down harder, kissed his fingers, and placed them on her name again. "Bye, baby. I love you. See you soon."

He pressed his fingers to his chest and felt the two of hearts. Karen had given him the card right before they'd wheeled her into the operating room, as she lay on the gurney outside of where she would die. She'd told him it represented them—two lovers who would always be together. Since that day it had never been out of his reach.

11

JACK SAT IN the gravel parking lot of Tarpon Stadium finishing what was left of the scotch. When it was gone, he tossed the flask in the backseat and headed for the ticket counter, where he treated himself to a box seat with ten of the thirty dollars he'd earned in tips today. Thank God not everyone was as cheap as the woman in the Mercedes. Hell, he still had plenty left over for food and beer. Maybe even for a few drinks after the game.

So he stopped at the hot dog stand outside Section 121 and bought himself a sizzling foot-long. Then smothered it at the condiment station across the concourse with mustard and chopped onions, the same way he always had at Yankee Stadium when everything was right between him and the game. The first bite was so good it hurt his jaw the taste sensation was so strong. He smiled when he made it to the end of the tunnel and the lush green canvas came into view. A baseball game, a box seat, a foot-long, a beautiful spring evening, and a genuine objective. It hadn't been like this in a long time. It was amazing how fast life could turn. On one thin dime.

"Hey, mister, good to see you again. You okay?"

It was the same old man who'd been here last night. "Hey there, my friend," Jack called back loudly. "God, yes, I'm fine. That was all a false alarm last night. People getting riled up over nothing. But thanks for asking. Mighty nice of you." The scotch had him in a great mood. "Good to see you, too."

"Glad to hear you're okay. We were all real concerned."

"Ah, I'm fine. You can't hurt me. I'm a tough old tank."

"Where are your friends tonight?" the usher asked.

"Friends?"

"The people you were here with last night."

"Huh? *Ooooh*. That was my daughter and her boyfriend," Jack explained. "They didn't want to come again so soon. Young people, you know how they are." He winked. "They wanted something faster and louder. You know?"

The usher shook his head sadly. "Don't I? I got a granddaughter just like that. Wouldn't come to a baseball game to save her life. She wants MTV and video games."

"Exactly." Truth was, Jack hadn't told Cheryl he was coming back tonight. He'd made up a story about going to dinner with some old codgers he'd met at Publix— which she seemed excited about. Probably because she figured he was finally starting to find a circle of friends, and she'd have more time to herself. "Hey, got a favor to ask you." He moved to where the usher stood and put his arm around the old man's bony shoulders.

"Shoot."

"You know any of the groundskeepers?"

The thing about groundskeepers was they always knew the players pretty well. They had to because they shaped the field for them. High grass if the team had speed so grounders took longer to make it to the defensive players; ridged first- and third-base lines if the leadoff guys could bunt so what they laid down was more likely to stay in play; fences moved in a bit if the team had power. Little things that over the course of a long season might win a few games—and make the difference between winning a pennant and finishing second. Groundskeepers talked to the players and the coaches all the time about what they were doing to the field, to make certain they got the changes exactly right. So meeting a groundskeeper might help him meet Mikey Clemant.

"Well, sure," the usher said. "Blaine Wilson is the head groundskeeper. Heck of a nice guy, too. Why do you ask?"

Jack glanced toward the outfield. Only fifteen minutes to game time, but Clemant was still out in center running wind sprints, long, dark hair flowing behind him like a lion's mane. Everyone else was back in the dugout sitting on their asses, but the kid was still out there working, still fighting to get better. "Just want to talk to him. Think you could arrange it?"

The usher gestured at two men leaning against the fence beside the Tarpon dugout. "That's Blaine down there on the left. Come on," he called, waving for Jack to follow him down the aisle.

Jack held his hand out when he was still five steps away, putting on his friendliest smile. "Hi, Blaine. Name's Jack Barrett. Nice to meet you."

"Uh-huh. What do you want?"

The man who'd been standing next to Blaine disappeared into the Tarpon dugout without so much as a wave, and the old usher headed back up the steps to his post outside the tunnel. Which was good. Jack didn't want anyone else in on this conversation. "I'll be straight with you, Blaine. I was here for the game last night, and I saw him play." Jack pointed out to right, where the kid had ended up after his last sprint. "Mikey Clemant. Saw the catch he made in the first and his walk-off homer in the ninth."

"Yeah . . . so?"

Blaine was sweating profusely. He was overweight, and when you were fat in Florida, you sweated while you swam. "I liked what I saw."

"That's great. Who are you?"

Blaine wasn't pleasant at all. He was one of those guys who needed to be impressed. "I used to be a scout for the Yankees."

Blaine straightened up. "Really?"

Amazing, Jack thought, watching Blaine's demeanor change before his eyes. Now he was showing respect. In the baseball world, working for the Yankees was like working for the pope if you were Catholic. It didn't get any better. "Yeah, thirty-four years." Jack raised his left hand so Blaine could see the World Series ring he'd worn tonight. He'd earned four of them—he'd been too junior to get them for the '77 and '78 wins against the Dodgers—but this was the only one left. It was from the win against the Mets in the 2000 Series—the most valuable of the four. Cheryl had reluctantly sold the other three on eBay to raise the down payment for the house. He hated showing off—hated people who did—so he rarely wore the thing. But tonight he needed what the ring brought with it: instant respect and credibility.

Blaine's eyes bugged out. "Wow."

Now Jack would get answers. "Tell me about the kid."

"Mikey's got all the talent in the world," Blaine said wistfully, still admiring the ring. "But he's got a screw loose."

"Seems like his teammates don't care much for him," Jack observed. "They didn't bother coming out of the dugout after he hit that walk-off dinger last night. Hell, even the guy he batted in didn't wait around."

Blaine nodded sadly, finally managing to pry his eyes off Jack's finger. "He's pissed 'em off, all right. Royally." He chuckled wryly, like the whole thing was a mystery nobody was going to solve. "But Mikey doesn't seem to care. It doesn't seem to bother him. And he's not a bad guy," Blaine added. "Just misunderstood. I know people think I'm crazy, but I really think he has a good heart under all that anger."

Jack took the last bite of the foot-long. "I want to talk to him," he said as he chewed. "What's the best way to do that?"

Blaine thought for a few moments. "Not here at the park, that's for sure. He might think you're press. Then you'd never get a word with him. He hates the press with a passion."

Jack didn't blame Clemant for that. He'd been raked over the coals himself by the New York press four years ago, when everything had gone down. Had his character assassinated by guys he thought were his friends. By guys he'd given inside scoops to for years so they could look good to their editors. They'd rushed to judgment in the name of a story, and that was one part of the bitterness he'd never get past. He had this gnawing suspicion that one of those guys might even be responsible for what had happened. At least had a hand in it. "Any ideas?"

Blaine nodded. "He goes to this bar down the street from here some nights after home games. They got the best cheeseburgers around."

From the looks of Blaine's belly, he was speaking from experience. "What's it called?" Jack asked.

"The Dugout."

"When's your father gonna be home?" Bobby leaned back, pulled the curtains to one side, and peered nervously out the window. He and Cheryl were sitting on the couch in the living room. "I don't want him coming in here and finding me like this. Christ, he'd be so pissed off if he caught me in the house alone with you."

"Oh, stop. It's not like I'm fifteen."

Bobby raised one eyebrow. "More like thirteen. At least in his eyes."

Cheryl waved. "Don't worry. Daddy won't be home for a while. A couple of hours at least."

"Yeah? How do you know?"

"He told me he was going out to dinner with some friends."

"That's impossible."

"Why?"

Bobby stole another suspicious glance out the window. "Nobody could possibly like him enough to want to spend a whole dinner with him."

Cheryl laughed. "You might be right about that." She put her hand on Bobby's knee, then slid her fingers up his thigh a little. Usually he made the first move. "I don't think he went out to dinner with anybody. I think he went to another Tarpon game. He wanted to watch that kid he was all into last night again."

Bobby turned away from the window. "Really? That's kind of weird, don't you think?"

She got on her knees on the couch beside Bobby and put both hands on his shoulders. "I would if it was anybody but my dad." She hesitated, uncertain of how much to say. Daddy had asked her not to tell the neighbors, but he'd never said anything about anyone else. "He was with the New York Yankees until a few years ago. A real important guy in the scouting group."

Suddenly Bobby wasn't at all interested in what was outside. "Really? Hey, that's pretty cool. What did he do exactly?"

"During the season he was usually a city ahead of the Yankees, checking out the next team they were playing. During the off-season, he'd go all over the country looking for talent. Down into Central America, too." She was sure she was never going to see him again when he made those trips. "Once he snuck into Cuba to watch this guy play and almost got caught by the secret police. He hitched a ride off a beach near Havana with some guys in a rowboat late at night and finally got picked up by the coast guard."

"Jesus." Bobby shook his head in disbelief. "He snuck into Cuba? That *was* crazy. Well, what happened? Did he retire?"

Cheryl nodded hesitantly. She wasn't going to tell

Bobby about that. "Yeah, but I guess he can't get baseball out of his system. It was his life for so long. It was everything to him," she said, hoping she wasn't sounding bitter. "He's amazing. He can remember games from years ago like it was yesterday."

"No wonder he nailed me on the pitch speeds last night."

A distant look drifted to Cheryl's face. "He saw that kid make those great plays last night, and he wants to get him to the Show." Before going to bed she'd followed her father's moves on the Internet and seen that it was the Tarpon home page he'd gone to. And the kid's personal page after that. "I know that's what's going on."

"'The Show'? What's that?"

Cheryl eyed Bobby suspiciously. "You know what that means. Come on."

"No, I really don't. What's 'the Show'? What's that mean?"

It had always been tough for her growing up—especially after she'd started dating. She always seemed to know more about baseball than the boys, so she'd learned to hold back and not say anything sometimes, learned to seem like she didn't know. Not say everything anyway, because a couple of times she'd embarrassed boys in front of their friends or dads with how much more she knew than they did. But Bobby didn't seem like the type who'd get worked up about it.

"It's what baseball players call the major leagues," she explained, her eyes narrowing quickly. Bobby was already grinning guiltily. "You jerk," she said, punching him gently. "You knew."

"Yeah, I was testing you," Bobby admitted, pulling her

close and kissing her. "Well, if your dad's so into baseball, why was it so damn tough to get him to the Tarpon game last night?" Bobby asked when they finished their kiss. "I mean, we basically had to put chains on him and drag him out there."

She shrugged. "I don't know. Maybe he had a hard time with it because he didn't really want to retire. But they have this mandatory thing," she said, hoping Bobby wouldn't pursue it.

Bobby pulled her close again. "Must have been tough for you growing up."

"What do you mean?"

"He was probably gone a lot."

Suddenly she regretted opening up a crack. Bobby had hit the nail on the head, and now the door was swinging wide open against a torrent of emotion.

Daddy had been gone a lot. A *whole* lot. And when he was home, all he wanted to do was spend time with David, her older brother. David had been a star baseball player in high school, then joined the New York City Fire Department. Now he was a decorated veteran who'd won all kinds of medals for his bravery at the World Trade Center, and many times since. He was the family favorite—at least the way she saw it. She'd spent her whole life trying to get her father's attention, spent her whole life competing with David for it. And rarely won.

She glanced around the tiny house. Maybe that was why she was here. There wasn't any competition. At least not right here, not right in her face.

She'd always figured she was here because she was so disappointed in her mother. Disappointed with the deceit, the sneaking around, the lies. Mom had denied it all, but Cheryl knew the truth. Mom had forced her to choose sides right before the divorce was finalized. Well, she must have wished she hadn't done that now. They hadn't spoken in four years. The calls from up North had finally stopped a year ago.

Cheryl had always hoped she was here simply because she loved Daddy that much and couldn't bear to think of him alone without his family or his career. Because she was afraid of what might happen in the early hours of a Florida morning after he'd guzzled a pint of scotch after convincing himself he didn't have anything to live for. She'd never have forgiven herself.

But maybe it really was because the competition wasn't here. Maybe that was the answer after all. She finally had Daddy all to herself.

"Must have been really tough," Bobby repeated, his expression sympathetic.

"Yeah," she murmured, "it was."

Bobby leaned over and kissed her hard.

Too hard. Cheryl had wanted to tell him to be gentler ever since their first kiss, but she didn't want to embarrass him, either. She kissed him back, trying to lead him to tenderness with her technique. But it didn't work; he was still rough. "Daddy thinks you're using me," she said, giving up for now. "He doesn't think you want a real relationship with me."

"*What?* That's ridiculous. You know how much I care about you."

"*How* much?"

He put one of his big palms on her soft cheek. "I love you, baby," he whispered, leaning forward to kiss her again. "I really do."

And for the first time his lips seemed soft, really soft, and she could tell he was serious. It felt so good. Daddy was wrong. That felt good, too. "Come on," she murmured, standing up and taking his hand. "Let's go to my bedroom."

"You sure?" Bobby asked, wide-eyed.

They'd been dating for a few months, but she hadn't made love to him yet. She'd given him other things to keep him satisfied, to keep him coming back, but she hadn't let him have her entire body. Now she wanted to. "Very sure."

The Dugout was a hole-in-the-wall wedged between a dry cleaner and a dive Chinese restaurant on a deserted side street a few blocks from the stadium. Just ten bar stools and ten Formica-top tables with baseball memorabilia everywhere. Covering the walls were signed photographs of famous players who'd spent time in Sarasota before going on to the majors. And there were autographed bats, balls, and gloves hanging from the ceiling. Beneath the clear cover of the bar were tons of baseball cards, some that were valuable, Jack noticed.

Jack signaled to the lone bartender. "Another one." There were only a few people in the place, and they were all at tables. He was the only one at the bar.

He was about to lift his glass and down the CD-thin sip of scotch remaining when the front door opened and Clemant sauntered in. The kid sat at the far end of the bar on a stool that let him rest his back against the wall—and keep an eye on the door.

Up close he was bigger than Jack had anticipated. At least six four and 230 pounds. He wore a gray sleeveless T-shirt, white nylon shorts that hung to his knees, flip-flops, and a plain blue logoless cap with the bill pulled way down. Muscles rippled all over him as he moved, like a big cat. He was a walking advertisement for the perfect physique.

Jack was careful not to make eye contact, just nursed what was left of his drink and took sidelong glances every once in a while. He wanted to make sure the kid had time to relax, time to settle in. The bartender said the kid usually drank a couple of beers with dinner, so Jack waited, hoping the alcohol might loosen him up. Waited until the kid had almost finished off two big cheeseburgers, a whole plate of fries, and three Miller Lites before casually walking over and sitting down on the bar stool beside him.

He hesitated a few moments, laying his left palm flat on the bar, giving Clemant a wide-screen view of the World Series ring. Finally he turned toward the kid. "Name's Jack Barrett," he said smoothly, holding out his hand. "It's a pleasure to meet you."

The kid took his time responding. Slowly finished the last French fry before wiping his palms thoroughly with a napkin and shaking hands. "Mikey Clemant," he said with a friendly smile.

"Saw your game last night." The kid's hands were so powerful. Like Thurman Munson's before he died in that tragic plane crash. "Two of the best plays I ever saw. The catch in the first and the homer in the ninth. And I've seen a lot of great plays."

"Thanks." The kid stroked his beard, then reached for his beer. "You at tonight's game?"

Jack nodded, glancing quickly into Clemant's eyes, trying to get a read without lingering. Just like you wouldn't look into a wild animal's eyes for long because it might set off the beast inside. But it was tough to see anything. The bill of the hat came way down, and the beard made the shadow from the hat seem even darker. "Yup."

"Not quite as good, huh?"

Clemant had gone oh for three tonight—two strikeouts and a pop-up—and he'd made a hideous throwing error. Jack shrugged. "That's baseball." Strange. It almost seemed like the kid had grinned for a second. Like he found his awful performance tonight amusing—even satisfying—in some way. Maybe that was why his teammates couldn't stand him. Maybe he was one of those guys who didn't care. Which was what athletes hated most in a teammate. And you couldn't teach someone to care. "Some nights that's just the way it goes."

The kid gestured at Jack's hand. "What's with the ring?"

Jack held it up for maximum effect. "I was with the Yankees for a long time."

"Doing what?"

"I was on the scouting side." Jack leaned toward the kid. The conversation was going even better than he'd hoped. Christ, from what everyone had said, he hadn't been expecting much. Well, it was time to attack. "Look, I know talent when I see it, and you're it. You got all the tools to make it big in the Show. And I wanna help you get there. You're wasting your time here in Sarasota."

For a long time the kid said nothing, just drew invisible shapes on the bar with his finger.

All right, he'd take another tack. "So, you're from

Minnesota," Jack tried. "I read that on the team's website. What's the name of—"

"Mr. Barrett," Clemant interrupted calmly, "I don't care how good you think you are at scaring up talent from small towns and bad teams." He stood up and dropped two tens on the bar beside his ketchup-smeared plate. "If you ever come up to me like this again, you're gonna be sorry. *Real* sorry."

He hadn't raised his voice, hadn't gotten angry. Just said what he had to say matter-of-factly. Like he was damn serious, Jack realized.

"Am I clear?"

Jack nodded ever so subtly.

And just like that the kid was gone. Out of the bar and into the darkness.

A shiver ran up Jack's spine as the door swung shut. The same way it did when the umpire yelled "Play ball!" at the beginning of every game. Only a few moments with the young man, but in those fleeting seconds he'd come to a vital and indisputable conclusion. Mikey Clemant could end up being one of the greatest baseball players of all time.

Part 2

12

IT WAS ALWAYS best to get to a loan shark early in the morning, before he had a chance to get out of his house and get moving. Otherwise you'd spend all day bird-dogging him. Crisscrossing New York City—from the Bronx all the way down to Staten Island—trying to catch up with him because he was constantly bouncing from borough to borough trying to gin up business or chasing down deadbeats. Mostly trying to collect as opposed to lend. Lending was the easy part of the racket. Collecting was the backbreaker.

Which was one of the reasons why the VIG—the vigorish, or interest rate—had to be so steep. To make up for all that running around, which most days didn't net you a dime. That and the risk factor. In the lender-of-last-resort market, you had to assume people were going to disappear on you despite what they knew could happen to them. Despite that scare-the-hell-out-of-them surprise visit you always paid the day after you loaned them the money even though technically they didn't owe you anything back at that point. When you showed them the bloody after-pictures of the last guy who tried to stiff the Lucchesi family.

Johnny knocked three times hard, then stepped to the side. Just in case the man inside the apartment decided the best defense was a good offense and blew a couple of shotgun shells through the door right before sprinting for the fire escape. You could never be too careful, even though Tony Treviso didn't have a reputation for being quick on the draw.

In fact, Treviso's reputation was quite the opposite. No one had ever actually seen Treviso draw, which was why the Lucchesi capos called him Timid Tony. He never did the dirty work himself. When somebody fell behind on a payment schedule, he called in the muscle side of the family to chop off a finger or slice an ear. And he didn't usually stick around to watch. Most guys in the family loved watching that stuff. Not Treviso. He just identified the guy and left. And when he had to take the ultimate step, those few times he had to make a mortal example out of a way-past-due credit, he *always* called in the brutes. Loan sharks were supposed to handle their own problems in the Lucchesi family—at least the initial slicing and dicing. But the rumor around was that Treviso didn't have the stomach.

Which meant he shouldn't have lasted long. But he had lasted. And it was because he made so much more than the other guys. He had an uncanny knack for sizing up a mark, for knowing who'd be terrified enough to repay the money—and who wouldn't. Which wasn't to say he didn't suffer his share of losses. Every lender in this market did. But his losses were dramatically less than everyone else's, so his profits were dramatically more, which was why the capos kept him around even though they called him a pussy behind his back, sometimes even to his face. They kept him around because he made them so much money, and, in the end, that was all that mattered. Even if he was a pussy.

Yeah, Timid Tony had always been a big money-maker.

Until that loan to Kyle McLean.

Johnny reached around and knocked again, pretty sure he wasn't going to get the shotgun-blast-through-the-door reception, but forcing himself to be cautious. You never knew how it was gonna go when a man felt trapped. Johnny had learned that one the hard way. He still had buckshot in his left thigh from a guy who'd flipped out on him a couple of years ago.

He'd thought about calling Treviso to let him know he was coming—to avoid a confrontation—then decided against it. He wanted this to be a surprise so he could gauge the gut reactions to the pointed questions, not hear canned responses.

And there was this one thing about Tony Treviso. This one footnote that belied the pussy tag the capos had pegged on him. This one story that made Johnny Bondano wary. Two years ago, Treviso was supposed to have murdered a guy he'd loaned fifty grand to—even though he'd gotten the money back. Then supposedly he'd sent the guy's severed head to his wife by overnight delivery service, with a dead rat stuffed in the gaping, bloody mouth. A few seconds after opening the box she'd collapsed and suffered a nervous breakdown. She was still in the psychiatric ward at Bellevue.

Nobody could confirm that Treviso had been behind the ghastly delivery. But when you asked him about it, he smiled in a way that he didn't smile when you asked him about anything else. In a self-satisfied, wicked way that convinced you he knew a lot more about that severed head than he was letting on.

Johnny knocked again. As hard as he could this time.

"Who is it?"

The hesitant, muffled voice was coming from someone who was standing well back from the door. So Treviso was worried that whoever was knocking might blow a couple of shotgun shells into the apartment. "Johnny Bondano."

"I never heard of no Johnny Bondano."

Which was crap. Just a ruse to try to throw whoever Treviso thought might really be knocking on his door off the scent. Johnny and Treviso had been together several times. The last time only a few weeks ago at a bar in Staten Island near where he'd killed the Capelletti guy. That was when he'd personally asked Treviso about killing the guy and sending the hacked-off head to the wife. When he'd seen for himself that strange smile skid across Treviso's thin face. When he'd felt the eerie chill run up his spine for himself.

He'd realized then that while most of the time Treviso was incapable of as much as setting a mousetrap, somewhere beneath the guy's pasty, pale exterior lurked a psychopathic switch that could turn Timid Tony into a man the devil would call a friend.

"It's the Deuce, Tony." Johnny tried to make his voice sound friendly—which wasn't easy. "I just want to talk to you, I just want to have a conversation." Marconi might get pissed if he found out about this meeting. He might not accept Johnny's excuse that he was simply questioning Treviso in another attempt to pick up Kyle McLean's trail. After all, if Treviso had any inkling of where McLean was, he would have tried to find McLean himself to get the hundred grand back. But Johnny couldn't just throw out his code. He'd decided that at the cemetery yesterday as he'd run his fingers over Karen's chiseled name. "Now open up. Nothing's gonna happen."

The door cracked a sliver. "I don't see nobody out there."

Johnny moved in front of the door and held his hands out to show Treviso he wasn't holding a gun. He could see the chain inside extending taut across the narrow opening. But nothing else. "How about now?"

The door shut quickly, then opened wide and Treviso stuck his head into the hallway. Like a frightened rabbit poking his head out of his hole. He checked in both directions, then beckoned for Johnny to come in. "How are you, Deuce, how are you? Jeez, I'm sorry about all that, but I gotta be careful, you know? You can never be too careful in this business."

Tony Treviso was a funny-looking guy. In his late twenties, he was an inch taller than Johnny but rail-skinny. Like he never ate. Or puked it all back up every time he did. He had thinning brown hair he wore slicked straight back without a part, a long nose, buckteeth, and a large black mole on his neck. He wore a food-stained tank-top T-shirt that was way too big and hung in sagging waves over his sunken chest like a flag on a windless day, exposing a patch of dark hair directly between his tiny pink nipples. And a pair of jeans that bunched together at his waist beneath an old black belt with a large silver buckle.

"Yeah, sure. Everybody's always gotta be careful in our business." As they shook hands, Johnny felt perspiration on Treviso's palm. "Samatta with you?" He knew what was wrong. "You okay?"

"What? Oh, *oooh*." Treviso held up his hand when Johnny nodded at it, then smiled nervously. "Well, it's not like I get a visit from Deuce Bondano at seven-thirty in the morning every morning. Kinda made me wonder what was up. Kinda made me nervous," Treviso admitted. "Know what I mean?"

"Yeah, sure."

Everybody greeted Johnny like this nowadays. Like he was the black plague and they couldn't wait for him to get up on his horse and ride right out of town. Like they were ready to turn and sprint wildly the other way if he so much as reached into his jacket for his wallet. He didn't have any friends anymore thanks to his reputation. Not any real friends anyway, no one he could confide in. He stuck his chin out. It was fine. He'd gotten used to working alone. *And* to living alone. It didn't bother him anymore.

Except after a few drinks. Then he started wishing he had someone to care about, someone to love. And if he had too many drinks, he'd start thinking about Karen. So he didn't drink much anymore.

"Yeah, sure," Johnny muttered again, touching his shirt and the two of hearts in the pocket. He heard a baby wailing somewhere in the back of the sparsely furnished apartment as he followed Treviso into the cramped kitchen. "You mind me coming here or something?"

"Of course not. Hey, *mio casa, tuo casa*." Treviso gestured toward a small round table beneath a window with dirty panes. The day's first rays were doing their best to fight their way through the grime. "Sit down. Please. Let's talk."

It was amazing how people feared him these days. Treviso was scared for his life right now despite the resident evil buried inside his soul. Johnny could see it plainly in the thin man's expression. And the beads of sweat lining Treviso's hairline were growing larger by the second. Pretty soon a couple of them were going to cascade down his forehead over his narrow eyebrows like tiny waterfalls and embarrass the hell out of him if he didn't do something quick.

"How about some coffee, Deuce?" Treviso asked. He picked up a paper napkin from a plastic holder in the middle of the table and wiped the perspiration away. "Or some water? Anything?"

"Nah."

A young woman balancing a toddler on her hip walked through the doorway on the other side of the kitchen, over by the refrigerator. If she was Treviso's wife, she was prettier than Johnny had expected. Much prettier. A prize, for Christ's sake. The goddamn trophy wife of a Fortune 500 executive. Not the wife of some two-bit Queens hustler. She was petite and exotic with beautiful olive skin and stark, jet-black hair that fell to her bare shoulders. The toddler had a clump of her hair in his cute, tiny fist and he was looking at it inquisitively as he babbled incoherent syllables.

Johnny caught the young woman's gaze for a moment, looked away, then quickly looked back again. "I'm fine," he said, his throat suddenly as dry as a perfect martini.

"Deuce, this is my wife, Karen."

Karen. Somehow he'd known that was going to be her name even before Treviso said it. God sure played some nasty jokes on his flock every once in a while, and this morning it was his turn to be the wool in the crosshairs. Karen. Jesus. Why couldn't it have been anything but Karen?

"Karen, this is Johnny Bondano. But we all call him Deuce. He's a business associate of mine."

She held out her hand. "Hi, Johnny."

For some reason he liked that she called him Johnny, not Deuce. Reluctantly, he took her slim fingers in his, summoning up his courage to gaze into those big brown eyes again. They were surrounded by long, curved lashes, and inside those lashes he saw the same intense curiosity he knew was in his eyes. Sometimes it happened this way. Sometimes two people were attracted to each other right off the bat and there was nothing either of them could do about it. Something nature had predestined, and that was that.

"It's nice to meet you."

Her soft voice was mesmerizing and her beautiful eyes expressive. "Nice to meet you, too."

"Why do they call you Deuce?" she asked, seeming to hold on to his fingers a moment longer than she should have.

"He carries a two of hearts in his pocket all the time," Treviso explained.

"Why?"

"Don't bother asking, honey," Treviso cautioned, easing into one of the kitchen chairs. "He won't answer. He's never told anyone. And I doubt today's gonna be the day he breaks his silence."

Johnny's shoulders sagged slightly, glad Treviso had laid out the ground rules. Even if the explanation had been laced with sarcasm. He hadn't wanted to seem rude.

"Maybe he'll tell me," she said, finally letting go.

Johnny's jaw clenched involuntarily, and he touched the card in his shirt pocket again. He didn't want to disappoint her, but he couldn't tell her. He couldn't break the bond. "Sorry."

"Maybe someday."

Johnny glanced at the toddler, then back at Karen, gazing into those mahogany eyes once more. She was talking to him through them; he could feel it. "Maybe."

"I doubt it," Treviso said loudly. "Johnny doesn't get this far out into Brooklyn very often. Do you, Deuce?"

It was a warning, plain and simple. Don't ever come near my wife when I'm not around. And it irritated Johnny. Treviso was in no position to threaten, even if it did have to do with his wife. "You never know," he said evenly. It was a stupid thing to say. There was no reason to get Treviso suspicious, but he couldn't help himself. The machismo had popped up out of nowhere, and he'd been unable to control it.

"Give us some privacy, will you, sweetie?" Treviso lit up a Camel no-filter he'd pulled from a half-full pack lying on the table beside the napkin holder. "We gotta talk business."

Karen moved to the refrigerator, leaned down, and pulled a jar of baby food off the shelf above the fruit drawer, then headed out the same doorway she'd come through. When she was far enough down the hallway that Treviso couldn't see her, she hesitated and looked back over her shoulder, locking eyes with Johnny for several seconds.

Johnny stared back, admiring the outline of her slim frame beneath the thin material of the strapless sundress. Unable to pry his gaze from her until she moved off when the baby started crying.

"Karen's a pretty girl, huh, Deuce?"

Johnny's eyes snapped to Treviso's. "Yeah, sure. Real pretty." Had Treviso known he was staring at her? Had Treviso picked up on the implication that he might drop in on Karen when she was here alone? "You know." He tried to say it like he wasn't really thinking about it. Like he was saying what anyone would say.

"A lot of people can't believe it when they see her, Deuce. They tell me I married way over my head." Treviso took a long drag off the cigarette, then tapped it on a glass ashtray sitting on the windowsill. "I say it's the other way around. I say she married way over *her* head. Her whole family's on welfare, for Christ's sake. She's living the dream now."

Johnny's eyes flickered around the cramped kitchen. "Yeah, the dream. Put out the cigarette, Tony. I don't like the smoke, especially this early in the morning." He really didn't like cigarette smoke, but he'd said it for another reason, too. Making Treviso put out the cigarette was a quick way of asserting dominance. "Now."

"What? Oh, sure."

Johnny waited until Treviso had tamped the burning end down into the ashtray before speaking. "Tell me about that thing that happened outside Marconi's house a couple of years ago." A thin column of white smoke rose toward the ceiling from the still-smoldering cigarette.

"What thing?"

"You know what thing." Johnny studied Treviso's face carefully, searching for the truth. "When his grandson was killed."

"Oh, *that* thing."

"Yeah, yeah. *That* thing. Tell me about it."

"What do you wanna know?"

"What happened?" It was obvious Treviso was stalling. Clearly he didn't want to talk about this, and he was trying like hell to figure out how not to. Marconi had told Johnny not to make any judgments, but that was impossible. He had to know what really happened. "Exactly what happened."

Tony leaned back and put his hands behind his head. "There's not much to tell, Deuce. A guy I loaned a lot of money to was way behind on his schedule. He lived close to there, close to Marconi's place in Queens. I was meeting Marconi to talk to him about something else anyway, so I told the guy to meet me there. I wanted to talk to him before I went in to see Marconi. Kill two birds with one stone while I was all the way up there in Queens."

"Kyle McLean, right? That was the guy's name?"

Treviso gazed at Johnny for a few moments, like now *he* was searching. Like his antennae had suddenly sprung up. "Yeah, I think that was his name. Why you so interested, Deuce?"

"Tell me about this McLean guy."

"What's there to tell?"

Johnny took a deep breath. He wasn't a man blessed

with a reservoir of patience. "Look, pal, you know I only work for one man in the family. I'm here as a personal favor to him. This isn't a family council deal. Now I want answers, I want your cooperation. I'd hate to tell Mr. Marconi that you wouldn't give me that." Johnny leaned back, exposing the butt end of his favorite pistol sticking out of the shoulder holster. He saw Treviso's eyes flicker down to the gun, watched them linger there for a few moments. "Come on, Tony. Stop fucking around."

Treviso nodded solemnly. "Yeah, okay." His voice was barely audible. "But can you at least tell me why you're here first? What Marconi wants to know?"

"Look, here's the . . . uh, here's the—" Johnny did a subtle double take as he stuttered. Karen was standing in the hallway outside the kitchen again, where Treviso couldn't see her. She was gazing straight at him with those incredible eyes, sending a message to him without actually saying a word. God, she was beautiful.

"What's the problem, Deuce?" Treviso wanted to know. "You all right? *Hey! Deuce!*"

13

JACK PULLED THE covers over his head to shield his eyes from the blinding light suddenly streaming into his bedroom. It was as if the sun were right outside the house. "What the hell's going on?" he grumbled.

"Time to get up, Daddy," Cheryl announced cheerfully, moving to the room's other window. "It's after seven-thirty, and it's a beautiful day. The calendar in the kitchen says you've got to be at work by eight. We both need to get going," she said as she raised the blind.

He sneaked a peek from beneath the covers, and he was instantly sorry he had. Now it was like *two* suns shining directly on him. He groaned. His head was killing him. He'd stayed at the Dugout last night until closing— until two in the morning—trying to get information about the kid out of the bartender. The guy hadn't said much, and when it was obvious he wasn't going to say any more and that he was getting suspicious, Jack turned his attention to a scotch bottle. Regaling the bartender with his Yankee glory days as he drank.

He cursed under his breath, realizing how pathetic he must have sounded going on and on about how he'd personally discovered some of the team's big names. It was true, but there was no need to brag about it.

God, he hated how alcohol did that to him. How it made him feel like he could spout off about himself to people he didn't even know and that they were actually interested. He was like that more and more the older he got, too. Like he was some flea-bitten old lion who still needed to hear himself roar every once in a while to convince himself he was still worth something. And people let him do it only because they felt sorry for him—or they wanted a good tip.

"I'm gonna call in sick today," he muttered, pulling the covers down slowly, squinting to let his eyes grow accustomed to the brightness. About the only thing happening for him at the store today was getting fired. He could face the music, all right; he had no problem with that. But he didn't want to do it with a migraine. He might go off on Ned, the store manager, and that wouldn't be pretty. No; he'd go in tomorrow to get the bad news. Besides, he was going to try for a new job today anyway. The hell with bagging groceries. "My throat's sore. I'm coming down with something."

"You're hung over, Daddy. That's all. You never get sick. You never missed a day in thirty-four years with the Yankees. Now get up. Come on."

"Please don't do this to me," he begged.

Cheryl sat down on the edge of the bed. "Where'd you go last night?"

"I told you. I met some guys at the store last week. We all went out to—"

"You didn't go out to dinner with anybody last night, Daddy. Don't lie to me."

She knew him so well. "Okay, I went back out to the stadium to watch the kid," he admitted.

"I knew it," she said triumphantly. "Why didn't you just tell me that was where you were going?"

"I didn't want your boyfriend tagging along. I didn't want to have to act all fake and play that stupid pitch speed game with him again." He reached for a glass of water on the nightstand. Cheryl must have brought it in because he couldn't remember getting it. Of course, he couldn't remember a whole lot about last night after leaving the bar. "Speaking of my favorite person, is he still here?" Bobby's SUV had been parked in front of the house when he got home. At least he remembered that much. He chuckled, remembering something else, too. Old habits died hard.

"No; he's gone."

"How late did he stay?"

Cheryl set her jaw defiantly. "All night. He left about a half hour ago."

Jack rose up on one elbow. "I don't remember giving you permission for him to stay over."

"I don't remember *needing* permission."

"Yeah, well, I make the rules around here," Jack grumbled. "You want to live under my roof, you abide by them."

"You may have made most of the down payment by selling your rings, Daddy, but I've paid most of the mortgage since we moved in."

"Still."

"And besides, who says I really want to live under the same roof with you anyway?" she snapped.

"Fine, then leave."

"Fine, maybe I will."

They gazed at each other intently for a few moments, neither one blinking.

Finally, Jack put the glass down on the nightstand and eased off his elbow until he was flat on his back, staring at the ceiling. "Christ." There was no way he was winning this argument, and they both knew it. "Next thing I know Bobby'll be moving in."

"So, how did the kid play last night?" Cheryl asked, starting to stand up, her voice still on edge.

"Not very well." Jack hesitated, appreciating the fact that she wasn't lingering on her small victory. "I tried to talk to him after the game, but the conversation only lasted about three minutes. It was weird."

Cheryl sank slowly back down onto the bed. "What do you mean?"

"I told him I thought he was the real deal, then he told me to get out of his face. Basically told me if he ever saw me again he'd kill me."

Her eyes opened wide. "Jesus, Daddy, you ought to call the—"

"I'm kidding," Jack said with a wave. "He was actually very polite. But he did tell me never to come up to him again." Jack held up his hand to show her the World Series ring. "I even wore this. You think he would have been impressed."

"That *is* weird," she agreed. "I mean, some guy wearing a World Series ring comes up to me and tells me he was a Yankee scout for thirty-four years and that he thinks I'm the real deal. I'd be pretty excited if I'm a minor leaguer."

"Yeah, exactly. But it wasn't like that at all. It was like I was the last person in the world he wanted to see."

"Where did you talk to him?" she asked. "At the stadium?"

"No; the head groundskeeper told me where the kid usually hangs out after games. It's this bar called the Dugout. By the way, the groundskeeper backed up what Bobby said about Clemant, too. That nobody likes him." Jack gazed at the ring for a few moments. He hadn't been able to get it off last night because his fingers were too swollen from the alcohol. He tried again for a few moments but still couldn't pull the thing over his knuckle. "Anyway, the kid came into the bar about an hour after the game. By himself, too. The bartender wouldn't say much about him, but he did say he'd never seen him come in with anyone else. He's always alone. Kind of weird." Jack shook his head. "So I told the kid I'd been to the game the other night. Told him I thought the catch and the home run were two of the greatest plays I'd ever seen. Then he asked me if I was at last night's game. I told him I was, and it was strange how he reacted. He smiled when he admitted that he'd stunk up the joint. Like he was proud of himself for playing bad."

"What do you think's going on?"

Jack hesitated, replaying the brief conversation in his head. "I don't know. But he's got all the physical tools, let me tell you. He's a big boy, bigger in person than he even looks on the field. I shook his hand. It was so damn strong. Like Thurman Munson's used to be." He suddenly noticed the red blotches on her neck. "Hey, what happened to you?"

"Nothing," she said, standing up and heading straight for the door.

"Cheryl, come back here. Hey! *Cheryl!*"

Bobby jogged down the sidewalk in front of the apartment building toward his SUV. He was on his way to an appointment with the head buyer of a sporting goods chain based in Tampa. If everything went right, he was going to make a big sale today and earn a nice commission.

He'd raced back here from Cheryl's place a little while ago, zigzagging through rush-hour traffic. Then showered and shaved in record time—he had a couple of nicks on his face to show for it. Despite all the dashing around, he'd still be half an hour late for the appointment, and the buyer was going to be pissed—he was a cranky old son of a bitch. But what the hell? He'd promise the guy World Series or Super Bowl tickets—which his company could easily get—and everything would be fine. It would be a pain to kiss the guy's ass for the first few minutes, but it would be worth it. He'd make some nice money on the deal and, besides, that last time he and Cheryl had sex this morning had been incredible. Best of the night. Worth a little ass-kissing.

He grinned as he aimed his keys at the Explorer and pressed the unlock button, thinking about last night. He'd finally slept with her, and, after a little prodding, she'd done it the way he liked—rough. Not real rough, just a little. Just a preview of what was to come. Which was why he was paying attention to her at all. He'd sensed that once she had sex with him, she'd do whatever he wanted. That she was one of those clingy girls who'd please a man any way he demanded after she'd given herself up. His instincts had been exactly right. She'd done exactly as she'd been told without any complaining.

He took a deep, satisfied breath. He'd dial the volume up on her a little at a time over the next few weeks. Get her to start sleeping at his apartment so he wouldn't have to worry about Jack hearing them. This was going to be fun, *really* fun.

He was about to hop in behind the wheel when he remembered that his briefcase was in the back. He wanted to go over some notes while he drove to Tampa, and they were in the briefcase. He hurried to the back of the truck, lifted the door, and started to reach inside.

"Jesus Christ!" he shouted, stumbling backward, his heart suddenly in his throat. He stared at the tan briefcase for a few moments, then realized that the coiled-up snake lying on top of it was fake. He leaned over, hands on his knees, breathing hard. "You suck, Jack Barrett. You suck."

Biff and Harry—the EMTs who'd raced to the stadium to help Jack—sat in the front seat of the ambulance, air-conditioning turned on full blast. It was still early in the day, but the temperature had already reached ninety. They were parked in a rest stop off Interstate 75 well east of downtown Sarasota. During their shift they didn't bother going back to base. Rescue calls came in fast, and this was a more central location from which to cover their territory. There were so many old people down here the heart attack calls never seemed to stop.

Biff yawned and stretched. He'd been out late last night, and there'd already been three calls since the shift had started at six this morning, two of which had required trips to the hospital. One old guy had already flat-lined by the time they got to him, but they'd made the trip to Sarasota General anyway. For nothing, of course.

Harry sat behind the steering wheel. "How long you think it'll be before the next call?"

Biff shut his eyes and nestled into the corner formed by the passenger seat and the door. Maybe if he got lucky he could snag a little shut-eye. "Seven minutes, Harry, seven minutes. Now how about some peace and quiet? I'm gonna try to catch a few Z's. Okay? I'm beat."

"Yeah, okay." Harry picked at his cuticles. "I'll take the under on that. I say it'll be less than seven minutes."

"Fine, damn it." Being tired and hung over had Biff in a cranky mood. That and being four months behind on his mortgage and two months behind on his credit cards, with no apparent way of bringing them current. The collection departments were starting to hound him, and he could only avoid them for so long. "How much?"

"A buck."

"You got it. Now shut the hell up."

"Okay, okay. Jeez. What crawled up your ass?"

Biff said a quick prayer, begging for help from above.

"So," Harry started up again, "how far you think the Yankees'll go this year?"

Well, he should have figured that would happen, Biff

thought. He hadn't been to church in more than six months. "*Jesus Christ*, will you please—"

"*All right*," Harry interrupted.

Maybe now he'd shut up.

But another thirty seconds later, Harry was at it again. "I hope that guy we helped at the stadium the other night is okay."

Biff sneered. "I hope he's dead."

"The whole reason he didn't go to the hospital was because he didn't have insurance. I heard his daughter say it. She was trying to keep it quiet, but I heard her. Poor guy must be broke."

"He'll be happier dead," Biff snapped. Being broke was no fun. He knew from experience. "Now, for the love of God, will you please give me some damn peace and—"

"Life Ride 7, LF 7," blared a female voice through the radio speaker. "Do you copy, LF 7?"

Harry grabbed the microphone off the dash. "We copy, we copy. What you got?"

"Heart attack at the Pelican Condos out on SR 91. The address is 11239 Atoll Road. It's the second left after you go through the front gate. Got it?"

"Yup!" Harry flipped on the siren and slammed the ambulance into gear. "Here we go, partner."

Biff groaned as he snapped his seat belt buckle together. There had to be a better way. There just had to be.

14

DEUCE. *DEUCE*."

Johnny checked the hallway again, hoping Karen would still be there. Praying Treviso hadn't noticed his subtle glance. "I, I want your help." But she was gone. "And I'm gonna get it," he continued, his voice growing stronger as he was able to refocus.

"I'll do whatever I gotta do," Treviso agreed. "Just tell me why you and Marconi are so fat on McLean. It's weird, you know? I mean, he's been dead a coupla years. He died in that damn car accident before I could squeeze the jingle juice out of him. I was out a hundred grand, for Christ's sake. It was the worst bang I ever took." He hesitated. "So what's up?"

There was no way around it. He had to explain what was going on. "There's a chance McLean isn't dead. Yeah, maybe he faked that accident after all."

Treviso's eyes opened wide. *"Huh?"*

Johnny grimaced. Treviso suddenly figured he had a shot at recovering the dough. A shot at climbing out of the bottomless pit he'd tumbled into after losing the hundred grand.

"How'd you find out?" Treviso demanded, rising from his chair.

"Easy, Tony."

"Easy? McLean cost me a hundred freaking grand, Deuce. I figured Marconi was gonna have me popped when he found out the guy croaked. If you know where McLean is, you better tell me."

Johnny's body tensed instantly. Nobody talked at him like that. Except Marconi. "Better? I *better* tell you?"

Treviso held out his hands apologetically, sinking back into his chair. "Sorry, Deuce. I, I didn't mean it like that. But you gotta understand," he continued quickly, "that was a big-ass loss for me. If you know where McLean is, please tell me. Gimme a shot at getting the money back before you ice him." Treviso took a deep breath. "I mean, I get it now. That's why Marconi's so interested, that's why you're on the case. The old man found out the guy who smacked his grandson might still be breathing, and he wants to take him down. Right?"

Johnny leaned back and lifted both hands above his head, like he was stretching. But he was really checking the hallway again, using his arms to disguise his true intent. She wasn't there, and he could feel disappointment tugging at his heart. How stupid was that? He'd met her only a few minutes ago. But he couldn't deny it. Besides, that's how it had been with his first Karen, too. Right away. As soon as he saw her. "Of course."

"He must want this guy bad."

"What do you mean?"

Treviso pointed at Johnny. "He put his top dog on the trail. He knows you'll finish it. You always do."

Johnny shifted uncomfortably. "Yeah, uh-huh." He'd never taken compliments very well. "And you're right, Marconi does want this guy bad. *Real* bad."

Treviso clasped his hands together. "Can you help me on this, Deuce?" he begged. "Give me a chance to get the money before you kill him. Please."

"No way, Tony. But don't sweat it. Marconi doesn't care about the dough no more."

Treviso's face contorted into an expression of utter disbelief. "Really?"

Of course Marconi still cared about the money. But Johnny was willing to say anything to keep Treviso on the sidelines. Even a blatant lie. "That's right."

"But he's still docking me, so he must—"

"*Look,*" Johnny interrupted loudly, "the boss is just out for blood. It's a revenge thing sweet and simple."

Treviso gazed out through the dirty windowpanes. Clearly not convinced, Johnny could tell.

"If you say so," Treviso finally mumbled.

"I do say so. *Now,* you gonna answer my questions?"

Treviso nodded solemnly. "Yeah."

"So tell me about this Kyle McLean guy." Johnny eased back in his chair.

So did Treviso. "He was already a hotshot high school baseball player outta Queens when I first heard about him. Had pro scouts drooling all over him after his junior year. He was a big kid. Tall, huge shoulders, even at seventeen." Treviso spread his arms wide. "He was a man among boys, Deuce. I saw a coupla games, and he was amazing. He'd crush the ball, a home run at least once a game. A lot of teams ended up intentionally walking him after a while. They said he was going to be the greatest high school player to *ever* come out of New York. And there's been some pretty fine talent to come out of here, let me tell you. He probably coulda played pro ball even at that point because he was—"

"I get the picture," Johnny said tersely. He wasn't into baseball, wasn't into sports in general. "Get on with it."

"Sorry, sorry. So anyway, it turns out his mother has cancer or something. I don't know the specifics. I never asked because I didn't care. All I knew was it was real bad and they were dirt poor and they didn't have health insurance because the kid's father had been outta work for a while. The father was sick, too. I think it was his liver." Treviso scrunched up his face, like it was painful for him to think back that far. "Anyway, they didn't have the money for the operation, and the kid was going nuts because if they didn't operate on her fast she was gonna croak. The kid and his parents were real close." Treviso grinned slyly. "I heard about the situation through my network, so I went up to him after a game one day. We talked a coupla times, and we worked out a deal." His expression soured. "At least I thought we did. See, I figured he'd be able to pay me back from some big signing bonus he got from a pro team right after he finished his senior year. It was perfect. It was a lot of money to ask Marconi for, but there was a clear way out of it. There usually isn't, you know? And I woulda made a lot a money if that thing had come through."

Treviso was looking off into the distance again. Undoubtedly thinking about how much better life would have been if the McLean loan had cashed out. "So what happened?" Johnny asked.

"The first time I hit McLean up for the VIG he jumps all big and bad with me. It was a month after I made the loan, and he tells me to screw myself right in front of one of my guys. Totally disrespects me."

"Who was the other guy?"

"Paulie the Moon."

Paulie the Moon was a Lucchesi soldier who worked in one of the Bronx gangs terrifying union officials and carrying out Marconi's run-of-the-mill hits. The rumor was he'd killed at least fifty people over the years, maybe more. Paulie got his nickname because his face was round as a full moon. He seemed like a gentle giant when you first met him, but he was a mean son of a bitch.

"McLean says I told him he didn't have to pay me anything for a year," Treviso continued angrily. "Which is ridiculous. I'd never say that."

Which made sense. No loan shark would ever let a mark go a whole year without at least paying the VIG. That would be stupid. But the kid might really have heard the deal differently. Might have thought when Treviso said he didn't have to pay the money back for a year it meant he didn't have to pay *anything* for a year. The VIG on a hundred thousand would be more than three grand a month, and it would be tough for a seventeen-year-old kid to nut that. Which Tony would have known. Which meant the deal would get renegotiated time and time again. Stretched out with more fees added and interest piled onto interest. So in the end the mark paid way more than he'd first thought he was going to. Sometimes loan sharks didn't explain everything very well—for obvious reasons. Especially an even slipperier-than-usual one like Tony Treviso.

"Yeah, okay, I get it," Johnny said. Now things were falling into place. There'd been a misunderstanding, which happened sometimes. Of course, when there was a misunderstanding, the other side never got any sympathy from the Lucchesi family. They always assumed the misunderstanding was just a mark's way of trying to wriggle out of the deal. That he was having selective memory about the terms of the transaction. Which was often the case, actually. "So what happens then?"

"So I start banging on him, I start getting tough. I tell him things are gonna happen if he doesn't start paying me something. Paulie helped me. He likes that kind of stuff."

Paulie *loved* that kind of stuff, Johnny knew. "You tell the kid you were gonna chop his mother's head off?"

Treviso grinned smugly. "Hey, why not? I'm supposed to be good at that, right?"

Johnny hesitated. There was one part of that story that had never made sense. "That guy paid you back. Right?" he asked. "All fifty grand."

Treviso looked up. "Huh?"

Timid Tony was playing stupid, but Johnny could tell he understood the question. "If he paid you back, why'd you still kill him? Why'd you send his wife the head with the rat in the mouth?"

Treviso fiddled with the mole on his neck. "You tell me why you always carry that two of hearts, and maybe I'll tell you about that thing."

The mole looked like it was hanging by a thread. Like

it was going to fall off in Treviso's fingers in the next few seconds. "Did you and Paulie kill the kid's girlfriend?" Johnny would never tell anyone why he carried that two of hearts in his pocket. Or what it signified.

"*What?*" Treviso's face twisted in shock. "No way."

Johnny pursed his lips. Treviso's words told one story, but his expression told quite another. "The truth, Tony. So help me God, I want the truth. Believe me, I'll know if you're lying."

"Look, Deuce, Paulie's got a mind of his own. Maybe he did something without telling me. I never asked. I don't really care, either." Treviso shrugged. "Maybe you should go talk to Paulie yourself."

"Maybe I will."

"Sure, sure, go ahead." Treviso reached, then hesitated, his fingers half an inch from the cigarettes. "Can I have just one?"

"When I'm gone."

Treviso's hand retreated slowly from the pack.

"So your story is," Johnny continued, "that McLean ran over Marconi's grandson after you met with him that night in front of the row house. Right?"

"Right. I remember it all real clearly now," Treviso said confidently, like his memory was suddenly turning crystal clear. "That was the night I told the kid I was gonna torture his mommy if he didn't start paying me. Gouge out her eyes, pour acid in 'em."

Damn. It was as if Treviso enjoyed thinking about what it would have been like to gouge out the poor woman's eyes. Like he was disappointed he hadn't actually had the chance to pour acid in the wounds. He'd caught a glint in Treviso's eyes and a twitch of the lips at both corners of his mouth. Johnny killed, but he took no pleasure in it. Just got satisfaction from erasing one more scumbag from the face of the planet. But it seemed like Timid Tony might actually enjoy killing. At least when that psychopath switch flipped on.

"Well," Treviso continued, "the kid hears what I'm gonna do and makes a move at me. Starts screaming about how he's gonna kill me first, before I have a chance to do anything. Lucky for me, Paulie's sitting in his car across the street, watching the whole thing. He comes running as soon as the kid comes at me. The kid sees Paulie, stops dead in his tracks, turns, sprints for his car, guns the engine, and squeals out. Just as Marconi's grandkid comes pedaling around the corner on his bike." Treviso held up his hands like he was gripping the handlebars of a bike, and moved his head from side to side, smiling foolishly. "And *bam,* that's that. The little boy's done. A bloody mess," he said, grimacing. "Of course, McLean doesn't stop after he nails the little guy, just tears off. Next day we hear McLean drove off a pier into the East River and drowned." Treviso shook his head. "And I'm out a hundred grand."

"That's your story? Your whole story?"

"That's it, Deuce." Treviso leaned forward and pointed at Johnny. "Now, if you catch up to the kid, he's gonna tell you something different. He's going to tell you he didn't hit a little boy on a bike."

"Jeez, why would he tell me that?"

Treviso shrugged. "What the hell else is he gonna say?" Not picking up on the fact that Johnny was being sarcastic.

"Then why did you tell me?" There it was. That old desire to be a lawyer, to force people into corners. Maybe it wasn't too late to be a white-collar guy, to be respectable. To put scumbags in jail instead of in the ground. "If it's so obvious that's what he's gonna say, I mean."

"Huh?"

All of a sudden Treviso looked like he'd been caught with his dirty hands in the cookie jar a minute in front of dinner. "Of course, he's gonna say he's innocent," Johnny said loudly. "That he didn't hit anybody. What? You think I'm stupid?"

"No, no, Deuce. I'm just saying, that's all. I'm just saying. That's why McLean faked his accident. Why he tried to make everyone think he drove off that pier. It all makes sense now. He knew Marconi would come after him for killing his grandson."

"McLean faked his death," Johnny said deliberately, "so you wouldn't kill his mother. Not because he hit a little boy. He wouldn't know it was Marconi's grandson he hit. It could have been anybody's kid as far as he knew." He raised one eyebrow. "If he actually did hit a little boy on a bike that night."

They stared at each other across the kitchen table for several moments. Suddenly there was no sound in the kitchen except for the gentle hum of the refrigerator motor. Even the baby wasn't whining anymore.

Finally Treviso stood up. "I gotta hit the can, Deuce. Gotta recycle some coffee. Be back in a minute."

"Sure," Johnny said, standing up, too. "Take your time." When it came right down to it, Treviso wasn't very smart, Johnny realized, watching him head out of the kitchen. He'd stepped into that trap so fast.

He pulled out his cell phone and checked his text messages, deciphering code as he went. It was probably driving the cops crazy reading his messages, but they'd never figure out what was really being said.

"Hi."

Johnny's eyes snapped to the left, toward the soft voice. Karen was standing in the other doorway, the one by the refrigerator. God, she was beautiful. So beautiful it took his breath away. "Hi."

She moved to him. "You felt it, too," she said in a soft voice, "didn't you?"

Nature. It was one hell of a thing. It always seemed to find a way. "Felt what?"

"Don't deny it," she said, putting her fingers on his arm. "You know what. You know *exactly* what."

For several moments Johnny thought about how wonderful it would be to have a companion again. Somebody he could love and trust and who'd love and trust him. Finally, he willed his eyes from hers. "Tell your husband I'll call him later." Then he turned and headed for the door.

Stephen Casey hadn't left his house or called anybody in two days. Not since the kindly old couple had untied him from the base of the streetlamp—where the guy who'd tortured him left him wearing just his underwear—and given him a ride all the way home at one in the morning. The couple had been coming back from babysitting their granddaughter in Queens when they'd spotted Casey. They'd even been nice enough to turn the heat way up in their old Impala because he was freezing. And waited around in their car until he found his spare house key under a brick in the garden beside the front door. They'd only asked him once what he was doing tied up to the streetlamp, and when he hadn't really answered the question, they'd let it go, hadn't asked him again. He'd gotten their names and address and was planning to send them something nice as thanks.

But first he had to get to his sister, to Kyle's mother, Helen. Had to physically get to her so she could warn Kyle.

He couldn't call Helen. He assumed her phone line was tapped, and he knew she didn't have e-mail—she wouldn't even know how to use it if she did. Besides, they'd probably be monitoring that, too. The question was how he was going to get to her. Whoever those guys were who kidnapped him the other night were out there watching, waiting for him to make a move. He could feel it. Those old constable-on-patrol instincts were kicking in.

Casey lifted one of the narrow slats of the blind hanging from his second-floor bedroom window and peered out. All the cars were on the far side of the street because the city cleaned the side his tiny house was on today. He gazed at the vehicles carefully, recognizing each one. It was a close-knit neighborhood, and everyone knew everyone else's car.

Finally he let the slat drop, brushing the dust from his fingertips. He hated dusting, hated cleaning of any kind. His wife used to do all that—she'd kept an immaculate home for sixteen years—until she'd left him for another man. Left him for another cop, a cop from the *same* precinct. Which was really why he'd retired. He couldn't bear to look at the uniform anymore. Everyone he worked with reminded him of what she'd done. It was as if she'd been with all of them.

He grimaced and shook his head, trying to rid himself of those awful memories. He had to get to Helen soon. He knew she was in terrible danger. And if they got to her, they'd get to Kyle.

15

JACK TOOK A quick belt of courage from the flask before climbing out of the Citation and heading into the store. Cheryl had finally persuaded him to go into work despite the headache splitting his skull, though she had no idea why he'd really bothered. She thought he was just doing the right thing.

It was eight-thirty; he was half an hour late. If they didn't fire him for yesterday's run-in with the woman, they were going to fire him for being late. It was the third time this month, and the store manager had warned him the last time that he wouldn't get off with just a warning the next time. Next time was *sayonara*. So one way or the other, he was gone.

Which was fine. What Jack wanted—the real reason he'd bothered to swing his aching knees out of bed despite the migraine—was the four hundred bucks the store owed him. It was payday, and every little bit meant something at this point. Which was deeply depressing.

He kicked a flattened soda can, sent it spinning across the pavement into a car tire. It was such a bite in the ass to have to put every penny under a microscope. To scrimp and save just to be able to buy a ticket to a Single-A baseball game. To work menial jobs because there wasn't much else he could do to earn a buck at this point in life. Well, he had a plan, a way to escape this desperate existence. Which was the other reason he'd bothered to get out of bed this morning.

Four years ago he'd figured he was set, hadn't thought he needed a plan. Figured he'd retire from the Yankees with his pension and relax on his beautiful sprawling back deck during his golden years, sipping fine scotch. But the front office had yanked everything away when they fired him—including his pension. They'd cited some barely legible legal jargon buried deep in his contract. Something about actions by the individual that were in direct conflict with the welfare of the team or that caused the team harm. Something he'd never bothered to pay attention to or have a lawyer pay attention to before he signed the contract because he trusted the people he worked for so completely. And in the blink of an eye his ten-thousand-dollars-a-month-for-life-starting-at-age-sixty-five retirement payment evaporated because he didn't have the money to fight the people in court.

Because his ex-wife, Linda, had crushed him in the divorce. She'd gotten the savings, the cars, the house, and everything in the house—except his clothes, his shaving kit, and his World Series rings. Turned out her lawyer was tight with the judge in the case, and the judge was a *huge* Yankee fan. When he heard what Jack was supposed to have done—how it was supposed to have blown the 2004 American League Championship Series with the Red Sox—the man in the black robe had exacted his own revenge for watching his beloved Yankees beaten by the hated archrivals. Exacted his own revenge after the Yankees were so close to being in another World Series. And Jack had paid a terrible price.

Jack had heard from some friends in the old neighborhood that Linda still owned the house, though she wasn't spending much time there. Apparently she was dating a rich banker from the Hamptons and living it up. Spending most of her time at his oceanfront mansion—when they weren't traveling. She hadn't called him once since they'd walked out of court. Not once. Forty years of marriage and it hadn't meant anything to her. Jack grabbed an empty shopping cart resting against a parked car and pushed the cart angrily ahead.

Linda had tried calling Cheryl a few times after the move to Sarasota. To try to repair the damage she'd done by making Cheryl pick a side. But as far as he knew, Cheryl had never returned the calls. Cheryl was usually the most forgiving person in the world—but not this time. Apparently Linda had even offered to help support Cheryl financially, but it hadn't changed anything. Hadn't even tempted her despite their nearly hand-to-mouth existence down here.

Jack shook his head ruefully as he pushed the cart across the hot asphalt, thinking about how much more attention he'd paid to David than Cheryl while the kids were growing up. Grimacing as he remembered her asking if they could have a quick catch together one evening just as he was headed out the door to go to David's baseball game—for the third night in a row. He could still see the hurt in her eyes as she stood there in the kitchen wearing her little Yankee cap and her little glove when she realized where he was headed—again. And after all that, here she was, taking care of him. Sacrificing her own happiness so he wouldn't be lonely. Being unfailingly loyal. And what had David ever done? Nothing. In fact, David was sitting squarely on the other side of the loyalty ledger.

Jack stalked through the store's main entrance, rolled the cart at two long lines of stacked ones, then headed through the second set of automatic doors. It was cool in here, a welcome relief from the sweltering heat. He saw Ned Anderson, the store manager, right away. Caught the other man's irritated look when their eyes met. It might be cool in here now, but it was going to heat up in a few seconds.

"Hey, Barrett!" Ned yelled across seven checkout aisles. He was standing by the magazine display in aisle eight, talking to the cola delivery guy. "Stay put. I'll be right there."

Jack watched Ned subtly accept a wad of cash. Undoubtedly this week's payola to maintain the end-aisle display—the best shelf space in the store. Ned was young to be a store manager. Only thirty-two, but he looked forty-five. He was bald on top and had deep crow's-feet at the corners of his eyes and mouth. He walked around with an air of self-importance that helped make him seem as if he were above everyone else, too. Most of the employees hated him, but the store was one of the most profitable in Sarasota. Ned wasn't going anywhere. Except up when he got promoted.

"Hello," Jack called when Ned was still three aisles away. Forcing himself to be cordial.

"You're late again, Barrett."

"Yeah, sorry about that." Jack caught Ned glancing up, toward the second-floor office, which overlooked the store. He looked up, too, but didn't see anything unusual through the long window. Just the guys who ran the produce and meat departments having a conversation. "Listen, Ned, I—"

"Hold on."

"Huh?"

"Just wait a second."

"But all I want to do is—" Over Ned's shoulder, Jack saw a door open. Behind it were the stairs leading up to the office. Then, like a terrifying apparition, the woman he'd gotten into it with yesterday in the parking lot loomed in the doorway. She was wearing a big, wide-brimmed red hat—and a face full of rage.

"That's him!" she shouted shrilly from the doorway, pointing a bony, diamond-drenched finger at Jack. "That's the man who dumped a whole bag of my groceries out on the parking lot. That's the man who called me a bitch! A *fucking* bitch!"

Ned stepped in front of Jack just as the woman reached him. "Easy, ma'am, easy," he said soothingly. "Is what she said true?" he asked, turning to Jack once he was sure the woman had stopped.

Jack looked around, aware that everything in the store had come to a halt. Cashiers weren't cashing, baggers weren't bagging, shoppers weren't shopping. Everyone was staring at what was going on at the end of aisle one. "I just came in to get my check," he said quietly. "I quit, Ned."

"You didn't answer my question. Did you call her a—" Ned interrupted himself. "Did you call her that?"

"I want my check."

"Answer my question!" Ned shouted, veins rising up out of his forehead. "Now!"

"Mr. Barrett didn't call her anything."

Jack, Ned, and the woman all glanced to the right quickly. It was the bag boy who'd been stowing groceries across the lane from where Jack and the woman had gotten into it yesterday. The young man who'd shown Jack the ropes on his first day at the store.

"Mr. Barrett was real polite to her," the bag boy continued. "She was the one who was rude," he said, pointing at the woman. "*Real* rude."

Ned gritted his teeth and cursed. Two seconds ago Jack had no way out. Now the old man was going to slip through the dragnet. "Don't get involved in this, MJ," he warned.

"I'm just telling you what happened."

Ned rolled his eyes. "Look, I—"

"Are you going to let this man get away with speaking to me like that?" the woman demanded, eyes bulging. "Are you?"

Ned's eyes flashed from the woman to Jack to MJ. "No, I'm not," he finally said. He pointed at the bag boy. "You know what, MJ? You're fired, too. You've been late four times this month." Then he pointed at Jack. "If you want your check, sue the company."

"You can't do that," Jack retorted angrily.

"I just did. Now both of you get the hell out of here before I call the cops."

Biff stood up as Harry continued CPR. There wasn't any point, he knew. The guy was dead. There would be no miraculous recovery, no back from beyond. The old guy had managed to crawl to the phone and dial 911 after the heart attack hit him, but that was it. He was probably dead a few seconds after he called for help. The 911 people said they couldn't raise him again, said the line was busy. Hell, he hadn't even had time to put the receiver back down.

So many people came to Florida to die. Maybe they didn't think of it that way when they moved, but for all intents and purposes, that's what they were doing. Yeah, yeah, it was just nature taking its course, but Biff was getting sick of facing it every day from the front row. Over and over.

"He's dead, Harry."

"I gotta keep trying," Harry answered, puffing hard as he pressed on the old man's chest with both palms.

Harry was a prime target for a heart attack himself. Soon, too. He was a decent enough guy, but he was stupid. He was forty pounds overweight, drank, smoked, and never exercised. He knew better than most people what could happen to him, but he still did all the bad things. Well, you couldn't have any sympathy for someone who knew what was going to happen to him but didn't do anything about it.

"There's nothing you can do," Biff called, moving toward the living room's sliding glass doors. "Nothing."

He unlocked the doors and moved out onto a small patio overlooking a pool four stories below. The old guy had died alone—and lonely. The super who'd let them in the condo had told them that the wife had passed away four months ago of cancer, and that the old guy hadn't been the same since. That he didn't have any other family members down here to keep him company. The sons and daughters were all back in Michigan or Minnesota or wherever with the grandkids, and the old guy rarely went out. Just sat around and stared at his television hour after hour, day after day.

Biff turned away from the pool. Harry was still at it in there, still trying to revive the old man. He watched the futility for a few more seconds, then glanced around the place. There were beautiful, expensive things everywhere—and probably a ton of cash in accounts all over town. The guy had spent his entire life working his ass off to get these beautiful things and all that cash, and now what good had it done him? Nada. Now he was headed back to Michigan or Minnesota in a pine box—or to a crematorium.

And suddenly, as he stared at Harry straddling the lifeless old man lying on the floor, it hit Biff like a golden lightning bolt from heaven. What he'd been trying to figure out for so long.

The better way.

Now he just needed a partner. Someone just as desperate as he was.

"Let me guess," Jack spoke up, "MJ stands for Michael Jordan. Your father's a huge basketball fan, so he nicknamed you MJ." One of the other bag boys at the store had told Jack MJ's real name was Curtis Billups. The thing about the father calling him MJ for Michael Jordan was a guess, but he had to get the conversation started somehow. This seemed like a good way to do it.

MJ smiled widely, displaying two rows of perfect pearly white teeth inside his dark complexion. "Hey, that's pretty good for an old white guy."

Jack glanced over at the young man sitting in the passenger seat of the Citation as they headed toward Tarpon Stadium. He would have taken a lot of satisfaction in being spot-on with his guess, but MJ's old-white-man zinger had taken the air out of that. "Forget the white thing for a minute," he said evenly, "we'll get back to that. What's age got to do with anything?"

MJ shrugged, his smile growing wider. "Nothing." He hesitated. "Everything."

"What's that supposed to mean?"

"Don't worry about it."

"Uh-huh. So, you got a problem with white people?"

"You got a problem with black people?"

Tall—a couple of inches over six feet—and lean with sharp facial features, MJ was a handsome kid. He had a cool air about him, too. Like he was always in control of the situation, never the other way around.

Jack sensed that no amount of digging was going to get him an answer about what age or being white had to do with anything. At least right now. So he took another tack. "How old are you?"

"Sixteen."

"Brothers and sisters?"

"Seven. I'm the oldest."

"Well, why the hell aren't you in school?" Florida high schools typically let out for summer earlier than those in other states. But as far as he knew, they hadn't let out yet. He was still seeing school buses around, screwing up morning traffic. "You should be setting an example. You know they look up to you."

MJ turned his entire upper body deliberately to the left. "You go to school?"

"Yup," Jack said proudly. "All the way through college. Paid my own way, too."

"Cost a lot?"

"One hell of a lot."

"Work while you were in college?"

"The whole time."

"Well, that's really cool. I'm impressed. Yup, really cool."

Suddenly Jack realized where MJ was headed. "It's not what you—"

"So," MJ interrupted, "you spent all that money and all that time and you ended up bagging groceries. Yeah, I should be going to school, all right," he said with a laugh. "Maybe I should go all the way, go for a Ph.D. Maybe then I could set my sights on being a garbageman."

"Look, you and I both know—"

"And don't try to tell me bagging groceries is just a hobby, old man. Just something you do to pass the time. It's pretty obvious you haven't bought any new clothes in years. That was a real job you just got fired from."

"I wasn't fired. I quit."

"Yeah, sure."

MJ was turning out to be damn smart. And you never knew if it was a good idea to hook up with somebody smart because in the back of his mind he'd always be thinking he could do it better than you. "All I'm saying is that you've got a much better chance of making it if you go to—"

"I didn't come along to get a sermon."

"No, I guess you didn't," Jack mumbled, suddenly aware that he might be putting his foot way into his own mouth. Maybe there wasn't a father around anymore. Just memories of the man who'd given him his nickname. Maybe MJ hadn't had a choice about dropping out of school. "You go to church?" he asked, thinking about how long it had been since he'd heard a sermon.

"Every Sunday."

"Really?" Jack hadn't been to church in ten years. That had been a Christmas service Cheryl had dragged him to. He respected people who were committed to their faith. He'd always wanted to find that for himself, even more so as he aged, but it had never come. And you couldn't force it, especially on yourself. It had to come naturally. He didn't know much about it, but he knew that. "That's good."

"You?"

"Nope." Jack slammed on his brakes before flipping on the Citation's left blinker just a few yards in front of a turn. He chuckled when the guy behind him who'd been riding his ass for the last mile had to slam on his brakes, too. "You know who you look like?" he asked, spotting the light towers of Tarpon Stadium rising over the palm trees.

MJ eased back in his seat. He'd braced himself on the dashboard with both hands when Jack hit the brakes. "Who?"

MJ seemed to have gotten a kick out of the slamming-on-the-brakes move, too. "A young Denzel Washington."

"I thought we all looked alike to you people."

Jack hid a smile. This kid was something else. Well, at least it was going to be fun working with him.

"Was that supposed to be a compliment?" MJ continued. "Was that supposed to make me feel good? Did you pick out a good-looking black guy and tell me I look like him to put me at ease? To make me like you because you think I look like him and you can admit that a black man can be good-looking?"

"Hey, what's your problem?" Jack snapped, suddenly not so sure they were going to have fun after all. "You don't want a sermon? Well, neither do I."

MJ held up his hands. "I'm just digging on you. Don't take it so hard, old man. You aren't the first person who said I look like Denzel."

"Don't call me old man, either."

"Little sensitive about the age, are you?"

Jack gritted his teeth. "A *lot* sensitive." The sudden emotion in the response surprised even him.

"So what do you want me to call you?" MJ asked.

"How about Jack?"

"Nah, Jack's a young man's name."

"There you go again." Jack spotted the stadium turn-in up ahead. "Calling me old."

MJ snapped his fingers. "I got it. I'm gonna call you Reverend from now on."

Jack furrowed his brow. "*Reverend?* Why? I just told you I don't go to church."

"Well, your name's Jack, and if we carry it out a little, it turns into Jackson. Like Jesse Jackson. Like the Reverend Jesse Jackson. Reverend for short. Yeah, I like that. It's way cool." MJ thought about it for a few more seconds. "Maybe even just Rev."

Jack wasn't sure he liked the nickname, but he wasn't going to argue about it. He needed MJ's help. "Why'd you help me back there at the store?" he asked, turning into the stadium's main entrance.

"Well, after all, you didn't call her a *fucking* bitch. Just a bitch. I couldn't let that one get by."

"The real reason," Jack said firmly. "Don't screw with me."

MJ hesitated. "You seem like a nice guy and all, Rev," he said, his voice taking on a sincere tone, "but I didn't do it for you. No offense."

"None taken, but I still want to know why you did do it. You're smart. You knew you were gonna piss off Ned. It was a no-win thing for you."

"Oh, I won."

"What do you mean?"

MJ curled his right hand into a fist and tucked it into the palm of his left. "I hate that woman. She didn't get her satisfaction. That was winning for me. She's everything that's wrong with people."

Jack swung the Citation into a parking space by the stadium's main gate, next to a sign that read "Executive Offices." So down deep the young man was way ahead of his years. Now that he was being serious he hadn't said "you people" or "you white people." Just "people." Life wasn't a race thing for him after all. Just a human thing. "Is your dad still around?"

MJ shook his head. "Nope. He left last year."

That explained it. As the oldest, MJ had been forced to drop out of school so he could work full-time and help pay bills. "Sorry," Jack said quietly. "Do you ever see him?"

"I don't want to talk about it."

"I'm cool with that." Jack exhaled heavily. "So let's get down to biz. I want you to—"

"*Cool with that?*" MJ interrupted. "*Biz?* How ancient are you?"

"That doesn't concern you."

"Well, you asked *me*."

"I don't recall saying this was going to be a two-way street."

"Fine," MJ said, opening the car door. "I'll get my own ride home."

"Wait a minute," Jack said quickly. "I'm sixty-three. What's the problem?"

"Look, don't try to act sixteen around me. Don't try to act cool. It ain't hip. If you want to know the truth, it's kinda scary. Just act your age. Okay?"

The kid was right. He'd scared himself, for Christ's sake. "Okay."

"Now, what were you going to say, Rev?"

Jack turned off the car. "I want you to go in and apply for the full-time batboy position."

At last night's game, Jack noticed the Tarpons advertising for a full-time batboy. And as he was standing in the grocery store listening to Ned go off on MJ, the idea had struck him. The idea of partnership. He could have a guy on the inside, actually in the dugout, picking up information about Mikey Clemant. Maybe then he'd figure out what was up with the kid.

"Okay, but how am I gonna get out here for games? I don't have a car. I rode my bike to the store because it was close, but I'm not pedaling all the way here."

"I'll be your taxi service. I'll get you out here and home every game."

"Oh, sure."

"I will." Jack gestured toward the stadium. "I'm gonna get an usher job while you get the batboy job. I'll have to be out here, too."

MJ smiled curiously. "Why? Why would you want to be an usher? What's this all about, Rev?"

"Let's get the jobs first," Jack suggested as they both climbed out of the car. "Then I'll explain everything."

"No. I want to know now."

It was clear the young man wasn't going anywhere until he understood the situation. Maybe it was best to tell him now anyway. Better to know sooner rather than later if MJ was going to have a problem being a spy. "I used to be a senior executive for the New York Yankees." It was interesting. Even people who didn't know much about baseball were usually impressed when he told them that. MJ didn't seem impressed at all. "On the scouting side. So I know talent." He gestured toward the stadium again. "There's a guy on this team who's good, *really* good. One of the best I've ever seen. I want to take him to the Yankees. But I can't reach him, can't get him to talk to me. It seems like he doesn't want to be discovered, doesn't want to make it out of Single-A. I can't figure out why. It doesn't make any sense, but I'm gonna get to the bottom of it." He pointed at MJ. "And you're gonna help me."

MJ's face brightened. "So I'm your mole."

"If that's what you want to call it."

"And this kid is your white whale."

Jack's chin recoiled slightly. "Yeah," he agreed hesitantly, surprised that MJ had ever read *Moby Dick.* "I guess you could say that."

"And you're Captain Ahab."

MJ was turning out to be a machine gun loaded with a clip full of surprises. "When did you read *Moby—*"

"I'm not calling you Rev anymore," MJ interrupted. "I'm calling you Ahab. That has a meaning for us."

Jack liked Ahab better than Rev, mostly because MJ liked that it had a special meaning between them. The young man had a lot of layers to him. He was a pain in the ass, but he was compelling. "Okay."

"You said you *used* to be with the Yankees," MJ called as Jack headed toward the executive offices. "Why aren't you with them anymore?"

"It's a long story," Jack yelled back over his shoulder. He definitely wasn't getting into that now.

"I got plenty of time."

"No way. Come on, let's go."

"All right," MJ agreed, following after Jack. "But you're gonna pay me four hundred bucks a week for this gig, right?"

"Right."

"Because this only pays twenty bucks a game, and they don't even take me to away games."

"Right."

"And you're going to pay me in cash. No personal checks."

"Yes, *damn* it."

MJ stopped and spread his arms. "Man, where you gonna get that kind of dough?"

"Good question," Jack muttered under his breath as he kept walking. "*Very* good question."

* * *

Stephen Casey reached for the doorknob of his front door, then pulled back. It was the third time he'd started to leave the house—then stopped. He wanted to go outside, knew he had to go out there so he could get in his car and make the short drive over to Helen's place to warn her that she was in grave danger. And that her son was in grave danger. He just hoped he wasn't too late.

He reached for the knob again—and pulled back again. It was the thought of what that guy had done to him the other night that was making him act like some terrified punk, not an ex–police officer. The thought of being tied to that plank at a downward angle, of the Saran Wrap encasing his face, of the water rushing into his nostrils, of that time he'd almost drowned. The thought of it happening all over again. It was killing him. Completely overpowering his courage, overpowering his desire to do the right thing.

He took a deep breath, shivered, then reached for the doorknob and turned.

Finally, he thought as he headed toward his car.

16

TREVISO POUNDED ON Angelo Marconi's front door with his small fist. It was a gorgeous spring day in New York, not a cloud in the sky. Still the slightest chill in the air—even at two in the afternoon—but the smell of new blooms was everywhere, even in this concrete jungle. He loved spring. He'd never told that to anyone but Karen. He didn't want to seem even weaker than he knew people already thought he was. But he always felt a sense of rebirth as May headed toward June and the daylight hours grew longer.

Treviso had spent all morning running around Brooklyn and Queens chasing a mark who'd turned into a greased pig a week ago—the way a lot of them did when their loan was due. But an hour ago, Treviso and Paulie the Moon had tracked the guy down to a greasy spoon in Astoria and surprised him while he was eating a meatloaf sandwich. Tracked him down thanks to a tip from a beat cop they paid off regularly.

They'd shaken twelve grand out of the guy. Everything Treviso was owed—four grand of principal, the VIG, even a cooked-up processing fee. The guy had actually started sobbing when they hauled his ass down a garbage-strewn alley behind the diner and Paulie pulled out a dentist's tool—a long piece of metal with a sharp hook on one end—and threatened to pull the guy's brains out through his nose. Treviso had no idea if that was even possible, but the mark must have believed it because he broke down immediately. He rode with them in Paulie's El Dorado to an electronics shop he owned where he grabbed a wad of cash from a safe in the back, then directed them to his brother's house, where he got the rest. It had been a long but rewarding day. Marconi was going to be pleased. Hopefully enough to grant a big favor.

The door opened and Nicky appeared. "Yeah, hey, Tony. Sorry it took so long, but I could barely hear you knocking."

Treviso saw a smirk flash across Nicky's face. Nicky had probably been thinking about calling him Timid Tony instead of just Tony. "Hey. How you been?"

"Okay." Nicky stood in the doorway, arms crossed, blocking the way.

"Oh, right, right," Treviso said, touching his forehead. "The password. How could I forget? It's ninety-one."

Nicky stepped back. "Okay. Know where you're going?"

"Yeah."

The smell of pizza drifted to Treviso's nose as he brushed past Nicky and headed up the narrow, creaky stairs. God, it smelled good. Marconi must be eating a late lunch.

Maybe the old man would share a slice. It was hard for Treviso to keep weight on, to stay at his normal 145, because of this intestinal disorder he'd been suffering from for a couple of years. He'd never bothered to find out what was wrong, just ate everything he could get his hands on. Nothing inside hurt too bad, so he figured it wasn't time to go to the doctor yet.

When Treviso reached the top of the stairs, he turned down the hallway toward the far bedroom and came face-to-face with Goliath. "The password is Knicks."

"Yeah, right." Goliath motioned for Treviso to put his palms against the wall and spread his legs. "You know the drill."

Treviso grinned and did so. Very few people in the family knew Goliath's real name, but Treviso did. He understood that Marconi didn't want people knowing Goliath's real name because then somebody might be able to get to him, might be able to bribe him. Then the old man's security could be compromised.

Goliath was so stupid. Marconi would assume you couldn't keep a guy's name secret forever. Not for long at all really, especially in the Mafia. And once the old man decided it had just about reached the time when people would find out the guy's real name, Goliath would be capped and dumped in the landfill the family controlled out in North Jersey. But Goliath didn't get it. He figured he had a job for as long as he wanted it.

"Okay, you're clean." Goliath turned and knocked on the door. "Boss?"

"Yeah?"

"Timid Tony."

"Let him in."

Treviso's grin grew wider. Not because he was about to meet with the number two man in the entire Lucchesi organization, but because he knew the whole frisking thing was a charade. There was a metal detector in the foyer downstairs, hidden in the doorway molding, which was why Treviso had taken off his belt with the huge buckle before coming in. The metal detector was a secret, just like Goliath's real name. You couldn't see the equipment even if you were looking for it, but it was there, all right. But Marconi was smart as hell. He knew that if certain people weren't frisked, they'd assume there was a metal detector somewhere, then try to find it and disarm it. That was the reason for the charade. The reason he had people frisked.

Treviso forced a serious expression to his face as he moved into Marconi's bedroom. Most people in the family thought he was a skinny, stupid little fairy. They had no idea he'd figured out Goliath's real name, or that he knew there was a metal detector in the foyer, or that he'd uncovered a hundred other things like that about the family. The same way he knew Deuce Bondano had been staring at Karen in the hallway outside the kitchen this morning. Staring at her lustfully, too, the bastard. As if he really had a chance with her.

"Hello, sir," Treviso said respectfully.

"Hi, Tony," Marconi replied through a mouthful of pepperoni pizza.

Treviso appreciated that Marconi never called him Timid Tony—at least not to his face. Which was all that mattered to Treviso, because he figured everybody cut down everybody behind their backs all the time anyway. Like the don of the family probably cut down Marconi behind his back. That was just how people were. Even good friends did it to good friends. It was a rotten world, but that was how it was, and there wasn't any changing it. It was just good to have a beautiful wife and a healthy baby boy to carry on his name. They were his world, all that mattered to him, and he'd do anything to protect them. Anything.

Which was the real reason he'd killed that bastard and sent the severed head with the dead rat in its mouth to the wife. Because the guy had asked Karen out. Tried to get into her panties.

One day she'd come along with Treviso to collect the VIG. At one point he'd headed into a bodega to get a pack of cigs and left her alone in the car with the guy for no more than five minutes. While he was gone, the guy had tried to get her to meet him later, tried to wet his snake. Karen had told him everything as soon as they dropped the guy off. Well, the guy had ended up damn sorry. So had his wife.

Treviso reached into his pants pocket, pulled out an envelope stuffed full of big bills, and placed it on the tray table in front of Marconi. "This is everything that guy down in Brooklyn owed us. The one I called you about yesterday. The one who's—" Treviso stopped when Marconi held up his hand. The hand that wasn't holding the oily piece of extra cheese pizza. "What?"

Marconi pointed at the television set. "Turn it up."

Treviso chuckled quietly as he turned the knob, his back to Marconi. Marconi was worth millions, but he was watching an *I Love Lucy* rerun on a vintage RCA you still had to turn up manually. "That good?" he asked, looking back over his shoulder.

"Yeah, yeah. Now get that chair over in the corner and bring it close to me so we can talk."

When Treviso was settled in, the old man patted his hand. "You done good with this," he said, holding up the pregnant-looking envelope. "You didn't take any for yourself, did you?"

"No, sir. I'd never do that. Never."

"Good boy. You have to scare this guy into paying you?"

"I did. Well," Tony interrupted himself, "I didn't exactly do it. Paulie the Moon helped me."

"He *helped* you?"

"Okay, okay. Paulie was the one who told the guy what would happen if he didn't cooperate."

"What was that?"

"He took this hook thing out of his pocket and told the guy he was going to stick it up his nose and pull his brains out with it."

Marconi laughed loudly, like it was the goddamn funniest thing he'd heard all day. Then he took another bite of pizza. "Good old Paulie," he muttered, spewing out a couple of small wet pieces of dough and cheese.

"Is that really possible?" Treviso asked, feeling his stomach churn. Marconi didn't close his mouth all the way when he chewed. The sight of what was going on in there combined with the thought of somebody's brains coming out through his nose was making him gag. "Can you really pull someone's brains out his nose?"

"Sure. I seen it done twice. It's a hell of a thing."

Treviso turned away and put his fingers to his lips.

"That bother you, Tony?"

"No."

"I thought you were supposed to have killed some guy and chopped off his head. Why would somebody's brains coming out through his nose make you wanna puke?"

"It doesn't."

Marconi cleared his throat. "How much is in there?" he asked, nodding at the envelope.

"Twelve grand."

"Remind me, how much was the loan for?"

"Four."

Marconi raised both eyebrows. "That's good. You're getting closer."

Since losing a hundred grand to Kyle McLean, Marconi had stopped paying Treviso his normal commission. Usually the Lucchesi loan sharks got 30 percent of the profits, but the huge loss to McLean had put Treviso in the penalty box. Since then he'd gotten only 10 percent, and it was killing him. But it was better than having his brains pulled out through his nose.

"Why don't you run down your loans for me while you're here?" Marconi suggested.

"Okay, sure. But first can I ask you about something?"

Marconi picked up the envelope off the tray table and tossed it on his bed. "What?"

Marconi suddenly seemed annoyed, probably because he wasn't used to anyone else setting the agenda. "It's like this. Well, I heard that the kid might still be alive. The kid who killed your grandson a coupla years ago. That kid Kyle McLean."

"How did you find out about that?" Marconi demanded, his tone turning surly.

"I heard it around," Treviso said quickly. "People talk, you know."

"How exactly did you hear?"

Treviso had been afraid of this. Of the old man demanding to know how he'd heard and not being put off by excuses until he had an answer he could accept. He'd been hoping the general answer would be enough, but now he was going to have to out Deuce Bondano. There was no choice. Deuce had called an hour after leaving the apartment this morning to warn him about saying anything to Marconi about their meeting. But who the hell was he supposed to be more afraid of? "Deuce Bondano came to see me. He told me about it."

Marconi pursed his lips. "Goddamn it."

"I won't tell nobody, I promise. I was just wondering if you'd let me and Paulie talk to McLean first. To see if we can get the money out of him. At least some of it, anyway. I gotta start earning some real money again or I'm gonna—"

"Meeting's over, Tony," Marconi interrupted.

"But sir, I—"

"Get outta here."

"But—"

"Goliath!"

Johnny eased the Seville to a stop half a block down the street from the house. He had no choice. He had to come here, he'd realized, pressing his arm against his body as he rose out of the car. Making sure the pistol was there. It was all window dressing, but Angelo Marconi wasn't a patient man. And the old man had eyes everywhere.

Johnny walked slowly along the sidewalk in front of the

small single-family homes lining the blue-collar neighborhood of eastern Queens, his eyes shifting smoothly about. Looking for anyone or anything suspicious. It was clearly a neighborhood in decline. No urban rehab here. The street was pocked with large potholes; dandelions were growing thickly through the sidewalk's gaping cracks; the cars that lined the street were old and corroded, and a few were even up on blocks; there was junk strewn across most front lawns; and almost all the houses showed visible signs of disrepair and neglect.

Broken glass crunched beneath Johnny's soles as he reached the wire gate in front of the small brick house. He checked up and down the street, then pushed open the gate just enough to squeeze past. The hinges looked rusty and he didn't want them squeaking as the gate swung back. He wanted the element of surprise.

One more check of the street—everything seemed normal—and he headed up the path toward the house. When he reached the door, he leaned against it and turned the knob. It opened right away, which surprised—and worried—him. He quickly drew his gun, holding it out in front as he moved through the quiet home.

When he finished searching the third and last bedroom upstairs, he was satisfied the house was empty. Except for a hungry cat meowing pitifully at his feet. Like it hadn't eaten in a while.

Either Helen McLean had made her getaway, or Marconi's patience had reached its limit. Those were the only two possibilities. He'd know sooner rather than later which it was.

* * *

"Why did you go to Helen McLean's house?"

Stephen Casey lay on the plywood board in an uncomfortably familiar position. On his back, wrists tied snugly beneath the board, neck chained to it as well, head eighteen inches below his feet. He wasn't bothering to struggle this time. He knew it was useless.

"Tell us!"

"She's my sister," Casey muttered. He was blindfolded again, so he had no idea when the water would come rushing down his nose. Somehow this time seemed worse because he knew what was going to happen, and he could feel his heart pounding wildly. The anticipation was driving him crazy. "Why do I need a reason to go to her house?" he asked, doing everything he could to keep his voice calm. He knew men like these thrived on seeing their victims terrified. "What's the problem?"

"Don't give us that bullshit."

Casey had always been good at remembering faces and voices, and he was certain that so far he hadn't heard the voice from the other night. That guy's tone had been naturally cold. A hundred times more intimidating than the loud, harsh Brooklyn accents he was hearing this time. These men had to *try* to sound intimidating. The other guy hadn't needed to try at all.

"Look, I don't—" Casey's words were suffocated by the first bucket of water splashing on his face. "I hadn't seen her in a long time," he sputtered when it cleared. "Hell, I didn't even—" The second bucket choked him off again. "*Christ,* please don't do this to me. I'm begging you." He could feel himself losing control, like some pitiful coward. Begging like a third-grade wimp on a playground. He hated himself for it, but there was nothing he could do. At least he'd gotten up the courage to leave his house and warn Helen. "I can't take it anymore. I'm gonna—" A third bucket. "Stop, stop, stop, I can't breathe! I'm trying to tell you I'm gonna—" A fourth bucket.

Suddenly Casey's chest felt like they'd dropped a truck on it. The fear of drowning evaporated, replaced by a different, even more imminent panic. He gasped several times and struggled madly against the ropes binding his wrists, the urge to clutch his heart enveloping him. He strained wildly against the chain securing his neck to the board until it felt like his eyeballs would explode from his skull. He gasped once more, exhaled heavily for several seconds, then his body went still.

The three men in the room glanced at one another, then one of them grabbed Casey's wrist.

"He's dead. Jesus Christ, he's dead."

"Heart attack?"

"No shit, Sherlock."

"Well, what do we do?"

The guy who'd searched Casey's wrist for a pulse shrugged, then smiled. "Take him home and put him in bed. Natural causes. It's perfect."

"What do you want, Deuce?"

Johnny settled into the chair beside Marconi. The old man seemed on edge this afternoon, probably because he didn't have something high in cholesterol heaped on a plate in front of him. "I wanted to let you know that I went to try to find Helen McLean today. The kid's mother. But she was gone. The house was empty. And it looked like she left in a hurry, like she wasn't coming back. At least not for a while."

"What do you mean?"

"There was an open suitcase in one of the guest bedrooms, and there were clothes spread out all over the bed in her room."

"How do you know it was her room?" Marconi asked.

"It was pretty obvious, you know? Pictures on the bureau, things in the bathroom. I mean—"

"Yeah, okay."

"And there was this cat. The thing was acting like it was going to take a chunk out of my ankle if I stuck around much longer. It was starving."

"You feed it?"

Johnny scoffed. "Of course not." In fact, he'd opened a can of tuna from the pantry and put it on the floor. Stroked the cat's head while it ate, too. "Why would I care about some stupid cat?"

Marconi grunted and waved like he didn't really care one way or the other. Like he regretted asking the question.

"There was one thing I didn't understand," Johnny said.

"What?"

"It didn't look like a man lived there."

"Huh?"

"I thought she lived with her husband."

"Bad liver got him a year ago." Marconi sighed. "Bastard."

Johnny looked up. "What do you mean? What did he ever do to you?"

"Nah, nah, I'm talking about that guy Stephen Casey.

He must have warned her, must have told her to get out."

"Weren't you watching Casey?" Johnny didn't know if they were. Marconi had never said anything. He'd just assumed.

"Of course we were," Marconi confirmed. "But we think he still got to her somehow. We picked him up earlier this afternoon and tried your technique on him. That waterboarding thing." The old man chuckled cruelly. "So it's pretty damn effective. Just like you said."

"What do you mean?"

"The guy up and had a heart attack on us while we were doing it to him." Marconi snapped his fingers. "Here one second, gone the next."

"What?"

"Yup, he's dead as a trash can."

"Holy Christ."

"Now what?" Marconi wanted to know. "*Now,* how the hell are you going to find Kyle McLean?"

Marconi rarely got mad. He didn't have to. But when he did, it was best to diffuse the situation quickly—or run. "I'll figure it out, Angelo," Johnny assured the old man. "You know that. One way or the other, I'll find this kid."

The old man pointed at Johnny. "You're not trying to make judgments this time, are you, Deuce? You're not trying to decide if you're going to do what I asked? I warned you."

Johnny gazed back at Marconi hard, making sure his eyes didn't wander. Hoping the old man wouldn't see the truth. Wondering where the question had come from, if it was just Marconi's suspicious nature, or if there was something more specific driving the interrogation. For a moment he thought about being proactive, about admitting to Marconi that he'd gone to see Treviso. Then quickly explaining it was all in an attempt to pick up Kyle McLean's trail. Not done in any way to help make a judgment about what had really happened to Marconi's grandson that night in front of the row house. He figured it might be best for him to bring it up first, even as thin as it would sound. But Marconi hadn't mentioned anything about Treviso, so maybe it was best just to let it go and get out of here as fast as possible.

"Of course not, Angelo," Johnny denied gently. "You told me not to make any judgments, so I'm not."

Marconi's eyes narrowed. "I'll find out if you are, Deuce. And if you are, I'll be pissed, *real* pissed. You just need to do your job, exactly like I told you."

Johnny nodded.

"You don't wanna piss me off, Deuce. You've been around long enough to know that."

"Of course."

"Good. Then get out of here and go kill Kyle McLean. That's what I want. I want him dead. *Fucking* dead. *Now*. Hell, yesterday wouldn't be soon enough at this point."

17

"SORRY, NED." IT took everything he had to say it, mostly because he didn't mean it, because he knew he wasn't wrong. And a little because he hated saying he was sorry about anything, even if he was wrong. "I really am."

Ned's office was the only one on the second floor of the store. Everyone else worked in cramped cubicles or out in the open. "What are you doing here?" he demanded, tossing his pen angrily into a cluttered mess of departmental reports. "Didn't I fire you this morning?"

Jack had worn his lucky Yankee cap to the store, brim pulled low over his eyes, and snuck up the stairway to the second floor when the cashiers weren't looking. He felt like a fool skulking around like this, but there wasn't any choice. He had to get his check. He needed the money so badly. "I want to talk to you about that."

"I'm trying to get out of here, Jack. Trying to get a few of these damn Memorial Day inventory orders off my desk so I can go home, prop my feet up, and drink a cold beer. Why are you getting in my way?"

"I'll apologize to that woman for what I did." Jack's jaw clenched involuntarily. "If that's what it takes, I'll do it."

"If that's what *what* takes?" Ned leaned back in his chair and smiled smugly, turning the crow's-feet at the corners of his eyes into puffy rolls. He put his hands up and motioned inwardly with his fingers. "Come on, say it. I can't wait to hear Jack Barrett eat a big piece of humble pie. Maybe with a scoop of I'm-a-prick-flavored ice cream on top."

Jack had gotten his usher job this morning without a hitch. There were lots of older men in Sarasota, but apparently not many of them wanted to lead people to seats in the sultry heat of a Florida evening wearing what looked like a bus driver's uniform. Name, address, and Social Security number on a short form, and he was in business with the Tarpons starting tomorrow night.

Sewing up the batboy situation hadn't been nearly as easy. According to MJ, the club already had fifteen applications when he applied for the job in an office down the hall from where Jack was fast-tracked to his usher position. And there were two kids filling out applications when the woman in charge handed MJ his form. Fortunately, Mitch Borden, the owner, had happened past at just that moment, taken an immediate liking to MJ, and hired him on the spot.

Which wasn't surprising. MJ had a way about him, an undeniable charisma you couldn't miss. And of course, hiring MJ gave the owner an opportunity to show the community he was an equal opportunity employer in an obvious way. Which didn't matter at all to Jack, even if MJ was resentful about it. Jack didn't care how it had happened, just that it had.

The only bad part about the whole deal was that MJ had turned into a damn good negotiator. Now he had the power, so he wanted a down payment. He wanted two hundred bucks in cash before he'd show up for tomorrow night's game three hours early to learn the ropes. To understand the complex nuances of retrieving bats, he'd said.

"Come on, Jack," Ned pressed, his grin growing wider and more obnoxious. "Let's hear it."

"I need that paycheck real bad," Jack admitted quietly. "I need those four hundred bucks. I'll apologize to the woman in person if you give me my money. I'll come here tomorrow whenever time you tell me she's going to be here, and I'll apologize. I'll get down on my damn knees and beg her forgiveness if you'll just give me the money. In fact, I'll kiss her fat feet if that's what it takes. And I don't even want my job back. Just give me the money."

"I don't care about that woman. I care about me."

"Huh?"

"Beg me, Jack."

"*What?*"

Ned stood up and moved out from behind the desk. "You've been a pain in my ass ever since you came here. I don't care if you beg her. I want you to beg *me*."

"Pain in the ass? What are you talking about?"

"Over the past few months I've had at least five customers come back in the store and complain that they smelled booze on your breath after you helped them load bags, but I didn't do anything. You're *always* at least a few minutes late, but I've looked the other way every time. And you've got to be the damn slowest bagger I've ever had in this store. But I chalked that up to you being so old." Ned chuckled wryly. "Even though you run a pretty fast forty-yard dash to your car at quitting time."

Jack frowned. "So I've got a couple of minor flaws. Nobody's perfect."

Ned rubbed his eyes, like he was tired and not just of Jack. "You're an old fart, Jack. I don't know any other way to put it. And there's not even anything cute about it. Usually old farts are cute. But not you."

"I'm a little cute."

"No you aren't. At least not to me. You only have one thing in this world going for you and that's your daughter."

Jack's eyes raced to Ned's.

"Cheryl's got to be one of the sweetest people I've ever met, Jack. And if she did anything with herself, she'd be one of the prettiest, too. But that's beside the point."

"When did you ever meet her?" Jack demanded.

"She came to the store a month ago." Ned snickered. "Goddamn, your wife must be a saint. That's the only way I can see how Cheryl could possibly turn out like she has."

"Cheryl came *here*?"

"Yeah. The day after you stumbled into my store three hours late with that flask in your pocket. She apologized for you, and told me how much you needed this job. Asked if I'd look out for you." Ned leaned forward so his face was close to Jack's. "And I have, damn it, I have looked out for you. But no more. I hit my limit when that woman came in here screaming about what you'd done. That was it. No more looking the other way, no more apologizing for you." He hesitated. "Tell Cheryl I'm sorry, but I'm sure she'll understand." He strode back to his desk and sat down. "You're an asshole, Jack. You've probably been one since you were born."

Jack swallowed hard, a big lump of pride stuck in his throat. He had to keep his eye on the objective: getting close to the kid. Right now he needed to pay MJ two hundred bucks pronto or he was going to lose a golden opportunity. He took a deep breath, thinking about how he ought to read Cheryl the riot act for coming in here like his mother and asking for pity. For interfering. For making him look like a jerk.

"Okay, I'm begging you for that check, Ned. Please."

"Get on your knees."

"*What?*"

"Get on your knees, I said."

"Forget it. Nothing's worth—"

"Fine," Ned interrupted. "No knees, no check."

"Jesus Christ." This was beyond swallowing his pride, but there was too much at stake. Slowly, he knelt down. God, the arthritis was killing his knees. "There," he said when he was on the floor. "You happy now?"

"You gotta ask me again. Now that you're on your knees."

Jack took a deep breath. "Please can I have the money? I'm begging you."

Ned's expression softened as the seconds passed. Finally he looked away. "Screw you, Jack. Like I said this morning, you want the check, sue the company."

"You son of a bitch!" Jack shouted, pulling himself back to his feet. "You goddamn son of a bitch!"

"Get out of here, old man," Ned ordered. "Just get the hell out of here."

And he did. He hobbled out of the office, down the stairs, and out the door because there wasn't anything else he could do. Ned was having fun just toying with him. Just trying to see how far he could get, how much of a monkey he could make out of an old man. Ned had no intention of ever paying him the four hundred dollars. Goddamn, he wished he was twenty years younger. He would have made Ned one sorry store manager.

As he passed through the outside door, the ATM on the brick wall caught his eye. "Ah, what the hell," he grumbled.

A few moments later Jack had pushed a few buttons and withdrawn two hundred and twenty dollars.

Leaving forty-two cents in his account.

"I'm glad you decided to come over here tonight, honey. I really didn't want to go back to your dad's place again."

Cheryl nestled down next to Bobby on the couch of his apartment. He'd been watching an Atlanta Braves game and drinking a beer while she washed the dishes. She'd cooked him a big steak dinner—a thick filet, mashed potatoes, and creamed spinach. His favorite meal, he'd told her last week. She was so happy to finally know he loved her she was willing to do anything for him at this point.

She didn't even care when he'd said the steak was "a little overdone," which she knew it wasn't. They'd talked five times on the phone today, and each time he'd been the first one to say the magic words: I love you. She was so happy she could barely stand it.

"It's my place, too," she said quietly.

"Sure it is," Bobby agreed, pulling her close and kissing her.

He'd finally learned to kiss tenderly. So many men never got it, even when you gave them step-by-step instructions. And if there was one thing that really drove her crazy about a man—other than being able to dance and make love—it was his kiss. Sometimes she actually enjoyed a long, passionate kiss more than sex.

There'd been this one boy back when she was nineteen who kissed better than anyone before or since. His lips weren't big and puffy, but when you closed your eyes and let him work his magic, they wrapped yours up completely like two silk sheets before he set you on fire with his tongue. Bobby wasn't anywhere near that good, but at least he was improving. Maybe with a bit more instruction and practice he'd get there. She was willing to make the commitment. She just hoped he was.

"You look nice tonight, honey."

She smiled up at him. "Thanks." That had come from nowhere. Maybe he wasn't as out of it as she thought. She'd brushed her hair for fifteen minutes before he showed up tonight so it literally gleamed. And she'd bought a fancy new clip to hold it up in the bun. It looked nice, she had to admit.

"What's so different?" he asked, checking the game on

the wide-screen, which took up one whole corner of his living room. "A little makeup?"

Cheryl punched him gently on the upper arm. "It's my hair."

"Your hair? *Ooooh*, yeah, your hair. Hey, it looks great."

She could tell he didn't really see a difference. He was playing along so there wasn't a bump in the evening. So he was sure to get sex. Men were so transparent.

"You know," Bobby spoke up, "you should spend a day with this woman from my health club. Her name's Ginny. She's really into fashion. She could take you around and help you pick out some new clothes. Maybe help you with some makeup, too. Introduce you to her hairdresser. Stuff like that."

"Who is this woman?"

"Just a friend."

"A *friend*?" Cheryl hated to admit it, but now that they'd made love she was getting possessive. She'd be the happiest woman in the world if she wasn't this way. But she was, and there was no getting around it or anything she could do about it. She'd always been like this, and it got worse the longer she was with a man. "How good a friend?"

Bobby held up his hands. "Trust me. Ginny and I really are just friends. She's nowhere near as nice as you. Or as pretty," he added quickly. "But she does the most with what she has. Know what I mean?"

"No." She wasn't letting him off that easy.

"Well, she dresses real nice and she uses makeup. That kind of stuff. Makes herself look better than she really is. Sometimes she uses too much makeup and then it's a train wreck, but you won't have that problem. You've got this incredible natural beauty she doesn't. You just need a few touch-ups here and there. Then you'll be awesome."

She liked his compliments, as backhanded as they were and as obvious as his agenda was. "I've always been kind of a tomboy, you know? I've never been into all that makeup stuff. But I think I look okay."

"You look great, not just okay. But why don't you spend a day with Ginny? Just to see what's what."

She nodded hesitantly. "I guess."

Bobby nodded approvingly. "Great. So, how's your dad doing? Still stalking Mikey Clemants?"

Cheryl laughed, imagining her father wearing a trench coat and a hat pulled low as he shadowed the poor kid all over town. "Yeah. Daddy was at some bar late last night trying to talk to him. But the kid bolted."

"Clemants is a head case," Bobby muttered. "I warned your dad about that."

"Yeah, I remember."

"Which bar was it?"

"I don't know." It was the Dugout, but for some reason she didn't want to say.

"Well, was it around the stadium?"

"I'm not sure."

Bobby gazed at the TV intently for a few moments, then grabbed Cheryl. "Let's make love, baby."

Men. First their stomachs, then a little farther below their stomachs, then sleep. "Don't you want to let your food settle?"

"Nah." He reached down and clasped her thin wrist with his big fingers. "Get up," he demanded, pulling her to her feet. "Come on."

She pulled away quickly. "Jesus, relax."

"Sorry, sorry. It's just that sometimes I want you so bad."

She rubbed her wrist. For a moment there she'd been scared. He'd grabbed her so hard. "I know you do." She stood up and smiled sweetly. "Come on, let's go."

Jack lifted the scotch to his lips. He was trying his best to nurse the damn thing, but that was getting harder the more he drank. After dropping off two hundred bucks to MJ on his way over here, Jack had only twenty-eight bucks left in his wallet—the remaining twenty from the ATM withdrawal, and what was left of his tips. This was his second drink, and there was almost no gas in the Citation's tank. Probably not even enough to get home. And he knew he was going to want that third drink bad.

"Did the Tarpons play tonight?" he asked. He knew they hadn't, but he needed to get the conversation started.

The bartender was leaning back against the cash register drying a glass. It was the same guy as last night. He had thick eyebrows and hairy forearms. "Nope. They're off tonight. They play down in Fort Lauderdale tomorrow. Why?"

Jack shrugged. "Just wondered." He saw that suspicious look creeping across the guy's face again. The same one he'd seen last night when he kept asking about the kid.

"Right." The bartender put the glass down and moved to where Jack was sitting.

Jack was on the same stool as last night when the kid had sauntered in. One with a perfect view of the front door. "Look," he said in a reassuring tone as the guy leaned over the bar, blocking his perfect view, "it's like I told you last night. I used to be with the Yankees. I think he's a talented kid. I'm just trying to help him."

"Help him what?"

"Get to the majors."

The bartender snickered. "The Tarpons are Single-A independents, pal. That's the bottom of the barrel. Clemant has a long way to go before he puts on pinstripes."

"I don't think so," Jack argued gently.

"That's the scotch talking."

"No, it's not," he muttered. "Look," he said more forcefully, "Clemant has a major-league bat and glove. He just needs some help with his minor-league attitude."

"Why do you care so much? What's in it for you, pal?"

That question had been hanging over Jack like a dark cloud. He hadn't dealt with it yet, not directly, anyway. But he knew at some point he'd have to. It was tough because two of the three potential answers—money and revenge—weren't very appealing. Downright ugly, actually. But painfully obvious, given the forty-two cents in his checking account and how piss-poor he'd been treated by people he thought would never do him wrong.

Then there was that third possibility. That altruistic, pure one. That he was doing all this simply for his love of the game. Simply because he wanted to see a man who could end up being one of the greatest players of all time have a chance to find out if he really was.

"I think he deserves a shot at the Show," Jack murmured. "And I think I can get it for him."

"You're out for money," the bartender said loudly. "That's all you want."

"No, I—" Jack interrupted himself as the front door opened and the kid strode in.

Clemant stopped short as soon as he spotted Jack. They gazed at each other for a few moments, then the kid turned around and headed right back out.

Jack hopped off the stool and hobbled toward the door as fast as his bad knees would carry him. But when he burst out into the warm Florida evening, the street was empty. It was as though the kid had been swallowed up by the night.

18

JOHNNY STOOD OUTSIDE the apartment door for several minutes, wondering if he could really do this. Wondering if he could destroy another man's world and live with himself. Which seemed so ironic because, after all, he killed men for a living, and killing a man was the ultimate destruction of a personal world. This was nothing when you compared the two. So why was he even giving it a second thought?

Maybe because those men he'd killed were all scum, all men who deserved to die. Johnny's expression steeled with resolve. If Tony Treviso really killed that guy, then sent the severed head to the wife with a dead rat stuffed in the mouth, he was scum, too. Worse than all the others put together.

Johnny raised his hand to knock, then hesitated. No one had ever proven that Treviso was behind all that.

Maybe Treviso had lucked into the tag and simply never denied it—like Johnny had never denied killing the guy who ran the liquor store down the street from Marconi's row house. Or maybe Paulie the Moon had chopped the guy's head off to help his timid friend. Maybe Treviso wanted so badly to be feared—instead of ridiculed—in a world dominated by macho men, he'd jumped at the chance to be pinned with something appalling. And been smart enough to know he couldn't openly accept responsibility for it because then the capos and the soldiers would be less likely to believe he was actually the person who'd done it. No one in his right mind would openly take credit for that crime because the cops might hear about it through the grapevine. Maybe Treviso was smart enough to realize that if he just smiled crazily when you asked him about it, you'd be more likely to believe he was guilty. Maybe Timid Tony wasn't so stupid after all. Or so timid.

Johnny knocked lightly, not bothering to step to the side of the door. Treviso was way up in the Bronx, boozing it up with Paulie the Moon. Johnny had gotten the word fifteen minutes ago from a friend behind the bar up there who was going to text-message him as soon as Treviso left. Even if he got the message in the next few minutes, he'd still have at least forty-five minutes before Treviso could get his ass this far out into Brooklyn.

The door swung open, and the sight that met Johnny's eyes literally took his breath away. Karen stood before him in a black lace teddy and high heels, hair falling down about her face to her shoulders. She was gazing at him so sexily with those huge brown eyes.

He moved through the doorway as if he were floating

and their lips met, pressed together gently at first, then harder and harder as their passion exploded. He never kissed the women Marconi sent him, just had sex with them. In fact, he hadn't really kissed anyone since kissing his first Karen just before they wheeled her away to the operating room. Thinking it would only be a few hours until he kissed her again. Now as this woman's slender body melted into his, he realized how much he'd missed that intimacy. And he realized he might not be able to live with himself for what he was about to do.

But there was no stopping at this point, no way he could resist her. She was the one who could finally rescue him from the abyss he'd been sinking deeper and deeper into for so long. He knew that because he hadn't been able to stop thinking about her since that first moment he'd laid eyes on her.

Johnny took a deep breath. He'd just have to live with the consequences.

Or not.

19

THE FASTEST WAY home was the interstate. It would have taken Jack less than twenty minutes using I-75, but then he'd run the risk of hitting a sobriety checkpoint, which the cops in the area were setting up more and more often. The number of fatal automobile accidents had skyrocketed in the county over the past year, and local politicians had demanded action. So Jack was taking the back way home to the coffin. Three times as long, but infinitely safer.

It wasn't like he was having a problem driving. Five drinks was no big deal, but that alcohol level would undoubtedly put him over the legal limit. Then he'd have only two choices when they pulled him over: take a chance and blow, or refuse and lose his license anyway. He'd bribed a Long Island cop a long time ago when he'd been pulled over late one night. Bribed him with cash and Yankee seats right behind the dugout for a twi-night doubleheader. But bribing wasn't an option now. He couldn't get Yankee tickets anymore—let alone box seats right behind the dugout—and he had only forty-two cents to his name.

Not even that, really. He still owed the Dugout fifteen bucks from tonight because he hadn't been able to pay the entire bill. So actually he had a negative net worth, exaggerated by the housing market going to hell over the past year. Thanks to that, his and Cheryl's equity in the house had disappeared. At this point they couldn't even sell the place for what they'd paid. Add on a Realtor's commission and they were way underwater.

Fortunately, the bartender at the Dugout had been decent about extending credit, probably because he figured Jack would be back again soon looking for Mikey Clement, and he'd be able to collect then. Collect or take a lot of satisfaction booting him out of the place when the fifteen bucks went unpaid.

The fuel gauge needle was riding on "E." Maybe even a little left of "E" if Jack put on his reading glasses. Thank God Cheryl had let him carry her cell phone tonight. Well, "let him" wasn't exactly accurate. *Made* him was more like it. She'd pressed the phone into his hand late this afternoon before Bobby showed up, given him Bobby's numbers, and told him to call if he had any problems. Told him she'd be at Bobby's apartment and she'd make sure Bobby answered.

Jack let out a frustrated breath. He'd seen those red marks on her neck this morning, but she wouldn't explain them. Damn it, he'd kill Bobby Griffin if there was any rough stuff going on.

Jack squinted against the headlights of an oncoming car. It was the first car he'd seen in five minutes. It was lonely out here in the barrens. Just an unbroken wall of pine trees on either side of the road fifty feet back across a sandy area covered with scruffy crabgrass. This would be a bad place to run out of gas. He just hoped there was cell coverage. Hoped Cheryl would come rescue him if he needed help. Hoped she'd be *able* to come rescue him if he needed help. Bobby seemed nice, but sometimes it was the nice ones you had to watch out for. Sometimes the clean-cut ones had more demons running around inside their skulls than the bikers with the long hair and tattoos.

He glanced into the rearview mirror as a car raced up behind him. The car was swerving from side to side right off his bumper, bright lights beaming into the back of the Citation and off the rear and side mirrors like the sun had beamed into his bedroom this morning after Cheryl raised the blinds. "Watch out!" he shouted, shading his eyes with one hand, praying it wasn't a trooper. Suddenly he realized he wasn't as sober as he'd thought. And the state boys down here could be mean as hell. You couldn't negotiate with them like you could in New York. "Hey, give me a break!"

He didn't have to wait long to find out if it was the cops. Seconds later the car blew past him. It turned out to be just a battered old rusty sedan. Then he realized there were two cars. Right behind the old sedan was a souped-up Mustang. Very quickly both sets of taillights disappeared around a bend up ahead.

Jack's shoulders slumped. He could feel perspiration seeping out of pores all over his body. He'd been certain that something horrible was about to happen, that he was going to jail or something. It had been such a strange and strong premonition. Thank God it had turned out to be a false alarm.

When he rounded another bend a few minutes later, he noticed a pair of taillights ahead. It looked as though they were stopped on the side of the road, in the sandy area between the asphalt and the wall of pine trees. He slowed down as he approached, slamming on his brakes when the same souped-up Mustang suddenly darted out into the road ahead. Then his heart skipped a beat. The sedan was flipped over on its roof.

He leaned forward over the steering wheel, his eyes narrowing as he saw how badly the old car was mangled.

"Oh Jesus," he whispered.

20

JOHNNY LAY ON his back on the bed. Karen's head was resting on his shoulder, her hand on his chest. She was fast asleep, breathing deeply and regularly. They'd made love twice, and it had been better than he'd even imagined it could be. She was incredible, and she claimed he was the best she'd ever had. Claimed she never enjoyed it with Treviso. That he was a klutz in bed. Didn't have a clue what he was doing and didn't give a damn about her—which sounded about right. And now that she knew what it could be like, how good it could be, she was going to want Johnny all the time. Suddenly he had a problem. A big problem. Because he was going to want her all the time, too.

He slid off the mattress slowly, doing his best not to wake her, letting her head settle gently to the pillow. He pulled the covers up over her slim shoulders when he was sure she was still asleep, still breathing regularly. Then he stowed her black lace teddy in a bureau drawer, put her high heels back in the closet, and got dressed.

He checked his watch after he'd slipped into his loafers. His cell phone had gone off ten minutes ago, alerting him to the text message warning him that Treviso had left the Bronx. He still had time to search the apartment.

He glanced back at Karen when he reached the bedroom door. She looked like an angel lying there. Christ, he was starting to fall in love.

Wrong. He already was in love. She was the one who could save him. There was no doubt about it.

The question now was: How far would he go? A shiver raced up his spine. He already knew the answer. All the way.

21

JACK SKIDDED TO a slippery stop on the dewy grass so his headlights were shining directly through the disintegrated rear window of the battered sedan. He threw the Citation into park, then frantically punched 911 on Cheryl's cell phone. "Come on, come on! Answer!" The phone shook crazily against his ear as he gazed wide-eyed at the wreckage. Why had the Mustang driven off without helping? There could be only one logical answer: whoever was driving it wanted whoever was in the sedan to crash. At the very least didn't care that they had, which was another reason to get people out here fast. Whoever was driving the Mustang might be back soon, might not appreciate someone stopping to help. Might have actually wanted whoever was in the sedan to get hurt, maybe even die. "Answer, damn it!"

"This is 911," a woman's voice crackled through the phone. "What is your emergency?"

"I just came up on an accident out here on Old Seacrest Road. I'm about five miles past that corner with the 7-Eleven and the Burger King," Jack explained, speaking fast, still trying to make certain the person at the other end could understand him. "It's bad, real bad. You gotta get people out here now."

"How many cars involved?"

"One. It's flipped over on its roof and smashed up 'real bad."

"Any injuries?"

"Yeah. I mean, didn't you just hear me? The car's flipped over and smashed up. I'm sure whoever's in there is hurt. I'm right behind what's left of it. I haven't gone up and looked yet, but I don't see anybody moving. Hell, they might be dead."

"Please go check and see if—"

"Get people out here, you idiot!" Jack roared.

"What is your name, sir?"

"Jack."

"Last name?"

He was involved, but he wasn't going to get *that* involved. If they wanted to track him down, they'd have to do it using Cheryl's cell number. "Are you gonna get people out here or what?"

"Is there a fire?"

"*Get people out here and get 'em out here now!*" he shouted, ending the call.

He climbed out and slid the phone in his pocket, hesitating as he gazed in dread at the tangled hulk of twisted metal lying on the ground before him. Unable to fathom anyone surviving. Not sure he wanted to go up there and find out. He could take the blood and guts as long as it was a man down. But not a woman. Or worse, a child. He glanced back the way he'd been coming, then into the darkness ahead, hoping to see another pair of headlights—as long as it wasn't the Mustang's. But no luck.

The phone rang, startling him. He pulled it out and checked the tiny screen. The 911 operator was calling back. He was about to answer and start yelling at her when he thought he heard someone calling faintly from the wreck. He froze and listened hard. There it was again. He tossed the still-ringing phone on the Citation's seat. He'd barely heard the voice the second time, too. In fact, he still wasn't sure he really had. It might just be panic playing tricks on him. Maybe he wouldn't have reacted to real bombs and bullets as well as he'd hoped. He put a hand to his head. This was one hell of a time for self-doubt.

"Help me. Please."

No doubt this time. And judging by the tone, who-ever was calling out was in terrible pain. No taking the easy way out and waiting for the emergency people to get here. It might be too late by then.

He hobbled toward the wreck, groaning as he dropped to his hands and knees onto the wet grass beside the smashed back window on the driver's side. He hunched down, searching the ruined interior. "Oh Christ," he mut-tered. It was his nightmare scenario. A young woman lay on the dashboard, wedged between the steering wheel and the windshield. As he crawled ahead, he could see that one of her legs was crushed, that she was bleeding profusely from it, and that blood was pooling on the ceiling of the car. One of her wrists was clamped tightly in the mangled steering wheel at a strange angle, too, obviously broken. And there was blood dripping from her nose and several cuts on her face, one of which appeared very deep. But her pleading eyes were open and she was sobbing weakly. She wasn't dead yet. There was still a chance.

"Can you hear me?" Jack asked loudly, aware of a faint siren wailing in the distance.

"Yes," she whispered in a Hispanic accent. "I can."

She moaned something more, something in Spanish he didn't understand. "What, *what did you say*?" A baby screamed, almost in Jack's ear, and he tumbled face-first into the grass. *"Damn!"* He scrambled quickly back up onto his knees and scanned the backseat, now aware of a strong gasoline scent. He spotted the baby when it screamed again. The infant was upside down in a car seat in the back on the passenger side.

"Help my little girl," the young woman said, moaning. "Don't worry about me. Just get Rosario out."

"I will, I will." Incredibly, the baby seemed unharmed. The little girl was screaming like mad, still terrified by the violent impact and from being upside down. But Jack couldn't see blood or any other signs of physical distress on her. "I promise you, I will." He lifted up to wipe off his palms—and saw the flames. Flickering orange snake tongues licking their way up through the bottom of the engine. His heart sank. "Oh, no."

Frantically, he tried prying open what was left of the door, but it was jammed too tightly into the frame and wouldn't budge. He limped as fast as he could to the other side of the car and tried that door—the one next to the baby—pulling like a wild man on the handle. It was jammed shut, too. And more bad luck. Somehow this window hadn't been shattered in the crash. If it had, he could have reached into the car and plucked the little girl out. "Damn it!" The sirens were growing louder—but the flames were getting higher.

He rushed back to the driver's side, dropped down again, and crawled carefully through the back window, trying not to rip his legs on the jagged pieces of broken glass rising from around the window frame like shark's teeth. "Ouch! Goddamn it!" A shard sliced his palm as he put it down on the roof. He stopped long enough to suck it from his skin and spit it toward the back, away from the baby, then kept moving. Now he felt a trickle of warm blood oozing from his hand each time he put it down.

When he reached the little girl, he held her in place with one hand and wrestled desperately at the buckles on the car seat with the other. But like the doors of the car, the buckles were jammed. "Come on, come on," he said, hissing. He could smell smoke now. A nasty, burning-rubber odor. "Easy, little one," he said, trying to calm her down. She was still screaming at the top of her tiny lungs.

"Hurry!" the young woman yelled from the front. "Please!"

"I am, lady, I am." He could feel the panic starting to sink in, getting in the way of his ability to think and act clearly. "Believe me."

Finally he was able to pop the belt holding the car seat in place. The car seat and the baby tumbled onto the roof in front of him just as flames started shooting out of the steering column. He grabbed the car seat and yanked it along as the young woman began screaming hysterically.

"*¡Fuego, fuego!*" she yelled. "Don't let me burn!"

The survival instinct had kicked in. Fire was such a bad way to go, Jack thought grimly.

"Please, God, don't let me burn!"

He dragged the baby quickly along the roof as he slid back through the window, slashing his pants, shins, and thighs on the glass around the frame. But he barely noticed the pain this time. A moment later he and the little girl were outside on the wet grass. He rose and carried her away from the burning sedan.

When he looked back, flames had fully engulfed the front of the car, and the young woman was shrieking pitifully. He stumbled back toward the fire, gasping for breath as an ambulance and a state police cruiser skidded to a stop on the side of the road. He dropped to his knees again, holding one hand to his face to shield his eyes from the intense heat. Then he took a deep breath, let out a guttural yell, and willed himself through the flames.

He burst into the car, grabbed the young woman by one shoulder and pulled hard, the sleeves of his shirt catching fire as he reached across the steering column. But she was wedged too tightly between the windshield and the dashboard. He couldn't pry her loose. He could see her lower legs burning, and he pulled madly at the wrist stuck in the mangled steering wheel, hoping she might be able to help him if he could free it. But it was no use.

Then she stopped screaming, even as the fire burned

her jeans off her lower legs, exposing her dripping flesh. She was just gazing at him forlornly now with those desperate eyes. God, he felt like his body was about to explode, he was so hot. How could she not be screaming, how could she not be struggling violently, doing anything to save herself? Shock must have set in. He mustered his strength for one more huge effort to pry her loose, but still he couldn't move her.

Suddenly he felt himself being dragged from the car. He glanced at her pretty face one more time; then she was gone and a burst of cool air hit him.

A moment later his body was being doused with something; then a state trooper and an EMT grabbed him by his wrists and dragged him away from the car—just as it exploded. The trooper and the EMT tumbled to the ground, and Jack rolled to his stomach instinctively as a searing wave of heat blew past them.

The trooper was up on his feet right away. He sprinted to the Citation, jumped in behind the wheel, gunned the engine, and raced it past the burning sedan to the road.

Jack rose on one elbow and stared at the burning hulk of the sedan, haunted by the awful look in the young woman's eyes. She'd known she had only seconds to live, yet she'd mouthed the words "thank you" as the flames engulfed her and he was pulled by the trooper and the EMT out of the wreck. Thank you for saving my baby, thank you for trying to save me. Those had been her last words. Jack hung his head. But she was dead. A sweet young woman with a beautiful baby, and she was dead. Trying hadn't been enough. God, what if this happened to Cheryl one night and whoever tried to save her failed?

What if that person's try wasn't enough? How could he go on living without her? Did this woman have someone who cared about her like that at home? Someone who would be so devastated by her death he wouldn't know how to keep going? He shut his eyes tightly. Too many damn questions to try to deal with now. Suddenly he felt older than he ever had. Like death was peering out at him from the flames.

"You're a hero, mister."

Jack glanced over at the EMT. "I don't feel like one." Damn. The guy looked so familiar. He checked the name on the shirt in the light from the blaze: Harry. One of the guys from the stadium the other night. The overweight one with the sad eyes. The one who seemed to sincerely care about his job.

"You saved the baby. That was all you could do. All anyone could have done." Harry smiled, recognizing Jack. "Hey, you're the guy we saw at Tarpon Stadium the other night."

"Uh-huh."

"Glad you're okay."

"Thanks."

"Better let me check you again after all of this," Harry suggested. "Can't be good for that heart of yours."

"I'm fine."

"That's what you said the other night, too."

"No, I really am." Jack gestured toward the wreck, starting to feel guilty that he'd wasted Harry's time the other night with the fake heart attack. Especially now that he'd experienced firsthand what this man had to deal with constantly. "There was a woman in there."

Harry grimaced. "I know, I—"

"Yeah, we saw her through the windshield," the trooper called, back from moving the Citation to safety. "There was no way you could have gotten her out in time, buddy. You did great just saving the baby."

Jack watched Harry crawl toward his partner, who was taking the baby out of the car seat and laying her on the ground to examine her. He recognized the other guy, too, and tried to remember his name. Biff. That was it. Now it was all coming back. Biff the prick. The one who looked at his job like it was a pain in his ass and didn't care if you lived or died.

"You okay?" the trooper asked, helping Jack to his feet.

"Yeah, I'm—"

"Hey, Tom!" Harry shouted.

"What you got?" the trooper yelled back, trotting over to where the EMTs were examining the baby.

Jack took one more look at the burning wreck, then headed toward the baby, too. He wanted to get a close-up look at the still-sobbing little girl.

"It's Rosario," Harry said to Biff. "Right?"

"Yeah, I think so."

Jack caught Biff's sidelong glance, then a quick sign of recognition in his expression, too. But there wasn't any friendly hello, like there had been from Harry.

The trooper exhaled heavily. "So that was Julia Hernandez in there," he said sadly.

"Must have been." Harry picked the baby up off the ground and held her to his chest. Her sobbing soon stopped. "So what do we do now?"

"Take her to Social Services," Biff said. "That's all we can do."

"Then he'll find her," the trooper cour ered, glancing at Jack, then quickly away.

As if he wished he hadn't said what he said, Jack thought. "Who'll find her?" he demanded, gazing at the little girl. She was adorable, probably no more than a year old. "What's going on?" he asked when nobody answered, sensing that they were holding back. "What are you guys talking about?"

"Julia's been calling 911 a lot in the past few weeks," Harry finally spoke up. "Her husband's been beating the hell out of her." A steely expression came to Harry's face as he stroked the baby's small head.

An expression that seemed out of place on Harry's face. It was the first time Jack had seen anything but compassion there.

"Rosario, too," Harry added.

Jack's eyes opened wide. "What?"

"Can you believe it?" The trooper's expression turned mean, too. Like he wanted to kill the guy. "Beating a baby?"

"Why didn't you arrest him?" Jack asked, aware of more sirens in the distance. "Why didn't she get a restraining order against him?"

"She wouldn't press charges," the trooper explained. "She wouldn't say that her husband was the one who'd beaten her when we got to the apartment. She was too afraid of losing him."

"Or getting killed once he got out if she did press charges," Biff pointed out.

The trooper nodded. "Yeah, right. Same old story."

"Well, if we don't do something quick," Harry spoke up, "Julia's husband is gonna ultimately get Rosario if we just turn her over to Social Services."

The trooper glanced at the emergency lights heading toward them in the distance. "That's probably right. Might take him a few days, but he'll get her."

"Why in God's name would this guy want to hurt his own daughter?" Jack asked, dumbfounded.

Harry and Biff glanced at each other, then at the trooper.

"Because it isn't really his baby," Harry explained. "Julia put his name on the birth certificate because they were together when Rosario was conceived, and he thought it was his kid when she was born. When the bastard found out it wasn't really his a few weeks ago, he went ballistic. Decided to take it out on both of them."

Jack plucked a couple of blades of grass, then tossed them away and watched them flutter to the ground. How could someone do that to a baby? Even if he'd thought it was his at first but really it wasn't. "Does Julia's husband drive a Mustang?"

The trooper nodded. "Yeah, a souped-up red one. Why?"

So Julia's husband had run her off the road and killed her. "She passed me a ways back," Jack said sadly, gesturing into the darkness. In the direction he'd been coming from when the two cars had raced past. "She was going like a bat out of hell, and there was a Mustang right behind her, right on her tail. It was souped up. I'm not sure it was red, but it had stripes down the side. A fat one between two skinny ones, I think."

"That was him," the trooper confirmed.

"Well," Jack continued, "when I came around the bend, the Mustang was hanging by the crash. When I got close, he took off. You can probably find his tire tracks in the ground around here somewhere."

"He ran her off the road, Tom," Harry said to the trooper. "He killed her. And he's gonna kill this baby if he gets his hands on her. He's off his rocker. We gotta do something."

Jack looked at the little girl again—she was so beautiful—then down the road. The flashing lights were getting close.

Harry reached out and grabbed Jack's arm. "Hey, pal, wasn't that your daughter with you at the baseball game the other night? I thought that was what she said when we first got there," he continued when Jack didn't answer right away. "Was it? Huh?"

"Yeah. *Why?*"

"She seemed real nice. Does she live here in Sarasota, too?"

"Yeah. She lives with me. Why?"

"Perfect." Harry's eyes flashed to Biff's, then to the trooper's. "You guys thinking what I'm thinking?"

"Absolutely," the trooper agreed. "Against the book, but we can't let the book get in the way. We can't let that monster get Rosario. I'd never forgive myself." He turned to Jack. "You gotta take this little girl and get her out of here, mister."

Jack couldn't believe what he'd just heard. "*What?*"

"You saved her life a few minutes ago. Now you gotta do it again. Otherwise that first time will be wasted. You'll have risked your life for nothing. You want that?"

"No, but what you're asking me to do is crazy. I can't."

The trooper motioned toward the emergency vehicles that were closing in. "You got to. Otherwise this little girl doesn't stand a chance," he said, picking her up and putting her back in the car seat. "It'll just be for a few days."

"But I don't . . ." Jack's voice trailed off. "Christ, I wouldn't know the first thing about taking care of a little—"

"You don't have to," Harry interrupted. "Your daughter'll help you. She's got a good heart. I could tell the other night."

Cheryl had a heart of gold, but how could Harry really have figured that out in such a short time?

"Do it, mister," Harry urged. "I don't want to have to respond to some emergency call and find this little girl black and blue and bleeding. Or drowned in a bathtub. *Please.*"

God, he'd never felt so old. So beaten up. "But I—"

"It'll be the best thing you ever do," the trooper cut in. "The best."

He nodded somberly after a few moments. "Okay," he whispered.

The trooper patted him on the shoulder and smiled, then turned, grabbed the car seat and Rosario and dashed toward the Citation. The next wave of emergency vehicles pulled up just as the trooper slammed the door shut after securing the car seat in the back.

"You're a good man," Harry said, patting Jack on the shoulder, too.

Jack barely heard the words. The magnitude of what he'd just committed to was overwhelming. "Thanks," he muttered. "Oh, Christ." He'd almost forgotten how low he was on fuel.

"What's the matter?" Harry asked.

He sure as hell didn't want to run out of gas with Rosario in the car. "Can I borrow five bucks for gas?"

Harry nodded compassionately and reached for his wallet. "Sure, pal."

"What's the matter?" Biff asked. "You poor or something?"

Jack's eyes dropped. He was feeling exhausted—and vulnerable. Feeling his sixty-plus years more than he ever had. "Yup. Just about broke."

22

CHERYL PULLED HER Honda to a quick, squeaky stop in the narrow driveway behind the Citation, then reached into the backseat and grabbed Bobby's bag. She was wearing some of his old stuff—an Oxford shirt with holes in both elbows as well as a pair of gray sweatpants. Her clothes were in the bag. The shirt and sweatpants were huge on her, made her look like a child. But she couldn't walk through the door wearing the clothes she'd gone to Bobby's in because she didn't want Daddy seeing how sexy they were. She didn't want him seeing the new red marks on her neck, either, so she was wearing the collar of Bobby's shirt unbuttoned and up.

Daddy was probably still in bed, but you could never be sure with him. Every once in a while he got up at the crack of dawn. She knew he was already suspicious of what was going on, and she was terrified that if he got another whiff of something bad, he'd steamroll right over to Bobby's apartment and start World War III. She was convinced she'd never see Bobby after that—and losing him would tear her heart out. She'd realized that while she was driving home. Realized how much she cared about him—despite his dark side.

She'd been adventurous last night while she was cooking. Worn an outfit she picked out yesterday at a high-end boutique near the office. A tank top that showed a lot of her full-C cleavage and a very short skirt. She'd felt positively naked, and predictably Bobby had loved it. Maybe too much. He'd been even more physical last night. Not abusive—not quite—but *very* aggressive. He'd pinned her to the mattress several times and slipped his fingers around her neck, whispering to her that he knew she liked it. She didn't, she hated it, but she'd made a commitment to him and she was going to live with it. She wasn't going to lose him. He might be her last chance. She was getting to that age where she had a better chance of being killed by a terrorist than marrying, she thought ruefully. And if you loved someone, really loved him completely, you accepted him completely. Meaning you accepted his desires—and his flaws—and gave him what he wanted. Really gave him what he wanted. No matter what it was. She wasn't a girl who went halfway when she gave her heart.

She was about to turn the key when a bright yellow service engine light caught her eye. She let her forehead fall gently to the steering wheel. She thought the engine had sounded funny on the way home, thought she'd heard a pinging noise she'd never noticed before. And the car had seemed to be jerking as it pulled away from red lights and stop signs. She'd hoped it was just her imagination, but obviously it wasn't. She didn't have money for a big repair job right now; she and Daddy were squeezed as it was. Money was always such a problem.

Of course, for the next two weeks money wouldn't be her biggest worry. Bobby hadn't used protection last night, said he hated dealing with that. And she hadn't been able to do anything about protecting herself because he'd forced himself on her and into her so strongly. He'd been irresponsible over and over—it seemed as if there was no limit to his energy—and she was right smack in the middle of that time of the month. A window that could produce a bad result. Then what would she do? She took a deep breath. More important, what would Bobby do? She turned the engine off, climbed out of the Honda, and headed up the cracked path toward the door. She couldn't bear to face that question right now.

When she opened the front door, she stopped and her mouth fell slowly open, amazed at the sight that met her tired eyes. Daddy was sitting in front of the TV in his lumpy old easy chair, and there seemed to be something wrapped in a pink blanket lying on his chest. Then she smiled. Another one of his pranks. It had to be. She knew him so well.

"You almost had me going there for a second." she called, laughing.

Jack held a finger to his lips. "I'll explain later," he whispered. "I think she's almost asleep."

"Oh, sure. Don't try to fool—"

At that moment Rosario opened her eyes and cooed.

And Cheryl dropped the bag of clothes and raced across the room.

* * *

Bobby opened his eyes slowly and stretched, awakening from a wonderful three-hour nap and an erotic dream. He'd kissed Cheryl good-bye this morning after giving her his shirt and sweatpants, then fallen into a deep sleep, completely satisfied by the long night of sex. Now he was refreshed and ready for more. He'd push her even harder tonight. See if she'd let him tie her up. Use some of that paraphernalia he had hidden in his closet. God, he couldn't wait. He could tell she wasn't enjoying it the way some women he'd been with actually had. But that made it even better. He liked that she didn't want to do it, but was being submissive and giving in anyway.

He grinned as he watched the ceiling fan rotate slowly. Life was good. Yesterday, the old codger up in Tampa had committed to a three-million-dollar order for his company's line of high-tech, skintight workout suits as well as a couple of million dollars' worth of weight training equipment. It had been the company's biggest single order of the year. The old guy had been pissed off when the meeting started forty minutes late, but after the promise of World Series tickets, everything changed. People were so damn predictable. Hell, the way things had turned out, he'd gotten an extra million bucks in the order he wouldn't have gotten without the tickets. So it had actually turned out *better* that he was late. And he'd gotten that last dip in Cheryl's pond. Everything always seemed to work out for him. Seemed like it always had. He was just one of those lucky guys.

His smile widened. His bosses in Los Angeles were ecstatic about the order, about how much product he was moving. Out of nowhere they were talking about a regional manager post—which would mean a big salary increase and an all-expenses-paid move to Atlanta. There'd even been a wink and a nod over the phone yesterday afternoon about him putting a few extra things on the move so he could suck more cash out of it. And the relocation wouldn't happen for another month, so he still had a few weeks to play with Cheryl. Then, one day, he just wouldn't be here anymore. Poof, gone. Result: another sobbing woman in his wake.

He laughed aloud. It was so beautiful. He'd kiss her at the door after a long night of rough sex like there was nothing wrong. Promise her that they'd go to a nice dinner that night. Then send her on her way, move out, change his cell number, and disappear forever. He'd never told her the real name of the company he worked for. Never told her his real last name, where he was originally from, or anything else about himself she could use to track him down if she turned out to be one of those fatal-attraction psychos. It was just so much fun playing with a woman's mind—and abusing her body. He never got tired of either one.

Cheryl put Rosario carefully down on the makeshift bed they'd built on the bedroom floor—several blankets and a ring of pillows so the little girl couldn't crawl too far when she woke up. It was as if Cheryl had suddenly gone to heaven, Jack realized, a sentimental smile creasing his face as he watched. She'd picked Rosario up off his chest when she'd gotten home and hadn't put her down since.

She'd even called in sick to work—something she *never* did—so she could stay home with the baby all day.

He backed out of the doorway and headed to the kitchen as Cheryl pulled a blanket over Rosario's tiny shoulders and kissed the little girl's forehead.

"She's amazing," Cheryl murmured, sitting in the chair across the kitchen table from him a few moments later. "It's just so awful about her mother."

Jack hadn't told Cheryl any of the gory details, just that Julia had died in a car accident. He hadn't told her that he'd been the one to pull the baby out of the wreck, either. It wasn't necessary. There was no need to pump himself up. He was already her hero. "Yeah, I know."

"Is it really only for a few days?" she asked.

She seemed so disappointed. Like that was way too short a time. Like if it had been for good that would have been fine. Harry had been right on with his prediction. "That's what the trooper said, Princess."

Cheryl pushed out her lower lip and pouted. "She's so beautiful. I don't know if I can let her go."

"Already you're like that?"

She shrugged. "What can I say?"

"Ah." He waved. Like it wouldn't be a big deal for him to give Rosario back. He didn't want to admit that he'd already fallen for the little girl, too. "You're such a softie."

"I'm a woman, Daddy. What do you expect?" She sighed. "I know it's not practical. Most days neither one of us is here, so it wouldn't work out. Still, I—"

"We couldn't afford having her around for long, either," Jack interrupted. He hadn't told her that as of yesterday he was going to be around a lot more during the day. Or that he had less than a dollar in his bank account. "Could we?"

Cheryl sighed again and opened her checkbook. It was lying on the table in front of her. "Do you really want to know?"

"No." He hated dealing with money, always had. He'd always let Linda take care of that part of the household. She actually seemed to enjoy that chore. Figured. Hell, she'd probably hidden half the assets ahead of the divorce. "But I guess I should," he admitted grudgingly. At least he knew beyond a shadow of a doubt he could trust Cheryl.

Cheryl tapped down the lines in the checkbook register with her finger, adding up expenses. "Here's the snapshot," she said when she was done. "In terms of savings, I've got about five hundred dollars in my account and you have"—she hesitated—"what, a couple of hundred?"

Not after giving MJ his down payment. "About that."

"It's not much, but at least it's a little bit of a safety net." She studied the register again. "I make forty thousand a year, which, after taxes, works out to almost twenty-seven hundred a month. You make almost sixteen hundred a month, which, other than FICA, you get almost tax-free. So, together, we've got about four thousand in cash a month to spend." She counted up the cash outflows in her head one more time. "The mortgage is about a thousand a month, including property taxes and insurance. The cars cost us a ton with the monthly payments, insurance, and maintenance. Utilities aren't too bad, but they still eat up a chunk. The food and miscellaneous column hits us pretty hard, and then there's always that credit card payment. Still, we should save a couple of hundred a month." She shook her head. "But it seems like there's always something we don't count on. Two months ago it was the roof. Last month it was the new refrigerator."

Jack got up and moved to the sink to pour himself a cup of coffee. "Talk to me about the house. What did we pay for it?"

"A hundred and fifty thousand. We put twenty down," she added hesitantly.

"Why do you say it like that?" he asked, taking a sip as he sat down again. "What's the matter?"

"Are you going to ask me what it's worth?"

"Well, I know the market's off some. What, like five or ten percent? You told me that." She'd actually said it was off more than that, but he was hoping it had come back since then. "Right?"

"More like twenty percent, Daddy," Cheryl said. "All the agents in the office are crying the blues."

"*Twenty percent?* Really?"

She nodded. "It's bad. The bottom line is that the house is worth only about one-twenty now."

"So we're ten grand underwater on it?"

"Yes," she agreed quietly. "It'll come back at some point. Real estate always does, especially in Florida. But that doesn't help us right now."

"Jesus," he muttered. He'd had no idea it was that bad. That the house was worth *that* much less than what they'd paid. "So we have a negative net worth, almost no savings, and we're barely breaking even every month."

She nodded gloomily.

Of course, that was assuming he made sixteen hundred a month. The usher job at the stadium wasn't going to pay anywhere near that. And on top of less money coming in, he had to come up with four hundred bucks a week for MJ. It looked like he was going to have to find another job fast if he wanted someone in the Tarpon dugout spying on Mikey Clemant.

"Well, at least it can't get much worse," Cheryl said, trying to smile.

Jack gazed at her. If she only knew.

23

HELEN McLean GLANCED fearfully into the rearview mirror again and again as she guided the old Dodge through northern New Jersey on the Garden State Parkway, searching frantically for any sign that someone was following her. Fifteen minutes ago she'd checked out of a terrifying, thirty-nine-dollar-a-night dive motel in downtown Newark that was being used mostly by drug users and prostitutes. A motel with a parking lot she'd had to pick her way through this morning to get to her car as if she were picking her way through a minefield because the asphalt was littered with rusty needles and used condoms.

Now she was headed to Perth Amboy to check into what was undoubtedly just as bad a place filled with exactly the same kind of clientele. Different names and different faces, but their lives would be mirror images of the ones she'd just left.

God, she missed her little brick house in Queens. Missed it so much she almost couldn't bear it. So much she was almost willing to go back to it despite the danger she knew was lurking in the shadows there. Not that the little house was anything great. But it was home, and at least she didn't have to worry about stray bullets tearing through paper-thin walls, or listening to a woman in the next room pulling two tricks an hour to support her crystal meth habit. But she had no choice. She had to move, had to *keep* moving to stay ahead of them. They were on to her.

She missed her kitty, too. She'd had to leave in such a rush there hadn't been time to find it. It had been outside somewhere in the neighborhood when she'd gotten the word. She'd called a couple of times from the door, but by the time the suitcase was packed, the poor baby still hadn't shown up. And she couldn't stay any longer. That had been made *very* clear. She had thirty minutes to clear out or she was dead.

The worst part of it all was she couldn't get messages to her son anymore. The bartender at the Dugout had told her Kyle wasn't coming in anymore because some guy who claimed to be an old Yankee scout was suddenly snooping around, asking a lot of questions. The bartender had told her not to call him again. That he was tired of being the go-between, that he didn't feel safe doing it any longer. He said he wouldn't go looking for Kyle to give him a message from her, either, because he didn't want to be seen with the kid, didn't want to be involved any longer.

Helen spotted the exit she was looking for and flipped on the blinker. She could feel the tears welling up again.

Like they had last night when she'd listened to the woman in the next room moaning for money, or when she'd been sure she'd heard gunshots in the parking lot. She had to help Kyle somehow. He'd sacrificed so much for her—his brilliant baseball future, his girlfriend, his safety. Sacrificed everything for her. And most important, he was her son.

Maybe she should just start driving south, toward Sarasota. Maybe that was the answer. Of course, if she did and they were back there, she'd lead them right to him. Maybe they were waiting for her to do just that.

Her tears fell in steady streams as she pulled to a stop at a red light. She desperately needed her brother's help. Needed Stephen to tell her what to do, like he'd always done after her husband passed away. But suddenly he'd disappeared, suddenly he was unreachable. She shivered. She understood what that meant.

Treviso dried off after a long, refreshing shower, patting his thin, dripping chest with a towel as he moved out of the steamy bathroom. He'd stayed out in the Bronx drinking with Paulie the Moon until three o'clock this morning, and he'd opened his eyes ten minutes ago to a raging hangover. He'd yelled to the kitchen for Karen to put the baby in the playpen and come service him right away. Sex usually helped his headache, but this morning it hadn't, in part because Karen wasn't her normal passionate self, so it hadn't been as pleasurable as usual. Of course, that tended to happen right before her period, so he wasn't concerned. She'd be back to normal in a few days.

He moved into their small closet and happened to look down, happened to notice something about her black high heels. He stared intently at them—lying snugly between a pair of sandals and her sneakers. They weren't properly arranged, he realized. The right shoe was on the left and the left shoe was on the right. The toes were pointing slightly out, not slightly in, as they should have been. All of her other pairs were positioned so the toes were pointing in.

Treviso ran his hands through his wet, thinning hair. Karen was a stickler when it came to the few pairs of nice shoes she owned. She took great care of them and always aligned them perfectly. And her black high heels were her favorite pair, her pride and joy, worth almost seventy bucks. He shook his head. His natural ability to pick up on such tiny details so quickly was his only edge in this world.

Marconi sat behind his tray table eating a big, greasy breakfast of scrambled eggs, bacon, hash browns, and a bagel with cream cheese. The beginning of an old *Dick Van Dyke Show* rerun was playing on TV, and he was trying to figure out if Dick was going to trip over the ottoman after coming in the front door during the opening credits—or avoid it. When Dick stopped, then twinkle-toed around it with a smug grin, Marconi laughed loudly, dropping the eggs and hash browns on his fork into his lap. "Motherfu——"

"Hey, boss."

Marconi dabbed at the food in his lap, irritated that

some of it had gotten on his freshly dry-cleaned maroon polyester pants. "What is it, Goliath?"

"Ricky Strazza's here."

"Yeah, okay, let him in."

Strazza was a Lucchesi soldier in one of the Manhattan crews. He was of average height and average build. Not outstanding in any way, so he blended into a crowd naturally. Which was exactly what Marconi wanted.

"Hello, sir," Strazza said when he was inside the bedroom and the door was shut. "How can I serve you?"

Marconi jabbed at the television, irritated at the interruption even though he had summoned Strazza to the row house for the meeting. "Turn it up."

"Yes, sir."

Marconi didn't even give Strazza the chance to sit, just motioned for the young man to kneel next to his chair and lean in close. He wanted this to go fast, wanted to get back to the show. "I got two things for you," Marconi said, leaning forward so his lips were close to Strazza's ear.

"Anything," Strazza whispered, ecstatic to be of help to this man.

Marconi gestured toward the door. "That guy outside."

"Yeah?"

"I want him dead by tomorrow night," Marconi ordered quietly. "You and your crew kill him tomorrow morning after he leaves here, then take him to New Jersey and bury him in our landfill out in Bergen County. Nicky can help you with the details. He knows what's going on."

Strazza smiled like a child who'd just gotten exactly what he wanted for Christmas. "Yes, sir."

"After that I want you on Deuce Bondano's tail like stink on shit." Marconi pointed at Strazza. "And don't ask me why I want you to do it, just do it. Report in to me three times a day about where Deuce goes and what he does. But under no circumstances do you let him know that you're on him. Don't fuck this up."

Strazza took one of Marconi's hands and kissed it. "Yes, sir. Thank you for letting me serve you."

Johnny knelt down in front of the gravestone and laid the bouquet of two dozen red roses on the ground, like he'd done so many times before. The cemetery's sprinklers had been on all afternoon and the ground was drenched, but he hardly noticed that his pants were soaking wet.

"Hi, sweetheart," he said softly, pressing his fingers to the letters of Karen's name the way he always did. "I love you." He looked out over the graveyard. The place was huge, at least thirty acres, but there wasn't anyone else around, not even workers. "I've done a bad thing," he murmured, "but you probably already know that." He bit his lower lip. "I was with another woman last night. Someone I actually care about. Not those girls I pay. Her name's Karen. Just like you." He rubbed his eyes, then touched his shirt pocket. "I'm sorry, *real* sorry." The lump in his throat grew big, and tears formed at the corners of his eyes. "I know I told you I'd never do that," he continued, his voice raspy, "but I've been so lonely." The first tear rolled down one cheek, followed quickly by several more down both. He brushed them away but more kept coming. "So lonely," he whispered. "Please don't hate me."

He took a few moments to gather himself. "I need to talk to you about something," he began again, trying to make his voice strong. "You always know what to say." He hesitated. "You know what I do for a living, you know I kill people. The way I killed that doctor who murdered you." A gentle breeze blew across his face, and he glanced up into the trees. The leaves weren't moving. He shook his head, wondering if that had been her. "I know it's not right, I know you wouldn't approve. But at least I've always killed people I figured deserved it. Murderers, cheaters, liars. But now they want me to kill somebody who doesn't deserve it. This kid." He put his face into his hands. "Please tell me what to do," he whispered, hoping the breeze would come again. But it didn't. "Please, sweetheart," he begged once more. "Please."

But nothing.

He'd never felt so completely alone.

24

"Curtis! Curtis Billups! Come here right now!"

MJ was lying on one of two bottom bunks in the tiny bedroom he shared with his three younger brothers. His three younger sisters had the room next door, which was only slightly larger than this one.

"*Curtis!*" his mother shouted again from the kitchen in her deep voice. "Don't make me take the Lord's name in vain. Don't make me do it, young man."

Anthony, MJ's ten-year-old brother, leaned over the side of the top bunk and peered down, a mischievous grin on his face. "You better get out there, MJ. Momma's pissed. You're in trouuuuble."

MJ rose off the bed and slipped the *Sports Illustrated* he'd been reading under the mattress. "Shut up, Anthony. Or I'll make you wish you'd never been born."

Anthony stuck out his tongue.

"Curtis!" MJ's mother yelled again. "*God help you!*"

MJ grabbed the dog-eared copy of *Tale of Two Cities* he was supposed to be reading off the cardboard box he and his brothers used as a nightstand and dashed for the kitchen. But not before giving Anthony a quick, stiff punch on the upper arm. "I'm here, Momma," he said breathlessly as he rushed into the kitchen, making certain to prominently display the paperback she'd borrowed for him from the library. "What do you need?" he asked, taking pleasure in the howls of pain coming from the bedroom.

She pointed at the book. "Were you really reading that or—"

"Man, it smells delicious in here, Momma." MJ put his head back and took a deep breath, then patted his chest. "You make the best country fried steak in the whole entire world." He gave her a big hug. "I love your cooking. It's awesome."

Yolanda Billups had been beautiful as a younger woman: tall and statuesque with long black hair and unblemished caramel skin. But the sands of time and seven pregnancies had done their work. She weighed almost two hundred pounds now, and her arms, shoulders, and legs had grown thick. But her face was still pretty. Expressive, too. She couldn't hide her emotions, so she didn't try. "Don't butter me up, Curtis." She ruled the house with an iron fist—at least most of the time. "I know what you're doing. It won't work."

MJ gave her his best hurt-puppy-dog look. She was still angry, but she was cracking. He could see that big smile of hers—where he'd gotten his—trying to break through.

Like the sun on a foggy morning. "Jeez, Momma, I'm not trying to butter you up. I mean it. You're the best cook ever. I can't even eat anybody else's—"

She broke out laughing, a deep baritone he-he-he-ha-ha-ha. She grabbed MJ and hugged him tightly. "I swear, I can't resist you. I love you so much, Curtis."

"I love you, too, Momma." MJ pulled back from the embrace, proud of himself. He was the only sibling who could consistently break her anger so quickly. His expression turned serious. He'd noticed how depressed she seemed lately, so he figured she needed some pepping up. "You take such good care of us." He held the book up. "I started it, and it's worse than *Moby Dick*. But if you tell me to read it, I will." He promised himself he wouldn't open the *Sports Illustrated* again until he'd finished the book he was holding. "I know you just want the best for me."

She wiped a tear from her eye. It had welled up fast. Of course, she cried at least a few times almost every day. Sobbed uncontrollably at church every Sunday during the recessional, hands raised in the air as she swayed back and forth in the pew with her two best girlfriends. "I do want you to read it," she said. "I want the best for you. I hate that you gotta work and you can't go to school because I need you to earn money because your damn daddy was a bastard." Her evangelical persona suddenly shone through. "By God, child," she said, raising one hand, index finger pointed to the sky, "I'm gonna see to it that you know more than all those other kids in school put together. I'm gonna make sure you're smarter than all of them. I know that book's boring for you, honey," she continued, "but white people will be shocked that you've even heard of it, let alone read it. God forbid you're able to discuss it intelligently. And I'm not saying I want you to be some yes-sir-no-sir Uncle Tom. That's not what I'm saying, child. But it's still a white man's world, and you gotta be real about that if you wanna get ahead. Like I always told you, conform, conform, conform. Until you're in charge. Then control, control, control. But not in a bad way," she added, raising her voice. "Not with malice or vengeance, young man. There's no place in this world for the devil's work. Right, Curtis?"

"Right, Momma."

"With fairness and equity. With benevolence. Remember, it's not a black world or a white world. It's just a world. You hear me?"

MJ nodded, remembering Jack's stunned expression when the old man realized that a dropout black kid knew who Captain Ahab was. It was the first time what his mother had been preaching for so long had made a real impact. Jack had treated him differently from that moment on. The change was subtle but undeniable. Knowledge really was power. People respected you when they knew you had knowledge. Some of them even feared you. He wouldn't tell Momma he understood that, though. "I hear you, Momma."

She took a deep breath, then reached into her apron, her contented expression fading. "We need to talk, Curtis," she said holding up a wad of twenties. "This is why I called you."

MJ's eyes bugged out. "Where'd you get that?"

"From your underwear drawer."

"Momma!"

"Anthony told me it was in there."

"Why, that little—"

"Don't blame him, Curtis," she warned, holding one hand up and wagging a finger. "And don't take it out on him later. He just loves you, he just cares about his big brother. Now tell me where you got this," she demanded. "There's two hundred dollars here and they're all crisp twenties, so I know this isn't tip money. I may be getting old, but I ain't getting dumb."

"You're not getting old—"

"Don't try to butter me up, child."

"And you'll never be—"

"It won't work right now, Curtis," she interrupted sharply. "Understand, I let you do that to me when I want to. Now isn't one of those times."

"Yes, ma'am."

"I know this isn't your paycheck because you always sign that over to me," she kept going. "Are you selling drugs, Curtis?" she demanded shrilly. "I swear, if you are I'll whip your little black—"

"I'm not selling drugs, Momma. I promise. You've taught me too well." He sighed, pissed off at Anthony. He'd wanted to keep this from her. Wanted to keep the surprise. "Momma, remember how I told you I wanted to get rich enough to own a pro baseball team?"

She gave him her here-we-go-again look. "Uh-huh."

"Well, I'm on my way."

"How's Rosario?"

Jack and Biff were standing beneath an oak tree on one side of an elementary school parking lot. "She's fine. My daughter's taken to her. Harry was right. Thank God, too," Jack said, shoulders sagging, "because I wouldn't have the patience. Rosario's a little cutie, but she's so much work. I'm too old for all that." Maybe this was how he could justify what Biff had suggested. He'd been wrestling with it so hard. Usually he was good at rationalizing anything, but this time it wasn't working. Of course, he'd never considered doing something like this before. Well, once. "It's damn expensive, let me tell you. Pampers, formula, food, clothes, all that stuff. Incredible." Cheryl had put it all on her credit card this morning. Fortunately, the charge had gone through. They weren't sure it would because the amount would push the balance on her card right to its limit. Maybe even a little over. "I had no idea."

"Don't tell me," Biff agreed, shaking his head. "You're preaching to the choir, old man. Got three kids of my own. All of 'em under five. My wife waitresses at Cracker Barrel so we got two incomes, but we still can't make ends meet. I just go farther in the hole every month. I'm trying to get another credit card because the ones I have are all maxed out. But I ain't having much luck."

They stood in silence for a few moments, neither one wanting to be the first to bring up why they'd really met.

"It's only for a few days," Jack finally spoke up. "Right? Then that trooper will come and get her."

Biff shrugged. "I guess."

"You *guess*? What does that mean?"

"It means I don't know. Call Tom and talk to him."

"Tom?"

"The trooper. Tom O'Brien."

"Oh."

"He gave you his number, right?"

"Yeah, I think I've got it somewhere." Cheryl would never forgive him if he called the trooper.

"He can tell you what's going on with all that," Biff continued, "that's not my department."

"But you were the one who—"

"I saw him at an accident earlier this afternoon. I think he said there was a problem."

"A problem?"

"The husband's going crazy trying to figure out what happened to the baby. Tom wrote in his report that Rosario died in the accident, but now the guy's pressing it. Says he wants to see the body."

"Jesus, I can't—"

"Look, are you in or out?" Biff interrupted.

Jack took a deep breath. "I'm in already, I'm in. The baby can stay with me and Cheryl as long as she needs to. I trust you guys. Okay?"

"I'm not talking about the baby," Biff snapped. "I'm talking about our business venture. I can't wait around any longer. I gotta know if you're in or out. If you're not, I got somebody else who's ready to go. I don't trust him much, so I'd rather it was you. But like I said, I can't wait around."

Jack stared into Biff's eyes, hoping to find remorse. But there wasn't any. Not one shred. Just a cold, selfish stare. "Yeah," he said quietly, hating that it had come to this. "I guess I'm in."

Part 3

25

"HEY, MISTER, FIND our seats."

Mikey Clemant was running pregame wind sprints in the outfield, and Jack was admiring how the kid was putting his heart and soul into every step. He wasn't just half-assing it, wasn't just jogging leisurely across the grass like most of the players. God, he could run like the wind, too. And his first step was like a cheetah's. Not a lumbering, locomotive start, like most big men. Jack took a deep breath of warm sea air, thinking how good the kid would look doing his warm-ups in pinstripes on the biggest baseball stage in the world. Yankee Stadium.

"Mister! Show us our seats."

The voice was louder and even more annoying this time.

"Hey!"

Okay, it was his job, but did it really take a rocket scientist to find your seat in a stadium this small? Besides, he'd noticed something different about Mikey Clemant tonight. A spring in the kid's step that hadn't been there before. Like something good had happened to him, and he was feeling his oats. It was nice to see, but it only deepened the mystery. Only made Jack more determined to get to the answer.

"Hey, bumblefuck, get your ass in gear and show us our seats. I'm not gonna ask you again nice."

Jack felt a hard tap on his shoulder.

"Or maybe we got it all wrong. Maybe you aren't an usher. Maybe you're a bus driver. That's what you look like, anyway. I bet your kids are reeeeal proud of you."

They were howling at him now, making a scene. He sensed people in the stands starting to get a kick out of it, too. No way to ignore it anymore.

Jack rose up deliberately off the yellow railing and gazed at the two teenage boys coldly. Smug attitudes, smug smiles, and, worst of all, youth. He focused on the one to the left, who had what looked like a volcano rising up from the left side of his nose. He winced and scrunched up his eyes as he stared at the huge pimple, like it was the most disgusting thing he'd ever seen and ought to be on display at a Ripley's believe-it-or-not museum.

The boy turned away quickly and grabbed his buddy by the arm. "Come on, Travis, let's go. *Come on.*"

Travis dished out one more impudent grin, then raced after his friend into the stands.

"Little bastards," he muttered. "Someday they'll figure out how tough life is. Just wish I could be there when they do."

"Hi, Jack."

He turned toward the raspy voice. "Hi there, Lester." Lester was the frail old usher who'd greeted him that first evening Cheryl and Bobby had brought him out here. The guy had to be at least eighty, but he still had a nice way about him. Most old people Jack knew didn't. Realizing their time was almost up and wishing they could do it over again usually made them bitter.

"How are you tonight?" Lester asked.

"Fine. Thanks for asking." Jack took another satisfying breath of briny air. "Just glad to be out at the ballpark."

"Learning the ropes okay?"

Jack pressed his lips together and shook his head, like he was having a tough go of it. "Well, this leading-people-to-their-seats thing is pretty complicated stuff. Right up there with putting a man on the moon and nanotechnology. But I think I'm finally getting the hang of it." Lester didn't seem amused. "Nice night, huh?"

"Beautiful," Lester agreed, his friendly demeanor quickly reappearing. "I haven't seen a night this pretty in a long time. Not so late in the spring, anyway. Cool, no humidity, no clouds." He nodded toward the gulf. "This kind of weather makes the water look so pretty."

Jack watched Clemant jog toward the Tarpon dugout after finishing his sprints. The kid tapped the second-base bag with his toe as he passed by, then made certain he didn't step on the foul line as he crossed it. In general, baseball players were a superstitious lot, so it was good to see that the kid was normal. At least in that department. "Yeah, real pretty."

"Looks like the sun's actually dancing on the surface, doesn't it?"

"Uh-huh."

Lester grimaced. "But it won't last."

"Nothing ever does."

"Pretty soon we'll be into the rainy season," Lester observed, paying no attention to Jack's philosophical waxing. "Humidity so thick you'll need a machete to get through it, and nasty thunderstorms every afternoon. Like they say in South Florida, if you don't start your summer golf rounds early in the morning, odds are good you won't finish."

Jack had heard that at least a hundred times since moving to Sarasota. And about how golfers were struck by lightning a lot down here because they didn't take cover soon enough.

"In fact," Lester continued, "I hear it's supposed to get hot again the day after tomorrow. Temps up into the nineties. Bad humidity. Ugh."

"Oh, well." Over Lester's shoulder Jack spotted MJ in the Tarpon dugout arranging batting helmets. "I'm thirsty. I'm gonna get a soda. Want one?" Lester seemed mortified. "What's the matter?" Jack asked.

"You can't do that."

"Why not?"

"No breaks until after the game starts. And you get only two a game. They can't last more than five minutes, either. Those are the rules. Didn't they tell you all that?"

Jack patted Lester's bony shoulder gently. The old man didn't understand supply and demand. The Tarpons couldn't come close to finding enough people to do this job. They weren't going to fire anybody for getting a drink. "You're a good man, Lester. There's darn few of us left."

Jack started toward the tunnel entrance, then stopped abruptly, remembering the deal he'd struck with Biff. And how he hadn't decided yet why he was really going after the kid. If it was just for money—or something better. Lately it seemed like he was doing everything for money. Or his lack of it.

He started for the tunnel again. Down deep, he'd always considered himself a good and decent man. Suddenly he wasn't so sure anymore.

MJ leaned over and undid the shoelace of his left cleat, then took his time retying it. While he was bent over, he tried to figure out what Mikey Clemant was staring at so intently. The kid was sitting off by himself at the far end of the dugout near the water fountain like he always did. But tonight he seemed to be grinning while he studied a small piece of paper he'd pulled from the back pocket of his uniform. Like he was in high school and it was a love note from a girl. Usually the kid wore a mean permafrown and stared everyone down. But Clemant had actually smiled when he strode into the locker room two hours ago. A real smile, not that fake one he usually dished out. It was the first time Clemant had even acknowledged MJ's existence, though they still hadn't spoken. At least it was a start. Jack was getting impatient.

Jack had turned out to be right about the kid. There was something strange about Mikey Clemant, something mysterious. It had been only a week since MJ had started the batboy gig, but he'd quickly become as determined as Jack to find out what was going on. Of course, he'd never let on. Then Jack might stop paying him, might figure he could get his information for free.

It was interesting that Clemant was in such a good mood, MJ thought as he finished the double knot. It wasn't like the kid was hitting very well, just hanging around that .250 mark. A hit in every four at-bats in Single-A was nothing to get hyped up about, nothing that was going to get him to the Show. Probably not even to Double-A.

MJ suddenly realized that Clemant was staring back, and he shifted his eyes quickly away, then began retying the other cleat. He had to be more careful. One thing about Clemant: he always seemed to be on guard, always seemed to be looking around. Watching his back the way a prey animal would. Which was odd for a big man. Little guys, sure, but not a man the size of Mikey Clemant. Maybe Clemant realized how much he'd pissed off everyone in the clubhouse, and he was worried somebody might take a sucker punch.

It seemed weird for the kid to call himself Mikey, too. Instead of Mike or Michael. Childlike almost. But a couple of the guys on the team had warned MJ on his first night to make sure he called the kid "Mikey." Otherwise, they warned, he'd get the evil eye. Maybe worse than that in the parking lot after the game.

That was another thing MJ had noticed about the kid. Despite his cautious and mostly polite manner, he scared people. Scared the hell out of them.

When the kid stepped to the plate in the home half of the first, Jack was helping an old man find the bathroom. The old codger said he couldn't understand Jack's directions and wanted to be led all the way to the damn door. Jack was about to do it—he wanted another drink and there was a concession stand near the bathrooms—when he heard that distinct smack of bat against ball. That unmistakable pop of perfect contact he'd heard in baseball stadiums thousands of times over the years. He whipped around just in time to see the ball rocketing toward the cow pasture. And Mikey Clemant taking the first few steps of his home-run trot.

It was a big crowd tonight, almost six thousand, and they were loud. The Tarpons were giving away free ice cream to kids carrying coupons from today's local newspaper as well as one free beer to all adults. Most were already on their second or third cold one. Plus, there was going to be a big fireworks display after the game, so the crowd was in a party mood. The ovation thundered around the park as the ball landed in the weeds beyond the fence, scaring a flock of seagulls. It was louder than any cheer Jack had heard at Tarpon Stadium. But as usual, none of the players gave the kid much of a greeting when he got back to the dugout. A few lukewarm high fives, but that was it.

The home run had been another monster shot, easily as high and as far as the one Clemant had hit that first night. But somehow it wasn't as awe-inspiring. Maybe, Jack figured, because he was expecting incredible things out of the kid every time up now.

Clemant eased onto the dugout bench near the water fountain, then leaned back and covered his face with his hands, listening to the crowd roar fade away as the next batter dug into the box. He could feel tears building at the corners of his eyes, and he didn't want his teammates seeing them. He knew they hated him, at the very least didn't understand him. And it killed him to be so distant, and to have them be so distant from him. He'd never been this way. He'd always been a leader, always been close to the other guys. Always been the first one to offer congratulations or consolation. The first to lend a hand. To come out early to the ballpark before a game or stay late afterward to work on hitting or fielding with a struggling teammate.

But it couldn't be that way anymore. He had to protect himself. Had to stay off to himself, removed from the camaraderie he craved. It had been like this for two seasons, and it seemed like it would have to stay this way as long as he kept playing. He had to play only for the love of the game now, had to simply enjoy making the bat and ball connect perfectly or making a spectacular catch. Of course, he couldn't even do that whenever he wanted because that would cause too much attention. And attention was what he feared most. What might allow the dogs to pick up the trail again.

Clemant pulled the bill of his cap down and wiped his eyes hard, then leaned forward, reached into the back pocket of his uniform, pulled out the crumpled piece of paper, and studied it. A scintillating thrill rushed through his body as he gazed at the scrawled words written there. The same rush he'd experienced this morning when he'd written it all down. He'd been anticipating tonight for months, for what seemed like an eternity. Actually crossed off days on the insurance calendar hanging on

the bare wall of his tiny, pathetic, stick-furnished apartment. Anticipated it intensely ever since coming up with
the plan one afternoon this past winter as he'd been waiting tables at a local Red Lobster. Ever since he'd checked
the records that night when he got home and recognized
this red-letter date in the scenario. He was worried about
the stir it might cause, but it wasn't like it was going to
happen again. There were no games like this for the rest
of the season. He'd be a star for one night, then fade into
oblivion. One night of glory wouldn't be enough for them
to find him.

He gritted his teeth. But then tonight might not be
enough for him, either. In fact, finally being able to cut
loose and be this good might end up being a very bad
outcome, he realized now that he was in the middle
of it. Maybe this plan hadn't been such a good idea
after all. Maybe it would whet his appetite so sharply,
might be such a tease, he wouldn't be able to resist
his thirst for more. Like a drug addict, he might suddenly need another night like tonight, even though it
wasn't in the record books that way. Maybe he'd be at
the plate tomorrow night and veer off course with no
warning. Suddenly diverge from the plan, unable to
control himself any longer. He could already feel that
awful possibility gnawing at him. He glanced up, past
the stadium lights, looking for an answer. Wondering
why he'd been forsaken. But the answer wasn't there.
Only darkness.

He carefully refolded the paper and stowed it back into
his pocket, then happened to glance to his left—straight
into the batboy's eyes. The young black guy looked away
instantly, but Clemant kept staring, wondering. It was

the third time tonight he'd caught MJ staring. He shook his head. It had to be that MJ recognized raw talent. It couldn't be anything else. They wouldn't recruit a black kid. It wasn't like them. They didn't trust blacks. As terrible as that was to say.

Clemant glanced down and spat. He liked MJ, liked the young man's confident attitude and that sharp look in his eye. He reminded Clemant of his best friend from home he hadn't spoken to in so, so long. Clemant felt the heat at the corners of his eyes again. God, he wanted a friend so bad. Somebody he could talk to, somebody he could confide in. Even if it was only a little talking and only for a little while. He hadn't told anyone anything remotely personal in two years. It was like being in a maximum-security prison without bars. It was a self-imposed island of exile, and he wasn't certain how much longer he could take it. He'd already noticed himself doing strange things: talking to himself constantly, forgetting where he'd put things, staring at people too long. He took a deep breath. Maybe all this wasn't necessary, maybe they didn't care anymore. Maybe time had healed the wounds.

Maybe he was as naive as they came.

Thirty minutes later, after two turns in the field, Clemant climbed the dugout steps and headed toward the plate. Halfway there, MJ handed him his favorite bat—the all-black, thirty-six-ounce maple with the two-and-a-half-inch barrel. It wasn't the same one he'd hit the home run with in the first. That one was made of ash and was heavier. There was always a seed of doubt with that bat. Always the remote possibility of something going wrong. But not with this one. Not with Black

Maple. He couldn't hit the ball quite as far with Black Maple, but he could hit it in the field of play anytime he wanted to. There was no doubt at all with this wand. It felt beautiful in his hands, like a perfectly balanced, razor-sharp sword in the hands of Achilles. He loved this bat, absolutely loved it, and he could do so much damage with it.

He nestled the toe of his right cleat into the depression at the back of the batter's box made by all those right-handed batters who'd gone before, took two practice swings, then brought the bat up into the kill position over his right shoulder. He wasn't going to take long with this turn. He was going to hit the first pitch that was even close. This was just a single and he wanted to get to the fifth, wanted to get to that second big shot. And God, it would be huge.

Don't intentionally walk me, he kept thinking as he dug in a little deeper. *Please* don't intentionally walk me. Please let me have all my chances tonight. He heaved a heavy sigh of relief when the pitcher nodded, accepting the sign the catcher had flashed, then went into his delivery.

He whipped Black Maple through the strike zone at the last moment, and smiled as he saw the white flash rocket toward the outfield out of his left eye. Perfect. Absolutely perfect.

Jack's mouth fell slightly open when Clemant laced the hard single to left, driving in a run. His jaw almost hit the yellow railing in the fifth when the Kid launched another monster shot over the center-field wall—the longest of the three home runs he'd witnessed—and the crowd went crazy. In the seventh he simply stared in awe when Clemant led off with a double to the wall in right and scored as the Tarpons batted around. And in the bottom of the eighth, in the Kid's final at-bat, when he laced another single, this time to right, driving in the last run of the game, Jack almost sank to his knees.

He caught himself on the railing in the nick of time, still completely awestruck by the Kid's talent. He'd never seen anything like it. *Never.* Then an eerie sense of déjà vu slowly overtook the feeling of awe as Clemant headed toward the dugout to retrieve his glove and cap for the top of the ninth after the next batter popped up to end the inning. MJ met the Kid in front of the pitcher's mound with the stuff, handing him his cap and glove and taking his batting helmet. Teammates usually brought caps and gloves to players left on base at the end of an inning, but Clemant had no friends in the dugout—MJ had confirmed this fact after his first game on the bench. The Kid usually sat by himself and rarely spoke to anyone in the clubhouse before or after the game, MJ had reported. The Kid had pissed everyone on the team off, just as Bobby had said that first night.

The déjà vu feeling intensified as Jack followed Clemant out to center, that spring in his step no longer there. Why? He ought to be ecstatic. He'd gone a perfect five-for-five tonight—five hits in five at-bats—two home runs, two singles, and a double. He'd driven in five runs, scored three himself, and made two incredible plays in the field: a gravity-defying, wall-scaling, home-run-robbing catch in the fourth and, in the seventh, a rifle throw from deep in right center to nail a runner who'd tried to score on a sacrifice fly. An unbelievable performance at any level of the sport. It had all been working for him tonight.

Jack cursed quietly, frustrated by the feeling that he'd seen it all before. Unable to remember where or when. He tried the old trick of not thinking about it for a few seconds, then refocusing on it. But that didn't work, so he went back to thinking about nothing but what he'd seen.

Suddenly it hit him. "Oh my God," he whispered, putting a hand to his head, elation, shock, and disbelief bursting through him at the same time. "That's it."

"It's getting late." Bobby was standing in the doorway of Cheryl's bedroom, holding a beer. He'd been watching a game on TV in the living room. "Let's go to my place."

Cheryl laughed like she couldn't believe he'd made the suggestion. "Are you kidding?" Rosario was lying on the bed playing with a bracelet. "Don't you see this package of huge responsibility lying in front of me?" she asked, starting to change the little girl's diaper.

"Yeah, I see it," he grumbled. He'd been forced to amuse himself most of the evening because Cheryl had been so busy with Rosario. He'd done a decent job of biting his tongue to this point, but now the game was over and he was getting frustrated. Since the baby had shown up, they'd had sex only once. "How could I miss it?"

"It's good practice," she said maternally. "I get to see how you'll be as a daddy."

He took a gulp of beer, then glanced warily over his shoulder back down the narrow hallway. "Your father's gonna be here anytime. Then the fun'll really be over."

"Oh, don't complain so much," Cheryl scolded good-naturedly, finishing the diaper change. "You're a bigger baby than Rosario."

"Why don't you bring her with us?" Bobby suggested. "She'll be fine. We can set her up on my couch. We'll put some pillows around her, and she'll be right at home. Snug as a bug in a rug."

"I don't think so."

Bobby made a face at the baby. "Shouldn't she be asleep by now?"

"She's had the sniffles the past couple of days, and it's put her off her schedule."

"Poor thing," he muttered sarcastically. "Well, it's put me off my schedule, too."

Cheryl gathered Rosario in her arms and moved toward the door. "Sometimes we all have to make sacrifices." She raised up on her tiptoes and gave Bobby a quick kiss on the cheek. "I love you." Then she slipped past him and headed for the kitchen. "I'm going to fix her another bottle. Maybe she'll go down after that. Then we can have some alone time."

"This is your brother's kid?" Bobby asked, following Cheryl to the kitchen. "That's what you said, right?"

"Uh-huh," she answered hesitantly. "Daddy and I are taking care of her while David and his wife are on a cruise."

"Oh?"

"Yeah. The ship left from Miami. They flew in here from New York, dropped Rosario off, then drove over there."

Bobby sat down at the kitchen table, in the seat beside Rosario's high chair. He made another face at the little girl. A friendlier one this time because Cheryl was looking. "Thanks for screwing up my sex life, kid."

"Don't talk to her like that."

Bobby cocked his head to one side. "She looks kind of . . . well . . . Hispanic, if you ask me." He gestured toward the living room. "Your brother's wife doesn't look Hispanic in any of those pictures."

"They adopted her," Cheryl explained, shaking the bottle. "David's wife can't have children." She slipped the nipple into Rosario's mouth, and her face lit up when the little girl grabbed the plastic bottle with her tiny fingers and held it herself. "Good girl," she said loudly.

"Yeah, good girl," Bobby echoed, standing up. "Maybe I can get a little attention now." He wrapped his arms around Cheryl. "Kiss me, sweetheart."

She gave him another quick peck on the cheek, then pulled away. "I need to run a load of wash."

"Damn it, Cheryl."

She stopped and turned back around. "What's wrong?"

"I'm outta here," he mumbled, stalking toward the front door. "I can't deal with this anymore."

"Bobby, stop!"

"Forget it."

A moment later he was out the door and gone.

Cheryl's eyes moved quickly to Rosario, who was sucking away on the bottle. Bobby was right; she had been ignoring him lately. She hadn't realized how much until just now. She heard the engine start up, then the SUV peel away. How could she have been such an idiot?

Well, she'd make it up to him. In a way he wouldn't forget.

"Can you believe the game Clemant had?" Jack asked breathlessly, not even giving MJ a chance to close the Citation door and settle into the passenger seat before starting in. "It was incredible." He'd barely been able to control himself while he waited for MJ to emerge from the home team clubhouse. "Five-for-five. Two dingers, five RBIs, three runs scored. He was on fire."

"Yeah," MJ agreed, swinging the car door shut. "On *fuego.*"

Jack's enthusiasm faded momentarily as the image of the young woman in the sedan flashed through his mind. She'd been screaming that word over and over as she burned. "Huh?"

"*Fuego,*" MJ repeated. "Spanish for fire."

"I know, but why'd you say it?"

"That's what they say on ESPN. On *SportsCenter* when somebody has a great game. You know, they shout '*¡Fuego!*' when they show a guy hitting a home run or making a great catch."

"Yeah, yeah. Now, look, I gotta tell you—"

"Didn't you know that?"

"Sure I did," Jack said confidently. Trying to revive the feeling of utter elation he'd been high on a few moments ago. Trying to forget the horrible image of Julia wedged between the windshield and the dashboard as the flames consumed her. It had been haunting his dreams every night. "*Of course* I did."

"No, you didn't."

Jack rolled his eyes. "It doesn't matter. Listen, I—"

"You say you're this big baseball guy and you didn't even know that? I mean, it's ESPN, for crying out loud."

"Will you please—"

"How am I supposed to believe that you're really—"

"Shut up!" Jack yelled. "Christ! Okay, okay, I didn't know. I never did watch ESPN. I was too busy—" He interrupted himself with a moan, irritated that MJ was *still* distracting him from what was literally causing his hands to shake it was so amazing. "Here's what I've been trying to tell you. Yeah, yeah, the Kid had a great game and all," he said with a flick of his fingers. "A *really* great game. But we already know he's a huge talent. Hell, I'm starting to think he could do that every time out if he really wanted to." An edgy smile played across Jack's lips. "See, here's the damn thing of it all. I think I've seen somebody have that same game before."

MJ had been rubbing at a dirt mark on his cleats. He was taking them home to shine them because the equipment manager did such a crappy job. "Say *what*?"

Jack guided the Citation out of the stadium parking lot onto the main road. "I know it sounds crazy, I can't even believe I'm saying it. But I'm almost positive I saw somebody else have that same game a long time ago. You know, five-for-five with two home runs, a bunch of RBIs, and a bunch of runs scored. Or at least a game a lot like it."

"Who?"

"Mickey Mantle," Jack answered, his voice hushed. "The Mick."

MJ shook his head. "How the hell could you remem-

ber a game from that long ago? Didn't Mantle retire in
the early seventies?"

"After the 1968 season, actually."

"Well, he must have had a ton of great games like that
during his career. How could you remember one in particular?"

"I remember him having the game in his last season,
in 1968. And believe me, he didn't have many games
like that in 1968. Maybe only that one. His knees were
so shot at that point he could barely run. Hell, *I* probably could have beaten him around the bases with these
knees," Jack said, patting them. "They moved him to first
from the outfield because of that. Those knees really
killed his hitting, too. And his eyes were bad, too, but
he wouldn't admit it. Anyway, in '68 his stats were terrible. Way below his career averages in every category.
Hits, homers, RBIs. So I know he didn't have many great
games that year."

"Yeah, but how do you know it was 1968?"

Jack's expression turned distant. "I know because I was
just about to go into the army when I saw Mick do it. I en-
listed in 1968, and I'll *never* forget that. I remember wondering all through the game if I'd made the right decision to
go into the service. Or if I was crazy for doing it. I remember thinking how when I got out I wanted to get a job with
the Yankees. That I would have done anything to work for
them. Started in the mail room, for crying out loud, just to
be able to say I was with the team. And the whole time I'm
thinking about how much I want to work for the Yankees,
the Mick is having this incredible game." He smacked the
steering wheel. "So it must have been late spring, too, right
around this same time of year, because I actually reported

to the army in early June." He knew how this was going to sound, but it was true. "You'll think I'm full of shit, but I can still remember a lot of games I watched no matter what year it was. What guys hit in the game, who pitched, who won. It's like the great golfers, like Nicklaus and Woods," he said. "They remember a lot of specific shots they hit in tournaments for years afterward. I can remember baseball games like they remember golf shots."

MJ shook his head. "Well, Ahab, at least you got one thing right."

"What?"

"You're full of shit."

"No, no, I'm serious. I have a great memory for that stuff."

"Worse, I think you're bullshitting yourself."

"What's that supposed to mean?" Jack demanded, angry that MJ wasn't buying into this. "Huh?"

"You want the Kid to have had a great game like Mantle because you think that'll help you get him a tryout with the Yankees. Like that might help you sell him to the guys up North."

"That's not it," Jack replied firmly. "It wouldn't matter to them."

"Okay, fine. Then who pitched for the Yankees the day Mantle had this great game?" MJ asked like a district attorney on cross.

Jack ran a hand through his hair as he drove, digging deep. "It was . . . it was . . . um . . ." He let out a frustrated sigh. "Christ, I—"

"All right, I'll give you a snow cone, a real easy one. Who was the other team that day?"

"It was the . . . the *Twins*," Jack blurted out, then shook his head immediately. "No, no, it was the Orioles." He banged the steering wheel again. "Nah, that's not right, either. Damn it!"

MJ snickered. "Yeah, great memory."

"I'm . . . I'm positive I remember the game," Jack muttered.

"Well, there's one way to check it out."

"Sure, go through all the Yankees' 1968 box scores. At least the ones for games they played around this time. But how the hell am I going to do that?"

"You could start with the Elias Sports Bureau."

Jack pulled to a stop at a red light. "Oh, yeah?"

Based in New York City, the Elias Sports Bureau amassed tons and tons of baseball statistics. Before the team had turned its back on him and he'd given up baseball, Jack remembered seeing the television networks credit Elias at the bottom of the screen whenever one of the announcers or analysts came up with an obscure baseball fact during a broadcast.

"That's a good idea," Jack agreed. "I'll call them tomorrow."

"Or," MJ continued, "you could just go on the Internet. I'll bet there's a site somewhere with old Yankee box scores on it. At least back to the sixties. People are nuts about that stuff." MJ grinned. "But you probably don't know how to use the Internet."

"I know how to use it," Jack growled, punching the gas pedal when the light turned green.

MJ snickered again. "Do you even have Internet connection at your house?"

"I got it. I been using the Net for years. I went on the Tarpons' site the other night."

"Sure you did." MJ glanced out the window. "It doesn't matter anyway. Even if you have it, you won't be able to find anything. You'll end up needing me." He rubbed his palms together. "Which means more money for me, more money for me."

"You'd actually charge me to go online and look for a website?" Jack asked incredulously.

"Absolutely. It's all about getting paid, man. Which reminds me," MJ said loudly. "You owe me six hundred bucks."

"Six hundred?"

"Yeah. Our deal was four hundred a week. This is the second week, and I've only gotten two hundred. You owe me six hundred dollars."

Jack had been waiting for this. He was actually surprised MJ had waited this long to bring it up. "Well, I—"

"Don't try to wiggle out of it, either," MJ warned. "My momma's pissed at me for doing this batboy thing. She doesn't believe it pays four hundred a week, like I told her. If I don't see some green soon, I'll be out. I swear."

"Yeah, well, if I don't get some information on the Kid soon, I won't care if you're out. I want something on him, and I want it fast." Jack pointed at MJ. "Don't think it hasn't crossed my mind that you're using me. It's a pretty good gig, you know. You're a batboy for Christ's sake. You're having a great time, *and* I'm paying you. I don't like getting used. I won't be used."

"You think *I'm* using *you*?"

MJ was pissed, Jack could tell. Really pissed all of a sudden. He could tell right away the emotion was sincere, but he'd needed to say what he said. It had been a while, and MJ hadn't come up with anything. "Hey, I don't know you that well."

"If you think I'm using you, then . . . then . . ." MJ clenched his teeth. "Then don't bring me out here anymore."

Jack heard the tone in the young man's voice change. It wasn't anger anymore, it was disappointment, almost sadness. Like he'd suddenly realized a good friend had been disloyal. "Listen, I'm just saying—"

"I'm serious. I quit. The hell with it. Find somebody else to do this."

This was a sixteen-year-old boy he was dealing with. He had to remember that. But sometimes it was hard because MJ seemed so much older, so mature. "I'm sorry. Okay? Really." Jack hesitated. "What's wrong?"

"Nothin'."

"Come on," Jack pushed gently. "What is it?"

"*Nothin'*, I said."

Then it dawned on him. What was really going on. "Did you give your mother the other two hundred dollars for the first week out of your own pocket? Did you front me?" From what Jack could tell, MJ's family probably couldn't last long if MJ's income dried up. They probably had even less in savings than he and Cheryl. "Did you?"

"It doesn't matter."

Jack caught MJ running a finger across his cheek under one eye. "From money you saved up, right? From tips you made at the store? You covered me, didn't you? You gave your mom the two hundred I gave you, then two hundred of your own? Didn't you?"

"I told you," MJ said defiantly, "it doesn't matter."

"Come on," Jack demanded. *"Damn it, come on!"*

MJ glanced down. "Yeah," he admitted quietly, "I did. I had to tell her what was going on; I couldn't lie to her. She started yelling at me when I told her the truth. Told me I couldn't do it because you'd welsh on me. Told me I had to get another job." MJ shook his head. "But I said you were a good guy, a real good guy. Said you'd never stiff me." He took a deep breath. "When you didn't pay up, I gave her the other two hundred out of my own pocket. I couldn't admit I'd been wrong. Plus she needs the money. She needs it real bad. *We* need it real bad."

Jack cursed under his breath. Now she'd be pushing MJ for the next four hundred, and he probably couldn't come close to covering it this week. He felt his palms sweating on the steering wheel as he pulled the Citation to a stop at the next red light. People, he thought. They never stopped surprising you. MJ had covered him and never said a word. Christ, now he *had* to get him the money. "What were you saving up for?"

"What do you mean?"

"Those two hundred bucks you covered me with. You must have been saving up for something if you had it lying around. Most kids your age spend money as soon as they get it unless they're saving for something. What were you saving for?"

MJ put his head back against the seat and closed his eyes. "Christmas," he answered softly. "We didn't have Christmas this year. No presents, no nothing. I don't want that to ever happen to my brothers and sisters again. And especially not to my momma."

* * *

"You're so beautiful." Bobby kissed Ginny as they lay on his bed. Ginny was the woman from the gym he'd wanted Cheryl to spend a day with going to the hair salon, nail place, and boutiques. They'd happened to run into each other forty minutes ago at a bar a few blocks from the apartment building. Ginny's husband was away on business for the next few days, and Bobby had jumped on the opportunity. There was no way he was going to introduce her to Cheryl now. Of course, now that he was moving to Atlanta, who cared? Better that Cheryl not meet anyone else he knew at this point. "I love your dark hair, I really do."

Ginny laughed sarcastically. "Bobby, you wouldn't care if I was brunette, a blonde, or a redhead right now. Hell, you wouldn't care if my hair was green. All you care about is that my husband's away, I'm bored out of my mind, and I'm in your bed naked. Don't lay all that sweet stuff on me. It insults me." She raised one eyebrow. "You're getting what you want, I'm getting what I want. Now let's do it."

The rumor at the gym was that Ginny got around, she didn't give a damn about her husband anymore, and when she hopped in the sack, she was wild. As Bobby moved his hands up her belly to her full breasts, she let out a little shriek.

"What? What is it?"

"Jesus," she said, with a hiss, wide-eyed. "What was that?"

"What was—" Bobby stopped at the sound of a loud knock on the apartment door.

"Get off me," she said, pushing him to one side and scooting over. "What are we going to do? Christ, what if that's my husband? What if he's having me followed?"

She put her hands to her face. "Damn it, I knew this was going to happen."

Bobby grabbed her arm, pulled her off the bed, made her gather her clothes up off the floor, then guided her toward the living room. "Get in the closet," he ordered, yanking open the hall door and hurrying her into the tight space beside a stack of luggage. "Go on. Go on!" He shut the door behind her, then his eyes flashed across the darkened living room as the knocking came again, louder this time. "Dear Lord," he whispered, glad that Ginny didn't wear a lot of perfume, "please get me out of this."

He hurried back to the bedroom, slipped on a pair of boxers, then retraced his steps past the hall closet toward the apartment front door. He hesitated with his hand inches from the knob when the knocking came again. He had a pistol in the drawer of his bedroom nightstand. If Ginny's husband was on the other side of the door, maybe he ought to get it.

"Who is it?" he asked loudly.

"Me, you dope."

Cheryl! Holy Christ!

"I've got a surprise for you," she called. "Something you're going to really like."

"Shit," he whispered, eyes flashing around. What the hell was he supposed to do now?

"Open up, baby," she called impatiently, "come on. I don't want to stand out here for long. You'll see why."

He had no choice if he wanted to keep having his fun, if he wanted to keep pushing her. He had to let her in. He crossed his fingers and opened the door. Here went nothing.

She stood before him wearing a raincoat and high heels. As he watched in amazement, she let the long coat slip from her shoulders and fall to the floor of the landing outside his door, revealing her naked body beneath. Then she stepped into the apartment, put her arms around his neck, and kissed him deeply.

"You can do whatever you want to me tonight," she whispered when their lips parted. "Anything."

He scooped her up in his big arms, carried her to the bedroom, laid her on the mattress, and kissed her passionately. "I love you. You're incredible."

"Well," she said softly, "it took me awhile to get my nerve up, but I'm glad I did."

"Me, too."

"It's crazy, but I told myself I had to—"

"Wait here one second, will you?" he interrupted, rising up off the bed. "I'll be right back."

"What's the matter?" she asked. "Where are you going?"

He smiled. "Don't move, sweetheart. Stay right there. I just need to throw out the trash."

Jack had inputted everything he could think of into the search engine: "major league baseball box scores," "Yankee box scores," "Mickey Mantle box scores," and a few more. But nothing was coming up. He wanted to throw the damn screen against the wall because MJ was turning out to be right—he didn't have any idea what he was doing. He almost pounded the table instead, but caught himself at the last second. He didn't want to wake

Rosario. Cheryl hadn't followed through on her threat to move the computer into the living room yet, and the baby was asleep on the floor in her makeshift bed just a few feet away, surrounded by pillows. He was the only one home, and he didn't want to be up all night with the little girl.

As reluctant as he'd been to let Cheryl go to Bobby's this late, he'd relented. He'd seen that desperate look in her eyes and felt terrible. The least he could do was give her a night off.

He let out a long sigh, thinking about Cheryl going over there this late. The bastard better not do anything to her. He might be old, but he could still take care of Bobby Griffin. Maybe he was no match for the young man physically, but that wouldn't matter if he took his gun.

He stood up just enough to peer over the pillows, just to make sure Rosario was still asleep, and instantly wished he hadn't. She was staring back at him with those big brown eyes. He ducked down, hoping she hadn't seen him, but she started cooing right away. A sure sign she wanted to be picked up.

"Damn it," he muttered under his breath. Rosario could be up for hours now, and she'd start screaming if he left her in here alone. "All right, all right." It wasn't like he was making any progress on the computer anyway. "Here we go," he murmured, reaching down and picking her up.

As he did, she broke into a huge smile and reached for his face with her tiny fingers. "Dada!" she said loudly. "Dada!"

Jack gazed at the little girl, that old uncontrollable

emotion bearing down on him. Like it had the night
Cheryl called him out for faking a heart attack at the stadium. When he'd been scared out of his mind she might
really leave him.

He pressed the baby gently to his chest. Maybe it was
stupid, but he didn't want Rosario to see him cry.

26

TREVISO LAY NEXT to Karen as she slept, admiring her beauty as he stroked her dark hair. Admiring himself for being able to marry a woman as beautiful as she. Finally he clasped her delicate chin with his fingers and shook it, rousing her.

Her eyes fluttered open and she looked around groggily. "Hi, honey," she mumbled. "What is it?"

He let his fingers fall from her chin, making sure he *really* wanted to say this because you could never be a hundred percent sure you could trust anyone—even your wife. "You awake?"

"Yeah."

"You sure?"

"*Yes*, Tony."

"Okay, okay. Look, you remember when you told me how that guy made a pass at you in the car when I was collecting the VIG from him that day? How he said he wanted to meet up with you later while I was in the bodega?"

Karen rose up on her elbow. "Of course I remember. Why?"

For a few moments Treviso relived the absolute hatred he'd felt for that man when she'd told him the story. The almost uncontrollable jealousy. And the intense pleasure he'd taken exacting his revenge. "I loved you for that. I mean, I love you for a lot of reasons, but I was happy you told me what happened. It made me feel good. It made me feel like I could always trust you."

She smiled at him sweetly. "I'm glad it made you feel good. You know you can always trust me." She stroked his cheek, waiting for more. "Is that why you woke me up, Tony? To tell me that?"

He took her chin in his fingers again and looked her straight in the eyes. "Can I *really* always trust you?"

"Of course. Why would you even ask me—"

"You know what I did to that guy, don't you?" he interrupted, his tone turning forceful. "You know how it ended up for him?"

"I, I—"

"You heard Paulie when he came over here that time, didn't you?" He and Paulie were close, but it wasn't like Paulie came to the apartment that much. Usually they met out. "You heard what Paulie said about that guy, about what happened to him. How his wife got his head in the mail?" They were in the other room when Paulie was talking about it, but it was a small apartment, and you could hear everything. Even if you were in another room and you weren't trying to listen.

Karen's eyes widened. Still, she said nothing.

"I love you so much, Karen, and I'd never blame you if a man came on to you. You're beautiful, and men are tempted real easy by women who are nowhere near as good-looking as you," Treviso added. "It's our nature." He shook his head. "But it doesn't matter. I could never forgive a guy who actually tried to make a move on you. They can look, but they can't ask." He let out a low breath. This was harder than he'd anticipated. "I don't know what I'd do to the next one. I really don't. And I got people who'd help me do whatever I decided to do, too. You know? Not just Paulie. There's others. You know that, don't you?"

She nodded.

This was what he was trying to tell her. The real reason he'd roused her from a sound sleep. "The only things I would ever blame you for are screwing around on me behind my back and leaving me. I'd never forgive you for those things, Karen. If I came home one day and you weren't here, or I found out you were screwing somebody, I'd go crazy. You know?"

She nodded again.

His fingertips tightened on her delicate chin. "I mean it," he said, his tone turning tough. "Do you understand me? Do you *fucking* understand me?"

"Yes," she said quietly, not trying to escape his fingers despite how tightly he was clasping her.

"I hope so because my boys would help me track you down. We'd never stop until we found you." He shrugged, like once the process had started it would be irreversible. Like there'd be no room for explanations or second chances when they found her. Like Marconi shrugged when he gave out a warning. Quiet but chilling. "And it wouldn't go well for you when we found you." It was something he'd heard Marconi say, and he loved how scary it sounded.

"No." Her voice was barely audible. "I'm sure it wouldn't."

"You can't blame me, can you? After all, I'm a man," he added lamely, "an *Italian* man. If you ever left me, I'd find you and I'd kill you. It's that simple."

"I know."

"I've taken care of you," he kept going, "I've given you a good life." He gestured around the dimly lit room. "I mean, look at this place. Look at all the nice things you have. And you were on welfare when I met you."

"I know. You saved me, you rescued me. You gave me a chance, a fresh start. I'll never be able to repay you. But I'll always be true to you."

Treviso hesitated. He liked how submissive she was being. It was turning him on. "You sure you understand me, Karen?"

"Yes."

"*Very* sure?"

"Very sure."

"Everything I've said?"

"Everything."

He let go of her chin and caressed her cheek gently. "All right, then." He lay down and pulled her close, wrapping one arm around her shoulder. "I'm glad we talked. Now we can go to sleep. Now *I* can go to sleep."

A few moments later Karen rose again so she was over him, so their lips were close. "Did you really do that, Tony? Did you really kill that man who came on to me in the car?" Her voice had turned husky. "I mean, I heard you did, but I never really knew for sure. And I didn't feel like I could ask you," she said, sliding her soft inner thigh over his leg. "Because you always told me not to ask you about exactly what you do. So, did you?" she asked again when he didn't answer, running her fingernails down his stomach ever so slowly. Moving her thigh even farther over his. "Tell me."

Treviso stared into her burning eyes, feeling himself becoming incredibly aroused. "Yeah, I did."

Then she was over him and he was inside her and they were going at it like two crazy teenagers in the back of a station wagon.

27

ROSARIO USUALLY WOKE at seven in the morning like a rooster on steroids. Singing and shrieking her soft-as-a-rose-petal bottom off. Then she drank an entire bottle of formula, ate a mush mix of prunes and apples or something else equally as unappetizing-looking, pooped like a human five times her size, ate more mush mix, teeter-tottered around the house in her drunken-sailor-hands-at-her-ears-just-learning-to-walk walk, and pooped again. By eight o'clock she was back in her makeshift bed in Cheryl's room taking her first nap of the day. It all happened before Cheryl left for work—which made Jack very happy. He was coming to love the little girl very much. He just wasn't much for the nuts-and-bolts stuff involved with taking care of infants—feeding, changing, entertaining. For God's sake, he hadn't been like that with his own flesh and blood. How could Cheryl expect him to be like that with Rosario?

Generally, he took the last fifteen minutes of the first morning shift, albeit grudgingly. Managing to crawl out of bed and trudge to the kitchen by quarter to eight so Cheryl could at least have a few minutes to herself before leaving the house. It wasn't a bad stretch of duty because it mostly entailed simply sitting at the kitchen table in his boxers, faded scotch-plaid bathrobe, and white socks and sipping a hot cup of coffee while he watched the baby teeter-totter around. All he had to do was make sure Rosario didn't pull anything breakable off tables or walls and smash it. Which would have been pretty much impossible at this point because they'd moved anything that wasn't nailed down off the tables and taken down everything hanging on the walls from three feet up all the way down to the floor so she couldn't get to them.

Jack liked to say they'd raised their standard of living since Rosario had arrived, because everything that had been anywhere within her reach was now higher up. Cheryl didn't seem to find that amusing. Probably, Jack figured, because she did the lion's share of caring for Rosario and therefore the lion's share of protecting their breakables. She was even coming home at lunch-time to make sure the baby was all right—and to get her fix. Taking a long time away from the office in the middle of the day, which worried Jack. They needed Cheryl's income now more than ever, and he could only assume that her boss wasn't happy about the two-hour-plus lunch breaks.

He'd finally told Cheryl what had happened, that he'd lost his job at Publix. It had been pretty obvious after a week. But probably because they had Rosario, Cheryl hadn't seemed as upset as he'd anticipated. Probably because she knew that if he was still working during the day, they wouldn't have been able to keep her. Money was going to be a real problem soon, but neither one of them had brought it up yet.

The state trooper who'd begged Jack to take Rosario "for a few days" at the accident had never called. Though, to be fair, they'd never called him, either. Once in a while Cheryl got frustrated with the constant responsibility of motherhood—the way any new mom would—but Jack could tell she'd also become permanently attached to the little girl. That it would kill her not to have Rosario in her life. So he'd never made the SOS call. He did check the local newspaper's metro section every day for any stories about a little girl being missing. It had occurred to him that they could be arrested for kidnapping at this point—a minor detail that could land them in the state pen for ten to twenty. But nothing had ever appeared in the press. The guy in the Mustang must have ultimately bought the story about the little girl dying in the crash along with his wife. Just like he'd wanted. The bastard.

Biff hadn't called with a live situation yet, either. Hadn't called with an opportunity to steal some poor old person blind when he or she was most vulnerable. Which was good—and bad. Jack owed MJ six hundred bucks. And he'd owe him another four hundred on top of that in a few days. Cheryl's thin cash reserves were quickly draining away, and his earnings as an usher were meager. Bottom line: they were staring at an imminent cash crisis. He needed money terribly, but he didn't want to do a terrible thing to get it. What Biff wanted him to do was worse than terrible, it was evil. But he couldn't take a day job—which would have solved their money problem—because of Rosario. Someone had to be home with her. And they didn't want anyone else taking care of her, didn't want to have to deal with prying questions about who she was and where she'd come from. As it was, Jack felt uncomfortable with Bobby knowing the little girl was with them. Sooner or later he'd start asking why Rosario was still around.

As he'd been lying in bed late last night watching minutes pass like hours on the digital clock sitting on his nightstand next to pictures of Cheryl and David, waiting impatiently for morning and his chance to call the Elias Sports Bureau, Jack had convinced himself he was still a good man. Convinced himself that his momentary self-doubt at the stadium last night in front of Lester had been unfounded, and that he really was trying to unlock the mystery of Mikey Clemant for pure reasons. That he was trying to understand what was going on with the Kid because he wanted to see a young man with so much talent have a chance at the big time. And for the big time to have a chance at a young man with so much talent. That he was doing it for the love of the game. Not for money, not even for retribution. That he wasn't doing anything just because he felt poorer now than he ever had in his life. That he wasn't being driven by the gut-wrenching fear of suddenly being destitute.

He rubbed his face as he shuffled down the hallway toward the kitchen. Wiping sleep from the corners of his eyes as he moved slowly ahead. Thinking hard about what he'd do if Biff called, how he'd feel about himself if he yielded to the temptation. Well, then he'd have no choice but to accept the fact that he was a bad man. A *very* bad man.

"Hi, honey," he said gruffly, moving toward a fresh pot of wonderful-smelling Vermont roast—his favorite. She was so good to him. She always made certain he was taken care of, even with Rosario in their lives now. "How are you this morning?"

"Fine."

Cheryl was feeding Rosario her second helping of morning mush, and her back was to him. "You okay?" Her voice sounded funny, and she usually trotted over before he started pouring his coffee and gave him a big good morning hug and a kiss on his cheek. Maybe she and Bobby had a fight last night. How great would that be? Maybe his luck was suddenly changing? It seemed like it had been nothing but rotten for four years. Maybe the law of averages was finally catching up. "Princess?"

"I'm fine, Daddy."

Jack poured a cup of coffee, putting his head slowly back and taking a deep breath as the warm, pleasing aroma rose to his nostrils. "What time did you get home?" he asked, taking a cautious sip of the steaming liquid. Almost instantly he felt his hands beginning to shake and a buzz permeating his entire body. But it wasn't just the coffee bringing on the sensation. It was anticipation, too. The hope that the call he'd make to New York in a few minutes would unlock the Mikey Clemant mystery.

He assumed the Elias offices would be open by nine, so he had only a little more than an hour to go. Only a little more than an hour before he might be able to get his hands on the 1968 May and June Yankee box scores to see if his memory had served him right. He'd already made his deal with the devil on this one. If whoever he spoke to at Elias confirmed that the company had the data but that it was going to cost him to get it, he'd pay. Then do Biff's bidding—and make restitution later. "Princess?"

"I got home around four, Daddy," Cheryl answered, picking up Rosario's plastic dishes and taking them to the sink. "Keep an eye on her for me, will you?"

"Sure." He began to unbuckle the baby from her high chair as Cheryl walked away. "Wait a minute," he murmured, the possibility hitting him hard. "Be right back, kiddo," he called over his shoulder to the baby, hobbling down the hallway after Cheryl.

"Daddy!" Cheryl grabbed a towel off a rack and quickly wrapped it around herself when Jack appeared at the doorway to her tiny bathroom. She'd been naked from the waist up, washing her face. "What are you doing coming in here like this?"

"Let me see your face," he demanded. She was turned away from him, positioned so he couldn't see her image in the medicine cabinet mirror, either. "Come on, Princess."

"No."

He grabbed her arm and tried to turn her. "Cheryl!"

"Get out of here, Daddy! *Get out!*"

"Look at me, Princess."

"No. Let me run my own life, Daddy. Stop running it for me. Stop keeping me all to yourself."

Jack could hear the baby beginning to wail from the kitchen. The little girl took her cues now from the woman who had become her mother. "Princess, I just want to—"

"Get out!" Cheryl shrieked, finally turning to face

him. *"Get out or I'll leave right now and I won't ever come back!"*

Jack staggered back several steps. Red blotches covered her neck. Fingerprints. Bobby's fingerprints. His hands had been wrapped tightly around her slender throat last night. "I'll kill him," he said, gasping. "And I don't care what the cops do after that."

"You won't go anywhere near him."

"I can't let him do this—"

"It's just sex, Daddy."

Jack turned his head and winced, like he was watching Rosario's mother burn on that dashboard again. The image of Cheryl being abused by Bobby was almost as bad. "Princess, please don't—"

"He's a little rough sometimes. But it's nothing I can't handle."

"It'll get rougher and rougher," Jack warned. He'd been a witness to this same scenario a long time ago. Had a front-row seat to this same horror show when he was a teenager. This was exactly how it had started with his father and mother. And it had only gotten worse and worse until finally his mother had "slipped" one night in the bathroom when he was fourteen—and never opened her eyes again. A terrible accident, the police called it. Which couldn't have been further from the truth. But what was he supposed to do? Turn in his father? "One night you won't be able to handle it, Princess. One night it'll get too rough. You gotta believe me."

"I love Bobby." Cheryl's voice was shaking, and there were tears perched perilously close to the edge of her lower lids. "I love him so much, Daddy. I'm going to give him everything he wants, everything he needs."

"He doesn't *need* to take advantage of you. He doesn't *need* to hurt you."

"He's not hurting me!" she yelled, grabbing her hair with both hands and pulling hard, like the conflict raging inside was driving her insane. The towel fell to the floor. "He loves me."

"Just let me talk to him, Princess," Jack begged. He wanted to tell Cheryl what had happened to her grandmother, how she hadn't really slipped on that bathroom floor so many years ago. The real reason he hadn't gone to her grandfather's funeral. "Just talk. That's all I'll do." He bent down, picked up the towel, and held it out for her. "Please."

Cheryl grabbed it and wrapped it around herself again, then pointed a shaking finger at him. "If I find out you talked to Bobby, even *tried* to talk to him, I'll leave you forever. I'll take Rosario and leave, and you'll never find us."

Jack stared at her for several moments, expecting her to rush into his arms the way she always did when they fought. Expecting her to realize how hurtful what she'd said had been and suddenly feel that avalanche of guilt she always felt. Please, Princess, he kept thinking, come to me and wrap your arms around me. I'll make everything better. Like I always do.

Then her chin began to quiver and the tears tumbled down her cheeks. He stepped forward, unable to wait any longer, but she took a step back and held one hand up.

"I've got to get dressed, Daddy," she managed to say, sobbing. "Go take care of the baby."

"Princess, I can't leave you like this. Can't we—"

"Go call my brother and talk to him about baseball. You always did love David more than me."

Jack spread his arms. "*What?* Where did that come from? How could you possibly think I love your brother more than you?"

"You sacrificed everything for him, Daddy," Cheryl whispered. "You gave up your life for him. You've never done that for me." She shut her eyes tightly, and the tears flowed like rivers. "Now *get out!*"

28

J OHNNY CHECKED HIS watch for the third time in the past five minutes as he stood in the Brooklyn parking lot beside his freshly washed Seville. He leaned against the driver's-side door and pulled out a pack of Parliament 100s he'd bought at a bodega up the street. He never smoked, *hated* cigarette smoke. Made people put out cigarettes in his presence—like he'd made Treviso put out the one at the apartment. Never smoked.

Except when he was feeling intense pressure.

Like those few minutes before he actually iced a man or right before he got to the graveyard with the two dozen roses on the passenger seat beside him. Johnny only smoked when he was *really* feeling pressure—like he was now. In fact, this was as bad as it had ever been. He could actually feel his hands shaking, feel himself sweating. And he *never* sweated.

He lit up the first cigarette as raindrops began spitting down from an overcast sky. "*Shit,*" he muttered, taking a long drag and looking up. "Of course, now that I had the damn car washed."

"Never fails," agreed a middle-aged woman with thick calves who was walking past on the sidewalk. She was pulling a cart full of fresh fruit and vegetables she'd bought at the stand on the corner in front of the bodega. "Know what I mean?"

Why was she being so friendly? Johnny wondered. This was Brooklyn, deep in Brooklyn. People didn't go out of their way to be friendly here. People didn't go out of their way to be friendly anywhere in New York City—except maybe in lower Manhattan sometimes. But not here. *Especially* not here.

He eyed her suspiciously as she tugged the cart along. What was her angle? Was she following him? He felt better when she grunted and gave him the finger. But that could all be part of the act, too.

He let out a long, frustrated breath. The pressure was getting to him. Plain and simple. *Way* getting to him. He was trying to keep too many balls in the air at once, and it was making him paranoid. Making him suspect everyone of everything. But it was a product of the life he'd chosen, which was the worst part about it. He'd always been sure he could keep everything under control—but he'd been dead wrong.

He took another puff off the cigarette. The premonition of peril was rearing its ugly head a lot lately, and he'd come to trust that premonition. Of course, maybe it was coming around so often because he was doing more things he had to hide than he ever had before. And maybe that thing Marconi always said was having its effect, too. That all deeds done in the dark eventually and inevitably came to light.

Who the hell was that guy leaning against the lamppost in front of the bodega? He seemed vaguely familiar, but then everyone seemed vaguely familiar lately. Jesus Christ. Jesus *freaking* Christ.

He checked his watch again. Karen was twelve minutes late. Something must have gone wrong. Terribly wrong.

29

JACK SAT DOWN glumly in front of the computer. It had been a seminal point in their relationship. The power had shifted completely in the blink of an eye, in the time it took to remember how much he loved the aroma of Vermont Roast wafting toward him down the hallway each morning as he shuffled to the kitchen, knees throbbing. Cheryl had made it very clear that if he confronted Bobby about the rough stuff, he'd be alone forever in this good-for-nothing ranch house. That she'd leave and never return. He'd seen in her eyes that she was absolutely serious. That she was finally so sick of him running her life she didn't care what Bobby did to her as long as she believed they were in love. And he knew she'd seen the fear of God in his eyes. The terror that she really would leave him, and he'd be completely alone.

He'd stepped toward her with open arms—the first

time he'd ever made the first move—but she'd stepped back. She hadn't even given him a kiss when she'd left a few minutes later. Just called from the front door that she'd see him at lunch. He'd lost his influence over her, every ounce of it. She could tell him to do whatever she wanted now, and he'd have to do it—or lose her. He'd finally pushed too far. The bitterness of being ordered around and made to feel guilty for so many years had ultimately reached a breaking point. And he was helpless to do anything about it.

The phone sat on the table beside the computer. His fingers trembled as he reached for it, but this time out of fear, not anticipation. The thought of Cheryl not coming home had shaken him to his core. He didn't know if he could do this anymore, didn't know if he even wanted to. His drive to do anything seemed to have suddenly evaporated.

"Christ," he muttered angrily, "make the call." He gritted his teeth and pressed the buttons, starting with the 212 area code. "You have to. This is all you got left."

"Information. How can I help you?"

Here went nothing. "In Manhattan," he said, "I need the number for the Elias Sports Bureau."

"The what?"

"The Elias Sports Bureau," he repeated, louder.

"Hold please."

The operator was back a moment later with the number. Instead of being directly connected, he jotted it down. He never liked being rushed into anything. After he collected his thoughts, he made the call.

"Good morning, this is the Elias Sports Bureau." The woman at the other end of the line had a shrill, nasal voice. She was peppy and full of enthusiasm. "How can I help you?"

"I'm . . . I'm looking for some information about baseball," Jack answered hesitantly.

"What kind of information?"

"I want to know a few things about Mickey Mantle."

"What about Mickey Mantle?"

"I'm trying to dig up some old box—"

"Hold, please."

"Yeah, but . . ." A moment later the line was ringing again.

"Baseball."

The male voice was hushed and secretive-sounding. "Yes, hello." Instinctively, Jack lowered his voice, too. He waited for the guy to ask how he could help, but there was nothing but silence from the other end of the line. "I'm looking for some baseball information."

"I know."

Jack took a deep breath. "Right, well, I . . . look, I—"

"What's your name?"

Jack held the receiver in front of him and gave it a curious look. "*Why?*" he asked after he'd brought it back to his ear.

"*What's your name?*"

"Jack Barrett. What does that have to—"

"What do you do?"

"I'm retired. Well, I mean I do some odd jobs, but I'm retired from what I used to—"

"What did you *used* to do?"

Why the hell was the guy acting so strange? Well, he wasn't going to feed the fire. Hearing he'd been a Yankee scout might make the guy clam up for some reason. "I was an insurance salesman." There was a long pause at the other end. "Hello?"

"What kind of information do you want?"

"Look, what's the big deal? Why are you grilling me?"

"What kind of information do you want?" the man repeated.

"Stuff on baseball."

"I know that. *Exactly* what kind of information?"

"Box scores. I want to see some old box scores."

"I thought this had to do with Mickey Mantle."

"It does. I want to look up some of his old games. I'm actually looking for one in particular."

"How far back do you need to go? Seasons, I mean."

"Nineteen-sixty-eight. His last." Another pause from the other end of the line. Even longer this time. "Can you guys help me?" Jack pushed. "Look, I'm willing to pay."

"I'm not supposed to tell you this," the guy finally said, his voice just a whisper. "But it would cost you a couple of grand to get this from us."

Jack's heart sank. A couple of grand? He was going to have to call Biff, not wait for Biff to call him. "It's gonna be tough for me to pay you that kind of dough. I'm living on a fixed—"

"Retrosheet-dot-org."

"Huh?"

"That's the website you want," the guy said evenly. "It's www.retrosheet.org. Everything you need is there. Okay? That's all I'm gonna tell you. Bye." Then the line went dead.

Jack slammed the receiver down and scrambled to Cheryl's nightstand for the pen and paper she kept there next to her phone. His hand shook as he wrote down what he thought he'd heard the guy say: w-w-w-dot-r-e-t-r-o-s-h-e-e-t-dot-o-r-g. Shook so badly he took a couple of breaths and wrote the website again because the first try was almost illegible. Then he hurried back to the computer, typed in the letters, and pressed "go." Almost instantly the screen flashed a message indicating that the site couldn't be found. "Damn it." He didn't want to have to call Elias back, didn't have any faith he'd get the same guy or, if he did, that the guy would spell the website out for him again. "Oh, shit." He noticed that he'd typed in www.rAtrosheet .org. No wonder. He corrected the typo, then pressed "go" again.

This time the site came up instantly. "Jesus," he whispered, his eyes widening. It was as if he'd just found the Holy Grail. "My God."

He slid the mouse to the third option down from the top—Box Scores—and clicked. The next page was called The Directory of Major League Years. On it were all years from 2008 back to 1871. He clicked on 1968. Next: Final Standings—the final record of all major-league teams in 1968. He clicked on the New York Yankees. Now there were several choices, but he slid the arrow directly to Game Log. As if someone or something were moving the mouse for him. Or maybe he'd just suddenly figured out how to skate quickly around the Web. Maybe it had finally hit him despite MJ's dire predictions. Either way, the experience seemed otherworldly.

When the next page came up, his fingers began shaking all over again. But this time out of elation. There were two choices: Date or Box + PBP. He moved the arrow directly to the second choice and clicked, and the world opened up in front of him. Suddenly he was staring at box scores for all games the Yankees had played in 1968. He scrolled down to May 30 and clicked.

"My God," he whispered as he gazed at the information, barely able to breathe.

On May 30, 1968, Mickey Mantle had gone five-for-five with three runs scored and five runs batted in.

Exactly as Mikey Clemant had yesterday. Exactly as Mikey Clemant had on May 30, 2008.

Jack scrolled down farther. Beneath the box score was an inning-by-inning account of the game. A play-by-play summary. He nodded as he read, his mind racing back to that day in 1968. The game had been played at Yankee Stadium against the old Washington Senators. Sure, that was right, he remembered now. The Senators. A few years later they'd moved to Texas and become the Rangers.

Jack touched the screen gently with his finger, following the progression of at-bats down. Fascinated by what he was reading. In the first, Mantle had hit a home run. In the third, he'd singled. In the fifth, he'd hit another home run. In the seventh, he'd doubled, and in the ninth, he'd singled again. Jack read through the play-by-play over and over, running through last night's Tarpon game in his mind. Going over the Kid's at-bats as he gazed at the record of Mantle's at-bats.

Suddenly Jack's eyes widened, literally like he'd seen a ghost. He clicked back to check the previous game the Yankees had played in 1968. It was on May 26. Must have been a couple of rainouts given the three days off, he figured. He glanced at the box score. Mantle had gone one-for-four with a single in the seventh. He stared at the stats for a second, then shot up out of the chair and headed as fast as he could toward the back door, where they kept the trash cans and the paper recycling tub right outside. When he was through the screen door, he knelt down and went through newspapers from the past few days until he found the sports sections for May 26. He thumbed through the pages, searching for the Tarpon box score. Finally he found it. Mikey Clemant had gone one-for-four with a single on May 26—just as Mickey Mantle had forty years before. The tiny gray hairs on the back of Jack's neck stood straight up.

Slowly Jack lay back until he was supine on the ground staring up at the blue sky, the prickly feeling taking over his entire body. On May 30, 2008, the Kid had posted the same hits Mickey Mantle had posted in his Yankee game forty years earlier—in *exactly* the same order. Home run, single, home run, double, single. And on May 26, 2008, the Kid had posted the same hits as Mickey Mantle had in his Yankee game forty years earlier. Again, in *exactly* the same order. Jack shook his head as he lay beside the recyclables tub. Coincidence? Not likely. A billion-to-one shot. And if it wasn't coincidence? Well . . . he shut his eyes tightly. He couldn't let himself think that. Not yet, anyway. He'd finish the research. Then maybe let his imagination run wild. If the Kid could hit a ball where he wanted to whenever he wanted to, there was no telling how good he really was. Even if this was Single-A.

30

JOHNNY WAS ABOUT to take the last long drag on his fourth cigarette, climb back into his rain-spotted Seville, get out of here, and be done with it. About to say the hell with everything and say good-bye forever to Tony Treviso and his psychopathic switch—and Angelo Marconi and his obsession. Then he saw Karen coming down the block on the opposite side of the street, pushing a stroller. And suddenly he knew why he'd found that tiny reservoir of patience to make it through four cigarettes. Why he probably would have waited here all day if he had to.

My God, she was gorgeous. So gorgeous the cigarette tumbled from his mouth and he didn't even realize it for a few moments. So gorgeous he suddenly became acutely aware of how careful they had to be. Tony Treviso was probably as jealous a husband as there was in New York

City. It had to have been a fit of insane jealousy that had flipped Treviso's switch to the on position that night. A mind-blowing, uncontrollable rage brought on by the mark making a move on Karen that had caused Treviso to temporarily lose his mind and chop the guy's head off, stuff a dead rat in the mouth, and send it to the wife. What the hell else could have made him do it? The mark had repaid the fifty grand. Paid every cent of interest and fees owed. Johnny had confirmed those facts with a Lucchesi contact in Brooklyn. What else could turn a 145-pound weakling who couldn't even watch his marks get roughed up into a monster who could carry out such an atrocity?

Treviso must have realized when Karen married him that he'd never find another girl like her. He must have realized she was way too pretty for him—and way too sweet. Must have understood then that his relationship with her was at serious risk anytime she stepped outside the apartment without him. Anytime she came into contact with another man who had more going for him than Treviso. Which was almost every other man she came into contact with. He also had to realize she was going to be taken away at some point, had to realize she would leave when a better offer presented itself. That there was no way he could hope to hold on to her forever. The outcome was inevitable.

Unless he did something about it.

Tony Treviso was a sickly little man. A man who would have been laughed at by even those coyote-ugly girls in the Brooklyn meat-market bars. And he had no career prospects. None whatsoever. He was gonna be a two-bit loan shark the rest of his life because the bosses would never let him get rich and never let him do anything else. That was how it went with loan sharks. You made okay money, but nothing spectacular because if you did too well, the bosses simply upped their percentage of your operations. And if you tried to leave the family with some money that wasn't technically yours, you'd be hunted down and killed, plain and simple.

So at some point Treviso must have made a blood oath with himself to kill anyone who tried to make a move on Karen. The bosses wouldn't rub him out for that. In fact, they'd love it. They wanted the Lucchesi family name to bring terror to the hearts of their enemies. What better way to do that than to have their enemies think that even the weakest of their members—a man who looked like a runt—was a psychopathic killer?

Johnny had told Karen about the man who'd been decapitated, about how her husband had been responsible for the murder.

She said she didn't believe it. Admitted hearing whispers about it, but she assumed it was just talk. Like most things mob guys said, she figured. Most of their stories were just exaggerations and distortions intended to intimidate others and build reputations—nothing more. This was just another of those stories.

Johnny tried to convince her that this time it wasn't just talk, that she needed to be careful. That at some point she'd have to leave Treviso or risk her own life the day he flew into a jealous rage when she couldn't resist any longer and happened to glance lustfully at another man. She'd asked Johnny if he was to be the one to rescue her if the story was true. He'd said yes—though not with conviction.

Because he wasn't being completely honest with her. He hadn't reached the point of no return.

Not yet, anyway.

The wild thing about it, the absolutely insane, *crazy* part about everything—he was actually considering it. Actually considering making his move, and taking care of Treviso's son like he was his own. In the short time they'd known each other, Karen had touched him so deeply he was actually thinking about it as he lay in bed at night trying to fall asleep. Trying desperately to erase her gorgeous image from his mind. She'd made him realize she could be the one to erase all those lonely nights. She could be the one he could love and who could love him. The one who could fill his hollow existence and make him whole again.

There was only one problem. Tony Treviso. And his psychopathic switch. That was the only sticky thing about this situation, Johnny told himself every time he edged closer to committing to this insane idea. The thing that made it all so complicated. If he stole Karen from Treviso, he'd have to kill Treviso. There could be no other way. Which wouldn't be a problem for an assassin like Johnny.

Except that Timid Tony was with the Lucchesi family. It wasn't like he was a guy that anybody who really mattered cared about on a personal level, but that didn't matter. As long as you were with the family, they took care of you. It was what kept everybody loyal to one another. Knowing they had protection. To kill Treviso and not have to worry about retribution, Johnny would need permission for the hit from Marconi, because no one questioned Marconi. And getting Marconi's okay on the hit shouldn't have been a problem, either. Marconi could be convinced. Unless, of course, the old man was starting to get suspicious about how the whole Kyle McLean thing was going. Unless Marconi had figured out that Johnny was sticking to his code of honor. Because he was more and more convinced all the time that Kyle McLean was no more responsible for the death of Marconi's grandson than Marconi himself.

Then getting Marconi's permission to kill Treviso would be a problem.

Johnny made it seem like he wasn't watching Karen as she moved past on the other side of the street, made it seem like he wasn't watching her slim, sexy body like a hawk. His eyes were hidden behind dark, wraparound sunglasses, and he made it seem like he was looking up the block at the bodega. But his eyes were actually straining to the far right side of his sockets, as far as they would go. Straining to keep tabs on her.

Then it dropped to the sidewalk. Something in a white envelope. Karen's move had been ever so subtle, but he'd caught it. Now the envelope just looked like a piece of trash lying on the sidewalk.

Johnny checked up the block. The guy who'd been leaning against the streetlamp was gone. Still he hesitated a few more seconds. When he was certain the coast was clear, he jogged across the street toward the target.

31

"MRS. BILLUPS, I can't tell you how much I appreciate this. You keeping the baby and all."

Jack had completely forgotten about this afternoon. The Tarpons were playing a day game, and the first pitch was scheduled for four o'clock. Fortunately, MJ had called twenty minutes ago, at noon, anticipating Jack's memory lapse. Jack just hoped this wasn't a symptom of a bigger problem. His father had suffered from Alzheimer's, and he'd been thinking more and more about that lately. Counting the times he forgot things during an average day. Unfortunately, the number seemed to be climbing. When he could remember.

"I don't know what I would have done without you," he continued. "You're a lifesaver."

MJ's mother cradled Rosario in one of her big arms. Her two youngest were grabbing at either side of her long skirt as they gazed up at Jack, wide-eyed with uncertainty, not sure what to make of him. "One more child around this place won't make much difference."

He chuckled. "Your little ones seem kind of scared of me."

"Just wary."

"Why?"

"They don't see many men like you around here."

"I don't know what you—"

"White."

"Oh." Jack hesitated. "Well, they sure are beautiful," he said earnestly, motioning down toward the little ones clutching her skirt. "What are their names?"

"Vanessa and Jeffrey," she said proudly.

"Well, Vanessa and Jeffrey," Jack said, bending over and putting his hands on his knees, "you're two of the cutest things I've ever seen." They were, too. He wasn't just saying it. "I hope you grow up as smart as your older brother." He raised back up slowly, feeling the tenderness in his knees. "If every sixteen-year-old was like your son, it'd be a much better world. He's a good kid."

She gave MJ a sidelong glance, trying to hide a smile. "You pay him to say that?"

"No, ma'am."

"I guess I'll keep him," she said, finally allowing herself the smile.

"You should."

"And who is this little girl, Mr. Barrett?" she asked, rocking the baby gently. "Your granddaughter?"

"Yes," he answered deliberately, trying to remember if he'd said anything to MJ about the baby. Anything that would conflict with the story he was about to tell.

He didn't think he had. "Rosario is my son David's baby. He and his wife are on vacation." They were all standing out in front of the Billups family's small, clapboard house—which was in desperate need of repair. The white paint on the walls was peeling, the front door was hanging by one hinge, and the shingles on the roof were rotting. There were probably a lot more things wrong, but that was all he could see. "My daughter and I are taking care of her while they're away."

"She looks Hispanic. Is your daughter-in-law Hispanic?"

"Uh, no, ma'am." Yolanda Billups didn't pull any punches, didn't beat around any bushes. Didn't miss much, either. "She's adopted. My son, I—I mean his wife," Jack interrupted himself quickly, barely remembering the story he and Cheryl had come up with. "She can't have children."

"Mmm." Yolanda gazed at him evenly. "Did you get my son fired from Publix?"

"Well, um, I . . ." Jack stammered. He should have seen this one coming. "I didn't really get M—I mean *Curtis*—fired."

MJ had told him to make certain he used Curtis and not MJ in front of his mother. She hated the name MJ. It reminded her of her husband because he was the one who'd given MJ the nickname, and she hated remembering anything about her husband. Like Cheryl had told him to make sure he remembered that it was David's *wife* who couldn't have children. He rubbed his eyes for a moment, frustrated. God, he could feel old age creeping up on him again. Like he had at the accident. He could hardly keep all these things straight. Five years ago—

hell, *one* year ago—it wouldn't have been a problem.

"It was just an unfortunate situation, Mrs. Billups," Jack spoke up, trying to make his voice sound strong. "Wrong place, wrong time kind of thing. If you know what I mean."

"You can call me Yolanda. You gotta be at least twenty years older than me, Mr. Barrett. Somebody that old shouldn't be calling me Mrs. Billups. Besides, it makes me feel old when you call me that and I don't want to feel old."

"I sure know what you mean," he muttered under his breath. He passed a hand across his forehead to wipe away the perspiration. It was hot as hell out here—Lester's sticky-weather forecast had come early. The stadium was going to be like an oven this afternoon, especially with that stupid bus driver cap on.

"Then you got him this silly job as a batboy out at Tarpon Stadium," Yolanda continued.

"I thought it would be good for him to get something else quick so you didn't—"

"And you're supposed to be paying him four hundred a week," she cut in, "aren't you?"

Jack nodded.

"Why?" she asked suspiciously. "Why would you pay him that much to be a batboy on top of what the team's paying him? What's your angle? Do you own a piece of the Tarpons?"

He only wished he owned a piece of a baseball team. *Any* baseball team. "No, I don't." He hesitated, appreciating that she recognized that there had to be an angle here somewhere. That few people in the world ever did anything purely out of the goodness of their hearts. Even people who seemed like they were. "It's, it's complicated. I—"

"Out with it," she demanded. "Otherwise Curtis ain't going anywhere with you today."

"Momma," MJ spoke up, "don't treat me like a—"

"Curtis!" Yolanda snapped back, wagging a finger at him. "Hold your tongue, young man. Don't go disrespecting me like that. Especially in front of a stranger."

MJ spread his arms. "He's not a stranger, Momma, he's—"

"He is to me." Yolanda glanced back in Jack's direction, a defiant expression on her face. "Why are you paying Curtis four hundred dollars a week to be a batboy? I need to know. Tell me or he stays here with me."

32

LMOST EVERYONE IN the Mafia had a fatal flaw, an Achilles' heel with the potential to do them in. A big mouth; a rampant alcohol, drug, or sex addiction; unmitigated greed; the inability to work alone. Something that would inevitably cause them to slip and enable the cops to collect hard evidence, haul them in, and make charges stick. Or something that pissed off a rival family member so much that the person became a target. It turned out Tony Treviso was no different. He had a fatal flaw, too. With Karen's help, Johnny figured out what it was.

Turned out it was a big black book he kept buried beneath some clothes in the bottom of an old moving box in a corner of his bedroom closet. A black book that documented all his lending activities. A diary that detailed each loan he made, each time he tracked a mark down for payment; where he finally found them; how much he collected; and how much they still owed. So if they tried lying about anything, he had a written record of everything ready to shove in their faces—along with Paulie the Moon's fist. It was vitally important for a loan shark to do all that. But it was even more important for a loan shark not to tell anyone—even his wife—where he kept the diary. So, ultimately, Treviso's fatal flaw was his inability to keep a secret.

Johnny was heading down the sidewalk toward the body shop. Yup, that would be Treviso's undoing, just as it had been for so many of his brethren. Johnny wasn't like Treviso and the others in that way. He didn't have that overwhelming urge to share his innermost secrets, which was what made him so good at what he did, so bullet-proof. He killed people and never told a soul. Not even when he drank. Sure, the rumors ran around, but they were never started by him. Which was why the cops could never make anything stick. That and the defenses those Harvard boys made.

Treviso probably had as many as twenty loans out at any one time, Johnny figured. That was about the average. And there was no way he could keep them all straight in his head. The problem for Treviso was, if anyone found the diary, they would know everything about his activities. Of course, Treviso never figured that would happen. Never figured in a million years Karen would roll over on him.

But she had. The diary was what Karen had dropped to the pavement in the envelope as she'd pushed the baby stroller past the parking lot where Johnny was standing. Karen was petrified Treviso would discover the missing black book, so Johnny kept it for only twenty minutes. He'd raced across the street when she turned the corner, grabbed the envelope off the sidewalk, raced back to his car, then squealed off to another parking lot a mile away to study it, darting in and out of traffic so no one could possibly follow him. When he found what he was looking for in the diary, he headed straight back to the original drop site and replaced the package, just as Karen was wheeling the stroller around the corner on her way home. The timing had been perfect. And much as he'd wanted to stick around and gaze at her incredible beauty as she walked, he hadn't. Instead, he'd jumped in the Seville and peeled out.

Yeah, she was petrified of Treviso finding out the diary was gone, all right. But she claimed she was even more petrified of him cutting her head off one day if she looked at some guy the wrong way. She wanted out of her marriage yesterday now that she was sure the story about the severed head and the rat in the mouth was true. Yeah, Tony had bragged to her about doing it, but she'd dismissed it as just another of his wild attempts to impress her. Now that she knew he hadn't been lying, she wanted Johnny's help. And she wanted it now. He'd told her his plan, and she'd agreed immediately to help him in any way she could. She'd told him she'd never fallen for someone this way before, either. He'd felt his heart warm like it hadn't in so long because he felt the same way about her. It was beginning to feel like fate, and it was familiar because it was the second time he'd experienced it.

Karen had mentioned the diary on the phone the other night, and Johnny had jumped at the chance to look at it. It hadn't taken long to find what he was looking for thanks to the fact that Treviso kept such meticulous records written in beautiful, tiny print. Days were clearly marked on the tops of pages so Johnny had been able to thumb right to the date in question. He'd called a few people and confirmed the date Marconi's grandson had been killed, then scanned that page in the diary. It was a perfect match.

Johnny knew how loan sharks often bartered with made-up fees supposedly associated with the loan. He was familiar with how they'd tell a mark after the fact, after the loan was made, that there was a processing or administrative fee that had to be paid along with the principal and the VIG, but that the mark could pay the fees off in services. That way the bosses could never accuse anyone of skimming. The VIG on each loan had to be specifically approved by the bosses before the loan was made and had to be completely covered in cash. That way the bosses knew they weren't getting ripped off. But everybody down the line understood that the loan shark was entitled to get what he could in barter off whatever fees he could convince the mark were also owed. Which was why Johnny had come to this body shop today. To see if Treviso had done just that.

"Hey, you," Johnny said brusquely. The young man kneeling in front of him was busy removing a smashed fender panel from the right front side of a Chrysler Le-Baron. "Where's Mr. Gates?" According to Treviso's black book, Gates was the owner of the body shop. At least, he had been two years ago. And his name was still on the front door.

The guy nodded over the hood of the LeBaron without taking his eyes off what he was doing. "In the back. Third office on the left." He smiled lewdly. "Miss April's hanging on the door. You can't miss her."

Johnny headed in the direction the guy had indicated, working his way around cars in different states of repair, around hoses hanging from the ceiling, around heavy equipment and tools scattered about the floor. He'd always liked body shops, especially the way they smelled— fresh paint, old grease, burning metal. He hesitated a moment in front of Miss April, admiring what God had given her. Finally he rapped twice on the door.

"Yeah?"

"Mr. Gates?"

"Yeah."

"I need to talk to you." Johnny heard what sounded like someone getting up out of a creaky chair. A moment later the door opened.

"Who the hell are you?" Gates demanded.

Gates was average height, heavyset, and thinning on top. He reminded Johnny of a larger version of Angelo Marconi, except that Gates had a graying mustache. "Name's Barton," Johnny answered calmly, subtly pulling his jacket back just enough for Gates to spot the pistol handle protruding from his belt. "I need a few minutes." Gates did a not-so-subtle double take. "Don't worry," Johnny assured him, "this won't take long."

Gates gestured back at his desk. The receiver of the phone was lying on it. "A friend of mine's on the line," he said in a shaky voice, jerking a thumb over his shoulder. "You do anything to me, Barton, and he'll—"

"Relax, Mr. Gates. I'm not here to start trouble. I just wanna ask you a few questions."

Gates gazed at Johnny for a few moments, then finally nodded. "Okay." He stepped to the side to let Johnny in, then made sure the door stayed wide open.

"Close it," Johnny called over his shoulder.

"But I—"

"Now."

Gates reluctantly did as he was told.

Johnny walked directly to Gates's desk, knelt down, and checked the cubbyhole for a weapon. A pistol taped to the inside of the desk that Gates could subtly reach down and fire. But it was clean. He stood up, grabbed the telephone receiver off the desk, and put it down on its base, ending the call. Then he moved in front of the desk, and dragged one of the two chairs to the side, to a position where he could better keep an eye on Gates and didn't have to worry that he'd missed anything in the cubbyhole. He nodded to the big man. "Okay, sit down. And do me a favor."

"What?" Gates asked as he sat in the wide leather chair behind the desk.

"Keep your hands on the desk. I want to see all ten fingers the whole time I'm here."

"Jesus, what's this about?"

This was about Tony Treviso getting his car repaired fast two years ago in exchange for Gates not having to pay some made-up fee associated with the Lucchesi family loan.

Johnny eased into his chair. "You ever borrow money from the Lucchesi family?" He knew instantly he had the right man. Fear spread across Gates's face like coffee spilling on a diner counter. "It's okay, pal. I know you paid it off. I know you're square."

Gates let out a visible sigh of relief. "If you know I'm square, what are you doing here?"

"The guy who loaned you the money. You remember him?"

"Are you a cop?" Gates asked. "Is this about me testifying or something? 'Cause I won't do it. I'd never testify against those people. I don't care if you throw me in jail for the rest of my life, I won't do it." An involuntary shiver shook his body. "I saw what they do to people who squeal on them. They showed me pictures."

"I'm not a cop."

Gates turned his head to the side. "Then who are you?"

"Just answer my question. Do you remember the guy who loaned you the money?"

Gates nodded grudgingly. "I'll never forget him. He's one of the strangest-looking guys I've ever seen. It was like he just got out of a concentration camp or something."

Euphoria surged through Johnny's body. Gates had to be talking about Tony Treviso. "Ever do any work on his car?"

Gates hesitated. "Why?"

Johnny glanced down for a few moments, letting Gates know in no uncertain terms that the stonewalling needed to cease immediately or there would be consequences. When he looked up, he made sure his eyes were mere slits. "If you remember the guy who loaned you the money so well, I'm sure you remember working on his car."

Gates swallowed hard, twice.

"Right?"

"Maybe . . . ahhh . . . no, no, I don't remember. I told you, I'm not squealing on anybody." Gates started to stand up.

But Johnny beat him to it. He was up on his feet in a flash, before Gates's ass was six inches off the seat, with the gun out aimed directly at Gates's fat chest. Being lightning quick had always come naturally to Johnny. Thing was, he could draw fast *and* hit people. That was the key. A lot of men could draw fast, but then they shot wildly. Could barely hit a barn door from a few feet away. Not Johnny. His aim was true.

"Listen, fat man," Johnny snapped, "I ain't putting up with this crap for another second." The barrel was perfectly still, wasn't moving at all, and Johnny could tell that that fact wasn't lost on Gates. "Live or die. It's your choice."

"Okay."

Johnny pulled the top of the Glock smoothly back, chambering the first round. "Now, did you work on his car?"

"Yeah," Gates answered meekly. "We did."

"What'd you do to it?"

"The front was all smashed up. We replaced the whole front end. I'll never forget. He wanted it done fast, too. We did the whole job in two days."

Johnny lifted the gun so it was pointed at Gates's face. "Anything else?"

"There was dried blood on the inside of the front end," Gates replied hoarsely. "Lots of it."

Johnny lowered the gun slowly. Now he had the proof, at least, enough proof for him. Tony Treviso had killed Angelo Marconi's grandson. Not Kyle McLean. There could be no doubt. "Good man. See how easy that was?" He slid the gun back into his belt without popping the round from the chamber. "I was never here, Mr. Gates. If I find out you ever told anyone I was, you'll be dead within twenty-four hours. You understand me?"

Gates nodded slowly.

As Johnny slipped out through the office door, Gates's eyes fluttered shut and he slumped forward onto his desk with a loud thump.

33

Y OUR MOM'S A piece of work, MJ." He'd meant it
as a compliment, but now that he'd said it, he was
worried the young man might take it wrong. "You
know?"

"Now, there's a hot story, Captain Ahab. I'll alert the
media."

MJ was a great kid heading the right way down a high-
way going in the right direction—thanks in no small part
to his mother. But he had a sarcastic lane to him, too.
Hopefully he'd lose that cynical side as he got older. Or at
least learn to control it. It was the only unattractive thing
about him. Of course, that was the pot blatantly calling
the kettle black, Jack realized. So it wouldn't do any good
for him to say anything to MJ about it. Maybe he should
have an off-line chat with Yolanda.

"I meant that I liked her style," Jack said quietly. "After

I was honest with her, after I told her why I was so interested in the Kid, she let you come with me. She appre-
ciates when people are candid. I like that. She probably
likes baseball, too."

MJ shook his head. "It had nothing to do with your
Mikey Clemant story. And she doesn't give a lick about
baseball. In fact, she hates it, thinks it's a waste of time.
Thinks all professional sports are a waste of time. Just
grown men and women playing children's games. She
thinks adults ought to be looking for cancer cures or the
next great technology instead of trying to hit a ball over
a fence or throw it in a hoop."

"She might have a point." Pretty good one at that.

"Of course she does. She's always right." MJ flashed
that charismatic smile. "That's why I love her so much.
That and the fact that she's never let me down. And she
never will."

"What do you want to do when you grow up?" Jack
had wanted to ask MJ that question for a while. Now
seemed a good time to get a straight answer because the
young man was pretty animated. For him, anyway.

"I'm already grown up," MJ answered right away.

Like he'd known the question was coming. Maybe
MJ had some sort of gift. He always seemed to have exactly the right answer ready to go right away. Maybe he
could read minds. Maybe that was what made him so
smooth. Things like that seemed more possible to Jack as
he was getting older. Strange gifts, aliens, the Loch Ness
monster, a shooter behind the fence on the grassy knoll,
otherworld existences. Maybe because he'd always hoped
there was a heaven, and now that he was sixty-three, he
really hoped there was a heaven.

"I meant, what do you want to do for a career?" MJ didn't say anything right away. Maybe he'd been wrong about MJ having a gift after all. "Haven't decided yet, huh?"

"Oh, I've decided. I just haven't decided if I should tell you."

That hurt a little. "Why not?"

"Well, now that you and Momma are getting along so well, I don't want you telling her what I tell you because you think that'll create an even stronger bond between you two. I mean, I've told her what I want to do, but she doesn't take me seriously. She might if she heard it coming from you, though, and I don't want that."

"I won't tell her," Jack promised, gazing out the Citation window at the brown landscape racing past. South Florida had gotten only a couple of inches of rain in the past few months. In a week or two the afternoon thunderstorms would start firing up and come every day until August and they'd have more rain than they could handle. But right now there were brush fires popping up all over the place because people were such lazy pricks. Throwing lighted cigarette butts out their car windows into the tinder. "I swear."

"Yeah, as long as you're sober."

"I won't tell her," Jack repeated firmly. "And I don't appreciate that. I've never let that affect—"

"Okay, okay. Look, I want to own a professional baseball team. I've always wanted to do that. I'll probably have to be a doctor or a lawyer for a while before I can afford it, but I'll get there. I love baseball. And by the way," MJ continued, his voice rising, "I've already told her that. But I don't want you saying anything to her about it. If she hears I told you, she might actually start to think I'm serious. Right now she thinks it's just a joke."

"I won't tell her. I promise."

"Good."

"Maybe you'll give me a job on the scouting side when you buy your team."

MJ grinned. "I doubt it."

"What do you mean?"

"Not if you keep thinking Mikey Clemant is so good."

Jack wanted like hell to tell MJ about everything he'd dug up on the Retrosheet website last night, but he didn't want to seem like a little kid who couldn't keep a secret, either. In fact, he'd found himself respecting MJ's demeanor more and more. It seemed like the young man was in control of himself and the situation all the time. Jack rolled his eyes but made sure MJ couldn't see him do it. Jesus, a sixty-three-year-old man wanting to be like a sixteen-year-old boy. How embarrassing was that? "So then why *did* she let you come today if she hates sports so much?" he asked, putting off the bring-the-house-down story about Mikey Clemant a little while longer. Prouder of himself every second he was able to hold off shouting the incredible news.

"Because she likes you."

That came as a shock. "Really?"

"She doesn't like many people, either," MJ continued, "but she definitely took a shine to you, Ahab. For the life of me, I can't figure out why."

"What's that supposed to mean? Why not?"

"There isn't much to like about you."

Jack caught a gleam in MJ's eyes. "There sure is. I'm cute. Damn cute."

"You're an old grouch."

"Maybe. But people can like old grouches. Especially ones like me."

MJ pointed at the Publix store where they'd worked as they passed it. "Ned Anderson sure doesn't."

"Ned Anderson isn't human," Jack retorted, thinking about how much he hated the store manager. "When I said everyone likes me, I meant everyone human. Ned turned into an alien when they made him a store manager."

MJ snickered. "You might be right. I thought I noticed a couple of bumps on his head one time. Maybe they were his antennae."

They shared a long, loud laugh.

Jack shook his head as the laughter subsided. "Your mom's a tough love. A couple of times I thought she was gonna pull a shotgun out from underneath that skirt and blow some buckshot in my ass while I was hightailing it for my car. The way she was carrying on and waving her finger at me about getting you fired and then convincing you to be a batboy." MJ was howling with laughter again. "Especially after I told her I wasn't sure when I'd be able to pay you." Laughing harder than Jack had ever seen him laugh. Out of control for the first time. "What is it? What's so funny?"

"She did that to Daddy once," MJ explained, wiping moisture from the corners of his eyes. "She chased him out of the house and nailed him in the butt from the front porch. Shot off half a cheek. Almost got his, well, you know. Which was what I think she was really aiming at. The doc in the emergency room said it was a heck of a shot. Daddy had to sleep on his stomach for a month."

"She go to jail?"

"Nah. The cops thought it was hilarious. They told her she'd shown a lot of restraint not shooting him somewhere else more important. They wrote up their report like it was self-defense. Like he'd been hitting her. They didn't like him much. Daddy didn't fight it, either."

"How come?"

"I don't know," MJ answered evasively. "He just didn't."

"Why'd she shoot him?" Right away Jack was sorry he'd asked. A dark cloud covered the kid's face, and his chin dropped. "My bad," he said apologetically. "It's none of my business. I shouldn't have asked, son." It was the first time he'd ever called MJ, son. But it felt right. "Hey, I got something I gotta tell you about—"

"It's okay," MJ interrupted. "She shot him 'cause she caught him in bed with another woman. With a friend of hers from down the lane."

Jack winced. "That sucks."

"She caught him doing it again a few months later with another woman, after his ass had healed. Caught him in their bed. He thought she wasn't gonna be back for a while, thought she was gonna be at a church picnic until sunset. But she came home early because Vanessa got stung by a bee. He got out of the house diving through the bedroom window, straight through the glass and all. But Momma trapped the woman in the bathroom until the cops got there. After they convinced her to let the woman out, they told Momma that Daddy was alley-catting around all over the place. She would have shot him for sure if he'd shown up at the house again." MJ hesitated. "But he never did. That was a year ago. I haven't seen him since." He shrugged. "I don't even know if he's alive."

Jack reached over and patted MJ's shoulder. He'd heard the depth of emotion in the young man's voice. It was as close as he'd ever heard MJ come to absolute honesty, to complete vulnerability. Most sixteen-year-olds didn't know what either of those were. "It's all right."

MJ gazed straight ahead through the windshield for a while. "Sometimes," he finally said, "when I'm out on my bike running errands for Momma, I think maybe I'll turn around and Daddy'll be standing there. We don't talk for long, just a few minutes. But he tells me he's okay. That he's got a job and a place to live. He gives me his phone number so I can call to check up on him. We end up hanging out together once in a while because we happened to run into each other that day. It ends up being a good thing." MJ cleared his throat. "Daddy used to take me fishing every Saturday at this little bridge near the house. We'd catch bluegill and bass. We'd be alone for a few hours because nobody else ever came there to fish. It was like our secret spot, and he used to tell me things those days, used to tell me how to look at life. What to watch out for, how to size people up, how to tell whether you could trust someone. Things I remember all the time, things I use all the time." His voice was barely a whisper. "You know, he wasn't much of a father, but he was a good dad." MJ turned toward Jack. "Does that make sense to you?"

This kid was something else. "Yeah, it does."

"I'd like to see him just one more time. Maybe go fishing with him again at that little bridge. I got some things I'd like to say to him. Nothing bitter, just things. Know what I mean?"

Jack nodded. He'd picked up the phone a thousand times over the past thirty-five years but never made that one call he wanted to make. He'd always put the phone back down before dialing that last digit because when he really thought about it, it seemed like it was better left a fantasy. Seemed like at that critical moment it was better not to know. Now that he was sixty-three, he wished he had made the call, wished he'd had the courage to follow through. But now it was too late. Now it had to stay a fantasy, had to remain an unknown. He nodded ever so subtly. Oh, yeah; he knew *exactly* what MJ meant.

They drove in silence for a long time.

When Tarpon Stadium appeared over the palm trees, MJ spoke up. "So, did you find it?"

Jack glanced over. "Find what?"

MJ was grinning from ear to ear. "The website. The one with all the box scores. Retrosheet."

Elation rushed through Jack's entire body. All the way to his fingertips and toes. "You found it, too?" he asked excitedly.

"Yup. Right after I talked to you on the phone."

But how? Jack asked himself. From the looks of the house, Yolanda Billups didn't have two nickels to rub together. "You got a computer at the house? And Internet?"

"I know, I know. You think we're too poor to have a computer. And we probably are," MJ admitted. "We probably shouldn't have spent five hundred bucks on it and we probably shouldn't be spending fifteen bucks a month on Web access, either. But Momma wants us all to be smart. She figures we need Internet to be smart these days. She figures it's the best way for kids to learn these days."

"Your momma's no fool."

"She's the best mom in the world," MJ said proudly. "So, did you look at it?"

"I had to call the Elias Sports Bureau first to find it, but *yeah, I looked at it.*" Jack whooped suddenly like he'd just struck out the last batter in game seven of the World Series. He couldn't keep it bottled up anymore. He wasn't like MJ. He had to show how ecstatic he was, had to let his joy run wild. "Could you believe it?"

MJ raised both eyebrows like it surprised him, too. "Which part?"

Jack caught the look. It was the first time he'd seen that expression on MJ's face. An expression of total disbelief. "The part about the Kid having the same game as Mickey Mantle on the *same* day. Same hits in the same order. Home run, single—"

"Home run, single, home run, double, single," MJ cut in, shaking his head. "I know. It's incredible. It's an incredible *coincidence.*"

"*Coincidence?*" Jack's jaw almost hit the steering wheel. "Coinci—"

"Look out!" MJ shouted, pointing over the dashboard.

Jack slammed on the brakes, and the Citation came to a grinding halt just inches behind a BMW stopped at a red light. He let out a relieved breath. He didn't have car insurance, either.

"Yeah, coincidence," MJ repeated firmly. "That's all it was. Don't get your hopes up, Ahab. I know what you're thinking."

"What's that?" Jack demanded, his heart still thumping from the near collision. "What do you *think* I'm thinking?"

"You're thinking this Kid is copying Mickey Mantle's 1968 season," MJ answered bluntly. "You think he's hitting exactly what Mickey Mantle hit in each game. Like anyone could really do that."

Jack nodded. Exactly. That *was* what he was thinking. "Yeah, okay. Look, I know it's crazy," he admitted, watching the BMW driver flick a cigarette butt out the window. God, he wanted to hop out, snatch up the burning cigarette, and toss it back into the BMW. He'd always wanted to do that once. "I know it's wild to think anyone could be that good at any level of baseball. I don't care if it's you or me playing T-ball against a bunch of six-year-olds." The light turned green, and Jack followed the BMW through the intersection. They were almost to the stadium turnoff. "I know how insane it sounds. But still. He had that game yesterday, and it's the same game Mantle had forty years ago on the exact same date." He flipped on the blinker. "All we have to do is get the Tarpons' play-by-play box scores from this season and match them up. I looked at the game Mantle had before the May 30 game," Jack went on, "and he was one-for-four on May 26 of 1968. The Kid had the same game four days ago, on the twenty-sixth. I couldn't tell if it was as exactly the same like it was last night because all I had was the newspaper box score. I couldn't tell if they had the same hit in the same inning or not because I didn't have the play-by-play, but we should be able to get our hands on all that stuff, right?"

"Yeah," MJ agreed, "we should."

Jack pulled into the stadium, then steered to the employee parking lot near the executive offices. "It'd be great if we could get the Kid to admit he's doing this,"

Jack suggested, putting the car in park and cutting the engine. "I know that's gonna be tough, but you can do it, MJ. Get close to him, drop a hint about what you know, convince him you're a good guy and you just want to help him." Jack puffed out his cheeks like he knew what a long shot it was. "I'm worried he might take off if he finds out I'm on to what he did last night. He didn't like the fact that I was with the Yankees when I talked to him at the Dugout. That seemed to scare him. But you're not gonna scare him." Jack's eyes narrowed. MJ was off in another world, apparently not listening. Jack tapped him on the shoulder. "Hey, you all right?"

"I'm fine."

"You hear what I said?"

"I heard, but it doesn't matter."

"*Doesn't matter?* What in the hell's your problem?"

"I don't have a problem. I just don't want to get caught up in a crazy fantasy."

"How can you say it's a fantasy? Facts are facts. I'm no statistics guru, but the odds are probably a billion to one that Clemant would have exactly the same game as Mantle on exactly the same day of the year. Hell, the odds are probably even higher than that. It's worth at least checking out, don't you think?"

MJ pursed his lips. "I took awhile coming out of the clubhouse last night. I didn't come out right after the game was over."

"I know. It pissed me off, too. So what?"

"I took awhile because Clemant pulled me aside, said he wanted to talk to me. He had me meet him in a training room down the hall from the locker room. We went there separately because he was worried about somebody seeing us walking together. I was kind of worried about the whole thing, worried maybe he was gonna smack me for something he thought I said about him behind his back. Or something he thought I did. But I went anyway because I'm supposed to be getting you information. Anyway, all he wanted to do was thank me for bringing his stuff out to him for the top of the ninth when no one else would. You know, his cap and glove."

"That's great," Jack exclaimed, remembering how MJ had met the Kid in front of the pitcher's mound. "Why didn't you tell me?"

"He asked me if maybe I wanted to grab lunch sometime and talk. Not about anything serious, just about baseball and regular stuff. He said he wasn't the bad guy everybody thought he was." MJ's voice was low. "Said he wanted a friend, someone to talk to. Said he couldn't open up to many people because of something in his past."

Jack could barely believe his ears, barely control his excitement. "That's *great*. You're in. I mean, we're as good as—"

"Then he asked me not to tell anybody. Asked me if I could do that for him. Asked me if he could trust me. Said people he cared about could get in trouble if I told anyone what he was telling me."

"Aw, that's a crock of—"

"I've already broken my promise," MJ interrupted, "by telling you all this. I think he was serious about people he cared about getting in trouble. I don't think it was a crock. He seemed real serious, seemed like he was getting emotional. Nervous, too. I feel bad."

They stared at each other for several moments, then Jack finally nodded. "Okay, fine. I respect your—"

"I'll only do it for you on one condition," MJ broke in.

"What's that?"

"Promise not to tell anyone. That it doesn't go any far-ther than the two of us." MJ drummed his fingers on his thigh nervously. "I promised to get you information. I don't want to let you down."

If they found out Clemant was really that good, how could MJ possibly expect him to keep it a secret? Not to at least try to get the Kid in front of people for a tryout? Then it hit him. "That's why the Kid doesn't do great all the time," he said, watching MJ pull something out of his pocket. "That's why Clemant doesn't have games like he had last night. *Jesus!*" he shouted. "That's why he'd copy Mantle's last season! It was terrible. By Mantle's stan-dards, anyway. A season no one would care about, espe-cially in Single-A."

"Yeah," MJ agreed, handing Jack what he'd pulled from his pocket. "You're right."

"What's this?" Jack unfolded the crinkled piece of paper and read what was scrawled on it, his heart sud-denly thumping hard. Home run, single, home run, double, single. And at the bottom of the paper in large letters: GO FOR IT. "My God," he uttered. "Where'd you get this?"

"Out of a trash can outside the locker room last night after Mikey Clemant tossed it in there. He had it with him the whole game last night. Had it in his pocket and checked it before each at-bat," MJ explained, open-ing the car door and climbing out. "I watched him do it each time," he said, leaning back down into the car. "He caught me staring once while he was looking at it. I thought maybe that was what he wanted to talk about in the training room." MJ's face lighted up for a moment. "I guess, in a way, that is what he was talking about. Anyway, after the game I saw him toss it in the trash can, and I pulled it back out when he was gone. Made a lot of sense to me when I went on Retrosheet before you came over today. By the way," he said, nodding at the paper, "you ever think about what else Mikey Clemant spells?"

Jack shrugged. "I don't know what you mean by—"

"Mickey Mantle. The same letters that spell Mikey Clemant spell Mickey Mantle." MJ made a pistol out of his right hand and pretended to fire it, then brought the tip of his index finger—the tip of the barrel—up in front of his mouth and blew, like he was blowing smoke. "Gotcha, Ahab."

As Jack watched MJ head toward the Tarpon clubhouse door, he couldn't decide whether to pump his fist in excitement—or cry. He was so close—yet still so far away.

MJ never put his cleats on until just before he went out on the field. They had long metal spikes and they were dangerous to walk around on in here. The locker room was carpeted, but the big bathroom area had a tile floor, and it was easy to slip on spikes in there, especially if the floor was wet. So he walked around in his team-issued flip-flops until he was ready to go out on the field. Like most of the players did.

Usually he was the first one to the diamond, making sure bats were arranged perfectly by the cage for the players before they started batting practice. But he was

late today because Jack and his mother had been carrying on for so long in front of the house. He'd already
taken a boatload of crap from the Tarpon's crusty old
manager, Lefty Hodges, and from a couple of the players.
But it had been mostly good-natured. This was the first
time he'd been late and, besides, everyone seemed to like
him, especially the owner. MJ knew why the owner liked
him—because he was black and the community could
clearly see that the team had no problems hiring minori-
ties. Being a poster boy for race relations had bugged him
at first, but it didn't anymore. He realized it was just good
business. Just the owner taking the right steps. A step he
might have to take someday as the owner of a baseball
team. In reverse. Besides, it ensured MJ's spot in the team
hierarchy because when the owner liked you, everyone
else *had* to like you.

MJ was zipping up his red Tarpon uniform pants as
he padded quickly out of the bathroom when he came
around the corner leading to the locker room. He happened to look up just in the nick of time. Zack Whitney, the team's top relief pitcher, was standing thirty feet
away in front of a locker staring down at a small piece
of paper. A moment later Whitney stuffed the paper in
his right front pocket, then quickly opened the lock and
the locker door and plucked a wallet from a pair of jeans
hanging on a hook inside.

MJ melted back into the hall leading to the showers
and pressed himself to the wall, then leaned around the
corner and peered into the locker room again. The problem was that Whitney was taking the wallet out of Reggie
McDaniel's locker. Whitney was stealing the wallet.

Whitney stuffed the wallet in the back pocket of his

uniform, quietly shut the locker door, then secured the combination lock with a quick upward motion.

As he turned to go, MJ pulled back out of sight and pressed himself to the wall again, praying the guy wouldn't head to the bathroom to take a leak. He didn't. A few moments later the locker room door squeaked open and MJ heard Whitney's heavy footsteps heading down the long tunnel toward the Tarpon bullpen. Not out the short tunnel to the field, which was the way all the players who weren't pitchers went.

When he was sure Whitney was gone, MJ let out a long breath. Now what?

34

THE GAME OF hide-and-seek was about to take a hairpin turn. The hunter was about to become the hunted.

Johnny had identified the tail. Recognized the sudden lane changes, swerves, and quick stops in his rearview mirror, and he couldn't stand it. Like a fighter pilot unable to shake enemy radar lock or an antelope sensing a pride closing in, the inevitability of it all was driving him insane. His stress was undoubtedly heightened by his situation with Karen, he knew, but that realization didn't help. In fact, it only intensified his mounting sense of grinding panic. Made him conjure up all kinds of crazy scenarios about who the stalker could be and why he was back there. Made his imagination run wild with thoughts of psychopathic mental switches, severed heads, codes of honor, rats, how gorgeous Karen was, and a boss who wanted death without judgment.

Johnny had tried desperately—without seeming desperate—to recognize the person behind the wheel of the trailing car. But that had been impossible. The chase car never came close enough—nor went away. It was like a specter that paced him maddeningly as he fled down an eerie, candlelit hallway. It seemed that his only option was decisive action. A scorched-earth response. Survival above all else.

So he parked the Seville in front of a large, nine-story apartment building near LaGuardia Airport in Queens and headed inside, literally whistling as he went, seemingly oblivious to the drama. He'd been with a call girl who lived here, so he knew the layout of the lobby. It was perfect for what he needed. There was another door opposite the main entrance and, by slipping out that door and going around back of the building, he could quickly return to the street where he'd parked without being observed.

The tail was down the street, parked ten cars behind the Seville, but still in front of the building. Which couldn't have worked out better. When Johnny came around the side of the building from the back, he was right behind whoever was tailing him. The guy hadn't gotten out—Johnny had made sure of that after moving through the front door of the apartment building—apparently content to wait for Johnny to reappear. Content to maintain the cat-and-mouse game when Johnny was on his way again.

The building lay directly in the path of planes taking off from LaGuardia and they were still very low as they went over, so each one made a horrendous racket. As Johnny crept along the passenger side of a pickup truck—which was parked directly behind the old Impala that had been tailing him—he tried to coordinate his move with the jet he assumed had just taken off. He'd spent the past few minutes timing interims between planes on his stolen Rolex, and each was almost exactly forty-five seconds. Hopefully the noise of the jet would drown out the gunshots and he'd get away clean.

At forty seconds he stopped and smoothly withdrew the pistol from his belt, feeling so much better with the weapon in his hand as he began to crawl forward again. His heart rate calmed noticeably and the crazy images disappeared now that his fingers were wrapped around the familiar grip. He was thinking clearly once more. He ought to be hearing the whine of a jet engine any second. Come on, baby, come on.

Sure enough, just as he reached the Impala's passenger door, a jet roared overhead, shattering the quiet of the street. He stood and without hesitation fired two shots through the passenger side window, hitting the unsuspecting victim in the right cheek and triceps. The first bullet ripped through the guy's mouth, blowing out the left side of his chin, and the second hit a rib, deflecting just enough to miss any vital organs, embedding in the driver's side door.

The guy frantically pushed open his door and tumbled to the street as Johnny fired two more times. But both shots missed.

Johnny jumped on the Impala's roof and scrambled across to the driver's side, aware that the guy had grabbed something from beneath the seat as he tumbled out. Assumed it was a gun. Johnny held the pistol over the side of the car and blindly popped off four more rounds at the spot on the street where he figured the guy was lying, then inched forward and peered down.

The first bullet from below tore through the roof and missed Johnny, but the second caught him in the left shoulder. He screamed and half-slid, half-rolled down the windshield onto the car's hood as more bullets exploded through the roof. For a split second he saw the guy's bloodied face through the window of the open driver's side door. Despite the searing pain in his shoulder, Johnny raised the gun smoothly, aimed, and fired, blowing a hole through the guy's left lung.

He jumped down to the street, groaning in agony as the impact of hitting the pavement ripped through his body. He hustled around the open door as best he could, gritting his teeth, aware of blood dripping down his chest inside his shirt.

Ricky Strazza lay sprawled on his back in front of Johnny, arms above his head, pistol a few inches from his twitching fingers, a pool of blood spreading out quickly beneath him. His eyes were open, and Johnny thought he saw him take a shallow breath.

"Strazza!" Johnny hissed. He recognized the guy from a meeting in Manhattan a few months ago. "You fucking bastard."

Strazza's eyes fluttered shut, but then he groaned and suddenly reached for the pistol lying on the pavement.

Johnny kicked it away quickly, stomped on Strazza's fingers, breaking two of them, then knelt beside the dying man, making certain to avoid the spreading pool of blood. "Who?" he demanded. "*Who?*"

Strazza gazed up at Johnny with glassy, melancholy eyes but said nothing.

"Tell me or I'll make your last few seconds worse than you could even imagine," Johnny threatened, pulling a

pen from his pocket and pressing the sharp tip against
one of Strazza's open eyes. "I'll push this thing down into
your brain so slow, Strazza. Now tell me who."

"Marconi," Strazza gasped. "Marconi. Now kill me.
Please."

Marconi. Angelo Marconi. *Holy shit.*

Johnny stood, aimed carefully, and fired one bullet,
this time directly into Strazza's heart. There could be no
chance of him surviving long enough to whisper his assassin's name into some Good Samaritan's ear while he
or she was kneeling next to him, keeping him company
during his last few moments.

Certain Strazza was dead, Johnny stumbled toward
the Seville, holding his left forearm in his right hand, his
shoulder on fire. He'd been shot before, in the lower leg a
few years ago, but this was different. It was a more intense
and frightening pain. This was a bullet, not buckshot.

He couldn't go to a hospital because all emergency
room cases involving gunshot wounds had to be reported
to the police. He just hoped he could stay conscious long
enough to get home. When he reached the Seville, he fell
inside behind the steering wheel and took several deep
breaths, then finally managed to get the key in the ignition and go, driving one-handed the whole way. Almost
losing consciousness several times.

When he got back to his apartment, Johnny applied
a dressing to the wound, stumbled to the couch, and
fainted.

A few hours later he awoke and managed to make it
back to the bathroom, crawling across the floor until he
reached the sink, somehow pulling himself to his feet
after a few tries. He stood before the sink, wavering un-

Forced Out

steadily, gazing at his blurry image in the mirror. Then he gingerly started to remove the dressing he'd applied when he first got home. It was time to change it. Fortunately the bullet had gone straight through, missing bones. But it had done a hell of a job on the soft tissue. He couldn't move his arm at all. At least it was his left arm.

He pulled the tape back from the sides of the square white dressing, groaning loudly and gritting his teeth so hard he thought they might crack when his chest hairs snagged. Then he pulled the tape from the top of the gauze, and the dressing slowly folded down—still held to his body by the tape at the bottom—revealing a dark red stain on the inside of the gauze and a perfectly round red hole a quarter of an inch in diameter in his shoulder. The wound was oozing now that he was on his feet again.

He closed his eyes and grabbed the sink, dizziness and nausea overtaking him, then slowly sank to his knees. For a full five minutes he knelt on the tiny black-and-white tiles of the bathroom floor, hugging the porcelain, sweating profusely, trying not to puke. He desperately wanted to crawl back on the couch and stay there until the pain eased—or he died.

But he had no choice. He had to get out of here. If he wanted to maintain that code of honor. And get the girl.

35

BAD VIBES WERE coming from every corner of the Tarpon locker room as MJ hustled through the door. They'd just lost a 4–3 heartbreaker thanks to Mikey Clemant dropping a routine fly ball to center with the bases loaded and two out in the top of the ninth. The error had allowed the other team to score twice, and the Tarpons had done nothing in the bottom of the ninth—three up three down—and that was that. Game over. End of story.

But it wasn't. Not for some of the players, anyway.

MJ heard the grumbling as soon as he pushed through the locker room door; he'd been cleaning up the dugout after the loss and was the last one in. The insults grew louder as he spun his combination lock right-left-right and yanked. As he opened the locker, he glanced over at Clemant, who was sitting in front of his. He'd already showered, had a plain white towel wrapped around his waist. Clemant was closer to his hecklers so he had to be hearing the insults: loser, quitter, steel hands, asshole, moron. But the Kid didn't seem to care. He was leaning back in his chair, enjoying a Milky Way bar, smiling serenely after each bite.

"Goddamn it! What the hell?"

MJ's eyes flashed toward the voice. Reggie McDaniel, the Tarpon first baseman, was furious. His street clothes and a few personal items lay strewn in front of his locker—now empty after he'd rooted through it violently.

"My wallet's gone!" McDaniel roared. He was a big man, almost as big as Clemant, with a fiery temper. He'd been ejected from four games this season, three more than anyone else on the team, including Lefty Hodges, the Tarpon manager. "I want it back, and I want it back *now!*" He glared around the room, his broad, bare chest heaving. All he had on were his uniform pants and game socks. "If I gotta go through every locker in here and shake everybody upside down by the ankles, I will. And when I find it, I'll kill the bastard who has it." McDaniel was only slightly more popular in the clubhouse than Clemant. "But if you give it to me now, there won't be any questions." The room had gone deathly still; no one was even moving. "Just toss it in the middle of the floor then walk straight outta here," he ordered. "But don't come back. I ain't puttin' up with no thief on my team."

MJ glanced at Zack Whitney, the guy he'd seen going in McDaniel's locker before the game. Whitney had been hurling some of the loudest insults at Clemant. Well, he sure had a hell of a poker face. If he hadn't seen Whitney take the wallet himself, he never would have guessed the guy was the thief.

"I had three hundred bucks in there," McDaniel muttered angrily, moving around his chair toward the middle of the large room so everyone could see how pissed he was. "And I'm gonna find it."

"He took it, Reggie!" Whitney shouted suddenly, pointing at Clemant. "Me and Hector saw him going through your locker right before the game. After everybody else was gone." Whitney jabbed a thumb over his shoulder at Hector Rodriguez, the third baseman, who was standing a few feet away from MJ. "We forgot a bag of practice balls, and we came back to get it. Everybody else was out on the field. At least we thought they were. When we looked in here through the door window, Clemant was closing your locker, Reggie. We didn't actually see him take anything because he was standing in front of your locker. So there wasn't anything we could say. But it sure as hell looked like he was going through your stuff. Right, Hector?"

"Right," Rodriguez agreed, nodding at McDaniel. "He didn't see us. We didn't want any trouble. Sorry. We shoulda—"

"You son of a bitch!" McDaniel yelled, rushing Clemant.

Clemant was out of his chair instantly and easily sidestepped the lumbering McDaniel, who slammed into the locker behind Clemant, bashing a huge dent in it. Several teammates tried restraining McDaniel, who was a raging bull, but he shook them off easily and made a second charge. This time he managed to grab Clemant's left arm on the way by, but Clemant countered with a lightning-fast right cross to the chin that sent McDaniel crashing to the carpet.

"He didn't take your wallet!" MJ yelled at McDaniel, who was staggering to his feet. "He didn't have anything to do with it." The locker room went still for a second time, and MJ felt every pair of eyes in the room race to him. "Whitney's lying his ass off."

"Keep your mouth shut, boy!" Whitney shouted across the room. "This has nothing to do with you."

"I'll say what I have to say," MJ retorted evenly. "And don't ever call me 'boy' again."

"I'll call you whatever the hell I wanna—"

"He stole your wallet, Reggie," MJ interrupted calmly, pointing at Whitney. "I was coming out of the bathroom, and I saw him do it."

"Stay out of this," Whitney yelled, veins in his neck bulging. "Or I'll kick your ass."

"You stole it. It was you."

"You got no proof," Whitney said with a hiss. "But I do. I got another witness. Right, Hector?"

Rodriguez nodded hesitantly, his eyes quickly moving from Whitney to McDaniel to Clemant.

"See," Whitney said confidently, folding his arms across his chest. He broke into a thin smile. "Maybe you were in on it, too, MJ. Maybe that's why you're sticking up for Mikey. We all saw you take his stuff out to him last night for the top of the ninth, you little ass-kisser. He has one good game," Whitney sneered, "and you decide to be his slave."

"I didn't take the wallet, Reggie," Clemant said loudly. "I may not be the best teammate in here, but I've never stolen anything in my life."

"Liar!" Whitney yelled. "You're a goddamn liar, Clemant. We saw you in front of his locker."

"Check his pocket, Reggie!" MJ yelled to McDaniel, stabbing in the air at Whitney. "The right front one."

"This guy's insane," Whitney retorted, pulling the stretch-tight game pants around his right thigh. "No wallet. See?"

"I'm not talking about his wallet," MJ said. "There's a piece of paper in his pocket with the combination to your lock on it, Reggie." MJ knew he was taking an awful chance. Whitney could easily have thrown the paper away. If McDaniel checked and there wasn't a piece of paper with a lock combination on it, this could get very ugly very fast. "Go on, Reggie."

Whitney, eyes widened as McDaniel made a move at him. So he made his own move—at MJ. "You little shit!" he yelled, dashing across the locker room. "I'm gonna kill—"

But Clemant caught Whitney before he'd gone three steps and hurled the smaller man over a chair and into the lockers, splitting open a deep cut on his forehead. Then Rodriguez and another player jumped Clemant just as McDaniel made it to Whitney. McDaniel clamped one huge hand around Whitney's neck and pinned him to the floor while he stuck the other into Whitney's right front pocket, searching for the telltale piece of paper.

Clemant was almost free of his attackers when two more guys piled on. Then everything went crazy, and it turned into an all-out brawl. Half the guys in the room were throwing punches.

"What the hell's going on here?" Lefty Hodges shouted from the doorway. The Tarpon manager was a stubby, potbellied, white-haired Irishman. Fifty-eight, he was

still feisty. Still not afraid to mix it up with the young guys if that was what the situation called for. And a lot of times in Single-A, it did. "Everybody stand down!" he yelled as his four assistant coaches waded into the melee, pulling combatants apart. "The next guy I see throw a punch is gone. *I mean it!*" Within a few seconds order had been restored. The players didn't like Lefty much, but they respected him. "That's better. Now somebody tell me what's going on."

No one said a thing.

Lefty spat chaw on the carpet and cursed under his breath, then pointed at Whitney. "You got the most blood on you, Zack." The right side of Whitney's face was wet with blood from the cut on his forehead. "Means you probably got the most to say." Lefty motioned inward with one hand. "Come on. Out with it."

Whitney picked himself up off the floor. He glanced uncertainly at McDaniel, who was holding a small piece of paper. "Clemant stole Reggie's wallet out of his locker," he said, sticking to his lie, "then he tried to pin it on me. He had MJ say I stole it." Whitney pointed at Rodriguez. "But Hector and I saw Clemant take the wallet. Clemant and MJ are lying. They're in it together. They probably split the three hundred bucks Reggie says was in it."

MJ spied the paper twitching in McDaniel's fingers, and he gave the big first baseman a what-the-hell look. But McDaniel didn't speak up. Maybe McDaniel hated Clemant more than he hated knowing Whitney was guilty. Maybe McDaniel figured this was a perfect way to finally get Clemant kicked off the team. The Kid didn't have any friends in here. That was more obvious than ever.

"I didn't take anything. These guys are—"

"Shut up, Mikey," Lefty snapped. "Put on some clothes, then get to my office." He gestured at MJ. "You, too. Move it. *Both of you!*"

It was almost seven-thirty, and the evening shadows were getting long. Jack was irritated and disappointed. Irritated because the game had ended more than an hour ago and MJ still hadn't appeared at the clubhouse door—usually he didn't take more than thirty minutes to shower and dress. Disappointed because Mikey Clemant hadn't copied Mickey Mantle at the plate today.

Before leaving for the stadium, Jack had checked Mantle's box score on the Retrosheet website. On May 31, 1968, Mantle had gone oh-for-two, grounding out in the fourth and striking out in the sixth, sandwiched between two walks. Clemant had gone oh-for-four today, and they'd all been lazy pop-ups to the infield. Nothing like Mantle's May 31 in 1968. On top of that, the Kid had made a horrible fielding error out in center in the top of the ninth that cost the Tarpons the game. He'd jogged apathetically out to the warning track beneath the long fly, then just dropped it. It was one of the easiest plays ever. It was almost like he didn't care about catching the ball, or he was drunk or on drugs.

Ooh. He'd never considered that possibility. Maybe the can't-miss-kid was an alcoholic or a druggie. Maybe some days Clemant came to the stadium under the influence. Maybe a lot of days. Able to convince Lefty Hodges he was fine, but unable to play anywhere near the level he was capable of. Some of the older guys like Hodges didn't get the drug thing, or looked the other way if they suspected anything because they didn't want to have to deal with it. Jack cursed under his breath. That could be it, all right. And nine times out of ten you couldn't reach a guy who was into drugs.

He'd seen it too many times, especially in the past few years. Guys who thought they'd go right to the Show after only a few weeks in the minors quickly tired of hanging out in bush-league towns like Sarasota when a few weeks turned into a few months. When it did, some of them headed down the path to ruin. To keep from going crazy, they told themselves, they rationalized. When the reality was they were buying themselves a first-class ticket on the express train out of baseball. Cocaine seemed to be the drug of choice because guys could still play while they were on it—sometimes pretty well even. But it could be anything: liquor, pot, XTC, crystal meth. Eventually cocaine caught up with them, too.

He flipped off the car radio, twisting the dial violently. He'd been listening to the postgame show on the local AM station, but he couldn't take any more. The on-air guys were hacks.

He banged the steering wheel impatiently. "Come on, MJ. Come on!"

MJ and Clemant had been sitting in Lefty Hodges's office for fifteen minutes, fidgeting, waiting for the old man to show. MJ was wondering if he would, or if this was, in fact, their punishment. To sit in the bowels of Tarpon

Stadium like a pair of morons until they finally figured out an hour from now—or whenever it was—that Lefty was not going to appear.

The office was small, just bare bones. Furnished only with a metal desk in front of a beat-up old chair that rolled on three squeaky wheels, the two rickety wooden chairs MJ and Clemant sat in, a fake plant behind the door set in a large tan-colored pot, and a bookcase next to the plant on which there was a bare-bulb lamp that was even dustier than the fake plant. The desk resembled a battlefield. It was booby-trapped by a platoon of large white Styrofoam cups half full of stale black coffee hidden among wadded-up sports sections, old lineup cards, and a big ashtray overflowing with cigarette and cigar butts. Lefty chain-smoked cigarettes before games—and after if they lost—and smoked one big, fat cigar after a win. All the way down to the nub.

MJ put his hands behind his head and leaned back. He and Clemant hadn't said a word to each other since leaving the locker room. "I wonder if the old guy's gonna show," MJ finally muttered. Funny how he thought of Lefty Hodges as older than Jack, even though Lefty was actually five years younger. Jack seemed more on the ball, more aware of the bigger picture, more into what was going on around him. All Lefty cared about was the Sarasota Tarpons. There was a rumor he had a wife, but no one had ever seen her. He was a laser-focused man, but it wasn't like all that focus did him much good. In seven seasons Lefty's winning percentage was below 50 percent. He'd probably lasted this long because he made only forty-five grand a year. "Maybe Lefty's just screwing with us."

"He'll show."

Another five minutes passed.

"I'm outta here," MJ said, standing up. He could picture Jack sitting in the Citation out in the parking lot, pounding the steering wheel. Another couple of minutes and there wouldn't be a ride home. "I'm gonna miss my ride if I don't go." He knew Clemant couldn't help with a ride. Clemant rode city buses to the ballpark. A couple of times he'd seen the Kid get out a few blocks from the stadium, like he didn't want anyone to know he didn't have a car. "If he isn't gone already." City buses didn't go anywhere near his house, so that wasn't an option, either.

"Don't worry. Your friend Jack Barrett's not going anywhere."

MJ sank slowly back down in his chair. "Huh?"

Clemant snatched an old lineup card off the desk. "Barrett won't leave you here," he said, scanning it. "He'll wait around as long as it takes. Hell, if you walked out there at midnight, he'd still be there. He might not be real happy, but he'd be there. He's too interested in what you might tell him."

"How do you—"

"Same as you know I ride the bus to the stadium," Clemant interrupted. "I've seen you get out of Barrett's car a couple of times. Out of that rusty old bucket of bolts he calls a car."

You always figured you were fooling people, always figured you knew more than they did, MJ thought. But more often than not, what you were really doing was fooling yourself. It was like his father had always said when they were fishing at that little bridge. People know 99 percent more than you think they know. If you accept that, he'd always say, really accept it, you'll do yourself a huge favor. Suddenly he missed his father a lot.

"What does Barrett want anyway?"

"What do you mean?" MJ asked innocently.

Clemant tossed the old lineup card back on the desk. "Come on, pal. Don't pull that crap on me. You and he are working together. It's pretty obvious. At least to me. Look, he came up to me a few days ago in a bar near here," Clemant continued without waiting for confirmation of the partnership. "Claimed he was an old Yankee scout. Told me how he could recognize talent anywhere, and that I was the real deal." The Kid hesitated. "Who is he really?"

MJ hesitated. "I don't know." He could tell the Kid was getting pissed.

Clemant shook his head. "So it was all bullshit?" he asked, biting his lower lip. "Bringing my stuff out for me last night in the ninth. That talk we had in the training room after the game. Sticking up for me in the locker room back there a few minutes ago? All that was bullshit, huh? You were just trying to make me think you were my friend so I'd tell you things. So you could tell Barrett."

"No," MJ said firmly. "No, I . . .". He grimaced. God, he hated liars. "Okay . . . okay, maybe I—"

"Is he paying you?"

MJ didn't answer. The truth suddenly seemed pretty unpleasant.

"Jesus, what is it you two think I'm gonna say?"

"Hey," MJ said sharply, "*you* were the one who told *me* people might get hurt if you said too much."

Clemant's shoulders sagged slightly. "Yeah, I did."

"That's a pretty weird thing to say."

Clemant nodded. "I know. It was just that . . . I wanted to . . . ah, the hell—"

"Look," MJ spoke up, "Jack Barrett really is a retired Yankee scout. I wasn't sure myself when he first told me. But I had a couple of long talks with the guy about the Yankees, then I checked out the people he talked about on the Internet. It's all good. Everything checks out. I even called some people in New York, some guys in the press up there. They knew him. Described that guy sitting in the bucket of bolts out in the parking lot down to a tee." MJ hesitated. "Plus, well, there's this game Jack remembers from way back in 1968."

Clemant eyed MJ suspiciously. "What game?"

MJ saw right away he'd caught the Kid's attention. "The same one you had last night."

Clemant's eyes opened wide. "How did you—"

"All right, guys." Lefty was standing in the office doorway, hands on hips. "I talked to some of the fellas," he continued, moving to the chair behind the desk and easing into it, sighing like he was completely drained. "And they all say they're pretty damn sure you took Reggie McDaniel's wallet, Mikey." Lefty spoke with an Irish accent. He was first generation. "Whitney and Rodriguez swear they saw you do it. A couple of other guys made it like you were guilty, too."

"Lefty, I'm not—"

"Keep your damn shorts on, Kid," Lefty spoke up, pushing back the brim of his bright red Tarpon hat with the smiling fish on the front. "I may not be the sharpest tool in the shed, but I ain't the dullest, either. I know a lot of this is because they all hate you." Lefty didn't pull punches. He wasn't smart enough to, and he knew it.

"But I can't ignore the fact that Whitney and Rodriguez claim they were eyewitnesses."

"They're lying, Mr. Hodges," MJ spoke up with conviction. "They didn't see anything. Mikey isn't guilty. I saw Whitney in front of McDaniel's locker right before game time, after everyone else went out to the field. He was reading the combination to the lock off a piece of paper. A piece of paper he shoved in his pants pocket after he opened McDaniel's locker. McDaniel got the paper from Whitney right before you came in the locker room, when everybody was fighting. I saw him holding it. Did you talk to him about it?"

Lefty nodded. "Sure. He said he thinks Mikey did it, too. There wasn't any piece of paper."

"He's lying," MJ said again.

Lefty threw his hands up, looked at the ceiling, and rolled his eyes. "Oh, right. Everybody's lying but you and the Kid."

"This is a conspiracy, it's a damn coup d'état." MJ saw both Clemant and Lefty glance up when they heard the words "coup d'état." Lefty because he didn't know what the words meant. The Kid because he was surprised to hear a high school dropout say them. Damn, Momma was so right. White folks had all these preconceived notions running around in their heads about blacks—even a young man like Mikey Clemant, who deep down seemed like a pretty good person. "Make me take a lie detector test," he said defiantly. "But make Whitney and McDaniel take one, too. You'll see who's telling the truth."

"Oh, sure, MJ. I'll have that all set up for nine tomorrow morning," Lefty said sarcastically, rolling quickly over to the bookcase on the chair. He grabbed a loose-leaf binder off the top shelf, then rolled back behind the desk. Completing the entire move in seconds, like he did it all the time. "Make sure you're there. I'm sure McDaniel and Whitney'll show." Lefty flipped back several pages in the binder and read for a few moments. Then he closed the binder and tossed it on the desk, knocking over one of the Styrofoam cups of stale coffee in the process. "I gotta make a decision here, gents."

MJ noticed coffee starting to drip down the front of the desk. "What do you mean?"

"I gotta do something. I can't just let this go."

"What are you gonna do?" Clemant asked quietly.

Lefty nodded at the book. "What the book says I can do without going to the owner. You're gone for two weeks, Mikey. *Without* pay. Go clean out your locker." His gaze drifted to MJ. "You, too. Same thing. Two weeks."

When MJ got back to the locker room, he didn't bother showering or changing out of his uniform. Just stowed his street clothes into a duffel bag, took off his cleats, and put on the pair of Nike high-tops he'd worn to the stadium this afternoon. As he banged his locker door shut, he glanced over at Clemant. The Kid was sitting in front of his locker, elbows on his knees, head down.

"You all right?" They were the only ones left. Everyone else was long gone. "Mikey?"

"Yeah, sure," Clemant muttered. "Never better."

"Don't worry. I'll talk to McDaniel," MJ promised. "I'm gonna get him to fess up to what he did. I know he found that paper in Whitney's pocket. I saw the look on his face after Lefty came in. I'm gonna get him to go to Lefty and admit everything."

Clement snickered. "Good luck. He hates me as much as everyone else on the team."

"Then why'd he go after Whitney? Why'd he bother getting the paper out of the guy's pocket? I saw him holding it, I swear." MJ had thought this through while they were cooling their heels in Lefty's office. "He wants his wallet back. That's the bottom line."

"He's probably already got it back."

"What do you mean?"

Clemant kicked his locker door. "I bet he followed Whitney into the parking lot tonight and pummeled his ass until he got the guy to fork it over. At least the three hundred bucks he was bitching about. That's why he got the piece of paper out of Whitney's pocket. He wanted to make sure you·were telling the truth about that before he went after the guy. But he figured he could get me in trouble at the same time. Win-win, you know?"

That sounded about right. "I'm still gonna talk to him."

"Uh-huh. Well, thanks for saying something to Lefty. At least you tried. I appreciate it."

"Yeah, sure." MJ turned to go, then hesitated. The Kid seemed lost. Like he was on the verge of suicide without a team. One thing about Clemant, he always had that confident air about him. Not an arrogant or cocky air, just confidence in himself and what he was capable of. Jack had pointed that out several times. But it was gone now. Completely. "You said something to McDaniel before Lefty came in the locker room," MJ spoke up. "About how you weren't the greatest teammate in the world. What'd you mean?"

"Just what I said. I'm not a good teammate. Simple as that."

"Well if you know it, why don't you try being one? Why don't you try getting to know the guys? Not ignoring them."

The Kid didn't answer right away.

"Why do you have a game like you did last night?" MJ kept going. "Five-for-five and two home runs? Then have a game like you did today? Four baby pop-ups to the infield?"

"That's baseball." Clemant shrugged. "Star one day, bum the next. You know that."

"Why make catches nobody else on this team could possibly make, then drop easy chances like that snow cone you sucked on tonight?"

Clemant shrugged. "I got ADD, and I don't know when it's gonna hit me. What the hell?"

"Why are you stonewalling me?"

"*What?*"

"How come the letters of your name spell Mickey Mantle?" MJ fired away, not letting up. "Don't tell me it's just coincidence."

"Hey, what the hell are you—"

"That game you had last night was exactly like a game Mickey Mantle had in 1968," MJ kept on. "Same hits he had that day. Even the same order he had them in. And on the *exact same day*: May 30. Don't even *try* to tell me that was a coincidence."

Clemant's face went pale. "How'd you figure all that out?"

"I didn't. Jack Barrett did. He remembered watching Mantle have that game in 1968 at Yankee Stadium. He was there that day. Said he'd never forget the Mick having such an awesome game as beat up by the years as he was at that point. Then Jack went on the Internet and checked it out. Sure enough, he was right. It matched right up."

"Jesus," the Kid whispered.

"What's going on, Mikey?" MJ demanded. "What's the deal? Why could people get hurt if you told me things? Why won't you tell me? *What* won't you tell me?"

Thirty seconds ago Jack was mad as a hornet for having to wait. It had been two hours since the game ended, and he was worried about Cheryl going crazy because Rosario wasn't home when she got there. Now he couldn't believe his eyes, could barely control his emotions. Mikey Clemant was standing right in front of him.

"Nice to see you again, Mikey," he said, extending his hand, trying to keep his voice calm.

"My name's not Mikey," the Kid replied, shaking Jack's hand with his strong grip. "But it sounds like you already know that."

"What's your real name?"

The Kid took a deep breath. "Kyle. Kyle McLean." His eyes dropped, and he shook his head. "Goddamn. I haven't introduced myself like that in so long."

The three of them stood in front of the Citation. It was dark now, but Jack could make out the Kid's face in the soft glow from one of the parking lot lights. "Why the alias with the same letters as Mickey Mantle's name?" Jack asked with a raised eyebrow.

"I know you know about all that," McLean said solemnly. "The five-for-five game, too. How you think I copied Mantle's 1968 game last night."

"I told him how you figured it out," MJ spoke up.

"Let me tell you something," McLean said before Jack could respond. "The whole reason I'm here is this guy." He gestured at MJ. "He stuck up for me today in a big way."

"He's got a habit of doing that." Jack gave MJ a wry smile. Now he really owed the young man. "What happened?"

MJ quickly explained the wallet incident and the two-week suspension Lefty Hodges had sentenced them to.

"I didn't steal the wallet," McLean assured Jack. "I'd never do anything like that."

Jack held up his hands. "If MJ says you didn't do it, that's all I need to hear." He hesitated. "So why'd you threaten me that night at the Dugout?"

McLean didn't answer right away. "Look, this is tough for me. I don't even know you guys."

MJ started to say something, but Jack cut him off. "Why don't you come home with me, Kyle?" he suggested. "My daughter'll fix us all a nice, home-cooked meal. You can spend the night at the house. It'll be relaxing. Something tells me you haven't been able to really relax in a while." The Kid had been running from something. The strain was obvious. He had that hollow, hunted look about him. "You could probably use the company, too." It wasn't much of a leap to infer that he'd been lonely. Probably very lonely. "Come on, Kid. You'll enjoy it. Low-key, I promise. We just want to help."

McLean finally nodded. "Yeah, okay," he agreed softly. "I'd like that, Mr. Barrett."

"Good."

McLean put his hand on Jack's arm before he could turn to get back behind the wheel. "Can I ask you a favor, Mr. Barrett?"

"Only if you stop calling me Mr. Barrett. Call me Jack. Okay?"

"Yeah, okay."

"So what's the favor?"

"Can you stop at a 7-Eleven on the way home so I can pick up a razor? I want to shave this damn beard off. I hate it."

Tears streamed down her face as she sat on the floor of Jack's bedroom reading letter after letter from a woman named Doris. Cheryl had been so angry at Daddy all day as she'd sat behind her desk at the real estate office, then exploded when she got home at five and he and the baby were gone without a note explaining where they were or what was going on. Which was just like him.

She'd always wondered what was in that box she'd seen under his bed every time she cleaned, and she was so mad by seven when he still wasn't back that she'd gotten up the nerve to look in it. She'd been in here for two hours now, reading and reading, unable to stop. Learning that Jack and Doris had met during their senior year in college, dated for a little while, then stopped when Jack had gone off to the army. How she'd married while he was away and how she'd regretted it ever since. How happy she was to hear that he'd achieved his dream, how he'd gotten further in the Yankee organization than he'd ever thought he would. How sorry she was that Jack's wife was having affair after affair behind his back but thought he never knew. How she wanted him to call her, how she desperately wanted to hear his voice. How she wished they'd made love just once.

Then the letters had suddenly stopped. She knew because each letter was still in its envelope in order by date, and the last postmark was four years ago. They'd all come from New York City.

Cheryl shrieked when she heard a car pull up in the driveway. She stuffed the letters back in the box, shoved the box back under the bed, and sprinted for her bedroom, wiping the tears from her eyes as she ran.

36

JOHNNY BREATHED A heavy sigh of relief as he guided the Seville into the parking lot of the Happy Go Lucky Motel. On the outskirts of Edison, New Jersey—a commuter town about twenty-five miles southwest of New York City—it was actually a pretty decent place. Safer than the fleabags he'd been sending her to until now. Not too bad to look at, either. What he could see of it, anyway. Not that he cared right now. His left arm felt like it was going to fall off.

While he was passed out on his couch this afternoon, the weather had turned awful. The bright, beautiful sunshine of this morning had given way to a steady downpour, which was making driving dangerous as the last gray rays of daylight faded into darkness. To make matters worse, he had to drive one-handed. He'd jerry-rigged a sling out of a pillowcase to help ease the shooting pains in his shoulder, but he still couldn't move his fingers on that hand. He'd almost passed out several times on the Jersey Turnpike—like he almost had on the way back to his apartment after shooting Strazza—but he'd been able to catch himself in the nick of time by shaking his head violently or pinching his thigh hard. He'd done it so many times his leg was black and blue in a couple of places. He reminded himself to climb out of the car slowly as he pulled into a narrow parking space and to walk deliberately to the door. He had to stay conscious. Had to.

After cutting the engine, Johnny stayed in the car for a few minutes, gulping bourbon from a rotgut bottle he'd picked up on his way out of the city. As he took another long gulp, he stared at the number on the motel door. Room 147. It was as far from the office as you could get—which was no coincidence. He took another deep breath and passed his palm slowly across his forehead. He was still sweating profusely, still fighting the fever. Which was a bad sign. He needed to stay levelheaded, needed to think clearly, needed to stay in control. His mind was his only advantage at this point, and if it wasn't sharp, this whole thing would turn into a disaster. An even bigger one than it already was. Like Treviso, Johnny had his own psycho switch. It had flipped on only a couple of times in his life, but when it had, no one was safe. Including himself.

He pressed his right arm against his side, making certain the pistol was deep in the shoulder holster, then checked his rearview and side mirrors. Marconi must know by now that Strazza was dead, but Johnny hadn't seen any signs of a replacement yet. No crazy zigzagging behind him on the turnpike as he'd raced down here. Still, you never knew. Marconi would be very careful this time, might even call in someone from the outside. Maybe a lot of people.

Johnny looked up through the windshield, hoping the rain had slowed a little. It hadn't. In fact, it seemed to be coming down even harder. He reached across his body with his right hand, unlatched the door, and pushed it open with his knee. Raw, damp air hit him as he rose up out of the car with a groan, then leaned back against it for a moment. His head started spinning, and he felt himself beginning to shiver. He'd worn a heavy raincoat on the drive down. Even with the heater in the car turned way up, he'd worn it. Suddenly, outside, he was freezing.

"Jesus," he muttered, "got to get inside." He slammed the car door shut with his foot, then staggered beneath the building-long overhang toward room 147, not bothering to lock the car. Something he *always* did. But these were desperate times. Routines went out the window now.

He fell against the room door, making certain his right shoulder took the brunt of the impact. Even so, painful shock waves coursed through him. The bourbon was counteracting the agony a little—but not enough. He knocked on the door several times, biting his lower lip hard and shutting his eyes tightly, pinching his thigh.

"Who is it?"

"Johnny."

The door opened, and Johnny all but fell inside the small, plain room. He staggered to the queen-size bed and collapsed onto it, taking several deep breaths before he could finally sit up and gaze at the woman. "Hello, Helen."

Helen McLean stared back at Johnny in horror. "What happened?" she whispered, grabbing his left shoulder. She couldn't see the sling beneath the raincoat.

"*Holy shit!*" he shouted, tumbling to the cheap carpet, lightning bolts of pain tearing through his shoulder. "*Oooh, Geeeoood!*"

"*What, what?*" Helen screamed, hands clasped over her mouth. "What's the matter?"

Holy Christ, she'd pressed right down on the bullet hole. Suddenly he was seeing nothing but yellow and green stars flashing in the purple darkness ahead of his eyes that were shut so tightly they could have formed diamonds from coal. It reminded him of the time he'd suffered a bad concussion in eighth grade when he'd fallen off the back of the motorcycle his uncle was driving. The intermittent flashes were bursting like fireworks in his head, like they had after he'd glanced off that telephone pole. "Holy Mother of Mary," he said with a hiss when the pain finally eased a little.

Helen knelt down next to him, sobbing. "What happened, Johnny? Please tell me."

"Help me up," he said, moaning. "But don't touch my left arm."

"Why not? What's wrong with it?"

"I fell," he explained, making it to his feet. Then easing back down on the bed. "I'm fine. It's nothing."

"Well, it doesn't look like nothing. It looks like—"

"Shut up," he said with a growl, suddenly sick of her high-pitched, whiny voice. "*Just shut up!*"

She put her hands over her ears and started rocking back and forth. "Johnny, please don't talk to me like that. What's happened, what's happened? *Oh God, what's happened?*"

With a herculean effort he lurched to the door, then turned and leaned back against it. God, he could barely focus. He was seeing three of her. Well, there wasn't going to be any waterboarding this time. It was going to be quick. Total intimidation and a fast answer—or death. He needed a bargaining chip, and he needed it fast. He didn't have time to take Helen to a seafood warehouse and interrogate her. Marconi was closing in. He could feel the old man making moves out there. That eerie pre-monition of peril still working for him despite the mind-numbing pain in his shoulder. His code of honor might be headed out the window: if Helen wouldn't give him the information he wanted, she would die. And if he re-ally was going to commit to Karen, if he really was going to take her away from Treviso and have her for his own, it would be all but impossible to hold on to his code, any-way. He'd need Marconi's permission to kill Treviso so he wouldn't have to worry about the little prick trying to get revenge. To get that permission, he'd have to kill Kyle McLean. Whether the guy deserved it or not. He wanted Karen. She was his code of honor now. The most impor-tant thing in his life. And he'd do anything to have her.

Johnny pulled his pistol out and aimed it at the older woman, directly at the chest of the middle image. He hated himself for this, but there wasn't any choice. Not if he wanted happiness. The hell with the code of honor. The hell with everything except Karen.

He'd tried, damn it, he'd tried. He'd gotten to Helen just ahead of Marconi's goons. Whisked her out of the little brick house in the nick of time and sent her to New-ark. Then gone back later and made another, more obvi-ous visit to the house—when he'd fed the cat. All for the benefit of the men he was sure Marconi had watching the house by then. So they'd go back and tell Marconi that he was on the level. He gritted his teeth. He'd tried so hard to do the right thing. But it wasn't going to happen.

Helen clasped her hands tightly out in front of her, so tightly her already pale hands went ashen. Tears rolled down her cheeks as she slowly crawled toward him, begging for her life over and over. He knew she didn't understand what was going on. How could she? He wasn't sure if he did.

"Don't come any closer," he said with a snarl, shocking himself with the callousness of his tone. It was as if someone he didn't know was talking, like he'd lost control of himself. "Or I'll kill you."

"Why, Johnny, why?" She sobbed uncontrollably, still slowly crawling across the floor toward him. "I don't understand. You said you'd take care of me. You said there were men who were trying to hurt me, but that you would keep me safe. Now you're hurting me. Why?"

"I lied. It's a damn awful world sometimes, you know? At least I got you this far. At least I bought you some time."

"Johnny, no. Don't do this to me. Please, ple—" Her last syllable was sucked into a horrific sob.

He moved two steps forward to where she was kneeling, adrenaline suddenly surging through him as his killer instinct kicked in despite the pain. "Sorry, Helen, but this is how it hasta be." He hadn't realized how sickeningly lost he was until just now. How *horribly* lonely he'd been for so long. Lonely enough to destroy the entire way he'd lived his life the past fifteen years. He wanted Treviso's wife, suddenly wanted Karen so badly. Wanted to feel her body against his every night, wanted her to share his life, wanted to give her everything he could, was even willing to accept her child—Treviso's child—as his own. And he was willing to turn his back on what had sustained him, everything he'd believed in for so long, to have Karen and the companionship he realized he so desperately craved now that he was allowing the walls to tumble down. "I need to know where your son is," he said, pressing the gun barrel to her forehead, surprised when she didn't shy away from the feeling of cold steel against her skin. Most people did. "I need to know where Kyle is. *Exactly* where he is. You have five seconds to tell me . . . or I pull the trigger."

Treviso stole quietly into the bedroom, then into the closet. Karen was in the kitchen with her sister and the baby. He'd have plenty of privacy. He needed to make a few entries in his diary to stay current, and this was a good time to do it.

He moved to the box in the corner and opened it, then peered inside. The diary had been moved; no doubt about it. He always put it back in a certain, exact way—with the spine of the book against the far wall. But now the spine was opposite the wall, now it was toward him.

He shook his head, and his thin lips curled into a wry grin.

37

J ACK REACHED FOR the knob—just as the front
door swung open. He pulled back, expecting the
same angry daughter from this morning. But the
rage was gone, replaced by sadness and compassion. He
could see the emotions etched into every nook of her
expression. She knew him like the back of her hand, all
right, but he knew her, too. Just as well.

"You okay?"

"I'm fine, Daddy. Sorry about this morning," she said
after a split-second delay.

"Me, too." He just wondered who she was feeling that
sadness and compassion for. But this wasn't the time to
talk about it. "I shouldn't have—"

"Where's Rosario?"

Jack broke into a wide smile and gestured over his
shoulder. "Right there."

A tall, well-built young man was striding up the cracked path carrying Rosario in his big arms, the baby's diaper bag slung over his shoulder. As he moved into the glow of the porch light, she brought her hands to her mouth. "Oh my God, Daddy. Is this—"

"It sure is," Jack confirmed, beaming. "Cheryl, meet the Kid. Kid, this is my daughter, Cheryl."

McLean cradled the baby in his left arm, waved with his right. "Ma'am."

"Hi, Mikey," she said hesitantly.

"His name's not really Mikey Clemant," Jack explained, his grin fading. "It's Kyle. Kyle McLean."

She took the Kid's hand for a moment, then reached for the baby. "Oh?"

Kyle slipped Rosario carefully into Cheryl's arms. "Yeah, well, I've been in kind of . . . well, for the past couple years—"

"Let's go inside," Jack suggested, grabbing the diaper bag off Kyle's shoulder. "Come on, Kid."

"I need to talk to you, Daddy," Cheryl murmured, catching Jack's arm as he followed Kyle into the house. "It'll only take a second."

He could tell right away that this was important. Maybe it had something to do with that sad expression she'd greeted him with. "What's wrong?"

She shook her head subtly.

She was telling him that Kyle was still too close. That she didn't want the Kid to hear. "Go on in the living room, Kid." Kyle had hesitated a few steps away. "I'll be right there." He turned back to Cheryl when the Kid headed off. "What is it, Princess? What's the matter?"

"Some guy named Biff called here a few minutes ago,"

she explained worriedly. "He says you need to get back to him right away. His number's on the pad by the kitchen phone. He said it was important. He was pushing really hard, Daddy. It was weird."

Jack grimaced. Then wished he hadn't. His reaction had only heightened her anxiety. He could see it right away.

"What's going on, Daddy? Who's Biff?"

"Don't worry about it, honey."

"*Daddy.*"

He took her hands in his. "Look, I gotta go out for a while. Just keep Kyle company." He could see she wasn't buying in. That there was still some bitterness left over from this morning. Still some need to let him know she was in charge of her own life. "I really need you to do this for me, okay?"

She pulled her hands from his and put them on her hips. "I was on my way over to see Bobby. I was hoping you'd watch the baby for me."

"Please, Princess," Jack begged. "This is so important. I don't want Kyle sitting around here by himself. He might get cold feet and take off. I'm so close. *We're* so close."

"Close to what?"

"I'll explain later. *Please*, just hang out here with him. Turns out he's a real nice guy. You'll like talking to him." He could see she was frustrated. "Please."

Cheryl crossed her arms tightly and stared at the ceiling for a few moments. "Oh, all right."

"Thanks, Princess." He gave her a quick hug. "You don't know what this means to me. To *us*. I promise I'll make it up to you." They spoke for a few moments more, then Jack gave her another hug and headed back out. "See you in a little while."

She watched him head back down the path until he disappeared into the darkness. "I sure hope so," she said under her breath.

After he'd started the Citation's engine, Jack adjusted the rearview mirror so he could look himself in the eyes. He didn't like what he saw.

"So you're from New York?" Cheryl asked, still carrying Rosario as she made her way into the living room. It was a throwaway question, just something to get the conversation started. Something Daddy had told her at the door. She sat down, then laid the baby on the couch beside her. The little girl was almost asleep. It was way past her bedtime. "From the city?"

"No, Queens."

"Oh. Well, we lived on Long Island before we moved here a few years ago."

"Yeah, I know. Your dad told me on the way over."

Cheryl saw him looking toward the door. "Daddy had to go out," she explained. "One of his friends is sick and wanted to see him." God. She'd known him only a few minutes and she was already lying to him. Great. Thanks, Daddy. "He shouldn't be long."

"No problem."

But she sensed that Jack had been right. If she hadn't

stayed, he probably would have been out the door. "I'll make you something to eat in a few minutes," she offered, pulling the little girl's pink blanket up over her chest. "Once the baby's really asleep. Okay?"

"I am kinda hungry, ma'am," the Kid admitted, smiling at her.

A sexy half smile she wanted more of right away. "How about a ham sandwich and some chips?"

"Maybe for an appetizer," he said with an easy laugh. "How about a big, thick steak and some mashed potatoes instead?"

"Well, I—"

"I'm kidding," he said good-naturedly. "A ham sandwich would be great. I'd really appreciate it." He patted his flat stomach. "It's just that I eat a little more than most people."

"I bet you do," she agreed, her eyes doing another quick scan. She liked the Kid, she couldn't deny it. He was young and maybe a little rough around the edges. But he had a disarming confidence about him. And then there was that body.

She'd convinced herself she was attracted to Bobby even though Bobby's inner self had turned out to be harder to find than a Manhattan taxi in a summer thunderstorm. Maybe she'd gotten past that empty spot in his personality because he was willing to say he loved her—a lot. And consistently be the first one to say it during their conversations. Unlike *any* of her previous boyfriends. And maybe she'd gotten past all Bobby's faults because he was by far the best-looking guy who'd ever paid attention to her. Which didn't make her feel great about herself, but at least she was finally admitting it.

Well, the Kid had already had a positive influence on her.

She was suddenly aware that she was staring at him—and he was staring back. She glanced down at Rosario and caressed her soft hair.

Kyle was handsome in a rugged way. Even more so if she imagined him without that beard. He had gorgeous gray eyes flecked with burnt yellow; a strong jaw; and, when he smiled, two very deep dimples. She liked the rock star long hair, too. It was wild and provocative. The beard had to go, but the long hair could stay. And up close, her father was right. Kyle was even bigger than he looked on the field. He was going to drive the women in New York City crazy if Daddy got him to the Yankees.

"Let me make one thing clear," she said firmly.

Kyle looked up apprehensively. "What?"

"I don't want you calling me 'ma'am' anymore."

"Why not?"

"It's aggravating."

"Huh?"

"It makes me feel old."

He looked at her like she was crazy. "*Old?* What are you, like twenty-five?"

So he was charming, too. "Now you're doing better," she said with a smile she couldn't control, gently pulling the pink blanket up around the baby's neck. Sometimes she switched the blanket out after Rosario fell asleep and slept with it herself, she loved the baby's scent so much. "Tell me about this game you had last night." Daddy had recounted the story at the door before leaving to meet with whoever Biff was. "When you copied Mickey Mantle. When you had the same hits he did on May 30, 1968.

In the same order." She watched his reaction. "Are you really that good?"

"Maybe I just got lucky."

She'd heard a defensiveness creep into his tone. "Is that what you were trying to do? Were you trying to copy Mantle's game in 1968?"

"Yeah, I was," he admitted.

She liked his voice, too. It was deep, gravelly. "Then why are you playing on a bottom-of-the-barrel Single-A independent team in Sarasota, Florida? My dad says you're one of the greatest baseball talents he's ever seen. And believe me, he knows what he's talking about. If you can hit exactly what you want in five straight at-bats, I have to agree with him."

The Kid was quiet for a few moments. "Was your dad really a scout for the Yankees?"

Cheryl nodded. She could tell he was searching for proof, could tell he wanted to make sure they were who they claimed to be. Apparently, as Daddy had guessed, there was something lurking beneath the surface, and before he spilled his guts, he was going to make damn sure who he was talking to. Which was smart. Well, if it was proof Kyle McLean wanted, it was proof he'd get. "Want to see the scrapbooks?"

"Absolutely."

"Okay." She rose off the couch, placed two pillows between the baby and the floor, then waved for Kyle to follow. "Come on."

He stopped at her bedroom doorway. "Okay if I come in?"

Now, that was a breath of fresh air, she thought. A guy who actually asked. "It's fine." She gestured for him to sit on the bed, then moved to the closet and pulled down a three-inch-thick scrapbook from the shelf above a line of wire hangers.

For twenty minutes they sat side by side, looking at picture after picture of Jack standing with Yankee greats in baseball stadiums all over the country. In Central America and Japan, too. Mantle, Maris, Munson, Catfish Hunter, Reggie, Bucky Dent, Goose Gossage, Guidry, Mattingly, Bernie Williams, Jeter. Three and a half decades of Yankee history. Of American history.

"Jesus," Kyle whispered as Cheryl closed the back cover. "That's amazing." He shook his head. "I wish I could be one of those guys."

"Daddy says you could be. He says he could get you a—"

"Why'd your father quit?" the Kid asked. "I mean, he had a pretty cool job, and he doesn't look that old. The Yankees have done pretty well the past few years, so I doubt there's been any major shake-ups."

Cheryl replaced the scrapbook on the closet shelf. She wanted to tell Kyle the story, but she couldn't. It was up to Daddy to decide to do that. "He got burned out," she said simply, sitting back down on the bed. "You know how much travel there is. It finally got to him."

He stared at her for a few moments.

Like he didn't really believe her. She looked away so he wouldn't see the truth. Those eyes of his were something. *Really* something. They searched you like a CSI team. Carefully and methodically. While they drew you in. "Let me ask you a question," she spoke up, trying to turn things around. "Daddy's tracked your games this season on the Tarpon website, and he's compared them to Mickey Mantle's 1968 season. He says a lot of them match up exactly to Mantle's but that some of them—"

"I can't always do it," Kyle cut in. "Sometimes the other team's pitcher walks me intentionally, or pitches me so far outside I'd have to reach London to get the pitch. Or sometimes he hits me. I can't control those things."

Cheryl felt a wild thrill rush through her. The Kid was admitting to what Daddy had suspected—that he could hit whatever he wanted to whenever he wanted to unless the pitch was in another time zone. At least, he could in Single-A. "But Daddy said today's game wasn't anything like the game Mantle had on May 31st in 1968. He said you popped up four times. Mantle didn't have a single pop-up in his game in 1968. And he said the guy was giving you pitches you could have hit."

The Kid smiled. "You sound like you know your baseball."

"You have to when your father is Jack Barrett." She'd heard the bitterness in her voice, wished she hadn't. But she couldn't help it, especially after this morning. "He's a wonderful man, and I love—"

"Do you have brothers and sisters?"

His voice was melodic, too. Not singsong, but comforting, even with his words washing over gravel. "A brother."

"Baseball player?"

"What do you think?"

"Pretty good high school player, right? But not good enough to make the pros. Probably good enough for college somewhere, but that would have been it."

Cheryl nodded, remembering the conversation at dinner that night when David had told Daddy he wasn't going to college. That he was going straight to the fire department because he knew he wasn't good enough to play in the big leagues. That if he wasn't playing baseball, there was no reason to go to college. "How'd you know?"

"Your expression," he answered. "I've seen it before so many times. I saw so many fathers at my high school games hoping like hell their sons could make it to the Show. Fathers who believed they could, believed their sons could be like me. Then they finally figured out it wasn't going to happen. But they held on to the dream even after their sons had already given it up."

Cheryl stared at the Kid intently. "Exactly," she said, her voice hushed. "That was how it was with Daddy and my brother, David."

"Then after the dads have that come-to-Jesus walk in the woods with themselves and they admit to themselves that the dream's drying up and blowing away like last fall's leaves, they try to make it up to their other kids by giving them more attention. But it's too late by then. So they go back to the son. Then the whole thing turns into a nightmare."

She didn't want to linger here. Kyle was getting too close to the heart of the matter, and she didn't know him well enough to go so deep so fast. "You're good at turning conversations around."

"I have to be."

"Because you have a gift."

The Kid nodded. "Yeah. If you wanna call it that."

She saw that in turn he appreciated her understanding of his dilemma. The way he'd innately understood hers. "But today. Why today? Why so different than Mantle?"

"I got worried," he answered, his voice growing tense for the first time. "The local TV station kept showing replays of last night's game over and over. They were still doing it this morning. The sports guys in town kept talking about the game. I heard the highlights even made it to ESPN." He looked down and shook his head. "I figured some people might hear about it. People who . . . well, people."

She took his hand in both of hers. "What people?"

His gaze turned defiant. "Bad people," he said quietly, his voice cracking. "Real bad people."

Jack watched from the shadows as Biff and Harry wheeled the stretcher down the path from the front door, emergency lights bouncing crazily off the lawn and the big house. The county cop had left a minute ago, and soon the house would be empty. They lifted the elderly woman into the back of the ambulance, then Harry hauled himself into the truck with her and pulled the doors shut while Biff retraced his steps to the front door. He was there just a few moments, then he jogged down the path again, jumped into the front of the ambulance, and the vehicle roared off.

It was the perfect setup, Biff had claimed excitedly on the phone. The mother lode. The one they'd been waiting for. A rich old widow who lived alone in a big house in a neighborhood that wasn't gated. Easy access and easy escape. He was going to leave the front door open so Jack could get in. There were jewels everywhere in the master bedroom suite. Dripping off the old woman's dressing table, nightstand, and the bathroom counter. Tens of thousands of dollars' worth, maybe more. They'd split it fifty-fifty tomorrow.

Jack took a deep breath and sighed, then moved out of the bushes toward the front door, head down. How the hell had it come to this?

38

"WHAT'S THE MATTER, Deuce?" the old man asked gruffly. "Why'd you have to see me right away? Why the panic attack?"

"Whadaya mean? Nobody's panicking."

"Yeah?"

"I'm fine, Angelo."

Marconi hesitated. "You sure you're all right, Deuce?"

"Of course."

Johnny was teetering on the edge of terrified as he watched the old man gorge on the last few bites of a thick, nearly raw rib eye. He was doing all he could to make it seem like everything was normal—despite the bullet hole and the dread—but it was tough. Nicky had claimed Marconi was fine with a quick meeting when they spoke earlier on the phone as Johnny was driving like a bat out of hell back up the Jersey Turnpike from Edison, fighting his body's urge to pass out. Nicky said Marconi was going to eat a late supper, then had one more meeting, at midnight. So coming by the row house at about nine-thirty wouldn't be a problem. When Johnny knocked on the front door a few minutes ago, Nicky opened it as usual, and was his usual respectful self. After Johnny had given the first password, it was smooth sailing up the steps to the second floor. Everything seemed fine.

Then things changed. There was a new guy standing outside Marconi's bedroom door. An even bigger and seedier-looking guy than Goliath. The guy asked for the second password twice and took a long time frisking him. Now Marconi seemed wary. When the old man was relaxed, his dark eyebrows were spread far apart. But when he got suspicious, they came together until they looked like one long caterpillar. The caterpillar was definitely coming to life.

"And whadaya mean, 'you sure you're all right?'"

"You seem jumpy. And you're sweatin' like a turkey outside a kitchen door on Thanksgiving. It ain't *that* warm in here." The old man pointed at Johnny's shoulder. "You got a problem?"

"Nah. Why?"

"You keep moving it. Like something's wrong with it."

Christ, Marconi never missed a trick. "I'm fine. It's an old injury from high school. From when I was in this motorcycle accident. It gets stiff when it rains, you know? I'm gettin' older. Sucks. You can understand."

"Yeah, sure." Marconi's expression turned grave and his eyebrows pinched even closer together. "So what's going on?"

It was a risk coming here. A *big* risk. Maybe all the nor-

mal stuff with Nicky had just been a well-choreographed
plan to get him here so they could kill him. Marconi knew
Strazza was dead at this point, and Johnny assumed the
old man would staple the guilt for the hit directly on him.
It only made sense. He'd been the mark, so he must be the
killer. That might be enough right there to get the death
sentence. Yeah, that feeling of terror he was trying desperately to fight was absolutely justified.

But offsetting the primal fear was one thing Johnny
figured at least gave him a fighting chance, at least gave
him an opportunity to bargain. Marconi's biggest objective in all of this was still to kill Kyle McLean, to get revenge for his grandson's death. Johnny was betting that
McLean's murder still took precedence over everything
else in Marconi's life right now. Even family business.
Mostly because the old man sensed that after all this
time he was finally close, about to get that long-awaited
payback. So it made sense for Marconi to let him come
here. Why the hell not let Johnny in the den? Why not
see what he was offering, understand why he'd begged
for the meeting?

The trick would be getting back out of the den—without doing it zipped up in a body bag.

To do that, to be able to leave here still breathing, he'd
have to offer something tasty. Something even more delicious than that nearly raw rib eye the old man had just
taken the last bite of. And Johnny was confident he knew
what that was. Felt certain he could negotiate his way
through the minefield. Just as long as they didn't cap him
before he even had a chance to start talking.

Of course, Angelo Marconi never—*absolutely never*—
negotiated with *anyone* over the telephone. Never even

spoke to anyone on the phone himself because he was ever fearful of the law listening in. Always had Nicky talk on the phone because he was terrified of spending his last few years wasting away in a federal pen. Which was why Johnny had been forced into taking this awful risk. Forced into entering the den. To make the offer, he *had* to make it in person.

"I need to ask you something," Johnny began, somehow making his voice sound strong despite the pain shooting through his body. He needed to clean the wound as soon as possible—there was dried blood caked all over the left side of his chest and stomach. But what he really needed was a month of sleep. Which, unfortunately, he wasn't going to get. Not anytime soon. In fact, he was booked on an early flight to Florida tomorrow morning. At least he'd get a little shut-eye before heading to LaGuardia. Then a few more hours on the plane before everything went crazy. "Angelo, I need your permission to—"

"Do you know where Kyle McLean is?" Marconi interrupted. "This whole thing has taken too long, Deuce. Way too long. Frankly, I didn't think it would take more than a week. And another thing, I thought you moved too slow on McLean's mother. On Helen McLean. You gave her time to get out." His eyes narrowed. "I just hope you didn't have anything to do with her getting out. I put some damn good people on tracking her down, but they haven't come up with anything yet, and it seems kinda odd to me that she's gone without a trace. I just don't think of a woman like that being Houdini. So lemme ask you again. Do you know where Kyle McLean is?"

Johnny knew his answer wouldn't go over very well, but he had to make certain Marconi understood right away this wasn't a Q&A session. That it was a negotiation. He just prayed to God he was right about Marconi's primary objective in all this. "Maybe."

Marconi's eyes bugged out for a split second, then he leaned back and smiled angrily, regaining control quickly despite the rage boiling inside. "Johnny, Johnny, Johnny." He chuckled like a father who was about to administer the belt to a pair of disobedient bare-ass cheeks.

It was the warning chuckle. Johnny'd recognize it anytime, anywhere. And it raised the hairs on the back of his neck. Scared him right down to his socks. It was the chuckle Marconi used right before he told Johnny who he wanted hit. It was the way he'd chuckled when he ordered Johnny to kill Kyle McLean a few weeks ago.

"Okay, lemme ask you another question." Marconi pointed a fat finger at Johnny. "You kill Ricky Strazza today?"

Johnny was ready to go right at this one because he'd come up with a perfect answer. He said a quick prayer, then began. "Yeah, I did. He was following me, Angelo, and it scared me. I figured he'd turned colors and was working for one of the other families. That was the only thing that made sense. I was gonna call you, but I didn't have time. I had my opportunity, so I took it. I shot him dead, that bastard traitor." Marconi was about to say something, then stopped. He could tell he'd headed the old man off at the pass with the traitor accusation. "I figured Strazza was gonna hit me. Figured he was working for the Capellettis. That it was payback for me killing that capo for you down in Staten Island. Like I said. That was all that fit. So I made my move. Figured you'd be happy about it. Not pissed."

Marconi gazed at Johnny for a few moments, touching his throat gently like it was sore.

Johnny knew the old man was trying to figure out what was truth and what wasn't. It wasn't like Marconi could have Nicky pick up the phone, make one call and find out if Strazza was a traitor. It would take more than a few calls and probably a week or so for him to get a straight answer. Thank God Marconi had far too much faith in the rumor mill to ignore it.

"Johnny," Marconi spoke up quietly, "I, I don't know what to say."

He'd never seen the old man at a loss for words like this. It was incredible, and he had to press his advantage. "Like I said, Angelo. I didn't have a choice. I had to protect—"

"All right!" Marconi barked, frustrated. *"Shut up and lemme—"*

The bedroom door burst open and the new bodyguard leveled a pistol at Johnny's chest. "Don't move, Bondano!" the guy ordered. "You all right, boss?" he asked, not taking his eyes off Johnny.

"I'm fine, I'm fine. But good work." Marconi smiled, obviously satisfied at his new bodyguard's lightning-quick response to his raised voice. He waved. "Leave us. But don't go too far."

"Yes, sir."

When the door was closed again, Johnny slumped down in his chair and took a deep breath.

"What's the matter, Deuce?" Marconi asked, pulling a long cigar from his shirt pocket. "Little strange being on the wrong end of a gun?"

"Yeah," Johnny whispered. It was, too. Though he'd been shot twice now, he'd never actually seen the gun aimed at him either time. The bullets had come from nowhere. Out of the darkness, so to speak. Like today, through the roof of Strazza's car. In all his years in this business, he'd never actually seen a gun pointed at him, he realized. Hoped he never did again. It was better when the bullet came from the dark.

"So where's Kyle McLean?" Marconi demanded when the cigar was lit.

Johnny drew himself up in the chair, searching for the courage to lay it all out. "I wanna kill Tony Treviso. I'll kill McLean first," Johnny added quickly when Marconi's eyes bugged out again. He didn't want Marconi to start yelling again and have that crazy prick outside the door bursting in here a second time. The guy might not show as much restraint the next time. For all his bravado, he seemed pretty inexperienced. Fidgety, too. Which was never good when a guy had a gun in his hand. Especially when he was aiming it at you. "McLean'll be dead in less than seventy-two hours, Angelo. I guarantee it. I'll bring a picture of him capped, like I have with the other guys. A close-up of the head shot. You'll know he's iced. Then I want to kill Treviso. I want your permission to do that when McLean is dead."

Marconi puffed on the cigar for a few moments, mulling it over. "Less than seventy-two hours?"

"Yeah. At most. I guarantee you. He's a dead man. All right?"

Marconi stared at Johnny hard, then gave him a half grin. "I like it."

Relief poured through Johnny. Words were one thing, but that half grin meant Marconi was really in. He recognized it the same way he'd recognized the death chuckle earlier. The caterpillar over his eyes was gone, too. "Good."

"Hey, why you wanna kill Tony Treviso?" Marconi asked.

"He's getting in the way."

Marconi snickered. "Timid Tony couldn't get in the way of anything. Wouldn't know how. I mean, I know about that rumor and all, about him killing the guy. It isn't true. Can't be." Marconi hesitated. "What's really going on?"

"I don't want any screwups. Treviso's gonna be pissed when he finds out McLean's dead and he didn't get a chance to—"

"You like his wife, don't you?"

"*What?*"

"Come on, Deuce, we all like his wife. She's beautiful. One of the guys on the council wanted to ice Treviso so he could go after her. He wasn't really serious, of course. At least I don't think he was. If he had been, I woulda said no. But for you, I could make an exception." Marconi gave Johnny a sinister smile. "Come on, tell me."

"Angelo, I don't—"

"All right, all right," the old man interrupted, sucking down more cigar smoke.

It was like Marconi wanted Johnny to want Karen. Like he was getting some kind of sadistic pleasure thinking about Johnny killing Treviso so he could have Karen. Like he was picturing what Karen would look like in bed nude.

Marconi shrugged. "Hey. You don't wanna tell me, you don't gotta." He pulled the cigar from his mouth and eyed the colorful band identifying its Cuban maker. "So you figured out McLean really did it? You're convinced he was the one who killed my grandson?"

Tony Treviso had run over the little boy. No doubt. Probably as he and Paulie squealed out to go after McLean, Johnny figured. The trip to the body shop and the owner's admission had proven once and for all who had killed the little boy. But it didn't matter anymore. Johnny had made his decision. He wanted Karen Treviso, wanted her for his own. And he didn't want her psychopathic husband and his ape friend Paulie the Moon trying to track him down the rest of his life. With Marconi's permission to make the hit, that would never happen. Treviso would be dead, and Paulie would never seek revenge if Marconi had okayed the killing. It was too bad for Kyle McLean— and Helen—but that's how it was going to be. He was waving good-bye to his code of honor forever. Nuking it. But maybe Marconi was right after all, maybe it was stupid. Killing was killing. There wasn't any honor when it came to killing. Maybe not even on the battlefield.

"Yeah," Johnny said quietly but firmly, "McLean killed him." He couldn't second-guess himself now. He had a passionate sense of purpose about something other than killing for the first time in a long time, and nothing was going to distract him from it. He wanted Karen Treviso, and nothing else mattered. If he tried telling Marconi the truth, that his grandson's killer was really Treviso, that might throw a monkey wrench into everything. Marconi might stop the process, might want to dig deeper for confirmation. No way in hell that was going to happen. This way it was all neat and tidy. He got Karen, he killed her husband himself with permission from the boss, and he made a million bucks. "There's no doubt about it."

* * *

Johnny lay sprawled on his back on the bed. Karen lay next to him on her left side, head resting on the pillow next to his. She was caressing his head with her long fingernails.

She'd asked over and over what had happened, what was wrong with his shoulder, why he looked so pale. He'd told her a story about falling down some stairs. The same story he'd told Helen McLean, who at this point was tied up tightly in the trunk of the Seville, a wash-cloth from the Happy Go Lucky Motel stuffed down her throat.

He'd been forced to be rough with Helen—very rough—to break her down fast. To get her to tell him where Kyle was. He'd done some awful things to her. Things he'd pay for dearly on Judgment Day. But there'd been no other way. She wasn't just going to tell him. He grimaced. He was almost as good at torturing as he was at killing. So maybe it wasn't Treviso the devil would call his friend, Johnny realized. Maybe it was really him. And the problem with being a friend of the devil was that he always turned his back on you in the end. It was simply a matter of time.

Turned out Kyle McLean was in Sarasota, Florida, playing baseball for some crappy minor-league team. Turned out he was playing under an assumed name: Mikey Clemant. It wasn't going to be real hard finding him now. Well, at least he'd done all those horrible things to Helen in the name of true love. He grimaced again. Jesus, how hollow and self-serving did that sound?

Treviso was up in the Bronx again with Paulie the

Moon, boozing it up at the same place as before. Johnny had the same eye behind the bar ready to let him know when Treviso left. He had it all worked out. He just wanted to see Karen one more time before he went to Sarasota. Seemed like Karen was the only good thing in his life right now, and he needed his fix of her to get him through the next few days. To make him feel better about what he'd done.

When he first got to Treviso's apartment, he thought about making love to her, but his shoulder hurt too bad. But damn, her fingernails felt good running through his hair and over his chest, even though he'd kept his shirt on so she wouldn't see the wound. Right now it felt almost as good as making love.

"You're warm, Johnny," she whispered. "Are you sick?"

"I'm fine." Amazingly, he really did feel better now that he'd been lying here for thirty minutes with the woman he loved. The pain in his shoulder had eased thanks to her gentle caresses. "Really."

"Can I fix you some coffee or tea?"

"Nah, but thanks. What you're doing feels great. Don't stop."

She rolled onto her back and started caressing him again. "What are we gonna do, Johnny?"

He glanced over at her. Hadn't she just heard him? "What do you mean?"

"We can't keep sneaking around like this, you can't keep coming here. Sooner or later Tony will figure out what's going on. We both know what'll happen then."

"I got it all worked out," Johnny said confidently. "Everything. We're gonna be together, Karen. You're not gonna have to worry about that prick husband of yours ever again. And I'm gonna take care of your kid, too," he added. "I mean it. I will. I'll treat him like he's my own. I been thinking a lot about this."

She rolled quickly back onto her side so she was facing him. "Are you serious?" she asked excitedly. "Really, Johnny?"

"Really, Karen. I'm committed." He was, too.

"Oh God." She kissed his cheek. "I love you so much."

"I love you, too. I really do."

"So what are you gonna do?" she asked excitedly.

"I'll tell you everything later," he answered, raising up with a groan and swinging his legs slowly to the floor. He hated to tear himself away from her touches, but it was after ten-thirty. He had to get back to his apartment and get some sleep. He had to be up at six in the morning to make his flight down to Florida. The good thing was, he'd be able to stay in his own place in Tampa. "When I get back from my trip, I'll lay it all out."

"Trip?" she asked, rising up on her knees, then shaking her long, dark hair. Arching her back and running her hands over her breasts and down her flat belly.

Johnny took a deep breath. She was so gorgeous. It was like being on a drug watching her. And now that he'd decided to have her, he started to understand what Treviso went through every day. That awful insecurity of wondering if today was the day she'd meet her next prince. If today was the day the natural selection process—nature's most powerful force—would make her move. "Yeah. I gotta go away for a few days," he finally said, promising himself that this would be the last trip he'd ever take without her. He wasn't going to give any man any chance to take his place. And he'd kill him if he tried.

"Please don't go," she begged. "I can't take three days without you."

"I got no choice."

"Take me with you."

For a few moments he actually considered it. "No, I can't."

"I wish you would."

"I'll take you next time, when it's not business," he promised. More to himself than her. "You'd like Sarasota."

"Where's Sarasota?" she asked, sliding off the bed and kneeling down seductively in front of him. "Forget it," she said as he was about to answer. "Right now I don't care where anything is but this," she murmured, unzipping his pants. She looked up at him sexily. "How's about a going-away present?"

Treviso stole down the narrow, pitch-dark hallway toward their bedroom, silently sliding the fingertips of his right hand along the wall to guide him. At the last second remembering to pull them away from the wall six paces past the front door to avoid the crucifix hanging there. He'd taken off his shoes in the corridor outside the apartment so he wouldn't make any noise walking on the wooden floor. He felt the pistol tucked into his belt beneath his shirt. Was aware of the cold steel against his belly despite how drunk he was. Thank God Paulie had driven him home. He wouldn't have made it on his own. He was way too drunk. Paulie was a good man. Always took care of everything.

He stopped outside the bedroom doorway, took a few quiet breaths, and listened. Then leaned forward, just far enough to see into the bedroom with one eye. Even though the shade was down, the rays of the streetlamp outside the apartment window were bright enough for him to see silhouettes. God, she was beautiful.

He moved across the floor, quickly removed his clothes, and slipped into bed. "Wake up, baby."

"Tony," Karen murmured, still half asleep. "Tony, is that you?"

"Yeah, it's me." He could feel himself becoming aroused. The touch of her body against his did it to him every time. No matter what part of her body was touching him. "Kiss me, honey. Kiss me hard."

For several moments their lips were locked together. Then he moved on top of her and she guided him in, moaning in pain as he entered her with one impatient stroke. "Did you find out?" he wanted to know.

"I got everything," she answered, biting her finger to keep from screaming as he began to move in and out. "He couldn't resist me. It happened just like you said it would. I knelt down in front of him and told him I wanted to give him a going-away present and he couldn't resist."

Treviso felt himself becoming more turned on, thinking about her kneeling in front of Deuce Bondano. The unsuspecting Deuce Bondano. "Where, baby, where? Where'd you do it?"

"In here. Right beside the bed."

Just a few feet away from where they were doing it now. Jesus. "Did you do what he wanted? Did you, Karen?"

She ran her tongue around her lips as his back-and-forth motion turned violent for a few seconds. "I did, baby. I did everything he wanted. Everything *you* wanted."

He shut his eyes tightly, imagining her on her knees in front of Bondano. Imagining what it looked like. The visual fantasy heightening his lust. "Christ!"

"He's flying to Sarasota, Florida, in the morning," she murmured huskily. "This guy he's going to kill plays for some minor-league baseball team down there. The Sarasota Tarpons. Says his name is Kyle McLean, but he's using another name."

"What is it?"

"Mikey Clemant."

Treviso felt that familiar overpowering sensation coming on, but this time it was different. This time it was like an earthquake. Way more intense than it ever had been. Even more intense than that first time so many years ago when he was twelve. When he'd gone down that lonely, trash-strewn alley with an old, toothless woman he'd paid twenty bucks to. Gone down the alley a boy—and come out a man.

It had been his ultimate act of self-control to make Karen give herself to Deuce Bondano, Treviso realized. He'd warred against every instinct inside to do it, but he'd finally prevailed. And now that it was done, now that everything had worked out perfectly and he was back in her arms, the sense of power was unbelievable. His wife had done exactly as he'd ordered her to do—gone against every natural instinct inside of her, too. But now he knew where to find Kyle McLean. Finally he had a chance to dig himself out of this terrible hole and get all that money back. On top of everything, he'd be the one to kill Kyle McLean for Angelo Marconi. Then maybe he wouldn't have to be a two-bit loan shark the rest of his life. For several exhilarating seconds he actually thought about being made, of maybe even being on the council someday.

He gazed down at Karen as he lost control. Sure, most people in the world would think he was a disgusting coward. But the hell with them. All of them. They didn't understand how disgusting it was just to be Tony Treviso.

And as the incredibly powerful climax finally exploded, his mind turn to only one thing: killing Deuce Bondano.

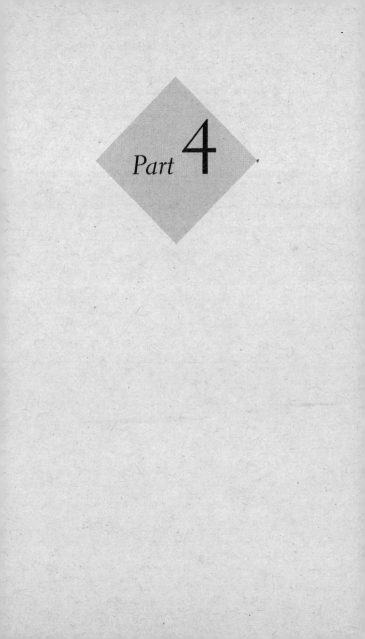

Part 4

39

JACK MOVED PURPOSEFULLY down the hallway from his bedroom wearing his plaid bathrobe, boxers, and white socks, barely noticing the pain in his knees as he gimped along. He held his breath as he came around the corner of the living room, then let out a long sigh of relief. Thank God. The Kid was fast asleep on the couch. Just like he'd been last night at twelve-thirty, when Jack finally got home. He took a deep whiff of the Vermont roast wafting toward him from the kitchen. He'd been so worried the Kid would be gone this morning. Or, worse, that this had all been a dream.

"You're up early," Cheryl said as Jack sauntered into the kitchen, feeling good about himself again. "It's only seven-fifteen."

Jack pulled a coffee mug down from the closet. Rosario was in her high chair. Cheryl was feeding her.

Everything seemed right with his world again. "Yeah, some trucker blew his horn going by the house a few minutes ago," he said, trying to seem pissed about it. "Bastard woke me up."

Cheryl scoffed as she steered a spoonful of applesauce into the little girl's mouth. "Nobody blew his horn, Daddy. You were worried Kyle was gone."

"I was not, I was—"

"What time did you get home last night?"

"I'm not sure," Jack answered tersely, pouring a cup of steaming black java, then heading for the table, irritated at the tone she'd interrupted him with. They were suddenly a lot more equal than they'd ever been. He understood why after the argument yesterday morning—but he still didn't like it. "So did the Kid say anything to you last night while I was out?"

"What time did you get home?" she repeated, her tone even firmer.

"Did the Kid say anything to you last night?" he repeated, even louder.

She stuck her tongue out at him, then smiled sweetly at Rosario.

He knew she didn't like him changing subjects, but there was no way he was talking about last night. Not yet, anyway.

"He wanted to make sure you were who you said you were," she finally answered. "He wanted proof."

"What did you—"

"I gave it to him. I showed him that scrapbook with all the pictures of you and the players. He was pretty impressed."

Jack eased into the chair opposite Cheryl's.

"He wanted to know why you quit the Yankees, too," she added, stirring the applesauce into a neater pile.

"What'd you tell him?"

"That they fired you because you were a mean, middle-aged man who makes his daughter cry."

"Hey, I didn't—"

"I told him you just got burned out and quit."

Jack brought the steaming mug to his lips. "Oh, okay," he muttered in a hat-in-hand way. "I'm sorry about yesterday, Princess," he said, gazing at the baby. "I've thought a lot about it since we had our, well . . . our little discussion."

"I wouldn't call it a *little* discussion. Maybe not even a discussion at all."

"Okay. Since our argument. There, I said it. Look, I'm not proud of what happened, but I meant well. You know that." He was hoping for some kind words back, but they didn't come. "I promise I won't try to run your life anymore, Princess." He couldn't believe what he was about to say. "And I won't say anything bad about Bobby anymore. I won't try to keep you away from him."

"But will you accept him?" she asked, her voice on edge. "I don't want you to just ignore him. I want to know that if we get married you'll love him like you should love a son-in-law."

Jack started to roll his eyes, then caught himself. "Are you already talking about marriage?" He tried using a tone that didn't sound like he was irritated, but it was hard.

"Bobby mentioned it last night on the phone."

"What do you mean, he *mentioned* it?"

Cheryl put the applesauce down on the table. "You're doing it again, Daddy."

Jack held up his hand. "Okay, okay. I hear you." It just seemed so wrong. He had such a bad feeling about Bobby Griffin. Or was it simply that he was going to have bad feelings about any guy she dated? He hadn't liked any of the losers she'd gone out with since they'd moved to Florida. But at least he hadn't had this gnawing sense of apprehension about any of them like he did about Bobby. "I'm working on it, all right?"

She took a long time answering. "All right," she finally said.

He glanced out the bay window in front of the table. It was another beautiful spring morning in South Florida. Warm and sunny, hardly a cloud in the sky. Of course, this morning was a little better than most, he thought, staring at the small storage shed where he kept the lawn mower and some other odds and ends. Actually, it was a *lot* better than most. Which was why he felt so good. Kyle McLean was safely under his roof, and hopefully would soon be listening to his advice. Then taking it.

He smiled, thinking about that other thing out in the shed. If the Kid hadn't been victimized yet, why not now? He ought to be glad about it happening here rather than at some big stadium in front of his veteran major-league teammates, who'd howl at him for days.

"Daddy?"

"Yes, Princess?" Her tone suddenly had a hint of desperation. "What is it?"

"I hate to bring this up so early in the morning," she said hesitantly, reaching for her purse and pulling out her checkbook. It was stuffed with envelopes—bills that needed paying. "I know how you hate it, but we've got to talk money."

She was right. He hated it *so* much. Suddenly he wasn't feeling as good about his world.

"We spent more on Rosario than I thought," she explained, holding up a few of the receipts. "A lot more."

"Ouch."

"Yeah, big ouch. On top of that, my car needs work on the cooling system or something. It's been making a funny noise, so I took it by the shop near the office. The guys are pretty nice there, and my boss knows them. So I trust them. They said I needed a new—"

"Ah, you can't trust anybody when it comes to fixing cars," Jack muttered angrily. "All those places are out to steal you blind. Don't you get that?"

"Yes," she said evenly, "I do."

Like she was placating him, he realized. Like she'd heard him go on and on about it so many times it wasn't worth arguing about it anymore. "How much are they gouging you for?"

"Eight hundred dollars."

There was no reason to argue—and no going back now. "I'll have the money for you tonight."

"What do you mean?"

"I mean I'll take care of everything this afternoon, and I'll give you the cash you need tonight."

"How are you going to do that?"

"Don't worry about it."

"Daddy, I—"

"Don't worry about it," he snapped. "You don't want me controlling your life. Well, don't try to control mine."

"I'm not trying to do that. I'm trying to keep you out of—"

"Princess!"

"All right, all right."

He glanced out the bay window at the shed again as the baby started to cry. He wanted to think of something fun. Not money and how they didn't have it. "Did Kyle say anything more about what was going on with him?" he asked in a low voice so the Kid wouldn't hear if he was awake. "About what he's doing here? About why he's using a made-up name?"

Cheryl picked the baby out of her high chair and patted her gently on the back as she held her to her shoulder. She stopped crying right away.

It was amazing, Jack thought. Rosario was so keyed into Cheryl's moods—and vice versa. Christ, what would Cheryl do if they came and took Rosario away? She might be suicidal. At the very least, inconsolable. There were so many damn moving parts to all this. Stay calm, he told himself, stay calm. But it was getting harder and harder to do that all the time, especially under the pressure. It was amazing—frightening—how much age affected you.

"Did he?"

"Yes," she answered quietly.

"Well, what did he say? *Come on*," he pushed. "*Please, Princess.*"

"He said a lot. The bottom line is that he's hiding out from one of the New York Mafia families."

Everything around her blurred to nothing until only her face was visible.

"He borrowed money from a loan shark to pay for an operation his mother needed," she continued. "A hundred thousand dollars. Neither of his parents had health insurance, and their savings were even less than ours. It was a life-and-death thing for his mom, and he thought he had a year to pay the mob back. He was going to use money from the bonus he figured he'd get on the contract he signed with a pro team after his senior year. People were telling him he'd get at least a million dollars. But the mob came looking for the money early. Way early."

"Keep going." Jack was on the edge of his seat. Literally.

"Kyle told them he couldn't pay. He thought they were bluffing. He'd never dealt with the mob before. How would he know? So they killed his girlfriend, the girl he was going to marry."

Jack shook his head. "Animals."

They were quiet for a few moments.

"Anyway," she continued, "after that the loan shark told Kyle they were going to start killing his family, too. The guy said they'd kill his mother first, then everybody else. He told Kyle he'd torture her before he killed her, too."

"Jesus Christ. The poor kid must have gone crazy."

"He told me he lost his mind, and he went after the guy."

"Bad idea." Jack didn't know much about the mob, but he knew you never won a fight with them. "*Very* bad idea."

"Especially because the loan shark's enforcer buddy was hanging around, though Kyle didn't know it. And this guy was bigger than Kyle. Which didn't really matter because the guy had a gun." Cheryl kissed the baby on the forehead and started rocking her gently. "So Kyle bolted for his car, jumped in it, and took off. He got away, but he knew he had a big problem. The next day the problem got even bigger."

"Why?"

"Kyle has an uncle who was with the NYPD. He told

him what was going on a few days before everything went nuts, so he was already trying to get inside information from his contacts. The morning after Kyle had his run-in with the loan shark the uncle got a call from an old informant who told him it all happened right in front of the house of one of the family's most senior guys. In front of a row house in Queens. The deal was Kyle killed this mob boss's grandson when he drove off in a panic. The little boy was riding his bike and Kyle hit him as he was trying to get away from the loan shark's buddy."

Jack banged the table loudly, scaring Rosario so badly she almost jumped out of Cheryl's arms.

"Damn it, Daddy. The baby was almost asleep."

"Sorry, but *now* I remember it all. Now I remember reading about that whole thing in the newspapers. The story was front page, even down here."

"I wouldn't know," she said, cradling the baby. "I never read those articles. It's like you said. They're animals and I don't want to know anything about them."

Jack raised both eyebrows. "Well, the great thing is, that all happened a couple of years ago. They've forgotten about it by now."

"I don't know about that, but Kyle swears he didn't do it. He says they framed him. He says he never hit a little boy on a bike. Never hit anyone. I believe him, too."

"But I'll bet his cop uncle told him at the time he had only one choice. To fake his own death and run."

Cheryl nodded. "Right. So Kyle drove his car off a pier into the East River, then came here to Florida and started living under the name Mikey Clemant. He doesn't stay in one apartment for long, he's broke, he doesn't—"

"He doesn't have any friends," Jack cut in, "doesn't get

close to his teammates, suspects everyone of everything. Yeah, I can understand him doing that for a while. But like I said, it's been two years. He doesn't have to worry about it anymore."

"Are you sure?" Cheryl asked uncertainly. "I thought those guys were supposed to have long memories."

"That's overblown these days," Jack said confidently. "Besides, if I'm remembering the story right, that mob boss was pretty old. Hell, he's probably dead by now."

Cheryl shrugged. "All I know is that Kyle told me he got scared after he had that incredible game."

"Because the local sports guys went on and on about it," Jack said, snapping his fingers. "They made a bigger deal about it than he thought they would. Then the national guys probably picked it up."

"ESPN," Cheryl said. "At least he thinks they did. He didn't see it himself because he doesn't have a TV, but people told him about it. He was even a little worried that somebody might figure out the Mickey Mantle thing, too. About him copying Mantle's 1968 season."

Of course. "That's why he dumped yesterday's game."

"Four lazy pop-ups," Cheryl confirmed. "Nothing like Mantle's May 31st game in 1968. And he won't ever have the same game as Mantle again."

"Did he admit that to you?" Jack asked. "That he had a different game than Mantle on purpose?"

"Yup."

Jack raised his hands to the ceiling, like he was thanking God. "It's a miracle," he murmured. He gestured toward the living room. "Did our young guest tell you what else Mikey Clemant spells? Or did you already figure that one out on your own?"

Cheryl thought for a few seconds, then her eyes widened. *"Mickey Mantle."*

Jack nodded. "Mantle was his father's idol. His father and just about everybody else in New York City during the sixties."

"Including you," Cheryl pointed out.

"He was," Jack admitted, a faraway look in his eyes. "He was the greatest player I ever saw." For a few moments he reminisced about some of the things he'd seen Mantle do on the field. Finally he shook his head. "So anyway, Kyle switched the letters around in his name to come up with his fake name."

"As a tribute to his father."

"Yes."

Cheryl put the baby back in her high chair. "He's had a couple of tough years, Daddy. We need to help him."

"We will, Princess."

"How?"

"I'm gonna get him a tryout with the Yankees," Jack answered. "Then I'm gonna help us." He gritted his teeth. "I'm gonna get my job back, and I'm gonna find out who screwed me."

Cheryl moved around the table and hugged him from behind, squeezing his shoulders. "Daddy," she said quietly, "there's something I need to tell you. I hope you won't hate me for it, but I looked in that box underneath your bed." She was ready for him to jump out of his chair and start yelling, but he didn't. "I know Mom made up all those lies about you cheating on her. I know it was really her cheating on you. That you were telling me the truth all along." She hesitated. She could feel his body starting to tremble. "I love you so much."

* * *

"Did you ride your bike all the way out here?" Mitch Borden asked. "All the way out here to the stadium?"

MJ nodded. "How'd you know?"

Borden pointed out the window. "I saw you ride up. How far is it from your house?"

"Nine miles."

"That's dedication, young man," Borden said with the faint smile of sincere respect elders didn't often give teenagers. "You can go a long way in life if you keep up that attitude."

Mitch Borden owned a string of Mercedes dealerships all over South Florida—and he owned the Sarasota Tarpons. He was a tall, gray-haired, distinguished-looking man in his late sixties. He'd been raised in a small Georgia town by a blue-collar father who'd been a devoted member of the Klan until the day he died. But Borden hadn't been poisoned by all that. He'd been strong of will and mind, an independent thinker even as a young man, and he'd turned his back on his father after leaving for college—which he'd paid for himself. Now he was worth millions, into many different businesses and investments. But his pet project was the Tarpons.

"I want to go a long way."

They were sitting in Borden's spacious office, which overlooked the baseball field on one side and the parking lot on the other. "Well, what can I do for you, son? Somehow you got yourself past Patty," he said, motioning toward the office door. "I don't know how, because usually she doesn't let anyone past."

"I got past her," MJ said politely, "because you wanted

me to get past her. I'm assuming you know what happened last night."

Borden nodded, his expression turning serious. "I did hear about that. At least I heard Lefty's version. I assume you're here because you have something you want to tell me? A different spin on it, I'm guessing."

"Mikey Clemant didn't do anything, Mr. Borden. He's innocent. Zack Whitney's the one who's lying." MJ hesitated. "Reggie McDaniel isn't coming clean, either. And Whitney's white and McDaniel is black. So you can see this isn't a race thing for me, okay?"

"Fair enough. Well, what do you think happened?"

"Pardon me, sir, it isn't what I *think* happened. It's what I *know* happened."

Borden spread his arms. "Okay."

MJ related the facts quickly.

When he was done, Borden nodded approvingly. "You're a good communicator, MJ. If you write and listen as well as you talk, I know you'll be a great success. Being able to communicate is essential for success."

For some reason Borden seemed fixated on telling him how far he could go in life, on being a mentor. Maybe that was just natural for older, successful men. Maybe they felt like it was their duty to help young people figure it out. "Thank you, sir. I appreciate that, but I—"

"I'll make you a promise, son," Borden interrupted. "I'll check out what happened personally. If I find out your version is the truth, you'll be back in the dugout for tomorrow night's game and your friend Mr. Clemant will be back in center field, too. And some heads will roll."

"How exactly are you going to check things out?" MJ asked skeptically. Judging from his reaction, Borden wasn't accustomed to this kind of scrutiny. But what the hell, this was important, and it wasn't like he was going to get another opportunity like this. It was the least he could do for the Kid after being on the take. "Details?"

"Don't worry about it."

It seemed like the odds were still pretty good that he and the Kid wouldn't be back in uniform tomorrow night. Well, at least he'd tried. "Okay." MJ started to get up.

"Why is Mikey Clemant so hard to reach?" Borden asked, his voice softer. "Why doesn't he want to be anyone's friend?"

"What do you mean?" MJ eased back into the chair. He could tell Borden was seeing right through the smoke screen.

"Don't try that with me, son. I'm helping you. Now you help me."

Borden was right. Fair was fair. "I don't know," MJ said apologetically. "I really don't. I'm trying to figure it out, too."

"Why? I mean, I've got an economic incentive. Why do you care so much?"

For some reason that was suddenly a tough question. Maybe in the back of his mind he still figured he had an economic incentive, too. Like Jack might give him more money if he kept helping. "I don't know. 'Cause he's my friend, I guess. At least I think he is. I know he doesn't have any other friends on the team."

"You know him before you started the batboy job?" Borden asked.

"No."

"Mmm."

MJ debated with himself for a few seconds about

opening up. He didn't know if he could trust Borden, but you didn't get many chances like this. "Look, Mr. Borden, I think Mikey Clemant could be one of the best baseball players who ever lived." MJ was careful to keep using the Kid's alias, even though he knew his real name now. "The world ought to see what he can do. And Mikey ought to have a chance to see the world." Jack had said that over and over. "You gotta help him. You can't let guys like Whitney and McDaniel ruin it for him."

"Well," Borden said quietly, smiling like he thought MJ was going overboard, "I don't know if Mikey Clemant can ever be as good as you say, but I do know this: you're a good man . . . and a good friend. And strong friendships can be made quickly. Don't ever think they can't. Two weeks is plenty of time to start trusting someone."

That really hurt. If Borden only knew his whole reason for doing this had been money—and that maybe it was still the most important thing for him in this—he wouldn't have quite the same high opinion. So many times MJ had heard Momma say life was all about the devil tempting you with money and material things. He hadn't really believed her, but maybe she was right after all. Why shouldn't she be? She was right about everything else.

"Speaking of caring, why do you care so much about me?" MJ asked. "Why are you willing to check out what really happened in the locker room yesterday for a poor black kid? Is it for the same reason I got the batboy job over all those other white kids? You got a guilty conscience?"

"Maybe," Borden answered honestly. "Maybe a lot

of white guys my age do. Even if we never did anything wrong. Is that so bad?"

A wide grin snuck up on MJ. Suddenly he liked Mitch Borden. Suddenly he liked two white guys in their sixties. Sometimes life was a damn trip.

The intercom on Borden's desk buzzed. "Yes, Patty?"

"It's that phone call you've been waiting for."

"Thanks." Borden rose from his chair, leaned over the desk, and held out his hand. "It's been nice getting to know you better, MJ. Should I call you or Mikey when I'm done looking into things?"

"Me."

"Do we have your number?"

The number at the house was on the application he'd filled out. Hopefully Momma had paid the bill this month. "Yes, sir."

"Good." Borden nodded toward the door. "Ask Patty to arrange a ride home for you. Somebody who can haul your bike. Tell her I said so."

"Thanks, Mr. Borden."

When he'd left the office and closed the door, MJ headed to Patty's desk.

"How can I help you?" she asked, looking up.

"Tell Mr. Borden I appreciated his offer." Maybe it was stupid, maybe he was just too stubborn for his own good, but he had too much pride to accept the ride. He had an overwhelming desire never to owe anyone but always to be owed. And maybe he needed nine miles of pedaling to think about why he'd gotten into this whole thing in the first place. "He'll know what that means."

* * *

"Well, look who it is," Jack called warmly as the Kid opened the screen door leading outside from the kitchen. Jack was by the shed, crouching beside a pine box the size of a large desk drawer. "How'd you sleep?"

"I'll tell you what, Mr. Barrett, I don't think I've slept like that in a long time."

"Call me Jack, will you please?"

"Yes, sir."

Jack liked what he saw. Kyle McLean seemed much more relaxed this morning. The beard was gone, too, and it was a big improvement. Cheryl was right. The Kid was going to need a team of bodyguards to protect him from the girls in New York. "Thanks."

The Kid smiled as he walked across the scraggly lawn. "I went to bed around ten last night, and here it is after eleven in the morning. I didn't wake up once. That couch is pretty comfortable."

"I know. I used to fall asleep on it all the time until I got that easy chair." Jack stood and held out his hand. "Hey, I'm glad you decided to stay."

"Well, like I said last night, all I got is this cheap little rental downtown. I hate it."

"You get what you pay for."

"You get what you can afford."

Jack smiled as he thought about the simple truth embedded in both statements. How most of the world's problems could be defined by one or the other. "Why don't you move in with us? At least until your suspension is over."

"I don't want to put you and Cheryl out," Kyle said politely, checking out the pine box on the ground.

"You wouldn't. Believe me."

"Well, it would help. When I got suspended yesterday, Lefty said I was gonna get docked on my pay, too. It's not like I've got much in the bank."

Jack patted the Kid on the shoulder. "So it's all decided. You'll stay with us."

"Thanks, Mr. Barrett."

Jack rolled his eyes. "*I told you, young man*, call me Jack. I hate that Mister thing."

"Yeah, okay."

Jack broke into a wide smile. "Hopefully you'll never have to play another game for the Tarpons anyway."

"What do you mean?"

"I'm gonna get you a tryout with the Yankees. The *New York* Yankees."

Kyle's wide eyes raced to Jack's. "No, no, I can't do that."

"Easy," Jack said reassuringly. "Cheryl told me about what happened back up North. About the mob and why you were down here using that other name." The Kid might be angry that Cheryl had violated some pact they'd made last night, but it was better to be up front about it.

"She told you?"

"Of course she did. She's my daughter. She tells me everything."

"Everything?"

"Sure. What would you expect?"

Kyle ran a hand through his long, dark hair. "Look, I really appreciate your offer, but I can't go back to New York. Ever. Those people are still looking for me. I know it."

"It's been two years. They've forgotten."

"No way. They haven't forgotten. Listen, I—"

"Let's not get into it now," Jack suggested calmly. "I

know you're worried about it. We'll talk, but not now. Okay?"

Kyle nodded hesitantly. "Yeah, okay."

"Good. Hey, look, I want to show you something." Jack pointed down at the box. "It's really cool."

"What is it?"

"Just look."

It was one of the oldest gags in the baseball book. When the top opened, a nasty-looking stuffed raccoon with bared teeth and claws came springing out, scaring the person who didn't know what was going on half to death. Big leaguers did it to rookies all the time. And sometimes front-office people did it to new front-office people. It had been one of Jack's trademarks.

"Come on," Jack urged, groaning as he knelt.

"You all right?" Kyle asked, kneeling down beside Jack.

"It's my arthritis, Kid. A lot of pain, but nothing to worry about. Now look at this," he said, his voice growing quieter the closer he got to the box, drawing the Kid in. There was a button on one side that released the door, the spring, and the stuffed raccoon, and he slid his finger subtly to it. "Closer, come on."

He was just about to push the button when he felt something on his shoulder. He glanced over. At the head of a huge snake.

"Jesus Christ!" he shouted, tumbling away from the box, pushing the button in the process, his heart in his throat. He thrashed about on the lawn for a few moments, finally grabbing the snake and tossing it toward the shed. "Damn it! Kill that thing!" he yelled at the Kid, making it to his feet as fast as he had in years.

Then he noticed that the Kid was bent over, hands on

his stomach, laughing uncontrollably. And that Cheryl was standing at the screen door, tears running down her face—she was supposed to have left for the office ten minutes ago. Suddenly he realized what had happened. The tables had been turned. "Fake, right?" he asked, his heart still pounding. Aware that the snake hadn't moved from where he'd tossed it.

"Very fake," Cheryl confirmed, trotting across the lawn and jumping into the Kid's arms.

Jack watched as the Kid caught her and spun her around twice before gently letting her to the ground again.

"Both of you in on this?"

"That's right, Daddy." She shook the Kid's hand. "Congratulations, Kyle. You got the master. Too bad we didn't take a video. Lots of people in the Yankee organization would love to have seen that."

Jack watched Cheryl and the Kid embrace again. Interesting. It wasn't bothering him. He couldn't remember the last time a guy hugging his daughter hadn't bothered him.

Johnny headed out of the Tampa airport in the rental car with the windows down, air rushing all around him. God, it was nice down here in South Florida. Eighty-five degrees and not a cloud in the sky. The air seemed cleaner and the sun seemed brighter. You started feeling healthier the moment you got off the plane, even while you were still in the terminal, even with a hole in your body. His shoulder was actually feeling much better.

He could move his fingers a little, and it had stopped bleeding.

Now if he could just lose this awful premonition of peril. It had hit him hard again as he was boarding the plane this morning at LaGuardia and had intensified with every mile closer to Florida he flew. Now it was as if it had attached itself to his heart because with every beat he was acutely aware of it.

Johnny took a quick check of his mirrors and pressed the accelerator. He just wanted to get to his condominium. Just wanted to get inside it and lock the door. Then maybe he'd feel safe.

40

J ACK CLIMBED OUT of the Citation and glanced up
at the sun, shading his eyes. It was after four o'clock,
but there still wasn't a cloud in the sky. It had been
one of those picture-perfect South Florida days, one
of the prettiest he could remember. Maybe it was an
omen.

He'd talked with the Kid for a while after the fake-
snake incident, and it seemed like Kyle might be letting
his guard down, might be softening his stance on going
back to New York. Like he was starting to convince
himself that the Lucchesi family wasn't so hot on his
trail anymore. And that if the Yankees gave him a big
contract, the organization could help with the situation
if the old boss—Angelo Marconi—was still alive and
kicking. Still looking for revenge. Maybe, just maybe,
Jack dared to consider for the first time, everything he'd

been dreaming of might actually be coming together.

He opened the back door and reached inside to lift Rosario from her car seat. When he raised slowly back up with her in his arms, MJ was heading down the rickety, warped wooden steps of the Billups' front porch.

"Hey, pal," he called.

MJ waved. "How you doing, Ahab?"

"All right. Where's your mom?"

"Fixing supper."

"Does she know I'm here?"

"I don't think so."

"What's she fixing?"

"Ribs and mashed potatoes."

Man, that sounded good. Suddenly Jack wished he wasn't on such a tight schedule. "I think I just drooled," he muttered.

"Stick around," MJ suggested. "There's enough for one more."

Jack wondered if that was really true. Or if he'd be taking food out of somebody's mouth. Well, either way, he was going to make a difference for the Billups family this afternoon. At least for the short term. "I'd love to, but I . . . I can't."

"Why? Because you don't want to have dinner with a black family?"

Now, that was crossing the line. "Come on, MJ, you know I—"

"I'm kidding." MJ grinned. "I just wanted to see if I could still get a rise out of the old man. I know where your heart is, Ahab."

MJ was a firecracker, no two ways about it. "You know I'd have dinner with your family anytime. Hell, I'd fix your family dinner at my house anytime. I *will* fix your family dinner at my house sometime soon."

"Yeah, yeah, we'll see. So how's the Kid doing?"

"Fine. He and my daughter are hanging out right now."

Jack had asked Cheryl to work on the Kid some more while she took him shopping for some new clothes, to get him more comfortable with the idea of the Yankee tryout and going back to New York. But she'd sort of balked at it. Hadn't rejected doing it out of hand, but Jack got the feeling she was still worried that the mob was after Kyle. Clearly she was starting to care for him, which, surprisingly, still didn't bother Jack. Even if she wouldn't help convince the Kid to stop worrying about the mob. It was weird. Jack even tried to *make* the idea of a relationship between them bother him. No luck.

"She took the day off to help him buy a few things."

MJ gestured at Rosario. "I know what that means."

"What?"

"It means you wouldn't mind having the Kid as a son-in-law."

"*What?* Are you out of your mind? She's thirteen years older than him."

"So?"

Jack tried to make it seem like the whole thing was crazy. But MJ had him pegged. Again. "How the hell did you come up with that?"

"Why else would you take care of the baby all day? You hate doing that more than you hate talking money. You did it because you wanted them to have some time together."

"She hasn't even known Kyle for twenty-four hours. My daughter doesn't fall for anybody that fast."

MJ smiled that broad, pearly white smile. "You haven't known him for twenty-four hours yet, either. But you're already in love with him."

Jack raised one eyebrow. "You might be right."

"I bet you'd rather have the Kid dating Cheryl than that guy . . ." MJ snapped his fingers a couple of times, trying to remember. "What's his name? Bobby something?"

"Bobby Griffin."

"You hate that guy, don't you?"

"I don't hate anyone." Which wasn't accurate. But it sounded better than the truth. "She's supposed to go out with Bobby tonight, which is why I can't stick around. I don't want to leave the Kid by himself at the house for too long. I don't want him getting lonely."

"Don't you have another commitment tonight?"

"What do you mean?"

"The Tarpons have a game. Or did you already quit?"

"Of course I did. I'm not dressing up like Ralph Kramden one more night I don't have to."

"Ralph *who*?"

"You know, *The Honeymooners*."

"You mean that movie Cedric the Entertainer did a few years ago?"

"Cedric the who?"

"That black comedian."

"*Black* comedian? No, no, no. It was—"

"I know, I know." MJ was cracking up. "Keep your shorts on, Ahab. You're talking about the character Jackie Gleason played. The bus driver on the old sitcom. The one Cedric the Entertainer *re*-created. My mother loves that old show." MJ shook his head. "Relax, old man."

Jack still couldn't always tell when MJ was putting

him on and when he wasn't. And he had to give the
young man credit. There weren't many people in the
world who could do that. "Point is I need to make sure
Kyle doesn't get any crazy ideas, doesn't talk to anybody
he shouldn't."

"All of a sudden you sound a lot like an agent, Ahab.
And a lot less like a hunter."

"Well, I hooked the whale. Now I just gotta convince
him to live in this big aquarium and perform every day."

"And give you a piece of the take."

That sure would be nice, but he didn't know anything
about being an agent. He'd mangled his own contract, for
crying out loud, given away his pension in the process.
He didn't want to screw up Kyle's deal. Nah, leave that
to a pro. To one of those big Wall Street lawyers turned
agents. He'd be happy just getting his job and his pension
back for bringing the talent of an era to the organization.

"He doesn't have to do that," Jack said quietly. "He's
under no obligation."

"But he should," MJ argued. "If he's any kind of man,
he will. If you got him that tryout and the Yankees got interested in him, he'd owe you big time. I mean, Single-A
straight to the majors? That's a big jump."

"He belongs in the majors. We both know that. The
jump would have nothing to do with me."

"Maybe not. Except now that he's been in Single-A for
a while, he's got a credibility problem. He's got stats, and
they aren't phenom stats."

True. Last season and the beginning of this one were
in the books. And the record wasn't very good. Of course,
when the front office confirmed that McLean had been

emulating Mickey Mantle almost perfectly this season, and saw him hit a couple of five-hundred-foot home runs in the tryout, the stats would probably be tossed out the window.

"He needs somebody like you to get him that tryout," MJ spoke up. "To make people believe he really belongs. It's not like he'd get his own tryout now. He'd have to work his way up through the ranks."

"It wouldn't take him long."

"Maybe, maybe not."

Jack shook his head, thinking about Kyle's situation. "Poor guy. The last two years he's had nothing to keep him going but baseball. No family, no friends, no money." It was amazing to think about. "Not even a television, for God's sake. He told me this morning he's read more books in the past two years than he's read in his entire life before this." The Kid had surprised him with how sharp he was. Jack hadn't been expecting much. "He's no dummy, either. He's smart." Jack grinned. "Not as smart as you, MJ, but smart. Of course, I haven't met many people smarter than you." He could see that MJ was suddenly struggling with his emotions. They'd developed a special bond, and now Jack had been the first one to actually say something about it. Which was how it should have been. Most teenagers didn't even know how to carry on a conversation with a sixty-three-year-old, let alone verbalize meaningful emotions between them. "And I doubt I ever will."

MJ kicked at the dusty ground. "Stop it, Ahab."

"I mean it."

"All right," MJ said softly. "By the way, the suspension's over."

"What?"

"Yeah. The Tarpons' owner called me ten minutes ago to let me know it was over."

"Mitch Borden called you? Holy crap. Why?"

"I rode my bike out to the stadium this morning to see him. We had a meeting."

"A meeting?"

"Sure," MJ said, as if it was no big deal. "I sat down with him and told him that the thing about the Kid stealing McDaniel's wallet was all bull. I told him what really happened. That Whitney was the crook. Borden promised he'd look into it fast. I guess he did, because the Kid and I are back in uniform tomorrow night. He said he wanted to talk to Lefty today, but we could count on being in the locker room tomorrow. Said neither one of us would lose any pay, either."

"How could he figure out what had happened so fast?"

"Cameras," MJ said matter-of-factly.

"In the locker room? What is he? Some kind of—"

"No, no. In the hallway leading to the bullpen. Said he had tape of Whitney looking at the wallet just inside the doorway to the bullpen, then hiding it in a vent or something. He's off the team. Gone."

Well, that was good news. Sort of. Jack had been kind of glad Kyle didn't have anywhere to go for a couple of weeks so they had time to really get to know each other while he was setting up the tryout. "Good for you. You want to call Kyle and let him know? I'll give you my daughter's cell number. You can talk to him right away."

MJ shook his head. "No. You tell him he's playing again. Make him think you got him back on the field.

I already told Borden that was how it was gonna be. He didn't get it, but he said he'd play along."

"But—"

"Kyle needs to feel like he owes you. This'll help."

"I haven't even paid you yet."

"You will," MJ answered confidently. "You won't let me down."

"You're right," Jack said softly. "More right than you know."

"What do you mean?"

Jack put Rosario down on the driver's seat, then reached into his pocket and pulled out a wad of bills. Twenty crisp one-hundred-dollar bills. "Here's two grand. This ought to settle us up."

MJ blinked several times in disbelief at the sight of so much cash. "That's more than you owe me, Ahab. Way more."

"It includes severance," Jack said with a smile, holding the bills out. "Sorry, but this ends the business relationship. At least for now. I wish it didn't, but I can't afford you anymore."

"I know."

"I'll help you get another job."

"Thanks." MJ took the money. "I'll probably do the batboy thing for a few more games. I actually like it. And I want at least one more chance to look Reggie McDaniel in the eye and tell him what I think of him."

"Don't go looking for trouble in life," Jack counseled. "Enough of it'll find you all on its own."

"Uh-huh. So where'd you get this?" MJ asked suspiciously, holding the cash up before slipping it in his pocket.

"Don't ask. It's too depressing."

MJ chewed softly on his lower lip for a moment. "How about you answer another question for me, and I won't ask you where you got the money again?"

"Depends on the question," Jack replied, smiling at Rosario, who was grabbing the steering wheel tightly with one of her precious little hands.

"What the hell happened in New York a coupla years ago?"

Jack's eyes flickered to MJ's. "What do you mean?"

"Why'd you get fired from the Yankees? I tried researching it on the Internet," MJ continued, "but there wasn't much there. The articles mostly just said you and the Yankees decided to go in different directions. There were a couple that implied you did something wrong, but there weren't many details."

Jack laughed harshly. "'Different directions.' What a crock."

"So what happened?" MJ asked again.

"I don't want to go into it." The weird thing was, he actually did. Suddenly he realized that enough time had passed, and he couldn't think of a better person to talk about it with than MJ. "I really don't."

"You sure?"

"It still hurts." Rosario was giggling as she grabbed the steering wheel with both hands. "I got framed."

"For what?"

Jack took a deep breath. Man, this was hard. "I was supposed to have given some information to the Boston Red Sox right before we played them in the 2004 American League Championship Series. Inside information."

"Jesus," MJ whispered. "About what?"

"About who," Jack corrected. "I was supposed to have given them an injury report on Derek Jeter, on the Yankee captain, on the main man. I was supposed to have told them that Derek had a bad right wrist that *nobody* knew about. So if you jammed him inside with fastballs and hard sliders, he wouldn't be able to get the bat around."

"*Whoa.*"

Jack nodded. "Yeah, whoa. Serious stuff. Because usually Jeter'll take you over the fence if you do that. But the Red Sox did pitch him inside with fastballs and hard sliders, and if you look at the tapes, he couldn't get the bat around. He went six-for-thirty in seven games. Terrible for him. Just one extra-base hit, a double. He didn't have a home run the entire series. It was a nightmare for him. A nightmare for the entire city."

"But how'd they pin it on you?"

"They found an e-mail on the server sent from me to some guy in the Red Sox organization."

"But why would you give the Red Sox that kind of information?" MJ asked, stunned. "You'd been with the Yankees for more than thirty years at that point. Right?"

"You'd think I'd get the benefit of the doubt, wouldn't you?" Jack asked softly. "Well, I didn't." His tone turned bitter. "Not one damn crumb of it."

"But it doesn't fit. There's something you're not telling me. Come on, Jack."

That was the problem with smart people. They were *always* smart. They recognized when you hadn't told them everything. That all the facts didn't fit. "Okay, look, here's what happened." Jack hadn't told anyone but Cheryl this. "I got a son named David. He's my only other child. He's with the New York City Fire Department, has been since he graduated from high school. He's one of those guys who went to the World Trade Center on nine-eleven and saved a bunch of people. He's been decorated so many times for bravery in the line of duty I can't even remember them all. He was getting pretty senior in the department by 2004, and he was up for a big promotion." This was so hard to think about. "Well, a couple of days before the 2004 ALCS with the Red Sox starts, I find out David's got a drug problem. He's doing cocaine. Lots of it, all the time."

"Damn."

Jack rubbed his temples, remembering how David's wife had called that night at three in the morning, hysterical. Sobbing uncontrollably because he wouldn't stop snorting the powder. She was terrified he was going to lose his job, terrified they were going to lose everything they had, mostly terrified he was going to die. Remembering how he'd raced to David's place in Queens. Thinking—praying—that somehow David's wife had to be wrong. His prayers smashed to bits when he saw David. Red-eyed and hopped up, pacing around the basement like a caged bear.

"Yeah," Jack continued. "Damn. So I gotta do something, and I gotta do it fast. If somebody at the Fire Department finds out what's going on—"

"He won't get that promotion," MJ cut in.

Jack scoffed. "The promotion wasn't even on the radar screen anymore. David woulda gotten fired faster than you can say 'fired.' They're real strict about that stuff. They gotta be."

"What'd you do?"

"I drove him to a detox center in Iowa I knew about

and told the department he was on vacation. I thought I had it all worked out. Until I got the call."

"Call?"

"The call that ruined my life. Some guy who claimed he was with the Red Sox," Jack explained. "The same guy I was supposed to have e-mailed. Turned out he knew everything about David's drug problem. Said he had a contact at the center in Iowa. Said if I didn't get him information about the Yankees he could use in the Series, he'd call the Fire Department and tell 'em everything." Jack shrugged and looked down. "And that's what happened."

"But you didn't send that e-mail. Did you?"

Jack shook his head. A sixteen-year-old kid he'd only known for a few weeks had more faith in him than people he'd played slave to for years. How much of a tragedy was that? And yet he still wanted to work for them again, was still unfailingly loyal to them. *God*, he hated being human.

"Nope," Jack confirmed. "I never would have done that. I never would have sent that information about Jeter to the Red Sox. Not even to protect my own son."

"Who did send it?"

"I don't know. Somebody who must have *really* hated me."

MJ moved beside Jack and patted him on the shoulder. "You know what I appreciate?"

Jack glanced up. "What?"

MJ tapped his pocket with all the cash in it. "That you gave me the cash outside without my mother seeing. You gave it to me, not her. I appreciate that a lot. You know I'll give it to Momma, but you gave it to me to give to her. That's important to me."

"I trust you, MJ. I really do." He could hear the emotion in his own voice, and it embarrassed him. But it would have been worse for MJ not to hear that. "And I don't trust many people."

"I know. I trust you, too." MJ hesitated. "Jack."

Treviso trained the high-powered binoculars on the condo building entrance. Deuce Bondano should be coming out anytime to head down to Sarasota—about thirty minutes south of here—to do the deed. To kill Kyle McLean.

Well, Deuce was going to lead him right to the prey, but the bastard wasn't going to be the one who finished McLean off. It was going to go down different than that. A lot different.

Since losing the hundred grand to McLean two years ago, Treviso and Karen had lived like paupers. The new cut on loan profits Marconi had imposed made it nearly impossible to live, especially with a baby. But he hadn't bitched about it to anyone besides Karen because he was afraid Marconi might decide to pop him one day if he heard he had a malcontent in the family. He'd been forced into a life of theft to survive. So when Deuce Bondano had shown up at the apartment that morning to tell him McLean was still alive, it was all Treviso could do to control himself. Not to bust out shouting and yelling. Finally a chance at redemption.

But Bondano wasn't willing to help. Didn't give a damn about helping a man in a tough spot.

Treviso had settled on his plan a few hours after Bondano left. It had taken him those several hours to convince himself he could really handle the thought of Karen having sex with another man, with Johnny Bondano. Sure, he'd seen that awful lust in Bondano's eyes as the bastard stared into the hallway, thinking the husband didn't get it. Sure, Bondano hadn't taken the bait right away when Treviso had sent Karen back into the kitchen to "touch him a little and get him heated up" while he claimed he was taking a piss. Sure, Bondano had managed to refuse then. But it had been like water building behind a dam. Inevitable. Ultimately Bondano couldn't resist Karen. He was just like every other man. Treviso had known Bondano would come around, though not as fast as he had. Bondano had called Karen that same afternoon, for Christ's sake. Then she'd called Treviso on his cell phone right after hanging up with Bondano. Called to tell him that Bondano wanted her bad. She was a good girl.

Then the question became: Would Karen really go all the way? Sure, she'd been willing to flirt a little in the kitchen. But would she go all the way? It hadn't taken long to find out. Turned out Karen was sick of living like a pauper, too.

Treviso thought back on their lovemaking session last night. When she'd told him in detail everything she'd done for Johnny Bondano. When she'd told him how Johnny had told her how he was coming down here to Florida to kill Kyle McLean. When Karen had told him how easy it was to get information out of Johnny when she was kneeling in front of him doing what he wanted. Treviso felt himself becoming aroused all over again just thinking about it. Maybe he was one sick-as-all-sin man after all, but he'd never experienced anything so physically and mentally powerful in his entire life. And he couldn't wait to feel it again.

It was all going to work out perfectly, Treviso realized. So little in his life ever had. But now, when it counted the most, it seemed like this would. Well, the sun couldn't shine up the same dog's ass every day.

He brought the binoculars down. The only thing about it all that bothered Treviso was that he'd never seen Karen so turned on, either. And for a split second it occurred to him that maybe she wasn't doing Johnny Bondano just for the money. Maybe there was something more.

41

"HI, PRINCESS." JACK smiled at Cheryl as he came through the front door of the house, carrying Rosario. "How are you?"

"Fine, Daddy. Here, I'll take her," Cheryl offered, holding out both hands. The little girl leaned toward her right away and broke into a big smile. "Hi, little one," she murmured, nuzzling the baby's velvety face.

After giving Cheryl the baby, Jack reached into his pocket and pulled out another folded stack of bills. This one was thicker than the one he'd given MJ. This time it was five thousand dollars. "Here. This should take care of the bills."

Cheryl gazed at the folded-over hundreds fearfully. "Oh, Daddy," she said with a gasp, "what did you do?"

It had been one of the toughest things he'd ever had to do. But it was better than stealing jewelry from a helpless, elderly woman who was being taken away in an ambulance by a Judas. He couldn't have lived with himself if he'd gone through with it. He'd actually gotten all the way to the door of the big house after Biff and Harry had driven off with the poor woman. Actually turned the doorknob to see if the house was unlocked. It was—and it had scared him to death. He'd turned and hobbled away as fast as his old knees would carry him. Back through an open field to the Citation—parked in a strip mall a mile away. He'd just wanted to get out of there as fast as he could.

"I sold the last World Series ring," he said hoarsely. "The Subway Series ring. When we played the Mets in 2000."

Cheryl's expression turned sad, like she'd lost a good friend. "I'm sorry. I know how much that ring meant to you."

It was the last thing he'd owned that proved beyond a shadow of a doubt that at least for a time he'd been an important cog in the Yankee organization. Now it was gone forever. Sold to some faceless guy on eBay.

"It's okay. You were right, Princess. I couldn't have lived with myself if I'd taken that woman's jewelry." He'd broken down and told Cheryl what Biff wanted him to do, and how everything was all interrelated. How Biff knew they had Rosario and how that was one way the guy could get revenge if Jack didn't take the jewelry. Unfortunately, he'd admitted to Biff how Cheryl and the baby had bonded so quickly. So Biff knew he had leverage.

"Does this mean the cops will be coming for Rosario?" she asked apprehensively.

"I don't know, but I'll find out tomorrow." Biff was

going to be one pissed-off EMT when he realized the deal hadn't gone down. But there was still a chance everything could work out. "Don't worry."

"Oh, sure," she answered, her lower lip starting to tremble. "You know me. I never worry."

He'd shoot Biff before he'd let the bastard have Rosario. "How was your afternoon with the Kid?" he asked, trying to distract her.

"Fun. He's nice."

He could see he hadn't distracted her at all. "Is he here?"

"Yeah. He said he was tired, so I told him to take a nap in your room. I didn't think you'd mind."

"No, of course not. Are you still going out with Bobby tonight?"

She nodded, then forced a happy expression to her face. "I've got a surprise for you."

"You got the Kid to agree to go back to New York." He assumed that wasn't it, but he had to keep pushing her. She might end up being the key.

"No. And I don't think he should, either, I really don't. But let's not talk about it now," she said, hoisting the baby into her left arm and taking Jack's hand. "Come with me," she said, pulling him toward the kitchen. "Come on."

As he came around the corner he saw a man sitting at the kitchen table. A white-haired, ruddy-faced man about his age. "Jesus H. Christ," he whispered. It was Howard "Fin" Olsen. His best friend in the world. "What in the world are you doing here?"

"Hello, Fast Jack," Fin said in his deep voice, standing up and spreading his arms. "As warm as ever, aren't you?" He laughed. "It's good to see you, old friend."

Jack smiled. "Good to see you, too."

They met where the kitchen and the living room came together and embraced for a long time. The way two old friends who hadn't seen each other in what seemed like forever ought to embrace.

Johnny moved along the concourse of Tarpon Stadium, checking the printed black numbers on his ticket stub against the painted red numbers on the cement walls. Looking for the tunnel that would lead him to his seat. He felt better, a lot better. He'd gotten almost five hours' sleep at the condo this afternoon, and though his shoulder was still tender as hell and he still didn't have much range of motion with his left arm, he could tell he was on the mend. It would take awhile to get back to normal, but there wasn't any sign of infection, which was the most important thing. He was still changing the dressing and the bandages religiously—he'd changed them twice on the plane from New York—and he'd keep doing that as long as the wound was raw.

He'd wanted to call Karen while he was driving down here from Tampa, wanted just to hear her voice for a few seconds. But he'd managed to keep his fingertips off the phone. There was no reason to risk Treviso finding out at this point. They were so close to getting what they wanted. He'd cap McLean tonight, snap a few pictures of the body with the digital camera in his pocket, then hop a flight back tomorrow morning and be in New York by early afternoon. Treviso would be a dead man in short order, and he and Karen would be free to live their lives happily ever after.

Johnny spotted the number on the wall matching his ticket and headed into the tunnel. When he emerged, he gestured at an usher wearing a red cap with a shiny black visor. An old man with age-spotted arms who was leaning on a yellow railing. "Yo."

"Yes, sir." The old man shuffled right over. "Let me see your ticket and we'll get you seated as fast as we can."

"No, it's not that."

"Oh, no? Then how can I help you?"

Johnny pointed toward the field and the players. "Which one of those guys is Mikey Clement?"

The old man squinted at the field, then touched his forehead. "Oh, gosh, none of them."

"What?" That didn't sound good. "Aren't those guys the home team? Aren't those guys the Sarasota Tarpons?"

"They sure are, but Mikey isn't out there tonight."

"Where is he?"

"Suspended."

"*Suspended?*" Holy shit. Wasn't that just par for the fucking course right now? What was he going to tell Marconi? "How long is he—"

"Don't worry, sir. At first I heard he was going to be out for two weeks. That was yesterday. But when I got to the ballpark today, I heard they settled everything this afternoon. He'll be back out on the field tomorrow night." The usher got a concerned look. "Unless you're vacationing and tonight is your last—"

"No, it's fine." Johnny let out a relieved breath. McLean's suspension meant spending one more night than he wanted to in Florida, but hey, things could be worse. This could be Arkansas or Rhode Island or some other shithole. "Thanks," he said, turning away from the old man and making sure not to look directly in his eyes so he wouldn't remember him. "Thanks a lot."

Kyle knocked on Cheryl's open bedroom door. "Hi."

She turned away from the mirror above the bureau. She'd been putting on an earring. "Hey, you, come on in."

He took two steps into the room, then stopped dead in his tracks. "God, you look incredible."

Well, that was nice. Unprompted, too. She moaned under her breath. Why did he have to be so much younger than she? So nice and so good-looking, too. Oh, well, what she had wasn't that bad. She caught herself wondering how far Bobby would take it tonight. "Thanks."

She'd finally taken the advice, finally decided to doll herself up. She'd just finished her hair—it was down on her shoulders, no more unruly bun, and styled. And she was wearing a sheer, clingy dress that fell halfway down her thighs along with a new pair of sexy heels. She'd bought the dress and shoes this afternoon at the mall while she'd gone off by herself for thirty minutes—thank God the credit card still worked—so Kyle wouldn't see what she got. She wasn't sure why, but she didn't want him to see until tonight—why she'd opened the door when she was almost finished. When she looked in the mirror, she had to admit it was quite a change. Judging from Kyle's expression and his reaction, it was a good change. A *very* good change.

"I . . . I really mean it, Cheryl. You look unbelievable."

"You should hang around more often." She was getting comfortable with him so fast. But thirteen years younger? A few years maybe, but *thirteen*. Besides, he probably didn't think about her in that way. She thought she'd caught him sneaking glances at her a couple of times at the mall, but it didn't make sense. She'd caught plenty of younger, very attractive girls gaping at him. Girls who were way more attractive than she was. "It would do wonders for my self-esteem."

"I'd be happy to," he said with a sincere smile. After a few moments his expression soured a little. "You going out with that guy tonight?"

She slid the other earring through the piercing in her left lobe. "What guy are you talking about?" Daddy must have told Kyle that Bobby was a loser.

"That guy you've been dating. Your dad says he's a real successful businessman in the area."

"Daddy said that?"

"Uh-huh."

Wow. That was amazing. Maybe Daddy was actually coming through on his promise. She grabbed her purse off the bureau, moved to where Kyle was standing, and gave him a kiss on the cheek. "I had fun this afternoon."

"Me, too."

"You sure you don't mind taking care of the baby tonight?"

"Nah. I used to babysit my cousins all the time. A couple of them were younger than Rosario. It's no problem."

Kyle was nice, really nice. And she still couldn't get over those eyes. It was like they were constantly searching the center of her soul. But not in a bad way, in a good way. "You'll probably be here alone. I'm sure Daddy's going out with Fin tonight. They haven't seen each other in a year."

"You mean that guy in the kitchen?"

"Yup."

"Who is he?"

"Daddy's best friend. They worked together for years with the Yankees. Fin reported to Daddy in the scouting department. His name's Howard Olsen, but Daddy calls him Fin because his family's originally from Finland. He's my godfather."

"Is he still with the Yankees?"

"Yup. Still works on the scouting side. He complains all the time about how bad the guy they brought in to take Daddy's spot is." She glanced at her watch. "Well, I better get going." She started for the door, then stopped. "You know, you ought to think real hard about going back to New York. I know Daddy feels like the mob's forgotten you, but I don't think it's really about the mob forgetting. I think it's about an old man never forgetting about his grandson."

The Kid nodded soberly. "I hear you."

She gazed into those eyes for a few more moments. "You've got my cell number if anything happens. If Rosario gives you any trouble at all, don't hesitate to call."

"Don't worry, I'll be fine. So will Rosario." He touched her arm lightly. "And hey. Don't have too much fun tonight."

Treviso had waited until he was certain Deuce Bondano was long gone before leaving the stadium parking lot. There was no reason to follow him back up I-75 to Tampa and risk being seen. There was still a little daylight left, and what if he passed Deuce unintentionally on the interstate and Deuce spotted him? After all, he knew where Deuce was going—back to his condo overlooking Tampa Bay. And he knew what Deuce knew: that Kyle McLean, a.k.a. Mikey Clemant, wasn't playing tonight because of a suspension but would be back in uniform tomorrow night. One of the ushers had told him everything. There certainly wasn't any reason to stick around here tonight. Trying to find McLean in Sarasota would be like trying to find Jimmy Hoffa's remains. Everything would have to wait until tomorrow night. Which was fine. He could wait one more night. After all, he'd waited two years.

Fin saw her first and stood up immediately.

Jack saw Fin's reaction, glanced over his shoulder, then stood up, too. "Princess," he said in a hushed voice as Cheryl walked into the kitchen, "you look beautiful."

"I'll say," Fin seconded. "I've never seen you prettier."

Cheryl smiled. "Thanks, Fin." She glanced at Daddy. "Kyle's going to take care of the baby tonight so you and Howard can go out."

"Who's Kyle?" Fin asked quickly.

"That would be me," the Kid answered, moving into the kitchen and holding out his right hand. He was cradling Rosario. The baby looked tiny tucked in his arm. "I'm the babysitter."

"And a heck of a baseball player," Cheryl added, instantly wishing she hadn't. She'd caught Jack's subtle slash sign across his throat an instant too late.

* * *

"What brings you down here?" Jack asked.

They'd come to a local watering hole near the house. They were both sitting at the bar, both drinking scotch. Like they always had. It was pretty low-key in here, not much atmosphere. But Jack liked that because the place never got too crowded.

"Sun and sand, Fast Jack, sun and sand."

"Don't give me that, Fin. It's June. Another two weeks and you'll have sun and sand up your way. Why'd you show up on my doorstep now with no warning?"

"The boy in the big office next to George's sent me down here. Apparently he was watching ESPN as he was nodding off to sleep in his Park Avenue penthouse the other night, and he saw a quick cut on some kid who had a phenomenal game in your town. Five-for-five with a couple of dingers or something. I've got it written down somewhere," Fin said, doing a quick but unsuccessful search of his pockets. "Anyway, he had me fly down here to check the guy out. It's probably a wild-goose chase, but I just shut up and do what I'm told these days. I want that pension, you know?" Fin grimaced. "Sorry."

"It's all right."

"You ever go to any of the games here?" Fin asked. "What's the team called, the Tarpons?"

"Yeah, the Tarpons." Jack shrugged. "I mean, it's Single-A," he said, watching Fin root around in his briefcase. "A crappy independent league, too. What can you expect?"

Fin donned a pair of reading glasses after pulling a piece of paper out of the briefcase. "His name's Mikey Clemant," he said, reading off the paper. "Ever heard of him?"

"Nah. I mean, I've *heard* of him, but I really don't follow the Tarpons. Like I said, it's Single-A. It's not worth it."

"Still haven't gotten back into baseball, huh? Still bitter about everything even after all this time?"

"Wouldn't you be?"

Fin took a sip of scotch. "You know you're never gonna figure out what happened up there. It sucks that the higher-ups pulled the trigger so fast, without even giving you a chance, but you gotta get over it, Jack. Otherwise it'll eat at you until the day you die. Might even *make* you die."

Jack actually considered it for a few moments, then waved. "Ah, what do you know?"

"Not much, I guess. Look at me, I'm sixty-three and I'm some forty-five-year-old guy's beck-and-call boy. He tells me to get on a plane, and I ask which one. Maybe I'm an old loser, but I'm trying to give my best friend in the world some good advice. Don't be angry all the time. It isn't worth it."

"How would you know?"

"I've had my own pain. Remember, Jack?"

"You still got your job."

"Yeah, but—"

"I'm sorry." Jack reached out and touched Fin's arm. "I . . . I guess I am still bitter. I wish I was still with the Yankees. I'm envious, you know? I'd take your job in a heartbeat."

Fin rolled his eyes and glanced over Jack's shoulder at the television mounted above the bar. "The guy I report to is such an asshole."

"Don't start." Jack hated to admit it, but it felt good to hear that. "How's Janet?" Janet was Fin's only daughter.

She was a year younger than Cheryl. "And those three grandkids?"

Fin didn't answer. He was staring up at the TV like he was watching a news bulletin about the president being shot. Jack turned quickly to see what was on the screen. And there was Kyle McLean's rugged face staring back. Still bearded because that was the press picture the Tarpons had. They were still talking about the game the other night—and how the suspension had been reversed.

Fin's fingers curled into a tight fist. "You son of a bitch, Jack."

Jack's eyes shot to Fin's.

"That's the kid I met in your kitchen tonight," Fin said, pointing at the screen angrily. "*You son of a bitch.* He didn't have the beard, but I still recognize him. Why didn't you tell me who he was? I thought we were friends. I thought we were *best* friends."

Jack hesitated. "Look, I—"

But Olsen was already headed for the door.

"Why do we have to come here?" Bobby demanded, following Cheryl inside. "Why can't we just go to my place?"

She dropped her keys on the table by the door. "Because."

"When's your father gonna be home?"

"Not until late," she answered, turning to kiss Bobby. He was back to kissing hard. The gentleness was gone. "He's out with an old friend from New York," she explained, pulling away prematurely. "He won't be home for a while."

"We're still gonna screw, right?"

Bobby'd been drinking. Hard. Maybe that was why his kisses were so awful tonight. "Do you have to say it like that? Can't you be a little sweeter?"

"Sweeter?" Bobby slurred snidely. "Jesus?" He pointed at her. "Take your clothes off. But leave the heels on," he called over his shoulder as he headed to the bathroom, unzipping as he walked. "I like that look. Just heels. It's hot."

Cheryl stood in the middle of the living room, hands on her hips, waiting for him to come back. He was so drunk he was talking to himself as he stood in front of the toilet. She could hear him telling himself how rich he was going to be and how she ought to kiss the ground he walked on. She glanced at the ceiling when he zipped up, then shouted, momentarily catching some very sensitive skin in the teeth of the zipper. He was just drunk. That was all. He wasn't usually like this. He'd apologize tomorrow and tell her how sorry he was and how much he loved her. Still, she was glad they were here and not at his place.

"I told you to take off your damn clothes," he said when he came out of the bathroom. "Now do it."

"Bobby, let's sit on the couch for a while," she pleaded. "Let's talk."

"I don't wanna talk." He moved to where she was standing, grabbed the bottom of her dress, and yanked it up to her neck, ripping it. "I want to fuck, I want to do it hard, I want to do it right now," he mumbled, shoving her onto the couch. Drunk as he was, he was on her in a second. "Come on, girl, give me what I want."

"Bobby, stop. Please. *Bobby, no!*"

He rolled her over onto her stomach, pressed her face into a pillow with one hand, and pulled her dress back up again with the other. "Goddamn, this is gonna be fun." He laughed, pulling her hands behind her back and holding them tightly together. "So much fricking fun that I— Awww, sheeeeeeit!" he shouted as he hurtled through the air. "What the hell!" He staggered to his feet when he finished rolling—and came face-to-face with the Kid. "Who the hell are you?"

"Someone you don't want to screw with, pal."

Bobby paid no attention to the warning—and lunged.

Kyle easily dodged the weak right, grabbed Bobby by the left forearm, spun him around, brought his wrist almost to the back of his neck, and forced his face to the wall. "What do you think you're doing to her, you asshole?"

"None of your— Jesus Christ!" Bobby shouted desperately as the Kid forced his wrist even higher.

Cheryl put a hand to her mouth. She'd heard something crack. Well, too bad. This had been the last straw. She wasn't going to stop Kyle. She'd had enough. She was just thanking God he was here. There was no telling how far Bobby would have gone. And though she wasn't proud of it, she was glad to see Bobby getting some of his own medicine.

Kyle pressed Bobby's face against the wall hard, then spun him around again so they were facing each other for a split second, and nailed him with a hard left to the chin.

Bobby crumpled to the floor like a sack of flour. It was over that fast.

As Bobby gasped for breath, Kyle grabbed his wallet from his back pocket, opened it, and pulled the driver's license out. "What's this guy's name again, Cheryl?"

She looked up curiously. "Bobby. Um, Robert Griffin. Why?"

Kyle handed the laminated card to Cheryl. "Take a look. Guys like this do it all the time."

The name on the license was Robert Turner—not Robert Griffin. "Get him out of here!" she snapped, suddenly so upset she could barely speak. She didn't know what was worse. How sad she'd feel for the next few weeks, or having to admit to Daddy that he'd been right all along. *"Now!"*

42

"YOU DIDN'T *WHAT*?"

"I didn't go in the house," Jack repeated, taking a step back as Biff's expression twisted suddenly and violently. They were standing next to Biff's beat-up old Pontiac. A good distance from where Jack had parked. But Biff could still see the Kid leaning back against the Citation's hood, soaking up morning rays, his huge arms folded across his broad chest. "I didn't rob the woman. I couldn't do it."

Biff's eyes flashed from Jack to the Kid. "Look, you old prick, I was counting on you. I left that front door open for a reason. What the *hell* is wrong with you? The jewelry was dripping off everything in the master suite."

"Maybe so, but I couldn't do it."

Biff was bursting at the seams, so primed to attack he could barely control himself. But the Kid was one tremendous deterrent, Jack could tell. Biff was chomping at the bit to beat the crap out of a sixty-three-year-old man. Seemed obvious he'd have no regrets, either. But he didn't want to get pounded to a pulp in return by a twenty-year-old stud, either. What a great guy Biff had turned out to be. Just another one of those bastards looking to pick your pocket any way he could.

"Could you really do that?" Jack asked incredulously. "To a poor old woman like that?"

"In a heartbeat," Biff answered curtly. "She's so rich she wouldn't miss anything. She's probably got Alzheimer's anyway. She'd never know the stuff was gone."

"Well, I couldn't do it," Jack said disgustedly. "Sorry."

"Sorry? *Sorry?* I got kids who need clothes, and a wife who's bitching at me constantly for a new washing machine." Biff's eyes widened. "Hey, I bet you really did take the stuff and you're lying to me. I bet you sold it and you're keeping the cash for yourself."

"Call the cops if that's what you think," Jack dared Biff. "Tell 'em to investigate. Better still," he continued, "tell 'em to call me." His eyes narrowed. "Nothing's gone, you prick. And you know it."

Biff pointed a finger in Jack's face, almost touching his cheek. Then brought it quickly down when the Kid rose off the Citation and glared in their direction. "I wanna pop you bad, Jack." He nodded toward Kyle. "That guy isn't always gonna be around." He sneered. "Have fun when Social Services shows up at your place. I hope your daughter doesn't blow her brains out when they take that little baby away from her for good."

Jack stuck his chin out defiantly. "You call yourself a lifesaver, Biff? You're a goddamn vulture. That's all you are. A pathetic vulture."

"Yeah, well, screw you and all your geriatric brothers and sisters, Jack. The rest of us would all be much happier if you people were wiped clean off the face of Florida. The only people who care about you are the ones who own hospitals, funeral homes, and cemeteries."

Jack glared at Biff for a few moments, then walked away. Thank God he'd been able to keep his mouth shut. Maybe he was finally learning.

Eyes narrowed and teeth clenched, Biff watched Jack walk all the way to the Citation. Finally he turned away, too.

Right into three undercover state troopers who'd snuck up behind him and who seconds later had him splayed flat out on the sun-baked hood of his Pontiac like he was doing a swan dive.

"Good job, Jack." It was Tom O'Brien, the trooper who'd been at the accident that night with Biff and Harry. He shook Jack's hand after climbing out of an unmarked car parked beside the Citation. "We got it all on tape. Biff's done."

Jack lifted his shirt so O'Brien could remove the wire. "Good. Damn good. But he said he was gonna—"

"Don't worry about Biff," O'Brien cut in confidently. "You won't have any trouble from him." He pointed toward the arrest that was still in progress. "My boys over there know all about Rosario and how your daughter's one of God's angels. She doesn't have anything to worry about. You or she think you see or sniff somebody who looks like Biff, you call me on this number right away day or night." O'Brien pressed a card into Jack's hand. "You sure your daughter wants Rosario for good?"

Jack shook the officer's hand again. "Yeah," he said, his voice hoarse, "very sure. But how can you do that? How can you give her to us permanently?"

"Rosario has no other relatives in this country besides her father, and we don't know who he is. In fact, there's no way we could find out. Her mother emigrated here a year ago from Venezuela and that's that. It's done." O'Brien's expression softened. "It's for the best. You and I both know that."

Jack nodded. "Okay. Well, I appreciate everything. Thanks."

O'Brien stepped back and saluted smartly. "No. Thank *you*, sir."

"Kid, Kid!"

Kyle looked up. He'd been about to head into the locker room. He let go of the door and headed down the corridor toward the white-haired older man who was standing next to the cinder block wall. "Yeah?"

"Can I talk to you for a second?"

"I'm late, pal. Only fifteen minutes to game time. My ride was—" The Kid stopped himself. Whoever this was didn't want to hear about how Jack Barrett had screwed up on the game's start time. "I'm sorry, I—"

"This'll be quick."

"Um, yeah, sure." Kyle was trying to be more approachable now that he'd made his decision, more like his old self. And not just to his teammates. He pointed at the man as he got close. "Hey, you're, um—"

"Howard Olsen," Fin said, shaking the Kid's hand. "We met last night in Jack Barrett's kitchen."

"Right." Kyle smiled. "How are you, sir?"

Olsen smiled back. The Kid was polite and respectful.

The higher-ups in the Bronx would love that. McLean would have to shear the shaggy hair if they gave him a contract, but a twenty-year-old who'd been living hand to mouth for two years could probably be convinced to do that. "I'm fine. Can we talk for a minute?"

"Um, sure."

"You know I'm with the Yankees, right?"

"Yeah, Cheryl told me."

"Good." Fin put his arm around one of the Kid's enormous shoulders. He could feel seventy home runs a year rippling through this body. Without steroids. "There's a few things about Jack Barrett you should know. I don't want you to ruin what could be a great opportunity. I want you to have all the facts before you make your decision."

43

MJ BURST OUT of the clubhouse doorway into the darkness, looked around for a moment, then took off as fast as he could across the vacant parking lot through the drizzle and fog. A thunderstorm had raced over Sarasota as tonight's game had ended—one of the first bad storms of the season, drenching everything. All that remained now were a few random showers and an occasional far-off jagged strip of lightning. He could barely make out Jack's figure standing in front of the Citation as he held his hand above his eyes and sprinted. Now that Jack wasn't an usher he didn't get preferential treatment, so he was parked by a grove of trees a good distance from the stadium. The Kid's incredible game of a few days ago had sparked a buzz, and a Tarpon ticket was suddenly a lot tougher to get. So parking wasn't as easy as it had been, either.

"At least you could have pulled up to the door!" MJ shouted as he neared the Citation.

"I would have, but the damn thing won't start." Jack was laughing so hard he could barely stand up. "And I don't care. I don't give a rat's ass that I'm standing here soaking wet and stranded."

MJ started laughing, too. A little at first, then uncontrollably, like Jack.

"Could you believe it?" Jack shouted, looking heavenward and spreading his arms wide. *"Could you believe it?"*

They high-fived twice, then embraced. It was the first time they ever had, but neither one of them hesitated for a second.

When they pulled back, MJ gazed up into the darkness and spread his arms, too. "It was amazing!" he yelled. "Amazing! Do you know what I felt like, Jack? *Do you know what I felt like?"*

"What?" Raindrops trickled down Jack's face. *"What?"*

"Like *God*!" MJ clenched his hands. "Every time the Kid went to bat he winked at me. As he was climbing the steps out of the dugout each time, he'd wink at me with this sly little grin. He freaking *winked*, Jack. I knew what was going to happen before it happened four times."

Jack nodded. It had been one thing to understand that the Kid was copying Mickey Mantle game for game after going on the Internet and matching Tarpon box scores with Mantle's 1968 box scores. But it was a whole different deal to tell the Kid what to do and then see him do it.

"I mean," MJ continued, "we told him to go one-for-four tonight. A pop-up, double, flyout, groundout. In that order."

"And he did it." Jack spotted the Kid emerging from the clubhouse door and starting to jog toward them. "In that *exact* order. You're right. It was incredible." He shook his head. "Here's the man of the hour now," he called when the Kid reached the car, clapping loudly. "You were un-believable tonight, Kyle. We were just talking about how amazing it was to know what was going to happen before it happened."

The Kid grinned. "Yeah, it worked out pretty well, didn't it? Black Maple was on fire."

"On *fuego*," MJ echoed.

Jack was about to say something when he noticed a dark figure move out of the trees at the edge of the lot. "Hey, what the hell?" he said, pointing.

As Kyle and MJ turned to see what Jack was pointing at, the figure drew a gun from inside his coat, aimed, and fired.

As the young black kid fell to the gravel, Johnny swung the pistol at the old man. He hadn't wanted there to be any ancillary killings, but he had no choice. There could be no witnesses, and he needed a head start out of here. If he didn't kill these other guys, they'd call the cops right away. Unfortunately for the black kid, he was the closest and therefore the most dangerous. So he'd been first to go.

"Jesus!" the old man shouted. *"What are you doing?"*

"It's the mob!" Kyle shouted. "They never stopped!"

"That's right, McLean," Johnny said with a hiss. "We

finally got you after all this time." He was about to fire again, about to get it all over with.

When there was a voice behind him.

"Don't shoot, Deuce. Just drop the gun and turn around real slow."

After the initial shock wave raced through him, Johnny did as he was told. He tossed the gun to the ground, then turned around slowly. And came face-to-face with Tony Treviso.

"I wanted to see your face before you died," Treviso said coldly, leveling a revolver at Johnny. "And I wanted you to see mine."

"Karen," Johnny said softly. He'd figured it out instantly, figured out that he'd been played the whole time. "Karen told you everything."

"You didn't really think my wife cared about you, did you, Deuce?" A mean smile crept across Treviso's face. "But look at it this way. At least I ain't gonna have the chance to chop your head off and send it to your mother, like I wanted to. At least it's gonna be quick."

Johnny gazed at Treviso. His dream girl had been a traitor all along. Everything he'd hoped to have, hoped to get back, hoped to live. It had all disintegrated in a few horrible seconds. "What do you think, Tony?" Johnny growled. "You think you're gonna get money outta this guy? He's broke. There's no money to get."

"Maybe not. But it really doesn't matter, does it? Because when Marconi finds out I killed Kyle McLean and I tell him you were gonna let him go, the old man'll let me off the hook. Hell, he might even give me my own crew. He might even—"

Treviso never finished. The bullet slammed through

his right eye and out the back of his skull, sending a crimson spray arcing into the night. He toppled backward, dead before he hit the ground.

As the man fell to the ground, Jack swung the pistol at the other guy. It was the pistol the first shooter had tossed to the ground a few moments ago. He'd always heard so many people say it was hard to kill a man, even when that man was threatening your life. He'd always heard it was hard to make that ultimate decision to end someone's life, to pull the trigger when you were aiming at human flesh. Even that crusty old army drill sergeant had said it so long ago in basic training. Well, they'd all been wrong. It hadn't been hard at all. Not after he'd watched MJ tumble to the ground.

The guy had never noticed him crawling toward the gun. Or, if he had, must have assumed he was crawling across the gravel to comfort a wounded friend.

Jack glanced at MJ's motionless body and felt tears coming on. MJ was the best friend he'd ever had, he realized, allowing the barrel of the gun to fall slightly.

In that split second, the man who'd shot MJ bolted for the trees.

Jack brought the pistol up again and fired—as many times as the gun would let him.

Johnny raced through the Tampa airport. He had five minutes to get to the gate to catch the last plane out to

New York City. He hadn't even bothered to stop off at the condo to drop off the guns he had in the back, just tossed them out the window and into deep water far below the towering bridge at the west end of Tampa Bay as he was speeding to the airport. He had to get back to New York as fast as possible if anything good was to come of all this.

Jack knocked on the door, barely able to hold back his tears. It was almost midnight, and he was emotionally drained. But he had to do this.

The guy who'd shot MJ was gone. Jack had fired eleven times, but all eleven bullets had missed. Moving targets were so much harder to hit.

The Kid had given chase, but the shooter had too big a lead, and he'd disappeared into the night. Jack had spent an hour with the police, and he'd have to go into the precinct tomorrow to work through some administrative details. But the detectives at the scene had agreed—when they'd heard the Kid's story—that Jack didn't have anything to worry about. It was a clear-cut case of self-defense.

The door opened a crack, and Yolanda Billups peered out. "Mr. Barrett? Is that you?"

Jack swallowed hard, trying to figure out where to start. "Yeah, it's me," he said, his voice barely a whisper.

She swung the door open. Two toddlers huddled at her knees. "What is it?" she asked, her voice rising. "What's wrong? Where's Curtis?"

Jack felt himself choking up, and his eyes dropped to the porch floor. "He's gone." It was all he could say.

* * *

"What the hell do you want?"

Jack was sitting in The Dugout, on the same stool he'd been sitting on the first time the Kid walked into the place. He glanced up from his glass of scotch at Howard Olsen. He hadn't expected Fin to come, but maybe he'd overestimated his old friend. Maybe he *should* have expected Fin to come. Not to make peace—to gloat.

"Sit down." Jack gestured at the stool next to his. "Please," he said contritely when Fin didn't move. "Just a few minutes. That's all I'm asking for."

"This better be good." Olsen eased onto the stool. "It's one-thirty in the morning, Jack. I oughta be doing something a lot more useful than talking to you. Something like sleeping."

"We've known each other for forty years." Jack waved at the bartender, indicating that Fin would have the same thing he was having. "We should try to work this out, try to talk through it."

It didn't take Fin long to get his scotch. There were only two other people in the bar. After he'd taken a long guzzle, he nodded. "Okay, talk."

Jack took a few moments to collect his thoughts. He thought about telling Fin what had happened tonight. About the shootings, about MJ. Then decided against it. It was none of Fin's business, and it didn't seem like he was going to be much of a shoulder to lean on. "Look, I'm sorry I didn't tell you about Kyle McLean. Sorry I didn't tell you I was close to him." He exhaled heavily. Why was apologizing always so hard? Even when he was actually wrong. "It was because the Kid is my ticket back to the Show, back to the Yankees."

"And you couldn't trust me with that?"

"I didn't want the word getting out on him."

"No. You thought I'd steal him."

"That's crazy, Fin. What I did was wrong, but I didn't think you'd take it so personally. I was gonna tell you." The apology wasn't going over as well as he'd hoped. "It was *really* wrong, but I—"

"Well, I hope you don't take this personally," Fin interrupted, finishing what was left of the scotch in two huge gulps. "I had a little talk with Kyle tonight, right before the game. I told him about you and what you did to the Yankees four years ago. About how much of a traitor you are. The kind of man you really are."

Jack's eyes widened. "You *what*?"

"Yeah, I told him everything. And Kyle's listening to *me* now. He's done with you. He was coming out to tell you that after the game when everything went crazy. That it's finished between you and him. I'm just glad you didn't get him killed."

"I don't believe it," Jack whispered. "All this because I didn't tell you who he was right away?" It didn't make sense. A piece of the puzzle was missing. A *big* piece. "You'd throw away our friendship over *this*?"

"You're damn right I would," Fin said firmly, standing up. Not bothering to pull his wallet out to pay for his drink. "Hell, I should have thrown our friendship away a long time ago, Jack. A *long* time ago. But better late than never."

What was missing suddenly became crystal clear. "Oh my God." Jack's hands began to tremble. "You found my letters to Doris."

"I sure as hell did, you son of a bitch. I found them four years ago in a box in the attic." Fin's face turned bright red as his fury boiled over. "My best friend and my wife." He gritted his teeth. "I almost killed both of you." He managed a wry chuckle. "But I didn't. I figured out a better way to get back at you."

"You!" Jack shouted. *"It was you!"* He stood up so fast the stool he'd been sitting on fell backward and crashed to the floor. "You were the one who sent the e-mail to the Red Sox from my computer. You knew about Jeter's wrist, too. And I'd told you all about David's drug problem. You knew everything." The explanation had been staring him in the face for four years, but he'd never figured it out. Probably, he realized, because he hadn't wanted to figure it out. "My best friend screwed me out of everything." He could barely breathe. "I can't believe it."

"Because *my* best friend was having an affair with *my* wife behind *my* back for forty years!"

Jack shook his head. "No, Fin. I never touched Doris, even when we went out in college. We wondered what it would be like all these years. Yeah, we were guilty of that. But we never did anything. We could never do that to you."

Olsen leaned in close. "It doesn't matter now, Fast Jack. Whether you did or you didn't. What's done is done. The only thing that matters is that Kyle McLean is working with me now. You're out of the picture, pal. He's *mine*."

44

PAULIE THE MOON lay on his back wearing just his white briefs, suspended from the ceiling of the seafood warehouse on a splintered plywood board. His feet were eighteen inches above his bulbous head, which was level with Johnny's knees. His hands and ankles were secured together by ropes knotted tightly beneath the board. And there was a chain double-looped around his neck. The ropes and the chain were stronger than the ones Johnny had used on Stephen Casey, and the board was another eighth of an inch thicker. Paulie was huge, powerful, and ax-murderer-crazy when he was furious or caged, and everybody here was worried he might bust through the bindings after the first bucket of water went gushing down his nose. Then it would be every man for himself, and that wouldn't be pretty. Nobody wanted to play sharks and minnows with Paulie the Moon playing the shark.

Johnny had already waterboarded the man who owned the body shop Treviso had taken his car to after killing Marconi's grandson, and the wimp had confirmed the whole story after just one bucket. Yelling at the top of his lungs about how this strange-looking little man with a disgusting mole on his neck had brought the car in and that there'd been a lot of dried blood underneath the bumper and the crumpled fender. The guy had been convincing, but Marconi wanted more. Wanted to hear straight from Paulie's mouth about how Tony Treviso had killed his grandson.

Paulie the Moon wouldn't be as easy to break as the wimp owner of the body shop. In fact, Paulie might not break at all. He was shivering like he was buried naked in a snowdrift, and parts of his body already seemed to be turning blue. But he hadn't bitched once. Hadn't pleaded for any kind of mercy. You had to give him credit for that, damn it.

It didn't seem like the first bucket even affected Paulie. Or the second one. But the third one started to rattle him. Johnny could see it in the way the big man's body tensed. The fourth bucket caused the awful panic Johnny was used to seeing in his victims after the first bucket— the body trying to move any muscle it could any way it could to escape. And after the fifth bucket washed over his face, Paulie was screaming like a baby. Admitting that Treviso had run the little boy down.

Johnny glanced over as Marconi emerged from the shadows, just as he was about to pour a sixth bucket down Paulie's nose. The old man nodded, then gave the slash sign. Johnny nodded back, pulled out a pistol, and shot Paulie in the temple. Paulie's body trembled for a few seconds, then went still. And everyone in the room breathed a heavy sigh of relief.

Johnny put the pistol slowly down on Paulie's chest. At least some good had finally come of all this. At least Kyle McLean would be able to follow his dream. It was the least Johnny could do for the Kid after killing his mother.

45

H OWARD OLSEN GLANCED at his watch, then across his desk. Kyle McLean sat in a big leather chair in the corner of Olsen's Yankee Stadium office, madly pushing buttons on his Game Boy. "I'd say don't be nervous," Olsen spoke up, "but somehow that doesn't seem appropriate." The Kid's tryout was less than an hour away. Right downstairs on the Yankee Stadium field.

"It'll be fine," Kyle said calmly, still pushing buttons, faster and faster. "Don't sweat it. I got my bats in the bag right over there." He motioned at a canvas bag in one corner of the room, then refocused on the video game. "They're all I need."

"You wanna change?" The Kid was wearing a ragged T-shirt, sweatpants, and high-top sneakers.

"Nah."

"They're gonna use Kenny Palmer to pitch to you," Olsen warned. "He's seven-and-one so far this season. With a 1.78 earned-run average."

"And he won the Cy Young Award last season," Kyle said as if by rote, rolling his eyes. "Won twenty-four and lost only six. He's got a ninety-seven-mile-an-hour fastball, a slider that changes directions like an F-16, and a curve that falls off a table six feet high. I know, I know. You told me twenty times. Don't worry."

"He's a vet," Olsen pushed. "He hates young guys."

"Of course he does. Tell you what: I'll smile at him real nice from the batter's box right before he throws me that first pitch."

"Don't take this so lightly, Kid."

Kyle ended the game. "It's okay, Fin, I'm not taking it lightly. I'm really not. Look, you have your way of focusing, I have mine. Okay?"

"Okay, okay." Olsen could feel his palms sweating. Everything important in life came down to a few precious moments. Wasn't that the old adage? Well, this was surely one of them. "And what are you gonna say when the tryout's over?"

Kyle cursed and tossed the Game Boy toward his bag of bats. "I'm gonna walk over to the dugout where everybody's standing, point at you, and tell the suits that if they want me to sign a contract with the New York Yankees, they gotta go through you." He hesitated. "Satisfied?"

Olsen broke into a broad smile. "Yeah, I'm satisfied."

* * *

Johnny knelt down and laid five dozen roses on the gravestone, then ran his fingertips across the chiseled letters. Karen Nicole Robinson. He missed her more than he ever had. He'd cheated on her and he'd broken his code of honor. There wasn't much left to do wrong. At least he'd done the right thing in the end.

When he'd kissed the creased two of hearts one last time, he pulled out the pistol he'd shot Paulie with and pressed the barrel to his chin. Then he looked up into the trees and waited for a sign, waited for the wind to blow. But it didn't. Everything stayed deathly still.

So he pulled the trigger.

The last thing he ever saw was the two of hearts lying beside him. Then everything went dark. And for the first time in many years, Johnny Bondano was at peace.

46

THE KID SAUNTERED toward the plate, still wearing his tattered T-shirt, sweatpants, and high-tops. It was three-thirty in the afternoon, less than four hours before the start of tonight's game against the Red Sox. Yankee Stadium was still quiet and peaceful beneath a partly cloudy late June sky. Six front-office suits, several coaches, and a couple of players milled around the dugout, making small talk while they waited for what they assumed would be a train wreck of cataclysmic proportions. Still, it was always fascinating to see someone crash and burn like this. It was like watching that terrible NASCAR wreck on television. Awful to watch the cars tumble over and over and burst into flames, but you couldn't pry your eyes from the screen even if you tried. The human struggle to survive was simply too compelling. Just like it would be here.

Howard Olsen sat by himself in a box seat a few rows up from the dugout, smiling smugly.

Other than Kenny Palmer, the pitcher; Tray Buford, the Yankees' second-string catcher; Olsen; and the people in the dugout, the stadium was deserted except for a few janitors sweeping aisles. Even they were slowing down, casting sidelong glances toward the plate, anticipating what was about to happen.

The batter's box was only a faint outline around the plate because the chalk hadn't yet been replaced since last night's game. The Kid hesitated when he reached it and looked up. He'd been to Yankee Stadium a few times as a boy, but he'd never been on the field. The place looked even bigger from down here.

"Scary, huh?" Tray Buford was just pulling his mask over his face.

Olsen had warned Kyle that Buford wasn't going to be very friendly. "Yeah, scary."

"You're gonna have to cut that mop off your head if you actually expect to sign a contract with us," Buford said, squatting down and banging the pocket of his glove a few times. "The Boss doesn't like long hair. Of course, there's that one small detail you'll have to get past before you have to worry about heading to the barber shop."

"Oh, yeah? And what's that?"

"Hitting my man Kenny Palmer," Buford answered, pointing toward the mound and laughing loudly. "My bet? You won't even make contact unless you try to bunt. And I doubt bunting's gonna get you much of a contract."

Kenny Palmer was staring sullenly back from the mound, obviously annoyed to have been tagged with what he considered a waste-of-time duty. He was wearing practice gear, and he looked like he couldn't wait to get back into the clubhouse. He'd pitched a complete-game shutout two nights ago, so there was no chance of him being in tonight's game.

Only an average-size man, Palmer was still damn impressive. His fastball popped Buford's mitt so hard during warm-ups the catcher was using an oversize glove—the one he used when the staff knuckleballer was throwing. And Palmer's curve really did look like it dropped off the edge of a tall table, looked like it dropped straight down the instant before it reached the plate. The worst thing about Palmer was you couldn't tell which pitch was coming, the way you could with most Single-A guys. Palmer's windup was exactly the same every time—no matter what he was bringing.

The Kid took a few practice swings, then moved into the box, excavating a hole with the toe of his right shoe.

"Good luck, Mr. Phenom," Buford said snidely, lifting his mask to spit a brown mess of chaw on the plate. "You're gonna need it."

Out of the corner of his eye Kyle checked the dugout. The small talk had stopped, and everyone was standing on the top step now, elbow on one knee. "I can't tell you how much I appreciate your support. Means a lot to me."

"You got it, Kid."

"The only thing is, Buford, from what I hear, I'll be taking your spot on the roster. So we won't have much time to get to know each other. But I'll e-mail you wherever you end up. Thank God for the Internet, huh?"

"We'll see, you son of a bitch."

The Kid took one more practice swing and raised his bat to the kill position. He wasn't using Black Maple today.

Today was all about putting the ball over the fence, where no one could catch it. Kyle knew that. Everyone knew that. So he was using the heaviest bat he had. His favorite long-ball bat. The Ash of Power. Of course, there was always that shadow of a doubt with the Ash of Power. Sometimes it didn't do exactly what it was supposed to do.

Palmer got the sign from Buford he wanted, nodded, wound up, and fired.

The pop from Buford's glove and the Kid's wild swing were met with a collective groan from the dugout and a glance heavenward from Howard Olsen. The fastball had blown past the Kid like a Lex Line express past a local stop.

"Nice swing, asshole," Buford shouted with glee, tossing the ball back to Palmer. "I bet they felt that breeze all the way down on Coney Island."

The Kid took one practice swing. "I just wanted your friend to feel good for one pitch," he said calmly.

Buford sneered as he put down the sign for the next pitch. "Okay, pal. Then bring it."

Palmer wound up and delivered.

This time, so did the Kid.

The ball rocketed over the fence in center. As did the next three. The Kid fouled off the sixth and seventh pitches, but the final three soared over the fence, too.

As the last blast landed in the monument area in left center, Palmer headed for the dugout, not even bothering to acknowledge the Kid. Just hurled his glove ahead of him and let loose a stream of expletives, then disappeared into the tunnel leading from the dugout to the locker room.

Kyle glanced down, but Buford was gone, too. Kyle

chuckled, gazed out over the lush green grass for a few moments, took a deep breath, then headed toward the dugout.

Several of the suits rushed out onto the field to shake his hand, but Kyle stopped and pointed to a spot above the dugout before they got to him. "See that guy right there," he said loudly, nodding. "If you want to talk about my contract, you go through him."

Jack smiled back at the Kid from where he was standing in the aisle, a few rows up from where Howard Olsen was sitting. He'd ambled down the stairs without anyone noticing as the Kid belted pitch after pitch over the fence.

"And the only way I'll sign a contract is if you fire that guy," Kyle continued, jabbing hard in the air at Olsen, who suddenly looked like he was having a heart attack. "Are we clear on that?"

One of the suits stepped forward and shook the Kid's hand. "As glass."

47

CHERYL AND THE Kid had been strolling through a sun-splashed Central Park for the past two hours. The first night in New York City they'd all stayed in a fleabag hotel in Queens because that was all Jack could afford. Now they were staying in the Four Seasons in midtown Manhattan—one of the best in the city—courtesy of the Yankees. On top of the three suites—one for each of them—they all had unlimited expense accounts.

They'd all met in the hotel restaurant for a delicious breakfast at nine this morning; then Jack had headed back upstairs. Back to his suite to negotiate with the Yankee suits who were coming down from the Bronx to meet with him. After pointing at Jack in the stands yesterday, the Kid had dug in against four more pitchers, delivering the same kind of towering blasts he had against Kenny

Palmer. Then he'd fielded fly balls for twenty minutes, making several spectacular catches against the blue out-field fence. After that he'd run wind sprints against the clock, power-lifted, and finally taken a complete physical, which he'd passed with flying colors. After the physical, the Yankees wasted no time. They'd seen enough. Especially Kenny Palmer. Palmer told the men in suits that under no circumstances would he ever pitch against Kyle McLean again in his career. Translation: make him a Yankee, and do it fast.

After Jack went back upstairs, Cheryl and the Kid had taken in some of the city's sights, done a little shopping, then headed into Central Park. They'd watched a group of middle-aged, overweight investment bankers and law-yers play softball against each other, then gone to Sheep's Meadow—an expanse of beautifully maintained grass in the middle of Central Park—and just hung out for a while. Not talking about anything important, just enjoy-ing the day. Now they were walking slowly back toward Fifth Avenue to catch a cab to the hotel, holding hands.

"You must be feeling pretty good," Cheryl spoke up. "A big contract in the works and no more worries about the Lucchesi family."

Angelo Marconi had called the Kid personally last night to let him know there would be no more trouble between them—as long as he got his hundred grand plus interest. Kyle had promised to pay it out of his signing bonus, and Marconi had agreed to wait two weeks.

"My mom's dead," Kyle murmured sadly. "That guy Johnny Bondano ended up killing her."

Cheryl shut her eyes tightly. "I'm sorry. I wasn't think-ing. I just—"

He gazed off into the distance for a few moments. "It's okay. I . . . I want to talk about it with you at some point, but not now. I'm not ready yet."

"Of course."

"Thanks, Princess."

Cheryl's eyes flashed to Kyle's. "What did you—"

"Princess," he cut in, squeezing her hand gently. "I called you Princess."

His hand felt so strong, but so soft, too. And she loved the way hers looked in his. Safe and secure.

"Is that okay?" he asked. "If I call you that?"

She nodded.

"You should be feeling good, too."

Once again her eyes flashed to his. "What do you mean?"

The Kid shrugged. "Well, I'm giving Jack ten percent of whatever I get. Seven percent on the side, because the standard commission is three for baseball agents. But he'll get it." He laughed easily. "If he does his job, you two shouldn't have to worry as much about money anymore. Right?"

She shook her head. "Do you think it was a good idea to have Daddy negotiate your contract? He was pretty nervous about it."

The Kid smiled. "I called a guy I know yesterday. A friend of a friend who's a lawyer here in town. I told Jack about him before he went upstairs this morning. He'll help your dad. He'll make sure about the details, and he won't charge too much."

Cheryl's shoulders sagged with relief. "I'm glad you did that."

"Well, I'm not an idiot." Kyle hailed a taxi as they came

out onto Fifth Avenue from the park. "You should feel good about that other thing, too."

"What?" she asked quickly, suddenly on pins and needles again. "What do you mean?"

"About being pregnant."

She clutched his hand hard and stopped, eyes flying wide open. "How did you know?"

"You have that glow, Cheryl. It's everywhere, all around you. I couldn't possibly miss it. Nobody could."

She stared at him in amazement, distracted by the ring of her cell phone as a cab pulled up in front of them. She wondered if he understood what had happened. "Hello."

"Cheryl, it's me."

"Hi, Daddy." She could tell by his voice he was excited. *Very* excited. "Get the Kid back here right away. And I mean *right* away."

Jack pointed to the line at the bottom of the page, and the Kid signed his name. Kyle McLean, in large, flowing script letters. The men in suits standing around the table clapped politely, and Jack smiled from ear to ear as Kyle stood up after putting the pen down on the page right below his signature.

"Five million to sign and six per for the next five years, Mr. Barrett," the Kid said, shaking Jack's hand. "Not too bad. You did a damn good job."

"With escalators based on performance," Jack reminded Kyle. "Based on incentives I know you'll blow away. Thirty home runs? I mean, *come on*."

The Kid looked out the window at the setting sun. It had been a long afternoon of details. "Don't be so sure I'll blow them away," he said, reaching into his pocket, taking out an envelope, and handing it to Jack. "Thanks for all your help, Mr. Barrett. You're a good man. Don't ever question yourself about that again."

Jack stared at the Kid for a few moments, an eerie feeling creeping up his spine. Then his eyes fell to the envelope, and they narrowed as he stared at the words written there. "Thanks," he mumbled.

"I want to go for a walk with Cheryl," the Kid said. "Okay?"

"Of course." The romance developing between them was obvious, and he was all for it. "Be back for dinner, all right?"

The Kid nodded. "She'll be back in a little while. Promise." He turned, strode into the next room, took Cheryl gently by the hand, and led her to the suite door. "Come on, Princess."

"Where are we going?"

"I'll tell you when we get there."

A few minutes later they were walking up Fifth Avenue hand in hand, Central Park on their left over a sturdy brownstone wall, the avenue to their right.

"Where are we going?" she kept asking.

The Kid wouldn't answer.

"Kyle." She punched him in the arm lightly. *"Kyle!"*

Suddenly he pulled her to him, slipped his arms around her, and kissed her deeply.

"You're really okay with me being pregnant?" she asked, gazing into his eyes when their lips finally parted. "I mean, you know, don't you?"

He smiled and nodded. "I do," he said, kissing her again. "And I'm fine with it. I love it."

She pressed herself as close as she could to him as they kissed again. She loved him so deeply, with everything she had. She couldn't imagine how she'd ever thought she could have loved anyone else. He was amazing. There was something about his way, about his ability to see into her soul. Whatever it was, she was addicted to it. She wanted more of it than she could get. Maybe that was how she knew she was finally really in love.

"I love you, Kyle," she whispered, melting into his embrace.

"I love you, too."

Then, with no warning, he pushed her away. So roughly she stumbled backward toward the brownstone wall separating the park from the sidewalk. She didn't understand, couldn't comprehend why he'd do such a thing in the middle of such a romantic moment. She'd felt his passion, his love. It was unmistakable. She couldn't deny it. Neither could he.

As she lost her balance and fell backward, she saw a taxi veer off Fifth Avenue from behind a bus. It climbed the curb, completely out of control, and hurtled down the sidewalk. Directly at Kyle. She screamed for him to get out of the way as it closed in, but her warning was cut short when the back of her head hit the wall. She tried to scream again when the cab's bumper was only a few feet from his body, as the cab hurtled into him, but no sounds would come. Then everything went black.

* * *

Jack had been lying on the king-size bed in his suite, catching a little rest. Not really sleeping, just relaxing, trying to come down off the high of the past twenty-four hours. When the phone on the nightstand rang, he reached for it, then stopped suddenly. He hesitated for several rings, wondering why he didn't want to pick it up. Within the first few seconds of answering he knew why.

After several minutes of trying to bring Cheryl down from the ledge, he spoke to a kindhearted policeman who promised to bring her back to the hotel himself.

When Jack finally hung up, he reached for the envelope the Kid had given him and stared at the words written on it: "To be opened in the event of my death only by Jack Barrett: The Kid."

Inside was a last will and testament, giving Jack every cent of the irrevocable signing bonus Kyle had just earned executing the contract.

Jack sank back onto the bed, his body shaking. Suddenly he and Cheryl had five million dollars. They'd never have to worry about money again. But the damn thing of it was, he would have given up every cent of that money if it would have brought the Kid back.

MJ. Now the Kid. Hell, he would have given up his own life if those two could have stuck around longer, he thought through his tears. Sometimes life didn't make a hell of a lot of sense. This was one of those times.

Cheryl crawled on her hands and knees to the spot where the Kid had been standing when the cab hit him. The policeman was beside her, bent over, begging her to let him take her back to the Four Seasons. But she paid no attention.

She ran her fingers gently over the bricks when she reached the spot, but there was nothing. No body, no blood, nothing to prove that he'd even existed. Her tears fell on her fingers as she caressed the bricks. Impossible, she thought. There was no way he could have avoided the cab, no way he could have avoided his fate. He was dead, but there was no proof.

She looked slowly to her left and, for a fleeting moment, thought she saw something up the block. Something familiar, something moving away that might explain it all. But a second later it had vanished like an apparition in the fog, and she realized that it had been only her imagination. Must have been only her imagination.

Then her tears fell for real.

48

YOLANDA BILLUPS MOVED slowly down the front steps of her dilapidated home as a blazing orange sun headed through a clear blue sky toward the western horizon, casting long shadows on the few scraggly blades of brown grass in her front yard. She was carrying her youngest little girl, and the next two were trailing behind her, just barely off the dusty hem of her long skirt.

"Hello, Mr. Barrett," she called softly.

"Hello, Mrs. Billups."

"I told you to call me Yolanda. I meant it."

Jack moved toward her on his bad knees. Cheryl stayed behind, back by the car. "You did," he agreed when they were close, "but somehow it never seemed right." He smiled sadly. "How've you been?"

"All right," she said quietly.

Not like she meant it, though. "You'd never complain,

would you? You'd never tell me how tough it's been." Jack rubbed his eyes. "Financially, I mean. I know how tough it's been without Curtis."

Yolanda brushed the little girl's hair for a moment. "You can call him MJ now, Mr. Barrett. I know you liked that name. I don't mind."

This was so hard. He wanted MJ to come walking out of the house with that wide, confident smile all over his face. He could only imagine how hard it had been for the woman standing in front of him. "I got something for you," he said, holding out a plain white envelope. He took the little girl from Yolanda so she could open it.

Her hands began to shake when she saw what was inside, when she saw the amount. "I . . . I . . . I can't accept this, Mr. Barrett. It wouldn't be right."

Jack nodded. "It *is* right and you *will* accept it," he said firmly. "There'll be no discussion."

She swallowed hard, then her knees buckled.

Jack reached with his one free hand to steady her, but she waved him off. "I'm all right," she said, putting a hand to her forehead. "My God, is this for real? A million dollars?"

"Oh, it's for real."

She shook her head hard, then held the check out for him. "I can't take it," she said, her eyes welling up with tears. "I can't profit from my son's death. The Lord would never approve."

"It isn't like that," Jack assured, pushing her hand gently away. "MJ earned it. It's his share of everything. Believe me. He earned it fair and square."

Yolanda stared at Jack for a long time. "Bless you, Jack Barrett," she finally whispered. "Bless you." She pointed at

Cheryl. "And bless your daughter and her unborn child. May God watch over them."

Jack smiled. "Thanks, Yolanda. That means a lot. At least coming from you it does." He handed the little girl back to her mother, then kissed Yolanda on the cheek. "Call me. I'll help you figure out the best thing to do with that money. Okay?"

Yolanda nodded and gave Jack a strong hug. Then he limped back toward where Cheryl was standing, her hands resting on her growing stomach. At least life made a little more sense now, he thought.

"That was a wonderful thing you just did, Daddy."

He smiled. Cheryl was so beautiful, the most beautiful thing in his life, the most beautiful thing he'd ever seen. She always had been, and he should have told her so many more times. He could feel his upper lip begin to tremble, and not long ago he wouldn't have been man enough to say the words.

"I love you, Princess. So damn much. I wish I'd told you so much more, but at least I—"

"I love you, too, Daddy," she interrupted, her voice trembling, too. She hesitated. "There's something I need to tell you."

"What?" he asked, looking down as he pressed moisture from his eyes. "What do you need to tell me?"

"I know you think this is Bobby Griffin's child," she said, rubbing her stomach gently, "but it isn't."

He glanced up, his eyes narrowing.

"It's Kyle's. We made love the night after he threw Bobby out of our house. This is Kyle McLean's little boy."

Jack's hands began to shake, and slowly Cheryl's image blurred in front of him. Suddenly life made sense.

Epilogue

JACK CLOSED HIS eyes and inhaled those deliciously familiar scents. Freshly mown grass, cigar smoke, and those sizzling hot dogs all blending together on the crisp sea air. Fifteen minutes to game time, and he was in heaven.

He opened his eyes slowly. But he wasn't in the stands anymore, he was on the field. He was in heaven.

Mitch Borden had fired Lefty Hodges at the end of last season and made Jack the manager of the Sarasota Tarpons. They'd won seven of their first ten games this year, and most important, they had a new star. A kid named Trent Forester, who was a pure hitter, like the Kid. Not as good, but then, no one ever would be.

Still, Trent reminded him a lot of Kyle. Which was good and bad. It was a ball watching him play, but the pro scouts were already circling. Trent probably wouldn't be around very long. But that was what happened in Single-A. That was the whole point. To get the really good ones to the Show as fast as possible.

"Hey, Granddad."

Jack smiled as Cheryl moved toward him. Rosario was peeking out from behind Cheryl's dress. She was growing more beautiful every day.

Cheryl held Kyle Junior out for him to take as they came together. "Someone wanted to see you."

Jack took the little boy in his arms and hugged him gently, bursting with pride. Junior was wearing a tiny New York Yankee cap, just like Cheryl used to do so long ago. It was the first time she'd brought him to the stadium. "Hey, Junior. Welcome to the greatest game in the world."

As he whispered the words, Jack touched the shirt pocket of his uniform. Inside there was the ticket stub from the first night he'd watched the Kid make that spectacular catch and smash that huge home run. It had never been out of his reach since that night. When Junior was old enough, Jack was going to give him that ticket stub.

And make sure it was never out of the boy's reach.

Acknowledgments

Special thanks to Cynthia Manson, Peter Borland, Judith Curr, and Louise Burke for making *Forced Out* possible. For allowing me to take this new direction which I am enjoying so much.

Special thanks to Dr. Brett Shannon for giving us peace of mind during Ellie's challenging time.

To Ellie, Courtney, Ashley, and Christina.

Also to Matt Malone, Andy and Chris Brusman, Kevin "Big Sky" Erdman, Jeanette Follo, Jim and Anmarie Galowski, Richard Green, Steve Watson, Nick Simonds, David Brown, Kathleen Rizzo, Bill Drennan, Skip Frey, Jack Wallace, Barbara Fertig, Jeff, Jamie and Catherine Faville, Bart Begley, Chris Tesoriero, Bob Wieczorek, Scott Andrews, Marvin Bush, Pat and Terry Lynch, Mike Lynch, Mark Tavani, Aaron McClung, Bob Wake, John Piazza, Chris Andrews, Bob Carpenter, Gordon Eadon, Gerry Barton, Mike Pocalyko, and Baron Stewart.

**Turn the page
for a sneak peek**

at HELL'S GATE,

**the next novel from
New York Times bestselling author**

Stephen Frey

Now available in hardcover from Atria Books

HUNTER LEE STOOD before the polished plaintiff desk to the judge's right, still wearing his sharp, pinstripe suit coat despite the heat of the packed courtroom. Even though the four attorneys at the defense desk had removed their coats hours ago when the judge said it was all right to do so. For some time he'd been gazing down at a single piece of paper lying on the desk, as though hypnotized by the typed words on it and the heavy, unique signature beneath the words. Finally he brought his dark, penetrating eyes to those of the white-haired judge.

"Your Honor, I call Mr. Carl Bach."

"The plaintiff calls Carl Bach to the stand," the uniformed bailiff announced in a booming voice.

A stocky, middle-aged man with a neatly trimmed, brown moustache rose from his seat in the middle of the third row. He excused himself in a low whisper several times as he struggled toward the center aisle over and around several pairs of knees. Finally free, he moved purposefully down the aisle to the witness stand, careful not to make eye contact with Hunter.

As Bach swore to tell the truth, the whole truth and nothing but the truth, Hunter thought back to how he'd honed his skills in those intimidating amphitheater classrooms at Virginia. By the end of his second year he'd gotten so good he could usually argue either side of an issue and win, he'd gotten so good none of his classmates would volunteer to take him on even with mountains of evidence on their side. Professors had to *force* other students to oppose him in class. That was what distanced him so remarkably from his classmates, his professors would tell the litany of firms seeking his services. That was what caught the attention of the big New York and Washington firms even faster than his gaudy GPA.

It was Hunter's father who had decided what his career would be early on in his childhood, even before Hunter really knew what a lawyer *was*. Robert Hunter Lee would be an attorney, his father would announce every evening as the family sat down to dinner.

As Carl Bach lowered his right hand and took a seat in the raised wooden witness chair, Hunter focused on his target. "Mr. Bach, please state your occupation for the record."

Bach rolled his eyes and gave Hunter an aggravated shake of the head, making it clear to everyone that he thought these proceedings were a charade. That they were a ridiculous way to spend a blistering hot summer afternoon in a stuffy Bozeman, Montana, courtroom with a broken air conditioner.

"I'm the chief operating officer of the Bridger Railroad," Bach answered stiffly. "I'm the second most senior executive at the company behind the CEO, George Drake."

"Mr. Drake also owns the company, correct?"

"Correct."

"Is Mr. Drake here today?"

"No."

Hunter gave the jury a puzzled look. Like it surprised him that Drake would miss such an important proceeding, like it was arrogant of Drake not to be here and, therefore, a personal affront to them.

He moved out from behind the plaintiff desk and headed toward the witness chair, leaving behind the piece of paper he'd been studying. "As the COO, you're an important person at the railroad." It was an obvious point but saying so for all to hear might put Bach off guard, might make him feel a connection to a hostile attorney, might cause him to drop his defenses at a critical moment. "A *very* important person."

"Ah . . . yes." Bach stroked the tips of his moustache with the stubby thumb and forefinger of his right hand. "Certainly."

"A person who should be up to speed on all important company matters. Especially matters related to the day-to-day operations of the railroad, especially as the *chief operating officer*."

Bach stole a wary glance at the jury, recognizing that he'd been deftly maneuvered into a tight corner right off the bat.

And the jury watched Bach silently remind himself that this tall, handsome attorney from New York with the deliberate manner and the intense eyes had a big-time reputation for a reason.

"Well, no one can really—"

"How big is the Bridger Railroad, Mr. Bach?"

"When you ask 'how big,' what exactly do you mean?"

"Let's start with how many miles of track you operate."

Bach pulled a white handkerchief from his shirt pocket and dabbed at the tiny beads of sweat forming on his forehead. "One thousand six hundred and forty-nine miles of main line. Four hundred twelve and a half miles of yards, spurs and sidings." The stocky man with the bushy moustache gave Hunter a smug grin. "Give or take a few feet."

A chuckle rustled around the courtroom.

"Thank you," Hunter said politely. Good. Bach was

giving specific answers. He'd taken the bait, felt he had to prove himself after being called out. Now the jury would expect crisp, specific answers to every question. In a few minutes Bach wouldn't be so specific, and the jury would wonder why. "Is all that track in Montana?"

"Most of it. We go a spitting distance into Idaho, Wyoming and the Dakotas, but that's it."

"So you connect with other railroads."

Bach nodded. "With the BNSF and the Union Pacific, with the big boys."

Hunter furrowed his dark, arrow-straight eyebrows. "The Bridger is what's known as a short line railroad. Is that correct, Mr. Bach?"

"A Class II railroad," Bach answered, using the official term. "As defined by the federal government," he added confidently. Clearly believing there couldn't be a land-mine buried anywhere along this path of questioning.

"Meaning?"

"Meaning," Bach continued, his voice taking on a pro-fessorial, condescending tone, "that we have annual revenues between $20 million and $280 million."

Hunter turned to the jury and let out a low whistle. "Wow. Two hundred and eighty million." It was so easy it was almost unfair, especially with the help he'd gotten from his anonymous benefactor. "That's big." To a New York jury that amount wouldn't sound very impressive. In Bozeman, Montana, it sounded like the gross domes-tic product of most European countries. "*Very* big."

"Well, actually," Bach spoke up quickly, realizing he'd been backed into that same tight corner once again, "it isn't that—"

"Mr. Bach," Hunter interrupted, "I don't want to keep you up here on the stand any longer than I have to. I know you're a busy man, and I know it's warm in here." Hunter broke into a friendly smile as he made eye contact with several jurors. Longest with an older woman wearing a faded blue dress and matching hat who was sitting all the way to the left of the jury box. He still hadn't won her over. He could tell by her rigid posture, stiff upper lip and cold expression. "Made a lot warmer," he continued, allowing his southern drawl to turn thicker and more potent, "by the fact that you're on the *hot* seat."

This time the courtroom erupted into a loud laugh. Even the older woman in the jury box cracked a thin smile.

The judge, too, Hunter noticed. Which fit. He'd been worried at the start of the trial that a Montana judge might make it difficult for a New York lawyer carrying a big reputation into his courtroom, but that hadn't turned out to be the case at all. The man in black had been completely fair, which Hunter had found was true about most Montanans. They were tough—because Montana was a tough place to live—but they were fair. Which was refreshing. It ought to help with the size of the award, too.

Hunter raised a hand, requesting silence, subtly taking control of the proceedings. Then he made a slow, sweeping gesture toward two children sitting in the front row just behind the plaintiff desk. Both of them wore stark, black eye patches.

"We all know why we're here," Hunter said firmly when the laughter faded, his voice turning stern as he moved toward the children. They were sitting between their parents, their tiny, dimpled chins buried self-consciously in their narrow chests. "We're here because fourteen months ago westbound Bridger Freight 819 tragically derailed just outside the small town of Fort Mason, Montana. I say 'tragically' because the four tank cars that jumped the tracks that May afternoon were filled with liquid anhydrous ammonia, a common fertilizer. As we heard the experts testify, those four tank cars derailed near the Murphy General Store off SR 72 and suffered catastrophic fractures when they smashed into several box cars sitting on a siding, Those fractures allowed the liquid inside the tank cars to escape, and, when liquid anhydrous ammonia hits air, it explodes into a gas."

The courtroom had gone deathly still. The judge was leaning forward on the bench, peering over his black frame glasses. The reporters standing shoulder-to-shoulder in the back had ceased scribbling on their pads. Those in the audience who'd been fanning their faces with newspapers had stopped fanning. Everything had come to a halt and everyone was staring at Hunter. They'd heard it all before during the past few days, but not like this, not so compactly and so dramatically. It was as if Hunter had magically transported them to the accident scene just as the train was roaring past and they could see for themselves how the tank cars had careened off the rails and slammed into the box cars on the siding, then tumbled over and over. It was as if they could see for themselves the steel cars rip apart like they were made of balsa wood, see for themselves how the liquid inside the cars burst into a huge, deadly, billowing cloud.

"Into a *monster*." Hunter's voice resounded throughout the courtroom. "A monster seeking water anywhere it could find it because that's what anhydrous ammonia does. It sucks water out of everything it comes into contact with. Like it did from the skin, lungs and eyes of those unlucky people in its path that terrible spring day in Fort Mason." Hunter pointed at the children in the front row. "Like it did from the eyes of these innocent children, blinding them as their lenses dehydrated like puddles beneath the Sahara sun."

"*Objection!*" One of the railroad's four attorneys shot up from his seat, unable to restrain himself any longer. "Mr. Lee's grandstanding, your honor. I mean, is there a question anywhere in our future?" The young man slammed the desk with his fist, totally frustrated. "*Objection!*"

"Overruled."

"Four people died when the gas singed their lungs bone-dry and ten were blinded, including these poor children sitting before us. Fortunately just in one eye for them." Hunter's expression turned sad, and he shook his head. "I can't believe I just said 'fortunately.' I'm sorry," he murmured, nodding solemnly to the little boy and girl, then to their parents. "Very sorry."

"*Objection!*"

"Overruled." The judge glared down at the railroad attorney. "Now, sit."

"Your Honor, please. This is—"

"I said, sit down, sir!"

Hunter glanced at Carl Bach. He was sweating profusely. "Those are the facts, Mr. Bach," Hunter said quietly, "and they are not in dispute. What is in dispute is who bears the blame. Was the engineer going too fast? Were the tracks the train was roaring down that day in desperate need of repair? Did the senior executives of the Bridger Railroad know the tracks were broken? As brittle as dead aspens in February." Hunter pointed toward the witness stand as he scanned the jury. "Did Mr. Bach know those tracks were broken? Or," he said, gesturing toward the four attorneys at the defense table, "is it as *they* would have you believe, as their experts would have you believe? That the tracks had been tampered with and that was what caused the train to crash. That, in fact, the Bridger Railroad was a victim in this horrible tragedy, too."

Hunter caught the judge's subtle hand signal. There needed to be a question soon. The objections hadn't been well received, but the point had been made. Enough orating.

"We've heard about chevrons in the rails, street gangs out to satisfy their hunger for random violence, even the possibility of foreign terrorists conspiring to murder the residents of Fort Mason." Hunter gave the railroad attorneys a did-you-really-think-anyone-would-buy-that-one look, slowly pivoting so that everyone in the courtroom could see his skeptical expression. "We've heard all manner of possibilities from that army of attorneys over there. One for each of the tank cars that derailed, now that I think about it," Hunter added, as if the fact had just dawned on him. Which, of course, it hadn't. "Ironic, huh?"

A murmur raced around the courtroom, laced with hatred for the railroad. It was a reaction that told Hunter he now had everyone squarely in the palm of his hand, even the older woman in the faded blue dress and matching hat. It was a reaction that told Hunter his father had been absolutely right to guide his son so forcefully into the law.

"Mr. Lee," the judge urged under his breath, "get on with it. Please, sir."

A sincere "please" from a judge? Had Hunter heard the man in the black robe right? His partners back in New York would never believe him. Where he came from, judges ran courtrooms with iron fists, not polite requests.

"What we haven't heard is the truth." Hunter moved back toward the witness stand. For several moments he stood before Carl Bach, staring down at the senior executive. "Did you know those tracks needed to be fixed?" he finally managed.

"No," Bach responded, his calm demeanor belying the anxiety etched into the lines on his forehead and cheeks. "In fact, they might have been fine. They probably were fine," he added quickly. "The cause of the accident could easily have been a hot box in one of the car's braking systems; a bad loading job in the coal cars ahead of the first tanker; or a shift in the load on the trip through South Dakota while the Burlington Northern had control of it. We just don't know, Mr. Lee." Bach spread his arms, appearing baffled. "No one knows. We dug through that accident scene for a week and nobody could figure out what happened. Us, the state boys, the federal agents. I spent two days over there myself. There was just too much damage to the cars and the tracks. There was lots of speculation, but nobody could ever say for sure what happened." Bach scanned the courtroom, searching for compassion, searching for just one friendly face. "What I do know is that all the main line tracks in our entire system had passed their regularly scheduled maintenance check the week before. With flying colors," he added. "With no exceptions and no maintenance orders filed. It's a stringent program we rigorously execute and document. You had access to all those records, didn't you, Mr. Lee?"

Bach had obviously been drilled on how to answer this question by his lawyers, but he'd practiced the response so many times the words sounded scripted now. Hopefully the jury would pick up on that. Hunter was confident they would because ultimately, juries were damn perceptive.

"Yes," Hunter agreed. "Your attorneys were very helpful in getting me those files."

"Good. I told them right from the start that you were to get everything you wanted as fast as possible. All the records, all the files." Bach's expression filled with sympathy for the two small children sitting in the front row. "The challenge, Mr. Lee, is that we can't possibly patrol every mile of track we operate every second of the day." Implying that the tracks had indeed been tampered with. "What happened was a tragedy, *is* a tragedy, is a *damn* tragedy. But there's bad people out there doing bad things more and more often these days. It's awful, but it's an awful reality, too."

Hunter nodded thoughtfully. "Yes, I see what you're saying." He paused. "But a question or two about what you just said, Mr. Bach. To set the record straight before you step down. Okay?"

Bach looked at Hunter suspiciously. "Yeah, sure."

"You just told the judge and the jury that all of those 1,649 miles of main line tracks are subject to a monthly maintenance program."

"Yes . . . I did say that," Bach agreed hesitantly.

"What about those four hundred twelve and a half miles of yards, spurs and sidings?" Hunter asked, boring in on his target. "Give or take a few feet here and there, of course. What about them?"

Bach shifted uncomfortably in the witness chair. It was obvious from his body language that he didn't like Hunter repeating the exact number of yard, spur and siding miles the Bridger Railroad operated. It was obvious that the precision coming back at him scared the hell out of him.

One of the railroad's lawyers shifted in his seat, Hunter noticed out of the corner of his eye. Then another one ran a hand through his thinning hair.

"What *about* them?" Bach asked.

"What's the maintenance program when it comes to the yards, spurs and sidings?"

Bach cast an SOS glance at his legal team. "Uh, it depends."

"On what?" Hunter was shooting questions at Bach faster now, speeding up the pace as he steered the COO into no-man's-land.

"On how much the tracks are used, on how old they are, on when they were last checked. On lots of things," Bach said, as if his answer should be obvious. "I mean, we're very diligent when it comes to those tracks, too, but we can't check them as often as we check the main lines. It wouldn't be cost-effective."

"*Cost effective?*"

"And it isn't necessary," Bach spoke up quickly, realizing how callous "cost-effective" had sounded in front of people who'd suffered so much. "Our trains go up to sixty, sometimes seventy miles an hour on the main lines, but on sidings the engineers are specifically ordered not to exceed fifteen so those tracks don't take nearly the wear and tear. And, if there is a problem with a siding track, what happens won't be so bad because the train is going slower. We're solid on this with all our people, we've never had a problem. Our safety record has been outstanding. Other than what happened in Fort Mason last year," he admitted in a low voice.

"The train in question was going over fifteen miles an hour that day. Right, Mr. Bach?"

The COO bit his lower lip. "I believe so."

"How fast was it going?"

"We don't know for—"

"*About* how fast," Hunter interrupted. He glanced at that piece of paper lying on the plaintiff desk, hoping Bach would catch the look. "Come on."

"Objection!" shouted one of the railroad attorneys. "The question calls for speculation on the part of the—"

"Overruled," the judge snapped. "We heard the experts testify. *Your* experts."

"Around forty miles an hour," Bach answered when the judge pointed at him. "Maybe fifty," he went on, almost in a whisper. "But it's a main line track so the engineer wasn't even going as fast as he could have been going."

"It's a double track main line at that point in the system, right?" Hunter asked. "Meaning two trains can pass each other at that point west of Fort Mason. Correct?"

"Yes," Bach agreed deliberately, as if he suddenly realized he had a problem. "It's a double track main line there," he confirmed, choosing his words carefully. "Then there are the siding tracks alongside the double main. The tracks those box cars were sitting on."

"Why are those siding tracks there?"

"The Brule Lumber Mill is about a half mile away, back in the woods. The sidings are a staging area for the mill. The long haul freights drop cars off there, then the local switcher takes them to the mill. And vice-versa."

"I see." Hunter rubbed his chin thoughtfully. "How far out of town on the west side does that double main go?"

"Huh?"

"How far west of town does the double main line go? When does it switch down to one track?" Hunter rested a hand on the railing that boxed in the witness chair on three sides. "What's the next big town west of Fort Mason?" he prodded when Bach didn't respond right away.

"Gordonsville."

"Okay. How far is Gordonsville from Fort Mason?"

"About thirty miles."

"Does the double main go all the way to Gordonsville? Are there two separate tracks from Fort Mason to Gordonsville?"

"No."

"Then how far does it go?" Hunter moved slightly to his right, blocking Bach's view of his attorneys. "Mr. Bach?"

Bach let out a measured breath. "Four miles."

"*Four miles!*" Hunter thundered, backing off a few steps and folding his arms across his chest. "That's all? You call that a main line? Isn't that really just a glorified siding, Mr. Bach? Just a place one train can idle while another one passes on the real main line?"

"It's a main line!" Bach shouted. "A *damn* main line even if it is only four miles long."

"Has that four miles of track always been classified as a main line?" Hunter demanded.

Bach's eyes opened wide, his expression went blank and his chin tilted slightly up. "I uh, I . . ." His voice trailed off.

"*Well?*"

"What's the point?" demanded one of the railroad attorneys, jumping to his feet. "What's this all about?"

"*Has it always been classified as a main line?*" Hunter fired again. "And I'm warning you, Mr. Bach, be careful about answering this question. Very careful."

"Yes!" Bach hissed, his knuckles going white as he clenched the arms of the witness chair. "It's always been classified as a main line."

Hunter stared at Bach for several moments, eyes flashing. The courtroom had gone deathly still again.

As if on cue, one of the dark-wood doors at the back opened, making what seemed like a huge racket in the stillness of the courtroom as it creaked on its hinges. Hunter didn't bother turning his head as an attractive young woman in a short dress slipped into the room and squeezed between two reporters. He didn't need to look, he knew what was happening. He kept his eyes riveted to Bach's, and he saw in Bach's forlorn expression exactly what he wanted to see. That it was over, that Bach was done, that suddenly he didn't want any more of this fight.

The woman had slipped into the courtroom as if she wasn't anyone special, which she wasn't. Except to Carl Bach—and to Hunter Lee.

"Are you sure you want to stick with that story?" Hunter strode toward the plaintiff desk and the piece of paper he'd been staring at before calling Bach to testify. He picked it up, then retraced his steps back to Bach's shocked, terrified expression and slipped the memo into the COO's trembling fingers. "*Are you absolutely sure?*"

"I . . . I . . ."

"That's your signature on the bottom of the page, isn't it?" Hunter asked, his voice dropping to a whisper.

Bach swallowed hard.

"*I didn't hear the question!*" one of the railroad attorneys shouted, pounding on the desk. "*Please repeat the question! What's on that piece of paper? Speak up, will you!*"

"Do you recognize that woman who just walked into the courtroom, Mr. Bach?" Hunter's voice dropped a notch lower, so not even the judge could hear.

Bach shut his eyes tightly and turned his head to one side.

"You don't want to keep going, do you?"

The executive hung his head. "No."

"We can't hear the questions," came a chorus of voices from the defense desk. All four railroad attorneys were standing now. "*Your Honor, please!*"

"Mr. Lee," the judge said, "please speak up."

"I'll ask you again," Hunter said quietly to Bach, backing off a little, offering the COO a horrible choice. His career—or his marriage. "The question you want to answer, not the other one. The one—"

"Ask me," Bach begged, unable to get the words out fast enough. "In Jesus' name, please ask me."

Hunter took another step back. "I'm going to ask you one more time, Mr. Bach." His voice was strong and clear again so everyone in the courtroom could hear him. "Was that four-mile stretch of track always classified as a main line?"

Bach stared straight ahead for what seemed like an eternity, eyes fixed on something in the distance only he could see. Then his lips began to quiver and his head to shake, almost imperceptibly at first, then with conviction. "No." He buried his face in his hands. "It was classified as a siding before the accident. We changed the track's maintenance classification to main line the day after those tank cars derailed." Bach began to rock back and forth in the chair. "Then we changed all the maintenance records from before the accident to make that four miles of track look like it had always been classified as a main line." Bach slumped down. "The train shouldn't have been going that fast," he mumbled. "It shouldn't have been going over fifteen miles an hour on that track. It shouldn't have been on that track at all. Those rails were rusty and cracked, they needed to be replaced. I saw it myself a few weeks before the accident. But we've been trying to save money everywhere we can." He gasped. "We've got *so much* debt on our books. We're so damned strapped for cash. I mean, we're almost bankrupt."

Hunter gazed at Carl Bach for several moments, watching the other man's tears come streaming down, thinking about how he'd just destroyed a man's career and wondering if he should feel some sense of remorse. Hadn't Bach deserved to be asked that terrible question, hadn't he deserved that terrible choice? Shouldn't people be held accountable for the awful things they did and wasn't that all he was doing? Wasn't that justice?

Hunter motioned to the judge. "I rest my case, Your Honor."

A few minutes later the judge had delivered his instructions to the jurors and they were shuffling out of the room, some of them casting hateful looks in Bach's direction as they left. They were headed to an anteroom to deliberate on how much money they would award the eight families who'd retained Hunter Lee. The litigator from New York City had lived up to all of his advance billings, to his big-time reputation.

When the last juror had disappeared, Hunter realized that he was thirsty. But, unlike the judge and jury, he had to exit the room like everyone else. Through those dark-wood doors at the back of the room, and the pack of hungry reporters who were already starting to shout questions at him.

As Hunter pushed his way through the chaos, a small man holding a letter-size envelope stood directly in his path. He didn't look like a reporter, Hunter thought to himself as the distance between them closed. He wasn't holding a pen and notepad.

"Robert Lee?" the man asked over the din of voices as they came together.

Hunter's eyes narrowed. "Yes."

"Robert *Hunter* Lee?"

"Yes."

The small man smiled thinly and pressed the envelope firmly to Hunter's chest. "Congratulation, Mr. Lee. You've been served."